I0676544

The Skin Territory

(Queen in Exile part 3)

By Oliver Strong

Smashwords Edition

ISBN: 978-0-9575457-2-4

Cover design by: **gerggerg@gmail.com**

Table of Contents

Chapter 1

'My name is Amar-sin, son of Mamagal. I was a great man living in the greatest system of the greatest civilization in the known galaxy. Until one day I crossed paths with fate, she was marked for the king and I an unknown destiny to travel the star filled night in search of the Amelatu.'

An old man translated his words to a blue skinned woman. The lady dressed in a brown, squiggly patterned tunic with skin tight leggings made a quizzical expression.

'Did she understand?' inquired Amar throwing his intricately sewn cape over one shoulder.

'I have no idea. They understand a little old Ur but until our AI deciphers her language it shall be many guesses.'

The blue lady scanned her guests she'd not seen anything like this outside an old Earth play performed by a traveling arts company for her family when she was but a child.

This young man reminded her of Hamlet dressed in stockings and strange boots. He wore some very flash yellow hose along with a ruffled shirt straight out of the 18th century. His cape was of black crushed velvet embellished with gold thread.

His elder companion was quite the contrast dressed in leather trousers and boots reflecting a gnarly sensibility. The young man his polar opposite was perfumed with an overpowering musk paralleling his gaudy sense of fashion.

These explorers appeared in the Ya'ax home system three days ago travelling aboard a vessel of unknown origin. Carrying a small crew it resembling two spheres welded together, one much larger than the other.

Living at the edge of civilized space the Ya'ax were subject to constant attack from various pirate nations picking at the edge of Xch'uup's influence. So upon witnessing this craft burst out of a white hole system wide alarms were raised. However, Itzel quickly realised it was not another pirate raid. This vessel was far too small for such an audacious attack.

Upon making contact it became obvious diplomatic relations were desired. Despite being totally foreign their language had much in common with old Tlillan and from there a relationship began.

The men on this star ship resembled Pixoa to one degree or another, similar to humans in size and individuality.

The Queen of Ya'ax was pleased to make acquaintance with any friendly species able to wield warships. Out here on the edge of space her people fought every day as their last. The beautiful blue skinned Queen had been pushing Triumvirate membership for many years now. With the protection of Xch'uup her people might no longer be traded at slave auctions across the Milky Way, Ya'ax females commanded amongst the highest prices.

'Amelatu?'

'Bazi, she doesn't understand, ask her again.'

'Amar, cool yourself. We must wait for our AI to process her language, when it is ready we shall discuss these subjects.'

'Ask her again about this ... woman.'

Bazi addressed Itzel in his best ancient Ur, 'Namlugallu asar Xch'uup baltu?'

The blue Queen thought for a moment. Bridge personnel stared the beauty up and down whilst Itzel spoke with her advisors.

After consulting language experts her sparkling blue eyed gaze met Bazi, 'Xch'uup la sinnis, Xch'uup Titaanis.'

The old bearded man gave a shocked expression as did one or two of the Ur crew.

'What did she say?' asked Amar.

'Titaanis?'

'Le'Titaanis.'

Itzel moved to a star chart depicting the Milky Way galaxy upon a slim pedestal beside the ship's Captain. She tapped the screen with both of her fingers before widening them to zoom in. Once focused on a specific area she tapped the Tlillan system, 'Xch'uup esharra.'

'What is she saying?' pushed Amar impatiently.

'She says that Xch'uup is not a woman but a God. She says that Xch'uup resides here, in this system.'

Amar gave a cynical sneer, 'That is ridiculous how could such an advanced people believe in Gods?'

'Have you met this Xch'uup?'

'No, of course not!'

'Then shut your mouth, you have already got us into enough trouble! The last thing I need is that tongue of yours arousing the ire of a God. It is a wonder you have not been struck down already!'

Amar shook his head, 'Do not tell me you believe such nonsense!'

'I neither believe nor disbelieve.'

Amar laughed, 'Really you do amuse me sometimes Bazi!'

The old man sneered at his young charge, 'If not for your father I would not have journeyed here to protect you. It is thanks to your fat mouth we are both lost in another galaxy searching for a myth. Now, if you can manage to shut up and go without offending these people or their God. Perhaps you might live to see the little whore you left behind in Ur, which you so pine for each night.'

Amar's eyes widened dramatically, 'How dare you speak of Puabi in such a manner!'

'Really? What do you propose to do?'

Amar unsheathed a jewelled dagger to which Bazi chuckled, 'Boy, by the time I was your age I had killed three men in battle with my bare hands! All you have achieved in your pitiful existence is smoke lotus, concoct bad poetry and violate the King's whores when he was away!'

The ship Captain moved between them pushing Amar away from Bazi.

The confrontation fascinated Itzel; she picked up a familiar word here and there yet struggled to understand what the fracas concerned. Eventually Amar sheathed his dagger the Captain pressuring him into taking a back seat for the rest of Itzel's tour.

Their vessel was little more than a massive engine room/power core/wormhole generator strapped onto a tiny bridge and living quarters inside a smaller sphere. Within half an hour they were back on the bridge again, Itzel was still smiling at a dejected Amar.

It had been three days before they achieved physical contact and now before an alien Queen the young herald from another galaxy had made an absolute horse's arse of himself.

The beautiful Queen chatted with Bazi their conversation eventually interrupted by many flashes of light. Itzel's wrist tablet bleeped urgently, she slapped it with all her might as vessels ejected from white holes surrounding the Ya'ax system.

'What is wrong?' shouted Amar.

'Shut up for a moment and I shall find out!' replied Bazi.

The Queen of Ya'ax put a hand on her head, 'Dakuiss, sarraqumis.'

'She says they are brigands.'

'What do they want?' asked Amar observing close to thirty pirate vessels of assorted shapes and sizes surround the star system.

'Etlu wabalu?'

'Maskab chun ek'tsab e wardumiss.'

'She says they come for slaves and something else ... iron from the stars?'

Amar thought for a moment, 'Iron from the stars, she means neutronium, they've come for neutronium and slaves ... can we get away?'

The Captain shook his head as his officers informed him of a wormhole nullifier preventing retreat.

Amar became frantic, 'No, no, no you must tell them! I am a herald from another galaxy, from the great civilization of Ur!'

'Perhaps you can tell them yourself when the battle is over, that is if you survive.'

Amar's eyes widened once again, 'Battle?'

Bazi took a perverse pleasure smirking at the terrified boy, 'Why yes, what do you think is going to happen Amar?'

Amar gestured towards the Ya'ax Queen, 'A negotiation, perhaps they will take some goods in exchange for leaving?'

The blue Queen was too busy speaking with her fleet Admiral to mind Amar, Bazi interjected, 'A good idea and may I say a generous one.'

'Generous?'

'Why yes, to offer your life for a people we have only just encountered is an excellent show of good faith from the people of Ur.'

Amar waved his arms, 'Oh no, THEY may offer slaves and neutronium.'

'I see.'

Bazi peered in the direction of the Captain, 'Do you think we can make a run for it?'

'34 enemy vehicles of various configurations the Ya'ax have three warships and us. We cannot make hyperspace there is an energy field creating a null effect upon our dark matter generator.'

Bazi spoke to Itzel, 'Abatu etlu?'

Itzel shook her head, 'Etlu daku, la'wussuru ul'naparsuddu. Simtum etlu kimah!'

Amar awaited a translation with bated breath.

'She says that they come for murder and pillage and it is our fate to die as warriors today.'

'I am not a fighter you must tell her this!'

'She is aware however the brigands,' Bazi pointed to a battle line of scum preparing to plunder the system, 'are not interested in co-operating. It seems that we must fight to the death … our deaths, or become slaves.'

The Ur Captain brought what few weapons his exploration vessel had to bear, the remaining friendly ships prepared for an onslaught.

Pirates cared not for bargaining often murdering her people before leaving with their booty; their next stop being the commodity markets of the Milky Way. Where anything and everything could be bought and sold outside of Xch'uup's jurisdiction.

Amar whispered to the heavens touching his forehead with his fingertips.

The bearded man laughed, 'I thought belief in the gods was foolish!'

Amar sweated profusely as pirate vessels closed in on the star's fourth planet, 'After deep consideration I have decided to open my mind to this Xch'uup or any other gods that may be watching today.'

Before Bazi could reply another wormhole opened up ejecting a long tubular vessel not far from the Ya'ax home world.

Itzel shouted into her wrist tablet, Bazi caught a little of her conversation.

'Who is that?' cried Amar.

'She says they are the men ... men of the Machine.'

'Are they friendly?'

'Makayuuk resussun?'

'La.'

'She says no, yet neither are they pirates.'

The Ur Captain jumped out of his seat to observe his navigation officer's readout. After a few seconds he shouted across the bridge, 'The brigands are in retreat!'

Amar tugged on Bazi's cloak, 'Why? What has happened?'

The old man turned to Itzel, 'Etlu Abatu, ammeni?'

'Makayuuk,' she replied pointing at the Makayuuk battleship which had just entered their system.

'Ammeni?'

'Makayuuk alal, iksuda gabbu.'

'She says these men of the Machine are great destroyers and conquers. The brigands fear these people.'

'But they have only one warship, why retreat?'

'Makayuuk isu isten, ammeni etlu adaru?'

Itzel narrowed her eyes, now she understood that these people weren't from around here. They hadn't heard of Makayuuk. Even the vilest brigands in the furthest part of the Milky Way listened to tales of Makayuuk.

The greatest warlords controlling massive empires built on plunder would baulk at the sight of just one Makayuuk ship entering their system. The Makayuuk's reputation preceded them wherever they travelled; and for the first time Itzel had met someone with no knowledge of the People of Machine.

'Makayuuk etlu ilat, ul'guddana Makayuuk ma baltu … isten baltu … Xch'uup. Makayuuk semu Xch'uup.'

The old man absorbed her broken language processing it in his mind, 'I think she is trying to say these Machine men are supreme warriors, none have defeated them in battle. She says only one fought them and survived that being Xch'uup whom they now serve.'

'Bazi! The null energy field is down we can fold space!'

Amar leapt over to the Captain, 'Quickly get us out of here!'

'Shut up Amar!' snapped the old man, 'Do not move the vessel, I do not wish to provoke these Machine men.'

'Will they kill us?'

Bazi ignored the young herald, 'Captain, power down your weapons.'

The Captain nodded as he returned to his seat. The pirates backed off folding space one by one in quick succession; returning to the den of filth and treachery they'd emerged from.

Itzel's wrist tablet bleeped, she informed the explorers of a Makayuuk request to come aboard.

'They want to come here?' asked Amar.

'Yes they do and I have allowed it.'

'Are these men not dangerous?'

Bazi sighed, 'Do you see danger around every corner?'

The young herald didn't reply.

Ten minutes later they waited outside an airlock on the smaller command sphere. As its thick hatch swung open Amar and Bazi both gasped.

Itzel dropped in a kowtow, 'Namaste Kalayuuk.'

'Liik'il,' replied Lian.

The explorers were frozen by a vision of beauty and power standing before them. A Valkyrie towered above their heads with a pair of steel eyed warriors flanking her on each side.

'Xch'uup welcomes you both to her kingdom.'

This Amazon, sword bound to waist, spoke their language with perfect clarity.

Bazi was the first to speak, 'Thank you, I bring greetings from the Kingdom of Ur.'

'The Kingdom of Ur? Don't you mean the Tamoanchan Territory?' grinned Lian.

'You have travelled to Anur?'

Lian nodded, 'How long has it been since you communicated with Andromeda?'

Bazi became a little uncomfortable at the question, 'It has been sometime.'

'Is Mammi aware of this expedition?'

'No, you must not inform Mammi!'

The tall Valkyrie dressed in her Tlillan ribbed suit and white frock coat smiled, 'Calm yourself, Xch'uup understands.'

'My name is Bazi, this is Amar-sin. We are heralds from a kingdom once the jewel of Andromeda. Today it lays dull and forgotten, we have been sent to find the Amelatu.'

'Amelatu?'

Amar chirped up, speaking before his elder could reply, 'A mythical race, great Nabus of the past spoke they will come from Mul.'

Lian looked hard at the young man in fancy clothes, 'Yet you believe in neither your Nabu nor the Amelatu.'

Amar did not reply.

'So why are you here risking your life in the unknown for something you don't believe in?'

Bazi cut in, 'Because he could not keep his sexual organs in his hoes!'

Everyone laughed except for Amar.

'And you, do you believe in the Amelatu?'

Bazi shrugged his shoulders, 'I have an open mind, we look and if the Amelatu are not to be found we may return home to grow old. May I ask how you speak our language so fluently?'

'You will accompany me. Xch'uup shall grant you an audience. If you wish you may bring your vessel or travel aboard mine.'

Bazi replied quickly, 'It would be an honour to travel aboard your vessel, Kalayuuk.'

Again Amar's eyes widened. Lian glanced at the young man with a grin, 'I'll be folding space in a few hours, gather your possessions and contact Asta when you wish to come aboard.'

The tall Amazon exited their bridge with the Ya'ax Queen in tow.

After the ladies had left Amar shouted spontaneously, 'Go aboard that? They could kill us? Or worse sell us to slavers!'

Bazi shook his head, 'Pack your things Amar, if she wanted us dead we would not be standing here. Did you not see that fleet of brigands retreat at the mere sight of her ship?'

'Yes but ...'

'Do as I say Amar and perhaps you will live to impregnate another of the King's concubines!'

An hour later and the pair sat aboard a shuttle heading towards a massive iron tube hanging in space. Bazi had only witnessed a space ship of this size when cargo vessels entered Ur on trade runs. Certainly he'd not seen a warship of this size since it would be rather impractical, why make yourself such a large target? The old man pondered this as its grey mass loomed larger; he came to the conclusion that since most ran in terror rather than fight it was a psychological tactic.

Entering a porthole their shuttle was captured by a magnetic net and guided in. Once its bay had been pressurised the two men thanked their captain for transport before saying their goodbyes.

Amar nervously clutched onto his bearskin baggage. The docking bay was large and as he looked around a door slid open revealing three men.

Asta and two of his officers dressed in traditional Makayuuk jump suits approached the anxious explorers of Ur. Asta greeted them, 'Namaste.'

Bazi reciprocated by pressing his palms together, 'Namaste.'

Amar watched his old family friend before dropping his luggage and quickly making the namaste gesture.

Asta spoke through a translation device in his collar, 'I am Asta 491 accompany me to your living area.'

After an icy greeting they followed these machine men through corridors of gun metal grey. So far this vessel was quite unremarkable from within; their quarters being more of the same.

Asta pointed to some steel bunk beds, 'You will sleep here for the journey to Otoch.'

As Amar placed his luggage down Bazi questioned the Captain, 'How long will this journey be?'

'Kalayuuk must visit outer systems first, twelve days without trouble.'

Amar spoke in a distressed tone, 'Twelve days? But look these beds have no mattress!'

Asta made a confused expression, 'Mattress?'

'Why yes a large textile filled with animal furs or feathers.'

Asta nodded his head, 'I understand the meaning but why would you require a mattress?'

'For comfort of course.'

Again the machine man furrowed his brow, 'Surely it is healthy to sleep on a hard even surface. A mattress will create spinal problems will it not?'

Bazi smiled, 'It is quite alright Captain.'

'I will provide you with mattresses it is not a problem,' replied Asta.

'Thank you very much,' said a grateful Amar.

'Feel free to tour our vessel, you are only restricted to quarters during a tunnel event.'

Bazi questioned Asta, 'Tunnel event?'

'The opening of a wormhole.'

'Ah, I see. Where is the bathroom on this vessel?'

Asta pointed to the far end of the room. A wall slid back, inside rested a shower unit. A moment later a toilet rose from the floor of the shower. Asta then pointed to a unit beside their beds, 'Food is dispensed from here, options are limited but you may eat whenever you wish.'

Bazi smiled, 'Thank you Captain.'

Asta pressed his palms, 'Namaste.'

Bazi and Amar replied before the Makayuuk men exited and the door closed.

Amar gave Bazi a look of horror, 'By the Gods this is torture!'

The old man wagged his finger, 'When I was a young man on campaign in the Traven Territory with your father ...'

Amar rolled his eyes, 'Yes I know you slept on catronium floors and ate insects, I've heard that story a thousand times already!'

Bazi shouted through his beard, 'You don't know how fortunate you are, if you were my son I would be ashamed!'

'Well I'm not your son and I like to have a little comfort in my life. I'll leave sleeping on hard metal and eating parasites to someone else.'

'You are a parasite!' scowled Bazi.

Before Amar could reply a crewman entered their room with mattresses, one under each arm.

'Thank you very much,' squealed Amar grabbing his cushion.

Bazi took his thanking the crewman.

Amar placed his mattress on its bed, delivering his comrade a smarmy grin.

Two days later and Amar was not grinning, 'My stomach hurts!' he moaned.

Bazi sat on his bunk with a plate of pink sludge, 'Then have something to eat.'

Amar lay outstretched, 'It tastes strange.'

'Well what do you expect?' asked the old man in an incredulous tone, 'We're in another galaxy!'

Bazi went to the food dispenser, pulled a tray out of a slot and placed it under the nozzle, 'Haanal.'

The nozzle fired a ball of pink gloop onto the tray. Bazi presented the tray to Amar, 'Here you haven't eaten properly in days. You cannot meet their leader in such a condition.'

The young man pushed himself up, leaning his back against the wall. Accepting the tray he looked at the thick sludge with disdain, 'Are there no eating utensils?'

'No, it is thick enough to use your hands. In fact it is not bad ... an acquired taste but nevertheless.'

Amar took a deep sigh and pulled a piece of the gloop off, rolled it into a ball and popped it in his mouth. He was so hungry that by now he could eat anything. The chewy Makayuuk cuisine was hardly fine dining but it did fill his stomach.

After a second tray Amar had recovered, the meal wasn't all that bad, it tasted something like a pudding he enjoyed back home.

Bazi placed both trays back in the wall unit to be cleaned, 'Let's have another look around this warship.'

Amar nodded, he needed to stretch his legs. The pair exited their quarters for another stroll. All of the obvious areas such as the bridge and engine room, they'd nosed around on the first day. Now they just wandered about to see what they might stumble upon.

At the corridors' end Bazi and Amar's ears detected chattering voices. Silently they looked at each other making for its point of origin. Turning a corner they walked into a mess hall.

The room had a circular sofa with a black circular onyx table as its focus. Makayuuk men and women filled the sofa along with Lian. They seemed to be engaged in a form of entertainment perhaps?

The pair observed as two people would place their fingertips upon the table, a hologram of a three dimensional shape then appeared in the centre. Next counters began to move inside a cube. A three dimensional game of Othello took place at lightning fast pace. Eventually the structure filled with counters of both black and white. After a tally had been made a winner was announced bringing laughter and celebration around the table.

After sipping her drink one of the Makayuuk women challenged Lian to a game of "Kuch". The Amazon refused politely but everyone egged her on, they wanted to see Xch'uup's Adjunct in action.

'Three versus one!' shouted Asta.

The crew roared in approval causing Lian to blush.

'Or perhaps she is afraid to lose?'

The tall lady looked down at Asta as if he were a naughty boy.

Asta grinned and the crew laughed.

Lian put down her drink, placing her fingertips upon the table, 'Fine, so who thinks they're tough enough?'

The machine men laughed as the first woman put her fingers down. After a second crewman entered the fray Lian peered at Asta, 'Well?'

Everyone laughed until the young man touched the jet black table's edge.

Cheers went out as a hologramatic ball of whirling particles popped up in the table's centre. It was evident Lian was taking on three challengers yet the nature of this game eluded Bazi for the moment.

'Begin when it pleases you,' stated the Valkyrie in a coy tone.

Her three opponents both pulled expressions of total concentration as particles swirled in a vortex. Three definite vortices formed but remained stationary, waiting for something to happen.

Lian smiled as a fourth vortex appeared nearest to where she sat, all observed the game unfold in total silence.

As Lian's vortex formed the other vortices moved in, it seemed they were attempting to swallow up their target. However on touching its edge they met stiff resistance.

The Makayuuk's concentration intensified as they attempted to consume their foe. This looked to be a game based on the power of brute mental force ... a game of will power perhaps?

The crewmen grimaced attempting to push Lian's vortex into submission, their faces contorting with mental strain.

As for Lian she smiled, music began to play in the room and Voice of Machine sang along as she defied the mental power of three Makayuuk.

Lian sang, 'Wave your hands if you're not with a man,' the half Tlillan beauty took one hand off the table and waved it in the air, 'Can I kick it?'

The backing singers on the music recording replied, 'Yes you can!'

Some of the observers began to grin. It was obvious to them that Voice of Machine would not fall tonight. She may not prosper in other contests but at the game of Kuch Lian remained undefeated. She sang to one of her favourite songs whilst pushing back her challengers' mental force. Lian allowed her opponents to persevere for a while before turning her attention to crushing them, one by one. She pointed to one of her adversaries and sang, 'If you can't get a girl but your best friend can it's time to move your body!'

Upon finishing that line her vortex bulged out swallowing his whole. Where her challenger's fingers had rested lights dimmed informing the Mack his game was over.

Voice of Machine pointed to a young lady totally focused on the task of defeating Lian, 'I don't wanna be sleazy, baby just tease me, got no family planned!' sang the Valkyrie as the ladies vortex was consumed.

Only Asta remained, he pushed as hard as possible but Lian gave no ground, 'Pimpin' ain't easy but if you're selling it … It's alright!'

The Valkyrie smiled and in time with the music she consumed Asta, dimming lights around his fingers. Everyone laughed and clapped even the challengers applauded Kalayuuk as she took a bow.

Lian noticed her guests, 'Greetings gentlemen. How are you tonight?'

Bazi pressed his palms together, 'Namaste Kalayuuk.'

'Please don't be so formal, come would you like to play?'

'If I could just watch that would be excellent,' smiled Bazi.

The Makayuuk shuffled up to make room on the sofa for their guests.

'Something to drink gentlemen?'

'Oh thank you,' said Amar.

The Valkyrie brought them two glasses of a yellow liquid similar in appearance to whisky. The heralds each accepted a glass goblet sipping the fluid inside.

Amar smacked his lips, 'Hmm, it tastes familiar … what is it?'

'Urine,' replied Asta.

Bazi placed his glass down politely. Amar spat any drink remaining in his mouth across the room.

'URINE! FROM WHAT?'

'I don't understand?' inquired Asta.

'From which animal?'

Asta attempted to calm his guest, 'Have no fear. It was taken from the crew.'

Amar went a funny colour as Bazi asked his host, 'Why do you drink urine?'

'It is a perfect mixture for rehydration, containing nutrients and anti-bodies strengthening the immune system. Why would you drink anything else?'

The bearded man looked at his glass and replied, 'Have we been drinking this in our quarters for the last two days?'

'Oh no, water is dispensed only from partially reprocessed urine.'

'So the ship's water is not,' Bazi went giddy for a moment, '100% purified?'

'Of course not, why remove the benefits of urine?'

'May I ask why this is yellow and the water dispensed in our cabin is not?'

'This is coloured and flavoured for the purpose of recreation.'

Amar's natural colour returned to his face, 'What have we been eating?'

Before Lian could stop him Asta replied, 'Processed protein.'

Amar gave a suspicious grimace as he wiped his mouth, 'Processed from what exactly?'

'Deceased Makayuuk, prisoners of war ...'

Before the machine man could finish Amar went green and vomited onto the onyx gaming table.

Bazi wasn't feeling too good however he apologised for his friend's son, 'Forgive him he is young and too familiar with soft living.'

The crew of the Machine warship grimaced as Amar wretched again and again. Despite the fact his stomach contents had already been ejaculated the young man couldn't prevent the reflex action as muscles contorted over and over again.

Amar spent the rest of the evening in a med bay groaning in pain whilst his stomach wrenched from one position to another. Bazi began to see the funny side as he chatted with Lian.

Once the pair reached Otoch, the first item on the list was to get a meal. Sitting in a Tlillan café with Lian, Amar and Bazi were ready to eat for an army.

A dish of nook'ol was served, Bazi tucked into the fattened grubs. Amar sneered at his plate of squirming insects until Bazi called out, 'What's the matter?'

'These are insects, live ones at that!'

The old man stretched his arm across the table, 'Don't you want yours?'

Amar snatched his plate. Holding it close to his chest he replied, 'Ahh! I didn't say that, did I?'

'Well?' asked the old man as he chewed on a fat nook'ol.

Amar put a maggot in his mouth, his brain acknowledged how disgusting this was yet hunger conquered any reflex to heave it back up.

That evening Amar and Bazi observed the city of Muul Kaah from the terrace of their hotel room, 'A city of pyramids, they seem to be fascinated by these constructions.'

Bazi nodded, 'Are you not fascinated by them?'

Amar examined many peaks through the twilight, 'I am.'

'Look at that one Amar how much effort do you believe it took to construct?'

The young man observed the peak of Muul Kaah itself, a mile high super pyramid, 'It depends on when it was built.'

'It is said the peak is eons old.'

'But how advanced were they upon its construction?' asked Amar as he stroked his chin.

'A good point,' smiled Bazi, 'perhaps there is hope for you yet?'

The following day the heralds were escorted into Muul Kaah itself, both were awe struck upon observing effigies of former Xch'uups decorating its interior. A luminescent moss lit the palace of sculptured deities staring down upon them.

Led by Nestor and his men they penetrated the Tlillan fortress, under intense observation. Matriarchs and Tlillan women sat on pews to the left and right. Upon a throne a woman rested in a long white dress. Bazi recognised her from mosaics in his hotel and restaurant. Her crown of feathers and sable locks of hair stood out on Otoch.

Russian soldiers fanned out taking their stations around Muul Kaah as Lian introduced the explorers from Andromeda. Amar could not take his eyes off a woman stood beside Xch'uup's throne. Her skin was darker than any Tlillan's; the tallest of her dark haired sisters by far.

Lian pressed her palms together, 'Namaste Xch'uup,' before taking her place upon a stone pew.

The entire palace waited with bated breath. Bazi realised they lingered on him and Amar. The bearded herald stepped before the Tlillan Queen's throne and greeted her as he would his King. Bending down upon one knee he stated, 'Ensi,' lowering his face towards the floor.

Amar quickly followed suit, bending his knee and addressing Malikah as Ensi, Ur for righteous ruler.

Malikah replied with the words, 'Uzuzzu,' something like 'rise' in Ur.

The awe struck explorers returned to their feet, 'I Bazi, envoy of the Kingdom of Ur, bring greetings from my King.'

'The Kingdom of Ur? Surely you are referring to the Kingdom of Telal?'

The old herald was disturbed, this Queen knew so much of his people and their language yet he knew nothing of the Tlillan.

Amar smiled, 'I am sorry, Telal?'

Malikah gave the young man a disappointed glare. Amitra smirked at such a weak bluff.

The sable Queen shook her head slowly from side to side, 'Do you take me for a fool?'

Bazi interjected, 'Forgive him he is young and naïve. I apologise if any insult was inflicted.'

Amitra spoke to the envoy from Ur, 'Xch'uup was only disappointed.'

Bazi gave his comrade a black stare before continuing, 'Xch'uup is correct. For many cycles we have been subjects of the Telal. I have been sent in search of the Amelatu.'

'Please describe this Amelatu,' stated Amitra.

'It is difficult … the legend was of the Etlu … the people of Ur many cycles ago. It is unclear as to whether the Amelatu is a species, race or single person; however the Amelatu is said to deliver the Etlu in their time of need. There is no exact description, the only words alluring to a depiction come from a Nabu long dead, "First came spirits followed by the grey mother chased by a condor of white. Until Roy D'effrayeur appears from eternity the Etlu will be slaves."'

Amitra spoke to Bazi, 'Xch'uup saw your arrival many cycles ago. In response an exploration vessel has been deployed to Andromeda. As we speak men and supplies are travelling to Masku Patu.'

Amar chirped up, 'For what purpose?'

'Masku Patu is now under Tlillan jurisdiction.'

The young man was shocked, 'What of the Kishar?'

Amitra shook her head silently.

'What of Telal?'

Malikah rose from her throne, 'We shall see. What I want from you is information.'

'Concerning?' asked a nervous Bazi.

'Every territory in Andromeda.'

'Surely you already have the information you require?'

'You can never have enough intelligence Mr Bazi, whether it be friend or foe.'

Chapter 2

'Namaste Xch'uup.'

Earth music played softly in the background as Malikah beckoned the long haired Indian inside a penthouse suite at the Plaza.

'Take a seat Amitra,' said the sable Queen glancing up from a tablet.

The Indian sat on a circular sofa, with a smile she asked, 'You still worry over your parents?'

Malikah nodded, 'They journey to Andromeda in three months from now.'

'Your mother is a very competent ...'

'It's not my mother which concerns me, it is my father.'

'Why?'

'He is a very stubborn man with a penchant for taking stupid risks. If only he and your father could be alike.'

'My father? He is as stubborn as a donkey. Besides is not danger always feared when distant but braved when present?'

'Braved?'

'You are both alike, ready to face danger head on for the benefit of others.'

The sable Queen smiled at her Grand Priestess, 'And she who removes terror from the mind is the greatest of friends.'

'You did not ask me here to speak on your parents. Arthur concerns you presently, yes?'

Malikah dismissed her tablet, 'How is he doing?'

'He is an excellent pupil quite the student of Socrates and Aristotle.'

Malikah pulled a disparaging expression.

'You disapprove?'

'Not of Socrates and Aristotle.'

'I believe his understanding of stoic logic will bring future benefits.'

'We shall see.'

The doorbell chimed to which Malikah called out, 'Enter.'

The door slid away, 'Namaste Xch'uup.'

'Come in Sandra.'

The sable Greek stood until offered a seat beside her Xch'uup.

'So what do you have to say on Arthur?'

The Valkyrie replied in a soft tone, 'He understands all he is taught, the boy's mind absorbs information as a sponge in the desert.'

'But?'

'He demonstrates no desire to learn any more than required. For him medicine is a chore.'

Before Malikah could speak further another chimed rang out, 'Enter.'

'Namaste Xch'uup,' bowed the short Marshal of Otoch.

'Come sit down Kaeo.'

The dark haired lady sat alongside her sisters, 'The boy?'

'What of his progress?'

'Progress! All he wants to do is listen to music and write poetry!'

'What of his swordsmanship?'

'Passable.'

'Oh?'

'The kid's a dreamer. He wants to be an artist.'

'What of his diplomacy skills?'

'Don't ask!'

Amitra and Sandra both chuckled at Kaeo's frustration.

'Greg has given me use of the Plaza's gym this afternoon. Arthur is waiting for us.'

'Pah, good luck with that!' snorted Kaeo.

Malikah arose from her sofa, her sisters followed suit exiting the room. They climbed some stairs and into a gym on the top floor of the most luxurious hotel in central New York.

Stepping through the door a young man, who looked to be in his late teens or early twenties by human years, awaited; part Tlillan, part human with short brown hair and green eyes. He possessed a startling resemblance to his father, Henry Jenkins, a feature most Matriarchs found quite disturbing.

Standing nearly six and a half feet tall his pale Darksider skin contrasted with chestnut brown hair, dressed in a normal pair of gym shorts and a green military t-shirt.

'Namaste Xch'uup,' bowed the young lad.

He spoke with what some might describe an English accent, though at times verbal inflections brought it close to that of a South African. Little contact outside a small family of Mictlantecuhtli precipitated this verbal aberration.

'Greetings Arthur, it is good to see you are punctual.'

'You wish to test me Xch'uup?'

'I do, Kaeo tells me you are deficient in self-defence is she correct?'

The young man fixed his eyes upon the short Thai, 'I don't know, Xch'uup.'

Malikah furrowed her regal brow, 'You don't know?'

'No Xch'uup, I don't.'

'Arthur, bring me a bokken.'

The young man jogged to the corner of the gym fetching his master a bokken crafted in the style of an 1852 sabre.

Malikah took the weapon, 'Thank you, now select one for yourself.'

The boy retrieved a similar weapon.

Malikah removed her frock coat handing it to Kaeo. Dressed only in a Tlillan ribbed suit she approached Arthur, 'Now we shall see if Kaeo spoke the truth, ENGARDE!'

The boy didn't react. He was taken aback at the thought of fencing with Xch'uup. Malikah quickly slapped his weapon aside before thrusting into the lad's ribs. Arthur fell to the floor with a cry of pain, his sable Queen gave a condescending Tlillan sneer, 'That was pathetic.'

Arthur returned to his feet taking an engarde position. His eyes began to fire as embers in the night.

Malikah smirked, moving in again she slapped his blade in a quick parry carte before striking the young man's wrist. Once again Arthur let out a cry of pain yet this time he maintained a pointed blade before rushing forward in a powerful lunge.

The sable Queen side stepped directing Arthur's blade away and leaving the lad outstretched, blade wavering in mid-air. Malikah kicked, knocking the boy flat on the floor.

'Is this it? I spend my time and effort educating you with the best this Galaxy has to offer and am repaid with mediocrity?'

Arthur scrambled to his feet but before getting there Xch'uup kicked him square in the face with the flat of her boot. Losing his vision for a moment Arthur dropped onto his back wiping tears of pain from his face in an attempt to restore his vision.

Malikah turned to Kaeo, 'You have failed me!'

Kaeo dropped to the floor in a kowtow, 'Forgive me Xch'uup.'

'Xch'uup does not forgive mediocrity.'

Before anything more could be said Arthur rose and in a fury charged Malikah from behind. The Empress spun around dodging his blade she grabbed Arthur's body and cast him to the floor with a mighty judo throw.

Malikah cackled as he lay beside a prostrate Kaeo.

Upon noting his surroundings Arthur spied the Grand Marshal's mantle, hanging from its sword belt.

Those present sensed an overwhelming desire to draw Kaeo's blade. Amitra, Sandra and Kaeo fell motionless awaiting the boy's next decision.

Malikah sneered in that condescending Tlillan fashion, 'Do it, don't take this humiliation ... finish me if you think you can!'

Arthur could not control his anger; in one of those moments we have all suffered where the heart overtakes any logical thought he snatched Kaeo's neutronium blade from its scabbard. Standing bloody faced before a condescending Xch'uup he roared, 'XCH'UUP! YOU WILL DIE!'

Malikah took a couple of steps back. Her sisters knew full well Arthur could not defeat her no matter what material his blade had been forged from.

Kaeo looked up in anticipation, if he attacked now it would mean the end of her toil. Secretly the half Tlillan desired Arthur leap into an attack, resulting in inevitable death. True bladesmanship came from the hand and mind wielding it, not the weapon itself.

Arthur breathed heavily through his teeth as blood ran down his face and fire leapt from his eyes. Much as the Goddess Lyssa sent Heracles into a fit of rage and insanity the daughter of Nyx filled Arthur's heart with thoughts of violence. Unable to control himself, just as the mighty son of Zeus, he rounded on the focus of his ire. Unlike Heracles Arthur's focus was not a weak woman or defenceless children. Lyssa drove Arthur into a stupor as if he were a rabid animal, hate and revenge coursed through his veins as hot lava erupting from Vesuvius.

Malikah peered through his eyes and into the soul of her young charge. Delving into a passion which swirled beneath the surface of all great artists hearts, 'You want to kill me, don't you boy?'

The lad didn't answer. Fury overwhelmed his senses leaving only revenge and hatred to be satiated.

'Well? Fight me! Or are you afraid of a woman? The son of a worthless whore and a stinking coward!'

He pointed Kaeo's neutronium blade at Xch'uup and just as he was to charge to his demise a voice reverberated throughout his entire body, 'ARTHUR!'

Detracting from his desire to plunge a blade into the Tlillan Queen's heart stood a beautiful woman dressed in golden armour. Hair of golden silk with perfect curls bouncing around a majestic face.

'Lower your blade,' spoke the Goddess in a Greek accent.

'SHE DESERVES TO DIE!'

Amitra and Sandra gave each other looks of puzzlement, it was unclear to whom Arthur was speaking. As far as they could tell he spoke to someone or something behind Kaeo yet nothing occupied that space.

'Take a hold of your mind boy! Malikah has brought down many great warriors in battle before now. She will destroy you before you have a chance to nick her arm!'

The sable Valkyrie was equally confused, 'Are you mad boy? Speaking to figments of your imagination? Your mother truly has failed her Xch'uup!'

Arthur snapped his vision back to Malikah his shaking hand vibrating the sword with uncontrolled anger.

Athene stood by his side, 'Only you can see me Arthur.'

'How?'

'Only those I wish may do so.'

'How?'

'Stop asking questions and listen. You will lower your weapon and after this foolishness is over you shall seek out Duncan McCann before he leaves for Andromeda.'

'Admiral McCann?'

'Yes, now lower your weapon.'

'I cannot, I will not suffer this humiliation.'

Athene moved between Arthur and Malikah. Her golden skin, sparkling blue eyes and cherry red lips were the perfect representation of a woman. She pushed his sword down, pressing her fingers upon its blade. Arthur could not resist despite his fury and enhanced Tlillan strength.

The Goddess whispered, 'When you see Duncan tell him that it is easy to be angry.'

'Who are you?'

'I am Athene but you shall not mention this to another soul, is that understood?'

'I understand.'

As Athene dissipated into the atmosphere her words echoed, 'Remember, it is easy to be angry.'

After the Goddess of Wisdom had left, Malikah, with a very puzzled expression, shouted in a deep voice, 'Come kill me you coward!'

Fire dissipated from Arthur's eyes, the Goddess Athene dispatched Lyssa's influence. Arthur dropped his blade upon the floor and taking a deep breath the lad walked for the exit as the Tlillan Queen heckled him, 'That's it, run home to mummy you coward!'

Before exiting Arthur turned back upon Xch'uup, bowed and said softly, 'It is easy to be angry.'

Once the lad had left Malikah looked down at Kaeo, 'You can get up.'

Kaeo rose to her feet retrieving her mantle, 'It is as I said.'

'He has little to no self-control. I'm unsure what halted him.'

Amitra stepped forward, 'Who was he speaking to?'

'Perhaps the madness is taking him?' interjected Sandra.

'Perhaps.'

Kaeo shook her head, 'He's dangerous I say put him in a control collar.'

'Arthur is not an animal.'

'Well I have business to take care of, if I may be excused?'

'Sure.'

Kaeo bowed, 'Namaste Xch'uup.'

After the short warrior left Amitra spoke, 'Did you sense it?'

'I did.'

'As did I,' reported Sandra.

'Do you think he is in love?'

'I believe he has deep feelings for her. If we wish to control him it must be done through Kaeo,' noted Amitra.

Malikah brushed her hair with one hand and discarded her bokken with the other, 'Is Kaeo aware?'

'I believe she is aware but denies the truth. Kaeo holds glory and honour in the highest esteem. Love is merely a vice, it distracts from that which is most important in life.'

Malikah nodded, 'Let him convalesce for a few months. Then we shall test the boy again.'

'And if he fails again?' inquired Sandra.

'Then drastic action is required.'

Taking his convalescent time Arthur got on the first flight to Geneva. Dressed in a polite two piece suit, cut for a young man, and carrying a small case he walked up the path of Duncan McCann's residence. Pressing his finger on the door the AI announced his presence.

Opening the door Ofra exclaimed, 'Whatever you're selling me I have one already!'

'I'm here to see Duncan McCann.'

Ofra suspected the boy's alien heritage but continued in a defensive demeanour, 'What do you want my son for?'

'My name is Arthur, Arthur Jenkins. Mr McCann is a friend of my father's, Henry Jenkins.'

Ofra took another look at the lad, 'You're the Tlillan boy aren't you?'

He smiled, 'Yes, that's me.'

Ofra grabbed the lad and dragged him inside, 'I remember when you were born. It was all over the news you know? The first male born to a Tlillan in centuries, all of those Matriarchs were furious with your mother!'

Arthur just smiled as Ofra led him through the house.

'DUNCAN!' shouted Ofra dragging her guest into the front room.

The Englishman was having a snooze on the sofa until rudely awoken by his mother, 'What the bloody hell? Why don't you shout a bit louder? They probably can't hear you on Mars!'

He rubbed his eyes to see Ofra with a young man, a young man who bore a striking resemblance to Jenkins, 'Who's this?'

'Don't be so rude to guests, this is Arthur.'

McCann dragged himself off the sofa, 'Arthur? Jenkins' boy?'

'Yes sir.'

'Well, well, well what are you doing here?'

Arthur looked down at Ofra who quickly got the message, 'I'll leave you two alone.'

After Ofra exited the room Arthur stated, 'I was sent here by a mutual friend of ours.'

'Oh? And who might that be?'

'Her name is Athene.'

McCann stopped dead. He was ridged as a plank of wood, 'I'm sorry?'

'I said I was sent here by Athene.'

'I'm sorry young man but I don't know anyone by that name.'

'She had a message I was to convey.'

'Really? And that is?'

'She says it is easy to be angry.'

McCann took a deep breath, 'I'm afraid you've wasted a journey young man.'

'Didn't I always say you were a poor liar my little Odysseus?'

The Englishman turned to his right, the Goddess of the flashing eyes had appeared. Golden breastplate and helmet in hand she grinned at McCann, 'You couldn't convince a child with that poor attempt,' mocked the warrior Goddess.

Turning to Arthur she smiled with her brilliant blue eyes, 'Greetings Arthur.'

Arthur pressed his palms together, 'Namaste Athene.'

McCann looked around the room suspiciously, 'Who are you talking to Arthur?'

Athene burst into laughter, 'He can see me but my little Odysseus trusts no-one … not even himself!'

Arthur spoke to McCann, 'Do you not see Athene? She is in plain sight.'

'I don't know what you're talking about.'

Athene approached the young man, 'He can see us both but fears he's being tricked by your Tlillan powers.'

'Mr McCann I give you my word there is no deception,' pleaded Arthur.

'I think you need to see a doctor, perhaps I should call one?'

Athene stepped towards the Englishman, her mood changed, 'Enough Duncan, I grow tired of this!'

Despite standing directly before him the Englishman ignored Athene. The Goddesses beautiful golden hair lifted into the air, strands glued together forming terrifying snakes. The Athenian's eyes changed from a sparkling blue to a stinging red as her bellowing voice filled the atmosphere, 'DO NOT IGNORE ME!'

McCann's body trembled with fear at such a terrifying display. Unable to speak he nodded as best he could in her direction.

Upon accepting recognition Athene's formed morphed back to that of the attractive goddess he recognised, 'This boy is destined to lead yet Malikah has failed in his education. It is now your responsibility to prepare him as you did your own daughter, for the trial. Malikah believes he is convalescing.

I will send his father with a man who will train Arthur in hand to hand combat. You shall give this man a place in your staff on the Discovery, is that understood?'

'Yes Athene,' nodded McCann.

Athene smiled lovingly, 'Good, he'll be here within a few weeks.'

'Understood.'

'Until then you'll train this boy in swordsmanship. By the time you leave for Andromeda I want to see a hardened Spartan warrior standing before me.'

'I understand Athene.'

The Goddess of the flashing eyes smiled. As she dissipated into the fabric of existence her voice echoed, 'Remember Duncan, it is easy to be angry.'

McCann turned to Arthur, 'That's a fine bloody mess you've gotten me into.'

Arthur made no reply.

'Alright young man, follow me and we'll get you settled in. Tomorrow we can start on your passage into manhood.'

The next day McCann brought Arthur along to an I.S.A fencing hall. At one end were racks of fencing weapons at the other hung protective fencing kit.

'So I take it Malikah has already taught you to fence?' inquired McCann.

'I've taken instruction from Kaeo for the last few years.'

McCann let out a sneer, 'Kaeo?'

'Is there a problem with that?'

'She's great with the blade there can be no doubt of that.'

'However?'

'However when it comes to instruction you could do a lot better.'

'Really?'

'What's your blade?'

'Sorry?'

'Epee, foil or sabre?'

'Sabre, I suppose.'

'Naturally,' the Englishman walked to a corner of the hall where an old fellow observed younger men practice; Charging back and forth in sabre duels, banging and crashing into one another.

'Gordon, I have a student for you.'

The bald fellow looked up at Arthur and gave a rather disinterested expression, 'No thank you Duncan.'

'Oh come on Gordon there's a bottle of Laphroaig in it.'

The old fellow stood up and looked the lad over, 'Have you fenced before?'

'Yes I was taught on Otoch by the Grand Marshal.'

Gordon chuckled, 'You must be quite the Zorro then?'

Arthur ruffled his brow, 'Zorro?'

'Never mind, how many years have you fenced?'

'Only three but I'm Tlillan, I can link with my instructor and learn far quicker than any human.'

Gordon grinned at McCann, 'Then why are you here?'

Arthur didn't reply.

'Why don't you fence Gordon?' suggested McCann.

The young half Tlillan looked down at the old fellow disparagingly. Gordon chuckled as he walked to the piste.

'Go get your kit on and pick a weapon lad,' instructed McCann.

'If you say so,' replied an overconfident Arthur.

Once on the piste the pair saluted, every sabreur stopped what they were doing to observe.

'Engarde,' shouted the referee, 'Ready? Fight!'

Sensors in the swords picked up and transmitted contact with the opponent's kit, there was no need for the wires used in the past. The kit was also sensitive to sword contact, lighting up in red or green at a firm touch. Arthur, confident in his physical superiority charged forward.

Gordon moved back slowly and once Arthur was in range he took the boy's blade in a bind before thrusting the tip of his onto his opponent's arm.

'HALT!' called the referee, 'One light to my right.'

The box in the middle lit up red on Gordon's side as did Arthur's kit on the area he'd been hit.

Arthur was quite confused, putting it down to luck. Surely this weak old man couldn't defeat a powerful Tlillan?

'Engarde, ready, fight!'

Again Arthur charged down the piste towards the frail old man. Arthur closed in on his target to make a strike. Gordon parried before elegantly placing the point of his sabre on Arthur's glove.

'HALT!'

This time both lights had been activated.

The referee quickly made his decision, 'Attack from my left, parried from the right, two hits, point right.'

Arthur swung his blade in frustration, 'WHAT? That was my right of way!'

The referee gave Arthur a grim stare, 'Attack parried right of way goes right.'

McCann shook his head, by the time the match was up Gordon had won 10 hits to 2. Arthur was furious, storming out of the hall after throwing his weapon to the floor.

Gordon smiled at McCann, 'I thought these Tlillans could learn anything in a day?'

'It seems humility isn't on that list.'

Gordon laughed then returned to his seat.

'Listen I need someone to train this lad, he's got three months until he has to go up against a Matriarch and win.'

'And you want me to do it?'

'Will you, please?'

'Three months? It's not possible you know that Duncan.'

'He's Tlillan, he can learn in a week what might take us years.'

'I know but that's not the problem is it?'

McCann nodded his head, 'That's my task, so will you do it?'

Gordon placed his mask on the floor whilst wiping sweat from his brow, 'I'll do what I can but you must teach him to control that temper or he'll get nowhere.'

McCann returned home to be greeted by one of his mother's black looks.

'What's that for?' inquired the Englishman.

'What did you do to that poor boy today?'

'I took him for a fencing lesson, why?'

'He returned all upset and wouldn't tell me.'

'Yeah, he probably didn't want it all over the city by evening,' quipped McCann.

Ofra tightened her mouth then snapped at her son, 'Shut your mouth! Now go and apologise to Arthur!'

McCann raised his eyebrows, 'For what exactly?'

'For whatever it is you did.'

The Englishman shook his head, 'Jesus Christ!'

'He's in his room and if you speak like that again you'll regret it!'

McCann sighed as he made his way upstairs, 'Yes mum.'

Arthur was in his room working on his tablet.

McCann stepped in, 'What's that you're up to?'

The young man lay on his bed tapping away at a screen, 'I'm composing.'

'Composing what?'

'Music.'

'Is it any good?'

'I'm sure you would find it quite deficient.'

'According to Malikah you're very talented with music and poetry.'

'Oh really? Has she been keeping tabs on me?'

'Yes, she's very concerned about you.'

'Really?'

'Really.'

'I think Malikah hates me.'

'Then why exert so much effort in your education?'

Arthur turned away from his tablet, 'You mean persecution!'

McCann shook his head slowly, 'Jesus Christ, listen to yourself you're the perfect victim aren't you?'

Arthur's attention returned to his work.

'There are people out there worrying about where the next meal is coming from. Some are going to sleep on an empty stomach tonight. Do you know how that feels Arthur?'

The boy replied coldly, 'No.'

'You've lived in palaces and five star hotels your entire life. Fed on the finest food the Galaxy has to offer. Educated to the highest standards possible and all you can do is whine like a spoilt brat.'

Arthur quickly sat up, Tlillan fire flickering in his eyes.

McCann mocked the lad, 'You couldn't defeat Gordon what makes you think you're a match for me boy?'

'Then why don't you just send me back to Malikah?'

'Because you're here to learn something.'

'What is that?'

'It is easy to be angry ...'

'I know that, I'm not a fool.'

'It is easy to be angry but to be angry at the right person at the right time ... that is hard.'

'Is that what Athene told you?'

'In a way.'

'So how do I learn?'

'Today you were humiliated, yes?'

'I was.'

'You humiliated yourself when you stomped off in anger.'

Arthur thought for a moment then nodded silently.

'While you're here with me you'll be humiliated every single day, do you understand?'

'I understand.'

'At some point you'll become numb to it, just as exposure to fear lessens its effects over time.'

Arthur nodded, after considering his actions the lad stated, 'I made a fool of myself today.'

'You did.'

'It won't happen again, you have my word Mr McCann.'

The Englishman smiled, 'Good, now we can get on to why you lost that match today.'

Arthur placed his tablet upon the bed, 'I don't know. I should have beaten him. He is old and physically inferior. My attacks should have overwhelmed him easily.'

'So why didn't they?'

'Each time he out fenced me, the more aggressive I became the easier he defeated me.'

'At least you see your mistakes.'

'But sabre is a weapon of aggression and attack, it doesn't make sense.'

'The sabre is a sword. The sword is a weapon of elegance and finesse not brute force. You must learn to control yourself then you may manipulate your enemy, much the same as Gordon manipulated you today.'

McCann returned to the kitchen where his mother had prepared a dish of fish and rice, 'How is Arthur?'

'He'll work it out.'

Placing dinner before him Ofra stated, 'Eat this.'

'Oh thanks.'

'Did Malikah send Arthur to you?'

Eating his meal the Englishman replied, 'No, he came here by himself.'

'What for?'

'It seems Malikah has dropped the ball.'

Ofra walked over to the fridge and took a fruit juice, 'All I know is that he's a very angry young man.'

'That's one of the problems but I've got a feeling it'll all be sorted out by the time he returns.'

'Well he won't get anything done on an empty belly. Call him down so that he can have some dinner.'

McCann put his knife and fork down as he got back to his feet, 'Yes mum.'

Chapter 3

On a street in London's East End a group of tired men stood in line on a cold spring morning. John Clayton numbered amongst them. Having fallen on hard times he slept beneath the heavens and ate on the charity of others.

Before this time he'd been a soldier, serving many years deep below Bandayuuk's surface but the war was over and there was little need for men of his ilk. Some became pirates, killing for profit on the edges of Triumvirate space. Some had been lucky enough to gain rank, providing a pension, others ended up on the streets.

Clayton didn't kill for money his morals wouldn't allow it. Despite many years served and medals earnt he'd failed to attain a monthly allowance from the SBS.

This was the fallout of the greatest conflict the Milky Way had witnessed, soldiers discarded upon the street to die in anonymity.

A caravan opened its shutters to serve a line of dishevelled men breakfast. When Clayton reached its service counter he recognised the woman serving him.

'Here, don't I know you?' said the Londoner.

'I don't recall having met,' replied a tall red headed lady in an apron.

'Clayton, John Clayton.'

'I'm sorry Mr Clayton I don't recall having met.'

'No, but you're Chanatico aren't you?'

Chanatico gave an odd expression, 'Why yes.'

'Yeh your Jenkins' missus, aren't you?'

'Yes Mr Clayton, now if you could move on there are others waiting to be served.'

'Oh of course, I mean it's thanks to your husband I'm here. That miserable old git had it in for me from day one!'

'Excuse me?'

Clayton pulled aside his dirty old trench coat to display a row of gleaming silver, 'See that? I fought for him and he demoted me three times. If it wasn't for him I'd be living the good life, drinking Martinis with some Tlillan bird. Instead I'm stuck out here eating from a bloody soup kitchen!'

'My husband had a lot of men under his command on Bandayuuk. I'm certain it wasn't anything personal Mr Clayton.'

'Well you tell him that you met John Clayton today, you let him know what's become of me thanks to his vindictiveness.'

Chanatico let out a big huff, 'I shall Mr Clayton now please move on there are others waiting, thank you.'

Clayton walked away but not before making a speech to the crowd of men waiting in line, 'Thank you, is that all I get? A thank you from his wife after I shed my blood for years in those bloody tunnels! I think that bastard owes me a job at least, what do you fellas reckon?'

Mumbles of agreement came from the line of men.

'Ah but he won't care. I'll just die of hyperthermia one night whilst he's snuggling up to his Tlillan missus!'

The men gave words of support for Clayton. Chanatico stopped dishing out soup, 'Mr Clayton, I'll speak to my husband tonight. If he remembers you I'll see what I can do, is that satisfactory?'

Clayton nodded.

'Will you be here tomorrow?'

Clayton laughed, 'I'll have to cancel tea with the King but I'm sure he'll understand!'

A line of vagrants laughed with the fallen soldier.

'Then we'll speak tomorrow.'

Since the end of Bandayuuk Henry Jenkins had retired from the military. Working for private security companies left him a very well to do man. Yet that he desired eluded him most, his son. Xch'uup possessed Arthur and Henry had to work around her schedule to see him. Being an SBS Brigadier was not compatible with such an arrangement.

Returning to his home in Kensington Jenkins retired his hat and coat before making his way into the lounge. Chanatico anticipated his arrival, dressed in a beautiful one piece lilac dress.

Jenkins raised an eyebrow, 'Well I'm either a very lucky man or in some terrible trouble!'

Chanatico smiled, 'What do you mean?'

'I've either forgotten something important or you're about to surprise me.'

'Hmm, a surprise.'

The security advisor let out a sigh of relief and kissed his wife, 'In that case I'll have a brandy.'

Resting in a comfortable armchair dressed in a three piece suit the former Brigadier took a glass of Cognac. Jenkins was poured an ample portion and immediately began to suspect something was a foot.

'Really Henry, why so suspicious?'

'I'm sorry dear, just human nature. What was it you wanted to surprise me with?'

Chanatico sat on the large comfy chair arm, draping her long legs across Jenkins'. She massaged his shoulder as he took a sip of the fine Napoleon Brandy.

'I met a man today who says he served with you, on Bandayuuk.'

'Really? What was his name?'

'He said you'd remember him.'

'Yes?'

'His name was Clayton, John Clayton.'

Jenkins was taking another sip of the fine French liquor when upon hearing the name he nearly choked, 'Clayton? Where in God's name did you see that bastard?'

'Henry! He was eating at a soup kitchen. He said he served under your command.'

Jenkins began to recover from the shock, 'Clayton, well I can't say I'm surprised that insubordinate is living rough!'

'Insubordinate?'

Jenkins got back to his feet and began to pace the room, 'Why yes, he spent 6 months in a bloody Glasshouse!'

'Glasshouse?'

'A military prison, he still didn't learn his lesson.'

'Why was he incarcerated?'

'Clayton assaulted an officer. If he hadn't been so effective at killing Makayuuk he'd of been discharged or jolly well hung there and then!'

'Did he assault you?'

'No, no, no it was a Captain. The order was given to execute some Macks and Clayton disregarded his orders. When confronted he head butted the Captain, breaking his nose in three places.'

Chanatico began to giggle as she stood up to massage her husband's tense shoulders.

'It wasn't very funny for Captain Brown.'

'Clayton says you demoted him three times, is that true?'

Taking a hearty swig of brandy Jenkins replied, 'Yes it is. Did he tell you that I promoted him three times as well?'

'No he didn't.'

'Of course he didn't, that miserable rascal. I promoted him to Corporal three times and had to demote him each time.'

'Why?'

'The man was impossible, constantly arguing with orders, sometimes outright disobedience!'

'Then why promote him?'

Jenkins displayed a callous visage as he recalled the past, 'John Clayton was the most merciless cold blooded killer I've ever had the misfortune to cross paths with. Put him in a tunnel with ten Macks and he'd come out alone whistling a tune.

I needed him, I'll admit that, but those days have gone and we all must look for another trade, Clayton included.'

Chanatico thought for a moment. Jenkins could see cogs moving in her cunning mind, 'What is it Chan?'

'I thought you could do with a butler.'

'A what?'

'Well you need your rest, you work so hard and I'm not always here. When Arthur is visiting it would be nice to have someone looking after the house.'

'Oh no, I'm not having that bastard living in here with my family!'

Chanatico ruffled her forehead, 'Why? Do you think he might steal the good silver?'

Jenkins took a hard slug of brandy, finishing the glass, 'No, Clayton isn't a thief.'

Chanatico poured another brandy for her husband, 'Then what?'

Accepting the glass he replied in a grim tone, 'Catch him in the wrong mood or look at him the wrong way and that bastard might just snap your neck.'

'Well how long did he serve with you?'

'More than four years.'

'Well he didn't snap your neck.'

'I was a Brigadier then!'

'Please Henry, give him a chance. He showed me his medals, don't you think he deserves one chance.'

Jenkins looked at his wife's eyes and couldn't bring himself to say no, 'Very well but the first sign of insubordination and I'll kick his arse so bloody hard he'll be shitting out of his nose!'

Chan kissed her husband, 'Thank you Henry, I'll let him know tomorrow.'

The next morning Chanatico was serving at the same soup kitchen. Sure enough Clayton appeared for his paper bowl of soup. Chan recognised the old soldier, 'Mr Clayton?'

'Yes Miss?' replied a hopeful man who'd long grown tired of sleeping in Hyde Park.

'When I'm finished here I want to see you, wait at the back for me.'

'Yes Miss Chanatico.'

Once her duties were concluded for the morning Chanatico stepped out the back, folding her apron she approached Clayton.

'I spoke with Henry, Mr Clayton.'

'Yes Miss?'

'He has agreed to take you on as a butler.'

'A butler?'

'Well if you you'd rather sleep rough on the streets of London that's up to you Mr Clayton.'

'No Miss Chanatico I'll take the job, anything's better than this.'

Chanatico smiled with satisfaction, 'Good, now here's some money,' she passed him a plastic card with a gold strip, 'get yourself cleaned up. You can purchase a uniform at this address.'

Clayton accepted the credit card and business address of a tailor, 'Thank you Miss.'

'I expect you to report for duty by five o'clock this afternoon.'

Clayton took another card with the Kensington address of Brigadier Jenkins, 'Thank you Miss.'

'Henry will speak to you once you arrive, try to be polite Mr Clayton. I had to press my husband quite hard to give you this chance.'

'I understand Miss.'

That afternoon John Clayton arrived dressed in his butler's outfit. Black shoes, straight black trousers, grey waist coat, white shirt, black butler's tie, white gloves and a long frocked black coat proudly displaying the medals he'd won in the tunnels of Bandayuuk. For the moment they were the only clean clothes in Clayton's possession.

The former soldier walked along an upper class residential street. White washed Edwardian terraced houses lined the pavement, it all seemed most proper. Clayton didn't look out of place as he marched up to Brigadier Henry Jenkins' abode and rang the doorbell.

The white door opened to reveal a smile from Chanatico, 'Oh you look fabulous Mr Clayton, do come in.'

'Thank you Miss.'

'Follow me. Henry is waiting in the lounge.'

'Yes Miss.'

Upon entering the lounge Clayton and Jenkins locked eyes for the first time in years.

Jenkins sneered as he stepped over to his new butler, 'So we meet again Clayton.'

'Yes Brigadier.'

Jenkins nursed a glass of Cognac viewing his new servant with suspicion, 'I'm not a Brigadier anymore.'

'Yes sir.'

Jenkins gave his former subordinate a black look, 'When you address me as Sir I want to hear some oomph behind it, not a weak croak!'

'YES SIR!' bellowed Clayton.

'That's better.'

Chanatico stepped up to her husband, 'Mr Clayton is very excited to be working for you my dear.'

Jenkins sneered, 'No he isn't, he thinks I'm an upper class parasite with no more right to live than a maggot ... isn't that right Clayton?'

'NO SIR!'

Jenkins maintained his sneer, 'He was a damned good liar too!'

Chanatico was quite shocked at her husband's attitude towards this poor fellow who'd fallen on hard times, 'Really Henry that's not a very nice way to speak to a friend.'

'Friend? He's no friend and besides he's my butler now, isn't that right Clayton?'

'YES SIR!'

'And I can treat him however I bloody well want, isn't that right Clayton?'

Clayton gave a worried look, 'Yes sir.'

'You just remember Chan the man you're looking at now was the most vicious, insubordinate bastard I've ever met in my life. If he manages a week I'll be bloody surprised!'

Jenkins eyed the medals hanging off Clayton's jacket, 'Amocualli itlan.'

'What does that mean?' inquired the young Matriarch.

'Why don't you tell her Clayton?'

The butler faced Chanatico, 'It means evil beneath, Miss.'

'I don't understand.'

Clayton replied with a rather embarrassed expression, 'I spent a lot of time in the tunnels on Bandayuuk, Miss.'

'I still don't understand Mr Clayton.'

Jenkins smirked, 'We discovered the location of a birthing station on Bandayuuk. Clayton here with a single squad of men fought their way down, deep into the crust. They entered the birthing station and dismantled it. Clayton murdered the newly generated Macks in their birthing tubes. The Makayuuk responded with a brigade of troops, didn't they Clayton?'

'Yes sir.'

'Yes sir, so sweet to hear those words pass your lips.'

Chanatico inquired further, 'Well what happened?'

'Tell her Clayton.'

'I don't quite recall, sir.'

'Lying bastard! You bloody well recall that day as well as the Makayuuk!'

'Tell me Clayton,' inquired Chanatico.

'We were surrounded. I used my knife to open a few Mack skulls.'

'Why did you do such a thing?' replied a horrified Chanatico.

'Makayuuk have chips, in the brain. We needed them to get out.'

'I don't understand.'

'All Macks have chips in their brain which transmit a signal to the closest hub network. I cut the chips from newly formed brains, leaving as many alive as I could. We used the transmitters to slip out whilst the Macks closed in on the birthing station. You see, they thought those dying Macks were us and we were them.'

'So how did you become so infamous?'

Jenkins took a slug of brandy, 'When they played the footage back there was only one man cutting those newly formed heads open. The other men in the squad didn't have the stomach for it, did they Clayton?'

'No sir.'

'Only true evil could commit such a horrific act, they named him Amocualli itlan after that. We gave him a medal and a transfer to the most elite squad on Bandayuuk.'

Chanatico looked quite ill, 'I see.'

'You'll be paid 50 credits a month, don't worry about the uniform I'll put that on expenses. If you like I can credit you with another 50 in advance.'

'Thank you sir.'

'You're expected to be on call from first thing in the morning until last thing at night, 7 days a week. You're permitted one weekend holiday of your choosing, per month, is that understood?'

'Understood sir.'

'Chan, take him downstairs and show him his duties,' he glared at Clayton, 'the first sign of trouble from you and you're out, understood Clayton.'

'Yes Sir, Thank you sir.'

Chanatico led the new butler downstairs into the servants' quarters. First she showed him the kitchen. A middle aged lady stood ironing clothes as they descended the steps.

'Annie, this is Clayton he's the new butler.'

'New butler? I didn't know we had an old one, Miss!'

'His name is Clayton and he'll be working here from now on, is that understood?'

'Yes Miss.'

'Now I want you to show him his room and get him acquainted with his duties.'

'Yes Miss.'

Chanatico smiled, 'Thank you and I'll see you later Clayton.'

'Yes Miss.'

The tall Tlillan returned to her husband, bending down to squeeze up the small parlour stairs.

Annie gave Clayton a grumpy look, 'So you're the new butler?'

'Yeh.'

'Done any of this work before?'

'No, this is my first time actually.'

'What'd ya do, tell them a bundle of lies to get the job?'

'No, I used to serve with Brigadier Jenkins.'

'Really? You must've been real pals if the most charity he could give is working as his manservant!'

Clayton gave an awkward grin, 'Yeh well we never was best of friends.'

Annie looked the man up and down suspiciously then pointed at his medals, 'Where'd you get those?'

'Bandayuuk.'

'I suppose that's where you met him?'

'Yeh.'

'Well the bedroom's in there,' she pointed to a small doorway, 'you can put your gear inside now.'

Clayton smiled, 'No need for that, this is all I've got.'

Annie looked him up and down, 'I see, well you can get to work peeling them potatoes. When the master calls for you you'll hear that bell ring,' she pointed to an old brass bell on a circular spring.

Clayton took his jacket off, removed his cufflinks and rolled his shirt sleeves up before getting to work peeling the potatoes on the main kitchen table.

'So, you saw much action on Bandayuuk?'

Clayton focused on his knife blade whilst peeling potatoes, 'Nothing to write home about.'

'So what'd they give you them medals for? Shining officers' boots?'

Clayton laughed as he picked up the next potato.

'You're like the Brigadier, trying to forget that place.'

The butler nodded as he worked away, 'Trying.'

'Then what are ya carrying them bleeding medals around for?'

Clayton paused for a moment, 'When I find that out I'll put them away.'

'You mean lay them to rest. You can't run away from ghosts Clayton.'

As the former soldier peeled potatoes he observed his knife glimmer in the light, it brought back memories of the past ...

Jenkins sat behind a desk in his office at camp Oscar, examining a tablet, 'Corporal John Clayton.'

'Yes sir,' responded a young man dressed in his SBS fatigues and holding a backpack.

'It says here you served in Mozambique, who with?'

'M squadron, sir.'

'Who was your commanding Officer?'

'Colonel Wright, sir.'

Jenkins smiled, 'Ah yes, old Wrighty ... never could keep his hands of those black women!'

Clayton began to feel awkward as the Brigadier reminisced.

'Turned out to be the end of him.'

'Sir?'

'Didn't you know?'

'No sir, I was transferred to X squadron in ...'

Jenkins returned to his tablet, '2121, yes I know. Well it wasn't long after that, old Wrighty was having his way with some young village girls; when the father and his 7 brothers arrived home,' the Brigadier began to chuckle.

'What happened to Colonel Wright, sir?'

Jenkins grinned at the Corporal, 'I think they had him with rice and peas for the main course.'

'They ate him sir?'

'Bloody animals, still he brought it on himself. Anyway you're here for your transfer to Captain Brown's Platoon.'

'Yes sir.'

'It seems you've been requested by the Bokors.'

'Sir?'

Jenkins stood up and made his way to a drinks cabinet, taking two glasses, 'Drink?'

'No thank you sir, not when I'm on duty.'

Jenkins nodded, 'Good man,' before pouring himself a Cognac.

Taking a sip the Brigadier examined Corporal Clayton, 'I had you promoted so that you could serve in the Bokors. The Bokors are a unit made up of men from various SBS and SAS squadrons, very much in the same vein as X squadron.

Since the SBS programme of implanting the Ixchel in all our troops, whether they be officers or not, something became evident; It seems the Ixchel is rather selective in who it takes to, 90% of our troops were found incompatible. At Geneva they managed to identify a single gene, without it the Ixchel will not take root. Well you have that gene Corporal some would call you a lucky man others would say you're cursed.

You've been transferred to what I consider my premier fighting unit on Bandayuuk. The Ixchel is a requirement, alongside a ruthless instinct on the battlefield. Underneath Bandayuuk it's kill or be killed, all those not possessing such a nature have failed to return.'

Jenkins paused to take a deep breath and an equally generous slug of Cognac, 'Officially Captain Brown is the commanding officer; however for all intents and purposes Sergeant Roberts is your CO. Do you understand?'

Clayton was rather confused, 'Not quite sir, nevertheless Sergeant Roberts is my CO.'

Jenkins continued, 'Since Bandayuuk all SBS and SAS reservists have been called up. Due to the influx of numbers new squadrons were formed. Most of them were either wiped out or forced to merge, due to low numbers. One of the few to maintain its membership was the Bokors.

Apparently you gained quite a reputation for yourself after that little expedition into the Mack nursery. Since your former squadron was decimated you've been split up to reinforce other special-forces squadrons. Roberts requested you and it was jolly difficult getting you here.'

'Thank you sir.'

'Don't thank me Corporal, just stay alive long enough to impress me.'

The doorbell rang and Jenkins answered, 'Enter.'

Sergeant Roberts marched in saluting the Brigadier.

Jenkins returned his salute, 'Roberts meet Corporal Clayton.'

Clayton stood to attention. Roberts smiled and in his Jamaican accent said, 'Good to see you Corporal.'

Jenkins pointed his glass, 'He's all yours Roberts … make sure he doesn't get killed too quickly. I pulled quite a few favours.'

Roberts saluted, 'Yes sir.'

'You can both leave now.'

Roberts and Clayton exited the camp commander's office. Strolling along one of the carbon composite corridors Roberts produced a large knife in a raw animal hide sheathe.

'Take this, every Bokor carries one and is expected to maintain it. Your kukri shall be inspected on a regular basis.'

Taking the large blade Clayton replied, 'Kukri?'

'A Nepalese weapon, one of our men was a Gurkha.'

Clayton pulled the knife from its sheathe to examine a 10 inch blade which bent inwards. Its handle was made from sandalwood with grips for his fingers. The Corporal's attention was quickly drawn to two small knives accompanying the kukri.

'One is for skinning and gutting animals the other for sharpening your kukri.'

Clayton replaced the blade, noting it had a wooden scabbard covered in untreated leather, 'Why carry a knife?'

Roberts chuckled as they walked through a door and into a second passage leading past the Mess, 'You carry one, don't you?'

'Well yeh but ...'

'But what? It saved your life in that birthing station.'

Clayton smiled, 'You've got me there mate.'

Roberts gave a big Jamaican laugh, 'You'll fit in good Clayton, just learn to use your kukri and keep it good.'

Corporal Clayton followed his CO into the barracks where he met the rest of Bokor squadron. The men were from various SBS and SAS squadrons. All brought to Bandayuuk for the purpose of defeating the Macks. Unfortunately the fight had gone below ground. Even Spetsnaz and Eastern States Special Forces struggled against an enemy with the co-ordination of an ant colony and fervour of jihadists on crack.

Xch'uup wanted Bandayuuk intact, her reason unclear. But it was their job to go underground and ferret out Macks fighting for Machine.

Body bags remained unused since men who could not exit the tunnels under their own volition rarely did. Bodies ended up processed into goo, feeding Macks and creating new ones in birthing chambers. Added to that a Makayuuk was "born" an adult, its brain an empty vessel for a mind inside Machine's matrix to possess; "New Macks" were not created due to the death toll of this war, many experienced minds waited in the matrix for vessels to be created in birthing chambers.

Each battle below Bandayuuk resulted in Mack numbers increasing. Although the I.S.A was unaware of the situation they understood their dead were being used to feed Mack soldiers. This didn't sit well back home when people discovered loved ones weren't coming home to be buried, rather, Macks were having them for lunch.

Roberts introduced Clayton to his squadron, 'This is John Clayton make sure he doesn't die lads … at least not on his first mission!'

Ripples of laughter could be heard around the room of bunk beds and lockers.

A young man handed Clayton a small bag, 'Take these Clayton.'

The Corporal's attention was grabbed by a soldier entering the showers. His face was bright red with black around the eyes and mouth. Around his mouth a design similar to rows of teeth; in fact his face resembled that of a red and black skull.

The fellow smiled before grabbing a towel and walking into the showers.

'Your locker and bunk are here.'

Clayton made his way over to the locker emptying his backpack into it. Finally he opened the small bag given to him, inside were two tins of face paint one red and the other black. It also contained his squad decals, a red and black skull below two kukris.

'What's this face paint about?' inquired the Corporal.

One of the men pointed to the tins, 'It scares the shit out of those Macks.'

Clayton pulled a dubious expression but his comrade laughed, 'You'll see Clayton, you'll see.'

A few months later and Clayton was fitting in at the Jenkins household. Despite the scepticism of Henry their new butler was working out very well. As far as John Clayton was concerned this was quite a nice number, he had free board and lodgings along with a very good wage.

In the parlour Annie was washing clothes. Clayton had his feet up reading a hard copy of "The Daily Mail" whilst puffing on a roll up cigarette.

'Do you know what the Master says about that newspaper?'

'No, but I'm sure you're gonna tell me,' replied the butler as he tried to relax.

'He says the only people who read that are right wing extremists.'

Clayton laughed as he pulled the cigarette out from between his lips, 'Really? He must have a bloody subscription to it!'

Just then one of the bells rang on the wall of the parlour. Clayton rose from his chair and put his cigarette out. Quickly slipping into his jacket and straightening his tie Clayton made for the steps.

Opening the front door the former soldier met with a deliveryman from the local post office, 'I have a delivery for Miss Chanatico.'

'Thank you, I'll take that.'

'I'm sorry, I need her profile before I can release it,' replied the man in a grey uniform and peeked cap.

Before the butler could reply a voice came down the hallway, 'Is that for me Peter?'

The postman smiled, 'Yes straight from Otoch!' he passed a large carbon cased package that had travelled 30,000 light years.

'Why thank you Peter, here take this,' Chanatico placed a gold sovereign in the palm of his hand.

The postman was embarrassed but accepted her gift. Clayton was rather intrigued by the reward.

'Thank you Miss Chanatico,' replied Peter.

The Tlillan beauty flashed her pink eyes as she turned inside with the parcel. Suddenly the postman realised he'd forgotten to take her DNA profile and reached for her forearm.

Noticing Peter's sudden move towards Chanatico, Clayton's instincts kicked in. Before you could wink an eye he snatched Peter's arm, breaking the postman's elbow joint via the ancient art of Pankration. First used by Spartan warriors and now by SBS soldiers.

The postman let out a cry of pain as Clayton brought him to the ground with the grace of a sprinting cheetah. As the butler began to twist the postman's head in such a manner his neck was sure to break, Chanatico let out a scream, 'CLAYTON!'

The servant stopped for a moment fixing his gaze upon his Mistress.

'What are you doing?'

Clayton looked down at the poor man he'd locked in a deadly vice, taking in the situation and realising what he'd done. The postman choked blood as he lay in tears of pain on the concrete floor. Clayton quickly released the man letting him flop onto the ground.

'He was about to grab you Miss.'

Chan dropped her parcel to assist Peter inside the house, 'Clayton, get this man some warm water and hot towels.'

'Yes Miss.'

The butler went downstairs quickly returning with steaming towels and a bowl of water.

Chanatico was pouring the wretched postman some of Henry's fine French brandy, 'I'm so sorry Peter, is it broken?'

The poor man screamed as Chan touched his arm.

'Clayton, call an ambulance and be quick about it!'

'Yes Miss!' the former soldier tapped his wrist tablet sending for an emergency response team, only available for residents in certain areas of London.

As Peter groaned in a delirium of pain, Chan accosted her butler with burning eyes, 'He was only trying to get my profile. I'd forgotten to sign for the parcel.'

Clayton recalled the pad dropped on the pavement outside, used to take the customer's DNA signature.

'Your actions are absolutely unacceptable!'

Later that day Henry stood in the lounge with a Cognac whilst Chanatico recounted the incident.

'Is he alright?'

'Clayton called an ambulance. He's in hospital with a broken arm and severe mental trauma.'

Henry began to laugh.

'What do you find so amusing?'

'Ah, good old Clayton he's a killer down to the bone. That postman was lucky to survive. Perhaps Clayton's losing his touch?'

'If I hadn't stopped him Peter would be dead now!'

Jenkins chuckled to himself, 'I did warn you about him my dear the man can turn into a demon at the drop of a hat. Even the Makayuuk feared him ... the evil beneath.'

'Well he can't stay here.'

'I thought he was your charity case?'

'I want him out of here by the end of the week and that's final Henry!' at that Chanatico stormed out of the room.

Jenkins stared at the doorway his wife had just marched through, 'If you say so my dear.' The former Brigadier walked towards the mantelpiece and pulled a brass chain hanging above it.

A minute later and Clayton entered the room in his uniform, 'You called sir?'

'I did, I was informed of your little fracas with the postman this morning.'

'I apologised to him and your wife, sir.'

'Yes well a simple sorry isn't good enough for the lady of the house, it seems you'll be leaving my employment by the end of the week.'

Clayton was very upset at the bad news, 'I understand sir.'

Jenkins took a sip of his brandy, 'However, I have something ... if you're interested that is.'

The butler perked up, 'Why yes sir!'

'An old friend of mine is going on an expedition and he could use a man with your aptitude in dangerous situations. I don't know the pay or anything of that nature but it's a job. Are you interested?'

'Why yes sir!'

'One other thing Clayton.'

'Yes sir?'

'My son, he needs something you can offer.'

'Yes sir?'

'Arthur has been under the tutelage of Xch'uup for some time now.'

'I heard sir.'

'Apparently he's already failed one trial.'

'I'm sorry to hear that sir.'

Jenkins pointed his glass at Clayton, 'Duncan is getting him up to speed on swordsmanship, you Clayton shall be showing him the ropes in hand to hand.'

'Understood sir.'

'You'll be getting the same pay as you do here. I want you to turn that lay about boy into a hardened Spartan warrior is that clear?'

'Quite clear sir.'

'And if he gets some bumps and bruises along the way, all the bloody better!'

'Understood sir.'

That weekend Clayton and Jenkins took an airship to Geneva. After landing safely and being towed to its hangar they exited their civilian flight. Unfortunately for Jenkins there was no more zipping around in hummingbirds, instead he was forced to sit with the rabble on air ships.

Taking a taxi from the airport they arrived at Duncan's home in 20 minutes. Before he could ring the doorbell Ofra was there, 'Hello Henry, it's so good to see you after all this time, how are you?'

'I'm very well, thank you, how are you young lady?'

Ofra laughed, 'Come in, don't you have any bags?'

'I'm sorry I have to get back to London today.'

'Who is this?'

'I'm Clayton, very nice to meet you Miss.'

Ofra had a beaming smile, 'So many compliments from young men, I might not be a single woman much longer!'

Jenkins smiled, 'I'm afraid I'm a married man Miss McCann, although Clayton here is single.'

Ofra locked her arm in Clayton's, 'Please tell me that you'll be staying.'

McCann came down the stairs, 'Well, well, well look who it is!'

Jenkins grinned and shook hands with his old comrade, 'Good to see you old boy, Clayton this is Admiral McCann.'

Before Clayton could salute McCann laughed, 'I'm only a Commodore now.'

Jenkins went a little pale, 'What in blue blazes?'

'Don't concern yourself old boy. I'm leaving for Andromeda and Bill needs an Admiral here, we can't have Admirals ten to the penny now can we?'

'I suppose not, is that irritating man still ...'

'Irritating?'

'Yes.'

'No, he's quite the easy going fellow nowadays. So what have you come all this way for, surely not to see me?'

'My son is training with you, yes?'

'Yes.'

'According to my wife he's come up deficient, she's rather concerned he won't pass his trial.'

'As is he.'

'Really? I thought all he cared about was his music.'

'It's his primary interest but while he's here that's had to change somewhat. He's getting along quite well. I've got the best bloody sword masters in Geneva working on the lad.'

Jenkins motioned towards Clayton, 'I've brought you this man, John Clayton is his name and he's a dab hand at self-defence.'

McCann shook Clayton's hand, 'Nice to meet you.'

'Now if you don't have room ...'

'That's fine he can stay here,' assured McCann.

'Thank you Duncan.'

'So Mr Clayton what'll you be teaching Arthur?'

'Pankration, sir.'

'Pankra what?'

'An ancient Greek martial art, sir. In English Pankration means "all strength".'

'Well first off you can drop the sir, secondly you can get settled in and tell me all about yourself.'

After Clayton had been shown to his room by Ofra and put his clothes away he joined Jenkins and McCann downstairs in the kitchen. McCann passed Clayton a coffee asking about Pankration again to which Clayton began a description.

'There are only two rules in Pankration, firstly no gouging, secondly no biting.'

The Commodore took a sip of his coffee, 'Is that it?'

'Yes.'

'Where on Earth did you learn that?'

'SBS were trained in Pankration, for Bandayuuk. We had these Spetsnaz fellas coach us for six months on Earth then six months on Bandayuuk. Most didn't live to finish the training though.'

'Why was that?'

'They died in the first months of fighting.'

McCann raised an eyebrow as he sipped his coffee, 'Are you going to see Arthur whilst you're here?'

Jenkins looked up, 'Is he in?'

'No he's at the gym taking instruction from Gordon. He won't be back for a few more hours.'

'I won't bother him, I don't have time anyway,' Jenkins raised his arm examining his wrist tablet, 'best be off soon.'

After 30 minutes chatting Jenkins had to leave. McCann showed his old comrade to the door. As they walked down the hall Jenkins pulled out a data chip.

'What's that for?' inquired McCann.

'A file on the latest member of your crew.'

'Oh really? Who's that?'

'Clayton, he's not a sailor but the man has medals for killing Macks with his bare hands.'

McCann took the chip, 'What else can you tell me about him?'

'The man's a bloody insubordinate.'

'So why am I being lumbered with him?'

'He was the worst soldier I've ever encountered ... yet ... the best killer. Give him a job and he'll watch your back.'

'What brings on his insubordination?'

Jenkins rolled his eyes, 'The man questioned every bloody order.'

'Why?'

'He had a conscience would you believe it?'

'You can't be a cold blooded killer and have a conscience old boy.'

'He did, anyway he comes with my recommendation you can scrutinize him whilst he's here.'

'Well thanks old chap.'

'And Duncan, make sure Arthur passes that trial will you?'

McCann nodded, 'I will, by the grace of the Gods.'

Chapter 4

A month later, standing in an observation lounge McCann overlooked an I.S.A gym. Coffee in hand he monitored Arthur spar with John Clayton. A tall Russian in his 40's holding a very intimidating stick scrutinized the pair.

Whilst enjoying his coffee Gordon approached, still in fencing attire, he often relaxed here after a few hours on the piste. Sipping his latte the old fellow snorted at the sight, 'My God, what's he using that for?'

'Using what for?'

'That bloody big stick!'

'Oh, he's the referee. The stick's used to keep order.'

'Keep order?'

'Apparently there are only two rules, you're not allowed to bite or gouge.'

Gordon wiped sweat from his forehead with a towel, 'A very gentlemanly discipline.'

'The trouble is your opponent is rarely a gentleman. You remember that Spanish bloke?'

'The one who stomped on your foot?'

'That's the one.'

'How could I forget?'

As the pair wrestled Arthur seemed to have the advantage, locking Clayton in a choke hold. The boy's forearm crossed Clayton's windpipe. Both men stood prone. Arthur crouched behind pulling his forearm back with his other hand, restricting his opponent's breathing in an attempt to force submission.

The referee looked on for any illegal gouging but all fell within the rules.

'It seems the lad has him,' commented Gordon.

'How's he coming along with you?'

'Much improved, it won't be long before he's the man to test your skills against.'

McCann chuckled, 'Worried he might knock you off your perch?'

'I'm more concerned about when I'll get that bottle of Laphroaig.'

'Don't worry old boy there's a bottle with your name on it.'

'I'll have the 30 year old you keep stashed away in your cellar, thank you Duncan.'

The Commodore raised an eyebrow at Gordon. A moment later his attention was torn back to the sparring below.

Clayton was in a very deadly choke hold, with Arthur's Tlillan strength the old soldier would soon pass out. In his prone position Clayton noticed Arthur had left the smallest finger of his hand limp. Detecting Arthur's mistake the Londoner took his opportunity, clutching Arthur's pinky finger he yanked it back on itself.

Arthur screamed in pain and released Clayton in reaction to a sudden shot of agony.

Clayton took his second opportunity, spinning around he put his opponent into a shoulder lock. His left arm entwined in Arthur's he held onto the lad's shoulder. His right arm had a firm grip on Arthurs's right arm, grabbing his wrist whilst twisting its palm to face the ceiling.

Arthur was down on one knee, his right leg locked by Clayton's right leg. As the old soldier pulled discomfort increased until Arthur was forced to fight back the agony with his mental abilities.

Despite superior strength the boy was unable to slip out of Clayton's exquisite hold; A 3,000 year old bind as good today as in Alexander's time.

Arthur raised his index finger and the referee call halt, tapping Clayton on the back. The old soldier released Arthur and they shook hands before the lad sought medical attention.

'My God, that's positively barbaric!' stated Gordon.

McCann nodded, 'Unfortunately not all disputes can be settled with a duel of honour.'

Ten minutes later Clayton was cleaned up, dressed and chatting in the observation lounge with McCann and Gordon.

'How's the boy progressing?' inquired McCann.

Clayton ran a towel through his short thin hair, 'He nearly had me today, a few more seconds and I'd have been a gonner.'

'That was pretty brutal. Breaking his finger like that.'

'His mistake, better he makes them now than when he's up against those Tlillans.'

'Who's the ref?'

Clayton sipped on a cup of iced tea, 'That's Vladimir, a mate from Bandayuuk. Arthur's gonna link with him tomorrow ... in a week he'll be able to take me down.'

'You sound disappointed.'

Clayton fixed his eyes upon the Englishman, 'I don't like to lose ... ever. But since this is the Brigadier's boy, I'm game.'

John Clayton nodded at Gordon, 'Gordon,' to which the old fellow replied in kind.

'May I be excused now, Mr McCann?'

'Certainly.'

John Clayton marched off to spend some free time on Lake Geneva fishing, his favourite past time.

'It seems to me that in a month we'll have a true son of Ares on our hands,' said Gordon.

McCann nodded as he drank his latte.

'Why are these Tlillans so obsessed with this child? I understand his gender makes them jumpy, but why?'

'Fear, the root of all emotion,' said McCann stoically.

'Why fear the boy?'

'He's the personification of a paradigm shift on Otoch. If a man can stand with a Matriarch side by side and earn the same privilege, it would shake society to the core; what of social order, what of the Matriarchs and most important what of Xch'uup if this boy proves himself in the trial?'

'Then why is Malikah interested in him completing the trial? Surely she'd rather him fail if he were a threat?'

McCann smirked as he watched the referee gather his things and leave the gym below, 'We all have a destiny my dear friend. Malikah has seen Arthur's, entwined with that of Xch'uup.'

'How so?'

'If he fails and is rejected by her Matriarchs it will lead to conflict. Bitterness and revenge will push a man in a direction he'd never have considered otherwise.

She wishes to bring him into the fold avoiding bloodshed on Otoch; even though she sees victory for herself ... it would be a pyrrhic victory. The Tlillan power structure would go to the grave along with Arthur and Xch'uups' authority with it.'

Gordon took a rest on one of the comfy sofas, 'So its control she wants?'

McCann nodded, 'Yup.'

'What do you want Duncan?'

'What do you mean?'

'You're not doing this for Malikah or her Matriarchs and there's more to it than helping the boy.'

The Englishman smiled, 'You always could read me, on and off the piste.'

'I think you want to send a man to Otoch. You want that boy to enter Muul Kaah and hit those Matriarchs for six at their own game, don't you?'

McCann only grinned at the old sabre master.

'Be careful Duncan, it's a dangerous game you're playing and Arthur's life is on the line.'

The Englishman looked down at Gordon, 'Arthur's life is on the line no matter what I do, her Matriarchs would be happy to see him gone.'

'Gone?'

'Yes, gone, whatever it takes for them to accomplish that. When he returns to Otoch he'll be protected by Malikah and able to hold his own against any challenge.'

As he finished his sentence Arthur entered the room in a space suit, still sweating from his previous match.

'How's the finger?' inquired McCann.

'Doctor Weissmuller fixed it up for me,' Arthur displayed his hand now locked in a carbon cast, little finger sticking out.

'It's a pity Sandra isn't here. She'd have set that right.'

Arthur smiled, 'Its fine. Nanites will have it as good as new by the morning.'

The lad turned to Gordon pressing his hands together as best he could, 'Namaste Mr Deveron.'

Gordon smiled, 'Good afternoon young man.'

McCann sat the boy down and congratulated him, 'Well done, it seems everyone has nothing but praise for you today.'

Arthur's eyes changed colour, 'Thank you, I'm trying my best.'

'You'll return to Malikah a proper son of Ares.'

'Son of Ares?'

'Yes, the Spartans believed they were sons of Ares … the Greek god of war.'

Arthur caught on, 'Ahh, I see. I thought you were referring to the ship Ares.'

Gordon shook his head, 'What are they teaching you in that Tlillan School?'

'Science, philosophy, history … Tlillan history.'

Gordon let out a snort before sipping on his coffee.

'So who were the Spartans?'

Gordon was shocked at the lad's ignorance.

McCann retorted, 'You've never heard of Spartans?'

'I know it refers to something of simple and utilitarian design yet durable at the same time.'

'The Spartans were feared throughout the ancient world, trained from the age of seven to be warriors. Those who survived the training became fearless sons of Ares. Something is considered Spartan because they lived only upon life's basics. Spartans did not indulge in pleasures but toughened themselves for hard campaigns. Everything they owned was likewise, an object with a utilitarian purpose that would last the rigors of war.'

'I see,' noted Arthur as he wiped sweat from his brow, 'this would be considered inappropriate material for my education.'

'Why's that?' asked Gordon.

'Kleos … that is glory and honour in battle … is only to be associated with Xch'uup and her servants.'

'So a man cannot earn kleos?'

'Gender is unimportant. A male or female may earn kleos but only through a Matriarch. Without Xch'uup's approval you may not earn kleos, to do otherwise is to challenge her authority.'

Gordon gave an expression of disdain, 'On Earth, if someone earns glory their leader is forced to recognise it. If not that leader undermines his or her own position. People do not respect those who refuse to honour true warriors.'

Arthur considered the opposing philosophies, 'The human approach is logical, glory and honour exist due to deeds in battle. A king has the choice to recognise that glory or not, either way its existence remains, he has no claim on another's glory.'

'So Xch'uup's claim is illegitimate?'

'Xch'uup's claim is illogical but her people make it legitimate by adhering to her law. You see the trick of a tyrant isn't to force people to be logical ... you wouldn't need a tyrant otherwise. The trick is to force people to do that which is illogical. If I can force people to gas other humans in death camps, launch nuclear strikes on innocent people, napalm children in villages then I have what I want ... control over their will.'

Gordon nodded his head, 'I see. Those that suffer are merely a consequence?'

'Something like that, yes.'

'These Tlillans are very cold blooded creatures.'

Arthur argued Malikah's case, 'Humans have been doing this since the beginning of recorded history. The only difference is that on Otoch they understand the manipulation and accept it.'

'I don't understand why they would do that?'

'In a totally cold, logical society how else would you display obedience to your ruler? The only method is by conforming to state sanctioned illogic. We do it constantly though only through ignorance and manipulation.'

'Give me an example,' requested Gordon.

'Alright, for example in the Eastern States their government took tax money and pledged to guarantee 20% of all mortgages, yes?'

'Yes they're still doing it now.'

'If I were a logical voter I'd protest this scheme since it uses tax payers money to inflate house prices into a bubble, which will ultimately burst and that public money shall be lost. In fact it is a transparent attempt to purchase votes in the next election.

Yet voters support this scheme, not because they are displaying loyalty through illogical acts that a sane person would otherwise refuse. They support it because they are stupid and believe they shall benefit from a government bubble in the housing market. Despite the fact history has demonstrated a 100% failure rate in these schemes.'

Gordon peered at McCann and chuckled, 'It seems the lad has a valid point, what do you think?'

McCann gave a smile, 'There's a reason people buy into Ponzi schemes, even today. On Otoch they'd laugh in your face.'

A month later McCann stood in the same observation lounge with several servicemen as a pankration tournament began. No weight classes, it was free for all.

Vladimir, who was refereeing, announced Arthur and his opponent, a rather large and hairy German.

The contest was fought in a circle no larger than a boxing ring, no rope only a ring marked on the mat. Vlad raised his stick and shouted, 'Fight!'

The pair stood much like two boxers, both making forward kicks on the other. This only pushed the other man back keeping him at a distance whilst searching for a weakness to exploit.

The larger German searched for an opening, looking to take Arthur to the ground. However the lad moved too quickly and obviously preferred to fight on his feet.

Arthur observed his bulky competitor and noted the man's bent knee as he prepared for the next front kick. Arthur moved in, advancing further than usual, bringing the heel of his foot upon his opponent's bent knee.

The German let out a mighty roar of pain as his bulk slapped onto the thin mat floor. A crunch reverberated around the hall. Arthur's superior Tlillan strength shattered his opponent's knee cap.

It was obvious Dr Weissmuller would be a busy man today as he stood ringside ordering staff in to treat their first patient.

Vladimir raised his stick to call a halt, declaring Arthur the victor by raising his hand.

Upon viewing Arthur's strength and expertise several men walked away from the contest; quickly culling the sensible from the brave or just plain foolish.

Arthur rested while those remaining completed the first round.

Meanwhile John Clayton entered accompanied by a fuming William Faraday. Everyone in the lounge greeted the Director of the I.S.A who made his way straight to McCann.

'What in the blue blazes is going on Duncan?' snapped the Etonian.

'I'm sorry?' replied McCann.

'I've just witnessed Staff Sergeant Hagen on a bloody stretcher being wheeled to an A&E unit!'

'Who?'

Clayton cut in, 'One of the contestants in today's tournament.'

'Oh the hairy guy?'

Faraday was furious, 'He was redeploying to the Adnoaran system in a week. Instead I see him on a stretcher in a pair of knickers screaming in agony!'

McCann furrowed his brow, 'I didn't force him to take part, besides Weissmuller will have him up and running in a few days.'

Faraday took a handkerchief from his jacket pocket and wiped his brow, 'I just pray he doesn't decide to take sick leave. I need him on Adnoara not in a hospital.'

McCann pointed at Clayton, 'Well it was his student that sent him there.'

The old soldier smiled, 'Why do you think I'm not taking part Mr McCann?'

As the three were chatting a muffled crack followed by a howl of pain came from the ring below.

Faraday glanced below to see Arthur, having been held in a bind from behind, breaking an SBS officer's ankle, 'Oh my GOD! That's Bates!'

'Sorry?' replied McCann.

Weissmuller's staff rushed in to carry the man away, grimacing in torture with a swollen ankle. A nurse administered morphine whilst Weissmuller worked his magic with medical nanites before sending the man to join Hagen.

'Captain Bates, he's been assigned lead of a drop squad in the Adnoaran system. Hagen was to be his Sergeant!'

McCann started to snigger.

'You may find this hilarious Duncan but I'm losing men to your damn boy,' Faraday pointed his cane at the group of combatants below as Arthur was declared victorious.

'Calm down Bill, no-one's gonna die today ... probably.'

The Director's eyes widened in fright, 'Die? People have died doing this?'

'Bill, people have died from eating a bad steak. You're not doing yourself any favours worrying about it.'

Waving the silver ball on his black cane Faraday retorted, 'Yes but if you knew the meat was rancid beforehand you'd throw it away!'

After the third round Arthur fought his way through the eliminators. Each crack of bone and wail of agony sent Faraday into further hysteria. The Director tortured himself over staff he may have to replace for the tour of Adnoara.

Without taking a scratch himself the young man brawled his way into the final. Each contestant experienced in the rigors of full on combat dropping to the wayside in order to clear a path to Arthur's ultimate goal.

By this time there was a great flurry of discussion in the observation lounge. Spectators were most impressed by the half breed's skill and discipline.

Clayton only grinned in the direction of McCann whilst Faraday refused to watch. Observing some of his best men trundled out on stretchers was more than he could bear.

In the final Arthur stood against a burly Russian man. Boris was a former Spetsnaz champion. His reputation being more than enough to convince most grown men Pankration was not for them.

He stood six and a half feet tall, eye to eye with Arthur. A bald head and grizzly face with a few days of growth, attached to a bulky yet athletic frame. The Russian's upper body was especially well endowed. Already in this competition he'd sent men to the accident and emergency room; Breaking their bodies before they had time to tap out.

Comparatively Arthur was quite thin, without his Tlillan heritage Vladimir would have stopped the fight before it began. A young teenage lad going up against a Spetsnaz killer was not something anyone desired to watch. However if Arthur was just some young 19 year old boy he'd never of made it past the first round.

'Ready?' called Vladimir.

Both men took a typical boxing stance and nodded.

'FIGHT!'

Everyone was captivated, crowds had gathered in the hall and upper lounge by this time.

Both men circled each other cautiously. A mistake here would have very painful consequences.

After front kicking one another for a few minutes Boris saw an opening. Arthur had a habit of slowly lowering his leg back to the floor once he'd executed a front kick. Perhaps it was due to tiredness or just an innate weakness in his training. Nevertheless it was there and upon the next kick Boris shot forwards.

Arthur was forced onto his back foot unable to retreat or strike with any balance. Boris moved in on the outside of Arthur's leg.

The Russian grabbed the lad's waist from behind and in one massive heave lifted Arthur off the ground. Captured in a waist lock he was thrown backwards as Boris bent and thrust the lad onto his side.

As Arthur hit the mat the Russian sped in to finish him off with a choke lock. Arthur reacted, quick enough to turn onto his back and face Boris yet unable to get to his feet before the burly soldier was upon him and dishing out strikes to the face.

To observers it didn't seem long before the lad would tap out or Vladimir put an end to this contest. Tlillan or not a man's face could not suffer that much punishment for long.

Stuck on his back Arthur had no leverage to make strikes so he attacked with a tracheal choke. Grabbing the Russians windpipe between his thumb and fingers, using his Tlillan strength he throttled the man.

Arthur suffered his punishment whilst reaching behind Boris' Adam's apple, crushing his foe's windpipe. Now it was a battle of attrition, who could take their punishment for longest.

Russian onlookers cheered Boris, encouraging him to punch harder. British onlookers rallied Arthur inspiring him to squeeze deeper and hold out against the Russian's brutal attack.

Faraday looked away. Clayton and McCann were hypnotized by the struggle below.

About ten seconds later the Russian's punches quickly lost their ferocity. Arthur's face bled profusely as he moved from side to side in an attempt to avoid the strikes.

Vladimir peered up to the lounge fixing his eyes on Clayton. The Londoner slowly shook his head from side to side. It seemed to McCann that Vladimir was asking whether he should end the fight or not.

Eventually Boris could no longer strike. His body could not maintain an assault without its vital fuel. The Spetsnaz champion peeled off to the side and collapsed onto his back in a semi-unconscious state.

Arthur rolled over to sit astride his body however Vlad called halt to the contest using his stick.

There was a roar of victory from the British contingent, the Russians weren't pleased.

McCann screamed, 'He did it!'

Clayton whispered, 'The Brigadier will be pleased.'

'Can I look?' said Faraday in a shaky voice.

'Oh, stop being such an old woman!' retorted McCann.

The Director peered into the hall to see one of his soldiers flat on his back, nurses checking vital signs through nanites. Arthur stood hand held aloft in victory, blood pouring from his face and two nurses waiting to check him over.

After his time convalescing, Arthur gazed out into space from inside the Athena. Hitching a ride to Otoch on board the warship; He found beauty in the spikey planet set behind the sleek and shiny Bohr space station.

Dressed in an I.S.A officer's uniform Arthur contemplated his fate as Athena sailed alongside one of its docking arms. The vessel came to a halt and the voice of Captain Kim announced that all those who were going ashore may do so.

Arthur moved to the closest port side airlock. The hatch opened and Athena's crew flooded out onto the Bohr docking arm. Inside waited Amitra but before Arthur could approach her Hassif was greeting his daughter.

'Namaste,' said the Amazon, 'but I'm afraid I am here for someone else,' her eyes were drawn to Arthur.

'I understand. Will I see you later?'

His daughter nodded with a smile and Hassif left.

'How have you been, Arthur?' asked Amitra.

'Geneva was a very interesting place, thank you.'

'What did you think of the lake and the jet d'eau?'

'A perfect setting for an artist.'

Amitra raised her brow, 'However you are not to be an artist ... Xch'uup awaits.'

Arthur followed in her path as she moved deep inside the Bohr. Along the way Tlillans were transfixed at the young lad's appearance. It seemed everyone on Otoch was aware of his trial.

Finally Amitra entered a pitch black room though Arthur used his Tlillan night vision to examine its contents.

The young man observed Malikah and her sisters, this time Lian was also present. As dim lights illuminated the room Arthur lowered his night vision.

'You've had time to consider your weakness?' echoed Xch'uup's cold voice.

Arthur pressed his palms yet before he might speak she cut him off, 'It is only us here there's no need for that.'

The young man raised his head and lowered his arms, 'It was most enlightening, thank you.'

In the corner lay a pile of bokken. Malikah's eyes moved in its direction and one of the wooden swords lifted up, shifting through the air to Arthur.

The lad snatched the wooden sabre levitating before him as another glode into the hands of Kaeo.

'Let me see how much you've forgotten during your holiday ... ALLEZ!'

The two combatants stepped into the centre of the large room. Kaeo charged her target whilst Arthur moved backwards looking for an opening.

The Tlillan Marshal made a cut, the young man blocked it. As Gordon had done many times before he put her blade into a bind.

Although an opportunity to either cut or punch Kaeo with his wooden guard presented itself, Arthur slipped away. Moving to the opposite side of the room he allowed Kaeo to recover from what should've been a painful lesson.

The other women stood at the side lines whispering between minds. All of them had seen Arthur's superior blade work and noted that without mercy Kaeo would have been bloodied.

The Tlillan Marshal charged her foe again in an attempt to redeem herself.

Placing his blade high and horizontal Arthur blocked Kaeo's attack, he then pushed into her body with his. Along with a helpful foot behind her heel he sent Kaeo onto her behind.

Despite the fact she sat on the hard catronium floor Jenkins' boy refused to deliver the final strike. Backing off once again he offered Kaeo room to recover.

The short Amazon rose up with fire in her eyes. The lad was fighting in a completely different manner since their last encounter.

As Kaeo prepared for another charge Malikah spoke, 'HALT!'

Kaeo eyes burnt bright with the humiliation of defeat.

'Kaeo, ENOUGH!'

The short Amazon cast her bokken back into the pile and silently moved in line with her sisters.

The Tlillan Queen stepped out this time, taking a blunt mahogany blade from the pile. She went into engarde.

Bearing down on Arthur Malikah made a lunge at his chest to which he swept the blade to one side in a parry, striking Xch'uup's wrist.

The sable Queen retreated in pain. This was certainly not the swordsman she'd fought three months ago.

Unlike his strategy with Kaeo, Arthur moved in taking advantage of the moment.

Malikah kept her blade outstretched pointing towards her opponent though it failed to intimidate the lad. He used a lightning circular parry followed by a lunge to the ribs pushing Malikah back further.

The Tlillan Queen shuffled to her side in order to get more room but the young man hounded her without pity; slapping her blade followed up by constant strikes, successfully blocked by Malikah.

After a minute or so of Xch'uup backing off Arthur stopped. With open arms he invited her to attack. The sable Queen moved in cautiously yet it made no difference to the outcome.

He knocked her blade away with a parry carte, came in on the outside and swept Xch'uups legs out from underneath with a single kick.

The Grand Matriarch fell flat on her back. When she glanced upwards Malikah found herself staring down a wooden sabre. She went to parry it but Arthur had one foot on her bokken.

'It seems I'm at your mercy young man,' stated Xch'uup.

Arthur offered an open hand to Malikah and she accepted his kind gesture. The lad lifted her from the floor with a grin on his face.

'I thought you were set on killing me?'

'That was then,' replied Arthur in a hushed tone.

'And now?'

'It is easy to be angry but to be angry at the right person at the right time that is hard.'

'Quite.'

The sable Queen narrowed her eyes, 'There is one last trial.'

He cast his bokken to the floor, 'I know.'

Malikah's eyes changed in pigment to deep burgundy as they locked onto Arthur.

The young man did likewise in an attempt to repel Xch'uup's mindscape. Pushing himself harder the pigment of his eyes went to that of black ink, stunning the Tlillan women present … except Malikah.

Xch'uup's hue followed suit, filling her eyes with the darkness of space.

Despite his heritage Arthur could not withstand the weight of Malikah's mindscape. A river of pain shattered his will. He felt the Acheron flowing into his mind, conveying the torment which Charon's boat sailed upon and forcing the boy to his knees. Just as the river God had been punished for refreshing the Titans in their battle with the Olympians now Arthur squeezed his head, letting out a great screech.

Yet Xch'uup pushed on, pressing her mindscape against his. The sable Queen wished to test this boy, probe his mind and perhaps find where his limits lay.

Arthur remained on his knees in utter torture as the greater mind crushed his. Squeezing his sanity as a machine might compress a rock of coal into a diamond. The underworld did call his name and Arthur sensed the pull of Acheron, the river all others sprung from in Hades domain, drawing him downward.

A hand touched Malikah's shoulder and a familiar voice graced her ear, 'That's enough, you've won.'

The Tlillan Empress pulled out of her trance. Wrapping her mindscape back behind its mental veil as Nyx is obscured by Helios, always there, always ready. Glancing down on the boy Xch'uup stated in a cold tone, 'You did better than I hoped young man.'

Sandra and Amitra stepped forwards assisting Arthur to his feet. Arthur looked his judge in the face, 'Yet I failed.'

'On the contrary, you have passed,' Xch'uup nodded at the dark skinned Tlillan, 'Amitra.'

Amitra pulled a golden chain with a red teardrop gem from inside her jacket, 'This is yours … but Xch'uup wishes you to select your clan.'

Arthur's eyes turned to Kaeo as Amitra placed the chain around his neck, 'I request a place in clan Teteo.'

Kaeo sneered at the lad yet before she might object Malikah spoke, 'It is done, you are now Arthurateteo.'

Arthur kowtowed to Xch'uup then his First, Kaeoateteo.

The Tlillan Marshal was furious yet contained herself, at least until out of Xch'uup's presence.

'Fine, come with me then,' snapped Kaeo as she led him out of the room.

Lian furrowed her soft brow, 'What is it with those two?'

'He's in love,' whispered Malikah.

'With Kaeo?'

'That's why he displayed mercy.'

Lian scoffed, 'I think it only made her mad, he's gonna have a rough time in Teteo.'

Malikah gave Voice of Machine a coy expression, 'It was his decision, to be close to the one he loves.'

Amitra approached the pair with a smile, 'His swordsmanship has improved by leaps and bounds, how were his mental abilities?'

'He is still young yet the boy is a sleeping dragon, we must be careful.'

Chapter 5

McCann concentrated on his cigar whilst his wife paced the room.

'Why do you desire this?' inquired the beautiful Ilam.

'You saw what it was like in there.'

'That is not your concern, Commodore,' She emphasised his rank though McCann was not to be swayed, he'd overlooked some terrible immorality in his past but this went beyond what he could ignore …

Upon exiting hyperspace the Discovery stumbled into an area of Andromeda set aside for those who wished to live in an anarchic environment. There was no big government bearing down, using its weight to bully citizens into living on a tax farm. No, this was a province where men lived and died by their own wits. Upon entering a very busy system McCann was stunned to see not so much as a proverbial eyebrow raised.

He likened this system to a central trade hub of what might be a great empire. Space stations littered the star system. Vessels of all sizes and constructions made journeys to and fro. Ilam was left speechless for a minute as she examined the wonderful sight of what could only be a Galactic Mecca.

'Discovery, make contact, let's see how long before we can decode their language.'

'Understood Commodore, making contact with the closest space station now.'

'How many Stations do you count in this system?'

'Initial Computation 593, Commodore.'

McCann narrowed his eyes at a black dome bulging from the ceiling of his bridge, 'That's impossible!'

Ilam stood behind her husband, 'Impossible? Why?'

'What in God's name would you need 600 space stations for?'

'As you so enjoy saying, there is only one way to find out my dear,' replied his lofty wife.

Minutes later a transmission emanated from a large octagonal construction. Ilam got to work immediately on deciphering the language. Along with Discovery she soon possessed a workable translation of the message.

Using the periodic table of elements as a Rosetta stone the analogue transmission explained simple concepts such as numbers from 1 to 1,000,000, the alphabet, man, woman, sun, water, planet and so on. Eventually more intricate concepts were possible and before long a passable programme was ready for use in their universal translator.

McCann examined a massive three dimensional octagon suspended in space, 'Ilam, send them a greeting and request permission to dock, let's see what they say.'

Shortly they received a reply, 'Play it Discovery.'

To everyone's surprise a very human face appeared upon the view screen, it then began to speak in a foreign tongue. Discovery dubbed the alien in androgynous English allowing her bridge crew to comprehend its dialogue.

'Stranger welcome into Kurgudwardum 57, I Mesan ready stay enjoy.'

The young man's image, dressed in a very smart white satin shirt and soft blue jacket disappeared.

'Commodore, they've certified a flight path to one of the station's docking arms,' noted Vezzali.

'Well I suppose it would be rude to decline now, send us in. I want a full bio-report before we open the airlocks, is that understood?'

'Yes Commodore,' declared Vezzali and Soasille in unison.

'Ilam, keep working on that translator I want to be speaking in smooth sentences by the time we set foot on that station.'

Ilam smiled at her husband with flashing pink, 'Of course I will my dear.'

McCann did his best to ignore her affections, though she persisted anyway.

Three days later and Discovery declared the station environment safe for crew members to enter without the protection of a space suit. Vezzali certified Discovery's findings before Ilam triple certified them. Discovery had transmitted a Rosetta stone of her own to the station command centre; Allowing them to decode the English language properly before distributing it to all merchants aboard.

Apparently it was not an odd occurrence for alien ships to appear unannounced offering trade.

McCann could not control his curiosity, they'd met a species almost identical to humans in another Galaxy; Added to that Discovery's appearance was no more than an everyday event for these people. They freely shared genetic data with the Discovery and according to Ilam were related to Tlillans. She was convinced these creatures must be descended from those who erected a network of beacons throughout Andromeda, the Milky Way and their many satellite Galaxies.

McCann prepared to board the station for the first time. As he put his gun belt on Ilam smiled, 'What is that for my dear?'

Fixing the thigh holster to his leg he replied, 'There's an old saying … you're more likely to get what you want with a kind word and a gun than just a kind word.'

'You're so cynical.'

Checking his pistol's xenon battery the Commodore sneered, 'I suppose you trust them?'

'Trust? No, yet arming myself may cause tension especially on first contact.'

McCann loaded a battery then checked his magazine of 50 small tungsten rounds, 'I was naïve once but I've learnt my lesson.'

Ilam pulled a coy expression, 'You were naïve? I must speak with your mother!'

'What on Earth are you blathering about woman?'

'I missed the first ten minutes of your birth, when you were still naïve!'

The Commodore gave a grim look as he flicked his weapon on, the whine of charging rails filled his cabin, 'Hilarious.'

Ilam embraced her husband, 'Oh I'm sorry, did I make you unhappy?'

McCann checked the readouts on his pistol. When satisfied his battery was properly charged and the magazine full he flicked it off, slipping it into his holster.

Ilam kissed him on the head, 'There let mummy kiss it better.'

The Englishman looked up at Ilam, 'I don't need my mother to kiss it better.'

'What do you need yakuntik?'

McCann slipped his hands around the tall Valkyrie's waist, 'Mak'taak hats'uts atan winklil.'

'You know how I feel when you speak dirty in Tlillan.'

The pair kissed passionately until the SI began to chime.

McCann gave a sigh as he pulled his lips away from his wife's, 'What is it Discovery?'

'First contact unit are waiting at airlock one as requested Commodore,' came her soft voice.

'And?'

'You are late Commodore. The alien delegation has been waiting for twenty minutes already.'

McCann put his military jacket on, 'All bloody right, tell them I'm on my way.'

'As you wish Commodore, Discovery out.'

The Commodore and Ilam stepped into airlock one. Mountbatten and Clayton awaited, both security men were armed.

'Ready?'

The men nodded, 'Ready.'

McCann peered at the ceiling, 'Discovery, open the airlock.'

A large circular hatch swung inwards revealing a passage to another opened airlock door and behind that a greeting party from the Andromeda space station.

'Ana biti sa eribusu,' spoke the first man.

McCann recognized him as Mesan, dressed in an expensive tight cut shiny suit and holding a black walking stick with a gold knob he stood out.

'Thank you Mesan,' McCann's collar translated his greeting, 'Gitmalu Mesan.'

For a moment Mesan pulled a puzzled expression but quickly approached the Commodore with a smile, 'Come walk with me, your name is?'

The group of four followed Mesan and his two men as McCann made first contact, 'My name is Duncan McCann this is my star ship.'

McCann gestured behind him, Mesan gave what the Englishman felt to be a rather slimy smile. It was obvious Mesan struggled to understand the universal translator. However the more they spoke the quicker the AI corrected itself and the clearer both parties understanding emerged.

The Commodore was under orders not to reveal his point of origin so when Mesan asked he gave a vague answer. Much to the Englishman's surprise Mesan smiled, 'My concern not, this Patu Masku, we only concern business.'

As they strolled down the docking arm towards the main station McCann felt his wife make contact with his mind. She divulged the meaning of Patu Masku ... territory of skin, the designation of the system they'd folded into. Next she noted the space station's name Kurgudwardum ... land of strong slave. According to Vezzali this whole system was full of slave traders. Furthermore they had entered an area of the galaxy which on appearances ran on the principles of true anarchy.

McCann decided to grill Mesan as he led them to a visitors' area, 'So what do you do here Mesan?'

The greasy fellow grinned, 'I am controller, area designator and regulation enforcer.'

'So you're the law around here?'

Mesan gave a sick expression for minute, 'Correct.'

One of his men chuckled. Unlike Mesan he dressed in a pair of leather trousers, tough boots wearing a white shirt made from cotton like substance. He carried a pistol of unknown specifications on a gun belt around his hip and held a sleek rifle.

The Englishman got the distinct impression Mesan wasn't telling him the full story.

'So what is the purpose of this place?' inquired McCann.

'Purpose?' replied Mesan in a stunned tone, 'You come purchase slaves, yes?'

'No.'

'Then why here?'

McCann didn't understand the question until his wife interjected, 'He's asking why you came here?'

Mesan eyed Ilam, 'How much for this one?'

'How much?'

'This female, I pay 1,000 guskin.'

'I'm sorry?'

'2,000 guskin.'

Ilam's eyes widened as their shade morphed hot as Hephaestus' hammer. Once Mesan witnessed her transformation he shouted, '10,000 guskin!'

'I'm sorry my wife is not for sale old chap.'

Mesan stopped walking, he eyed Ilam as a butcher examining a piece of meat, 'All females have price, how much you want Duncan McCann.'

'I'm not here to sell. Besides if I sold her I'd never hear the last of it from the mother-in-law!'

Mountbatten chuckled along with Clayton, Ilam was not amused.

Mesan seemed rather upset, 'I understand must keep harem quiet.'

The station controller returned to his walk, 'Come follow Duncan McCann, we must speak on skin game.'

The party was led into an area close to the docking arm. Kurgudwardum was titanic by even Tlillan standards, easily comparable to the Bohr.

Its walls were built from carbon composite, coloured in a very light brown they made quite a pleasant stroll. Its atmosphere became smokier as they proceeded down the hall. Light levels slowly declined until similar to a side street on a dark night.

Eventually they reached the end of the hall. Mesan stopped at a closed hatch, 'Prepare yourself for pleasure and profit!'

The hatch swung open to reveal a long boulevard dotted with strange establishments; all emitting odd words in neon lights as they illuminated the dark avenue. Small transport vehicles with barely enough room to seat 3 adults sped to and fro, weaving around pedestrians who barely acknowledged their presence, unless flagging one down.

'Come let me show favourite here,' ejaculated a merry Mesan.

As they stepped inside a blue neon doorway, music began to play. McCann's translator deciphered an approximation of the song, 'Well she was only 13 ... but I begged for mercy ... she was the most beautiful love slave I'd ever seen!'

Before it could go further McCann tapped his wrist tablet, muting the AI's translation.

Scanning the establishment and its patrons he felt a cold chill run down his back.

'This way,' called Mesan pointing to a table large enough to seat their entire party.

Walking towards their destination the I.S.A sailors gawked in shock at an assortment of weird and wonderful women dancing on stages pitted around the establishment. Each one surrounded by men, some there to bid for possession of the numbered slaves others for more nefarious purposes.

Before reaching their table a short fat human, reminding McCann of a Mexican bandit due to his moustache, slapped Ilam on her behind, 'How much guskin for tonight?' he laughed.

Hephaestus' hammer smashed against its anvil once more, red sparks igniting Ilam's eyes. Grabbing his neck she lifted him clear off the floor much to the entertainment of patrons.

Staring into his terrified eyes with coals of fire she barked, 'Far more than your life will ever be worth.'

After making her threat his amigos arose from their table hands on pistol butts, ready to draw.

Music died down, bar girls stopped dancing across the massive hall, all watched the scuffle intently.

Mesan scooted to Ilam's side, 'Please let go, no trouble good.'

Ilam noted the men ready to draw and fire. She could hear her husband and his security men as their pistol rails charged behind her.

The Valkyrie controlled her anger releasing the fat man. He scurried away much like the insect he was, nursing a sore throat.

Ilam smiled at his amigos, 'My apologies Gentlemen.'

They smiled before returning to ogle young dancing girls. Music resumed and the establishment heaved a sigh of relief.

Eventually the party reached their table. A small stage filled the opposite side from where they sat. Its intention was obvious once the floor disappeared and a young lady ascended.

Mesan gestured to the bar, a tray of drinks were dutifully supplied to their table, 'Compliments of the station,' stated the controller.

McCann eyed the blue liquid before dipping his index finger into its tall thin glass and placing a drop of fluid upon his wrist tablet. After his tablet completed an analysis a bleep emanated. The drink was akin to an Earth cocktail with only 10% alcohol, 'Its fine to drink,' stated the Commodore.

The party began to sip their drinks. It tasted similar to sweet plums. Ilam pointed out she did not drink alcohol and Mesan had something close to grapefruit juice brought to the table.

'Why no drink alcohol?' inquired Mesan, still fascinated by the Amazon.

'It would distort my perception of reality,' replied the beautiful Tlillan.

'Reality? You are oracle?'

McCann cut in, 'My wife is a seer, she can see into the future and the past.'

It all clicked into one place for Mesan, 'Ahh! Mesan understand, female is Nabu, prophet … yes?'

'My name is Ilamachutli and I suppose you could say that.'

'Mesan apologise Ilamachutli, not understand she Nabu,' the station controller quickly turned to McCann, '50,000 guskin, last offer cannot go higher.'

The Englishman shook his head, 'Sorry old boy but she's worth more than any man could offer me.'

Ilam fixed her pink smiling eyes upon McCann.

Mesan noted the change of pigment again and with a frown took a shot of his drink, 'What you think of slaves? Here best in territory.'

'Some of these slaves are children.'

'Why you come here, yes? We offer all, whatever desire.'

'I don't think it is moral to buy and sell children, certainly not for the purposes these scum have in mind.'

'You like boys?'

McCann frowned, 'Certainly not!'

'Then what desire?'

'I desire information.'

'Concerning?'

'This galaxy.'

'I not understand.'

'I want star charts, trade routes, information on civilizations. Military strengths, laws, languages and so on, can you provide that?'

Mesan gave a wide grin, 'Mesan understand, you come to find buyer yes?'

'I'm sorry?'

'You find client here, raid slaves in Tamoanchan, he purchase.'

Before McCann could reply Ilam responded aggressively, 'TAMOANCHAN?'

Mesan was taken aback by the mighty Amazon, 'Tamoanchan, all know, yes?'

Ilam bellowed over the music, 'No I don't, tell me.'

'But all aware of Tamoanchan ...'

Ilam snarled at the station controller, 'I have no time for this little man. You shall answer my questions or suffer. Now describe to me Tamoanchan!'

'Tamoanchan territory of Telal. This territory of skin trade, many different territories.'

'Describe the Telal and their territory to me!'

'Telal, demon, evil demon. All understand this.'

'I do not,' pressed Ilam, 'describe a Telal … physically.'

'Telal no good slave, Telal old, shrivelled. Mouth like Azag …'

'Azag? What is Azag?'

'Azag serpent, many teeth.'

'Describe the Telal further,' pressed Ilam in a tone which caught her husband as fearful.

'Small, necklace of skulls, man skulls. They come here long time ago, take Etlu territory. Name it Tamoanchan.'

'When? When did they come here?'

'I give you facts.'

'Just tell me when they arrived little man!'

'First one maybe 500 great cycles ago I give all information, Mesan promise.'

Ilam relaxed back into her seat with a stoic gaze.

'Must leave now, important business,' Mesan peered worriedly towards Ilam as he stood up.

'Thank you very much Mesan, I hope to see you and your information soon.'

The station controller nodded before scuttling off with his guards. McCann turned to his wife as a girl danced naked before the I.S.A staff, 'What was all that about?'

'I hope I'm mistaken Duncan, that's all I can say now.'

McCann replied in a sardonic tone, 'Marvellous.'

Ilam turned off her translator, 'We cannot trust Mesan.'

McCann did likewise, 'Agreed.'

'I have an idea of whom we might trust here.'

'Yes?'

'First we must procure some local currency.'

'Well I doubt they take I.S.A credits but I had Bill load up a stash of sovereigns in the Discovery's hold before we left.'

'Excellent,' the Valkyrie looked towards Clayton, 'Go back to Discovery and return with at least two full sovereigns, understood?'

Clayton stood up and replied in his cockney accent, 'Yes Miss,' before saluting the Commodore and leaving.

'Where did you find him Duncan?'

'Jenkins recommended him to me.'

'A good soldier?'

'A good killer.'

'I see.'

'So you think we can get some of this guskin for gold?'

'Gold is a universal unit of exchange. It must be worth something even as far away as Andromeda.'

McCann smirked at his wife, 'Failing that we could always pawn you off to one of these perverts for fifty grand.'

Ilam returned his smile, 'And you would come to my rescue, yes?'

'I was more inclined to you throttling him to death once you were both alone … after the cheque had cleared the bank.'

'Naturally!'

Upon finishing their drinks Ilam approached the bar and spoke to its tender, 'I'm looking for something specific. I wondered if you might assist.'

'You want drink?' replied the old man unloading clean glasses from a dispenser.

'No, I'm interested in purchasing a slave.'

'You speak to Anu,' he gestured across the room to a table filled with several armed men.

Ilam nodded to the barman, 'Thank you.'

The mighty Valkyrie moved with great strides towards Anu's table. The men sat around it dressed in similar brown leather trousers. Ilam noticed all wore blue handkerchiefs around their necks. Something else struck the Amazon on her way over, no girl performed for the men.

As Ilam came to a halt the table went quiet, all eyes fixed on her.

'I'm looking for Anu.'

A man dressed in black with the same blue handkerchief tied around his neck spoke, 'You've found him.'

Anu was quite well kept compared to his friends. Although she found his stubbly face and long thin lotus cigar detestable.

'I'm looking to make a purchase, something different.'

Anu grinned as his friends began to cackle in an excited manner, 'We have everything you need sweet one.'

'I'm looking for a slave, a mature slave.'

One of the band laughed, 'Mature? You mean it can walk?'

Several of Anu's men found him amusing, Ilam did not, 'I'm looking for a female who has matured beyond the ability to give birth.'

The table went still before everyone burst out in laughter. They obviously thought this was a joke.

'Be serious sweet one, slaves like that are spaced each day.'

'I wish to purchase one.'

They laughed again before Anu pointed to the exit, 'You go Dock 17, get one for nothing sweet one.'

'Thank you,' spoke Ilam.

Before she could leave one of Anu's greasy men squeezed her backside and shouted, 'You are welcome sweet one!'

The Amazon sneered at the moustachioed fool before delivering a mighty kick to his face. Knocking the slime ball backwards he tumbled along the floor a few times as Anu's band laughed hysterically.

The idiot slowly gathered himself, placing a hand upon his wooden pistol grip, 'You dirty whore!'

Anu leapt to his feet, 'Aea!'

The bleeding man ignored Anu, pulling his pistol from its holster. Before anything could be done a shot was fired and Aea went down like a sack of potatoes, a hole occupying his forehead.

Anu stood pistol drawn, wisps of smoke rising from the barrel.

From what the Amazon could gather it was something like a pulse pistol. Using an electrical charge to fire a solid object ... crude but effective.

Anu spun the pistol on his index finger before slipping it back into its holster with great finesse. He'd obviously used this weapon before.

'Dock 17, you find slave for free.'

Ilam nodded before returning to her table, much to her husband's relief.

Walking out of the hell hole McCann fixed a dark look upon Ilam. The Amazon sighed, 'Duncan, you may stop that.'

'Stop what?'

'That stare.'

'Whatever,' snorted the Englishman.

Ilam ignored his attitude, 'We must find Dock 17. Apparently we may procure what I'm looking for there.'

'And what is it you're so intent on risking your life to find?'

'A slave.'

'Well there's more than enough to choose from right here.'

'I need one that has lived for some time, so that I may link with it. It seems Mr Anu only deals in children.'

'Pah! MISTER ANU!'

'Duncan, this is a different galaxy. How they conduct themselves may be peculiar yet you cannot pass judgement upon their morality so soon.'

McCann shook his head, 'Look who's talking!'

'Duncan this is a different environment, we must fit in with them.'

The Englishman looked around as they walked down a massive boulevard lit up with sleazy slave trading joints and casinos, 'This is something like Amsterdam and Tombstone combined.'

Ilam accosted a passer-by for directions to Dock 17. Sending co-ordinates to Clayton the party followed the mighty Amazon. After 20 minutes they stepped into a large cargo area, cleared of any produce.

Inside groups of men gathered each carrying chained prisoners. They waited at a large reception desk that rested before a group of airlocks. Five men and women worked the desk, taking money and details from customers who received tickets in exchange.

McCann strolled in observing the odd scene before it all became clear. A loud speaker declared, 'Customers 150 to 173 please bring refuse to airlock 4.'

Men with chained prisoners in one hand and appropriate tickets in the other walked past a security desk towards armed staff, guarding a corresponding airlock.

The first customer, after having his ticket checked unlocked shackles from the necks, wrists and ankles of three naked women. The women all of varying species were escorted into an airlock at gunpoint. Similar events transpired concerning other customers all delivering naked prisoners of varying ages, species and gender. The customers walked away with their shackles.

Next the massive hatch to airlock 4 closed sealing its contents as a klaxon sounded; once shut an outer port was opened and its occupants evicted into the freezing void of space.

The customers collected their paperwork and left as a new batch offered money for the privilege of spacing prisoners. This activity continued night and day inside the massive cargo bay.

Before McCann could note his disgust Clayton appeared with a handful of sovereigns, 'Here I got the coins for ya ... what the bloody hell's going on here?'

'Murder,' replied McCann solemnly.

Ilam piped up, 'You don't know their crimes Duncan, please restrain your prejudice.'

'Crimes? What crimes might a little old woman have committed to deserve execution?'

'Oh give it a rest Duncan!' snapped Ilam before marching towards one of the desks.

The beautiful Tlillan noticed a woman in her 60's shackled by the neck. The Valkyrie addressed the fellow holding her chains, 'Excuse me but what is this ladies' crime?'

'Crime?' replied a tanned man in his fifties, 'This my wife, soon my ex-wife!'

There was a ripple of laughter in the docking area, now converted into a convenient method of disposal for slaves, criminals and unwanted wives.

'Why is she here?' inquired the Amazon.

The short fellow shrugged his shoulders, 'Anu sell me new wife, I tired of this old donkey.'

McCann stepped up beside Ilam and eyed the chubby piece of dirt about to space his wife, 'Well we've all felt like spacing our wives at some point, I can attest to that but why not divorce her?'

The chubby man gave a puzzled expression.

'You know have the marriage annulled?'

'Ahh, why I do that when I space for only 10 guskin?'

Ilam forced a smile, 'Well we can take her off your hands for free, how would that be?'

The naked lady dropped to the floor grabbing McCann's knees. Yanking her chains from her executioner's grasp she pled, 'Please sir, I serve you as a god if you take me. What you want I provide, never complain.'

Her executioner laughed, 'Hah! If she like this before I might not space her now!'

Another ripple of laughter passed through the dock.

'Must refuse, need to space, family insurance policy … good profit.'

The old grey haired woman trembled as she wept, gripping the Englishman's knees for dear life. McCann could sense Clayton's disgust, his desire to snap this slime in two was powerful and the Commodore agreed.

'Give me your wife,' stated the Englishman.

'What? This MY wife! I do with what I want! I come this station buy new wife!'

'I said give me your wife,' McCann snarled as the crowds moved away from the drama.

The executioner placed his hand on a pistol. It resembled a small Walther PPK not something you'd expect a gunslinger to carry. McCann flicked his pistol on charging its rails. It seemed that in these parts people kept weapons charged permanently, something he'd imitate in the future.

The Commodore stared him in the face, 'Well, go on, shoot, if you think you're fast enough … you filthy piece of shit!'

Tension filled the air, Cronos stretched out the fabric of space and time dragging each second through the dock kicking and screaming. Seconds ticked as minutes and minutes as hours until the temporal deity lifted his sickle, allowing time to flow its proper passage.

McCann's opponent thought for a moment, contemplating his limited options and their likely outcomes he weighed up his chances.

The Englishman was certain this man wasn't a fighter just a coward with barely enough guts to pay someone else to space his wife.

'That's what I thought. You don't have the nuts to pull that thing, do you?' The Englishman slapped his face with the palm of his hand, 'Well? Do you?'

His opponent didn't move, again McCann slapped him causing the fellow's lip to bleed, 'Is that it, you're gonna just gawp at me while you bleed?'

The slime's hand moved away from his pistol, his wife's chains tumbled to the floor. He walked toward the exit in silence and his wife shouted, 'I always knew you were too afraid to fight a real man, PIG!'

Something snapped inside him, the fat man spun around yanking his pistol from its belt.

At the same time McCann pulled holding down the trigger and firing three tungsten rounds consecutively, all three entering the target's chest. The ex-husband crumpled onto his back as a pool of hot blood surrounded an unfortunate corpse.

Shaking her fist the old woman heckled the deceased, 'Hah hah hah! Now you have an ex-wife! And you won't require my guskin where you are going, you stupid donkey penis!'

The rest of Dock 17 were aghast yet did nothing about what had just taken place. McCann took the ladies' chains and handed them to Ilam, 'Here, I'm sure you two will get along like a house on fire.'

Back on Discovery the old lady was clothed in a space glove. Her chains removed she spent the rest of the day linking with Ilam.

'Commodore McCann,' came Discovery's soft voice.

'Here,' replied the Englishman resting on the bridge of his docked vessel.

'Transmission from station controller Mesan.'

McCann got to his feet, 'Put him on.'

Mesan's image appeared on the view screen, hair slicked back into a pony tail, 'Duncan McCann?'

'What is it Mesan?'

'I have a warrant for your arrest.'

'Arrest?'

Mesan's eyes moved down to read a tablet before him, 'For the murder in cold blood of Citizen 398PXB ... I'm hereby requesting you hand yourself in for immediate trial and execution.'

The Commodore furrowed his brow, 'Trial and execution?'

'I don't issue warrants for innocent men.'

'That doesn't make sense.'

'We shall discuss after you've handed your weapons in at nearest control station.'

'That man was about to space his wife.'

'He using a method of female disposal sanctioned by Kurgudwardum 57.'

The entrance to the bridge slid open and in stepped Ilam with the old lady he'd rescued.

The old woman shrieked at Mesan, 'Female disposal?'

'Who is this female?'

'My name is Gianna-atir-sinnis-ash the third what is your name young man?'

'I am station controller Mesan.'

'Station controller HAH! Anu controls this god forsaken toilet floating in the void of darkness!'

Mesan became uncomfortable, 'Duncan McCann, silence this female so men may speak with civility.'

The old lady turned to give McCann a grim look, McCann made no reply.

Gianna returned her gaze to Mesan, 'You may keep my husband's vessel but I want my possessions brought to this ship.'

'His star ship impounded all contents are to be liquidated at auction tomorrow.'

Gianna snarled at the pony tailed Mesan dressed in a purple shirt, 'Send my daughter here immediately or I'll contact my lawyers in the Vega territory you filthy bandit!'

'Your daughter is one of the assets to be liquidated ... still a few years of love before hard labour,' smirked Mesan.

'You fiend!' shrieked Gianna

'I might purchase myself and Duncan McCann don't step on this station again, leave now, never return, this matter forgotten.'

McCann nodded silently as Mesan's figure disappeared from Discovery's display.

'Communication ended,' said Vezzali, working more than one station on this small vessel.

'Prepare to cast off, the sooner I see the back of this place the better.'

'What of my daughter?'

McCann fixed his eyes on Gianna, 'What of her?'

'That fiend Mesan he'll auction her off to skin traders and then god knows what may become of my little Edna.'

McCann wasn't interested, 'Listen Granny I've got my orders and they don't include rescuing your daughter.'

'You bastard!'

The Englishman was taken aback by the little woman's forwardness. He said nothing in reply only moving to retire to the Officer's Mess.

'Do you have a daughter, Duncan McCann?' cried a desperate Gianna.

The Commodore stopped in his tracks as the crew waited for his response.

'Yes.'

'If she were to be auctioned off would you do something about it?'

McCann looked back at Gianna, 'I would.'

'She is your daughter now Duncan McCann.'

'I'm sorry?'

'When you shot my husband I became your wife, that's Vega Territory law!'

'I'm not from the Vega Territory, Granny.'

'Well I am and you took me as your wife when you saved me.'

'I already have a wife.'

'Now you have two!'

Vezzali wiped her eyes as she listened to Gianna's heartfelt plea.

'Listen Granny one wife is more than I can put up with most days. Two would have me swinging on the end of a rope before Christmas.'

Gianna stomped up to him, reached up as high as she could and slapped the Englishman around the face, 'You heartless bastard!'

Again McCann remained motionless.

'Then give me a firearm, I'll go and teach that fiend a lesson!'

'So all that talk about doing whatever I desire was just a heap of shit to get out of a bind?' stated McCann in a sardonic tone.

Gianna slapped him again, 'Watch your language there are ladies present!'

Both Vezzali and Ilam were touched by Gianna's desperation. She'd lost everything and her daughter was about to be auctioned to slavers.

Next a voice emanated from behind the Commodore, 'Sir, if it's all the same to you I want to help Granny out.'

Clayton was dressed in a Tlillan white frock jacket, standard issue for a non-military mission, with a pair of pistols hanging below his hip.

'Clayton you're under my command and this is an information gathering expedition. Not some hunt in the tunnels of Bandayuuk!'

'Sir, Ilam says she'll be sold and raped until she either dies or is too old.'

McCann gave his wife the evil eye then bellowed at Clayton, 'It doesn't matter. We have the information we need and must move on.'

Clayton was unfazed, 'I'm sorry sir but it does matter, she's up for auction because of us and I want to do something to stop it.'

Gianna marched over to Clayton entwining her arms around one of his, 'Good boy, I'm glad to see there are some decent folk out here!'

Chapter 6

That night in Discovery's Mess a plan of action was formulated. They'd wait until tomorrow's auction to purchase Gianna's daughter. No blood, no fight just a clean trade.

'I'll have to stay aboard the Discovery,' noted McCann toying with a shot glass at the bar.

'Don't you worry about Mesan,' said Gianna as she entered the Mess, 'he hasn't got the guts to come after you. He's only brave when it comes to bullying women!'

Clayton approached her with a smile, 'Come here Granny, can I get you a whisky?'

'Whisky? What's that?'

'Sikaru,' stated Ilam.

'Oh, no young man, I'm from the Vega Territory we certainly don't drink.'

'Why not?' inquired Clayton.

'Well I wouldn't want to cause any offence ...'

McCann gave a loud snort raising several grins amongst the ship staff.

Gianna gave the Englishman a black look, 'But where I come from only ruffians and bandits drink. Respectable folk keep clear of such vice ... no offence intended.'

'So what are respectable folk from the Vega Territory doing here spacing their wives and purchasing sex slaves?' sneered McCann.

'I thought we were going on a holiday to the Quasar belt, it was supposed to be our second honeymoon. I'd always wanted to see it and he promised me a month long cruise. Of course when we exited hyperspace I looked at the navigation map and we were in the Skin Territory! That villain drugged me and his own daughter, when I awoke I was naked and in chains!

He arranged to space me at Dock 17, they would provide a legal death certificate permitting him to cash in on my insurance. He'd claim all of my money, if I die under suspicious circumstances he gets nothing you know.'

Clayton shook his head, 'Sounds like a real bastard to me, I think he got what he deserved.'

Gianna nodded her head, 'Quite right! And now Duncan McCann is a wealthy man.'

Clayton ordered a fruit juice for Gianna, 'Why's that?'

'Well he's my husband now and when I die my daughter will look after him I'm sure. My family are respectable prospectors in the Vega Territory you know? We made a fortune on the Neutronium Rush … before it became the Skin Territory.'

Clayton shook his head, 'I don't, tell me about it.'

McCann sighed until Ilam slapped his back, shutting him up.

'Many millennia ago this system was one of several with stars rich in neutronium. All the stations you see here today were mining camps, established to capture neutronium cast from the star.

Oh men would risk their lives trying to get closer than their rival, to be first when neutronium belched out. Some would be vapourised, I remember my great grandfather telling me how he saw one man and his seven brothers killed; when a lump of neutronium too big to catch in the magnetic net crashed into their mining ship. They all died risking their lives. One year and you could leave a wealthy man for the rest of your life.'

Clayton passed a drink to Gianna, 'So how did it end up like this?'

The old lady took a sip of her juice, 'They strip mined that star with graviton beams. First the neutronium ran out then the people left and before you knew it this place was a grave system!

Illegal traders, villains and fiends bought up these stations, selling lotus, guns and slaves. No-one cared though. It was outside of any civilized Territory so they were left to their own devices. I think a lot of politicians are so heavily invested in the Skin Territory they refuse to come in and clear it up.'

McCann took a sip of his whisky, 'So tell me about this Mesan and Anu.'

Gianna pulled a grim expression on hearing their names, 'Mesan is a puppet, that ponytailed freak can do nothing without Anu's permission.'

'So tell me about Anu.'

'He runs the Blue Necks, the gang controlling this station, they all wear blue handkerchiefs. If anything happens on this floating den of vice he has a hand in it.'

McCann placed a single gold sovereign in Gianna's hand, 'Is this worth anything?'

Gianna picked the coin up with her index finger and thumb before examining it closely, 'Hmm, looks to be 90% pure about four guskin in weight. I've not seen this coin before, where did it come from?'

McCann was taken aback at how accurate the old lady was, 'It's 91.6% pure and it's from a very distant system.'

The old woman handed back the sovereign, 'I've seen every coin in circulation young man and this is not one used; however you'll get about four guskin for it.'

Ilam passed a dark blue coin into the possession of Gianna, 'What about this?'

The old lady eyed it in the same manner, 'Neutronium, pure ... 160 million guskin,' Gianna examined the profile of Xch'uup struck into the coin, 'Who is this?'

Ilam grinned with satisfaction 'That is my daughter.'

'She must be somebody.'

'Her predecessor fought the Telal, banishing them to this place.'

Gianna gave her a hard stare, 'No-one can defeat the Telal.'

'Who told you that? The Telal?'

'It's a fact; they have not lost the Chihuaz for nearly half a million cycles!'

Ilam gave a puzzled look, 'Chihuaz?'

'You're really not from around here are you?'

'Please explain.'

'Each cycle in the Tamoanchan Territory the Chihuaz is staged. If nations, planets, systems, territories have a dispute they may ... settle it.'

Ilam was still none the wiser, 'I'm sorry I don't understand.'

Gianna let out a sigh, 'Their leaders fight to the death rather than declare war, if you wish you may challenge for the seat of Topixque.'

'Topixque?'

'The Chihuaz seat of power, whoever holds it rules the Territory absolute. My husband used to watch religiously, it's the top rated programme in the galaxy; of course I never watched that kind of trash, because ...'

McCann removed a Trinidad Reyes from its tubos, 'Decent folk from the Vega Territory don't do that sort of thing?'

Gianna made a black look in McCann's direction, 'Why yes and I hope you're not going to smoke that disgusting thing in my presence?'

The Englishman placed his cigar back in its tubos, 'So these Telal turned up, seized victory and have held it ever since?'

'Yes.'

'They must be pretty mean fighters? Either that or they cheat.'

Gianna shook her head, 'Have you ever seen a Telal?'

'No.'

Ilam stepped forward, 'But we fought them in the past.'

'And won?'

'The battle raged for days until Xch'uup,' Ilam pointed at the neutronium coin in Gianna's hand, 'met the Tzitzimeh in a duel.'

'Tzitzimeh? You mean Telal.'

'Their true title is Tzitzimeh. We banished them after the greatest battle ... before Bandayuuk.'

McCann looked at his wife, 'If these Telal know what's good for them they'll steer clear of us.'

'They are a demon of pure evil, enough to terrify even the most hardened of Matriarchs. I doubt a human could handle but one.'

'Well I'd say we've done a damn good job of picking up your slack so far!'

'Calm yourself Duncan. It was not intended as a jibe.'

McCann finished his whisky and stepped closer to both Ilam and Gianna, 'Well you just show me one of these creatures that makes you all piss your pants,' the Englishman slipped his pistol from its holster spinning it around a few times before slipping it back with perfect grace, 'and I'll show you how we dealt with demons on Bandayuuk!'

Ilam rolled her eyes.

Gianna pointed toward the Englishman, 'You've had far too much to drink Duncan McCann. You need to go to bed and sleep it off you won't be much help to my daughter with a hangover!'

McCann sneered before exiting the Mess.

Gianna looked up at Ilam, 'Does he drink often?'

'You have no idea,' replied the Valkyrie.

'Well I'll have to see what we can do about that. I'm not having a drunk for a husband.'

The next morning McCann awoke beside his wife. Slipping his arms around her they engaged in a long kiss. Once finished he called to the AI, 'Lights.'

The room slowly illuminated, as it did the Englishman waited until his wife's beautiful face became clear. As the level of illumination rose the Englishman noted something odd. Using vision gifted to him via the Ixchel he examined the person lay naked beside him.

McCann realised it was not his wife but in fact was Gianna. The Englishman leapt from his bed, 'What on Earth are you doing here?'

Gianna sat up in the large comfortable bed she'd spent the night in, 'I'm your wife, where do you think I should sleep?'

'In your quarters?'

'These are my quarters, aren't they?' the old woman looked down with a smirk, noting McCann was undressed.

The Englishman followed her eyes and quickly threw on a space suit, 'You need to leave.'

'Why should I leave?'

'I'm married and my wife ...'

'Ilam said it was fine. Apparently she doesn't enjoy the stench of whisky. I find it quite invigorating myself.'

After throwing his suit on McCann turned slowly to look at a naked Gianna smiling in his bed, 'We didn't?'

The old lady smiled, 'Now don't tell me that you don't remember Mr McCann?'

The Englishman was so shocked he couldn't speak.

Gianna got out of bed and he was horrified.

'I'll leave first Mr McCann, that way no-one will know about our little soiree last night,' the old lady slipped into a black ribbed space suit and left with a cheeky wink.

McCann was silent for a few minutes. He looked up, 'Discovery?'

'Yes Commodore,' replied the SI in a soft voice.

'Do you have last night's footage, from my cabin?'

'I'm sorry Commodore you requested it be disabled.'

'Why?'

'I have no idea Commodore.'

'Was I alone when I disabled it?'

'No you had a guest.'

'Who?'

'Gianna-atir-sinnis-ash the third was present at the time of your request, Commodore.'

McCann muttered to himself, 'Marvellous.'

Strolling to the Mess McCann rubbed his face, awaking his mind from the madness of Dionysus. Upon entering the Mess Gianna was sat at a table next to his wife, the old lady had a big grin on her face as did Ilam. Doing his best to ignore their antics he got himself some eggs on toast and sat next to Clayton.

'Mornin' Commodore.'

'Good morning Clayton, anything happen last night I should know about.'

'Nope everything's running ship shape.'

'Do you have the location of Edna's auction?'

'Yep eleven hundred hours she'll be up for sale, what do you plan to do?'

'We've a large stash of sovereigns. I think I'll try to buy her first.'

'And if that doesn't work?'

McCann chewed on his breakfast as he considered the question, 'In that case they'll take a down payment in tungsten.'

Clayton nodded, 'Let's hope they see sense first.'

After breakfast McCann, Clayton and Mountbatten stood at an airlock. Each man had prepared himself with thigh holsters, pistols loaded with 50 tungsten rounds. Dressed in typical black cargo pants, navy issue boots and white Tlillan frock coats the men checked their weapons. Whilst certifying their I.S.A issue pistols the sound of boots clinking on the catronium floor approached.

As the group looked up from their firearms Ilam and Gianna appeared, both dressed in Tlillan ribbed suits and white frock coats. The towering Tlillan carried a pair of ion weapons made on Otoch.

'What on Earth are those things?' stated Mountbatten noting the rifles Ilam carried, one in each hand.

'Tunnel sweepers,' replied Clayton.

'I'm sorry?'

'It's a plasma weapon that uses an Ion battery, after charging up gas in the atmosphere it fires a ball of plasma. We called it a Tlillan tunnel sweeper. On Bandayuuk you could flush out Macks like a turd with one of them.'

The Valkyrie gave a serious expression, 'I'm coming and Gianna will be with us to identify her daughter.'

McCann didn't disagree. He planned on buying Edna then leaving peacefully. However if needed be he'd require all the help he could get.

Ilam peered down at the old lady beside her, 'Gianna, have you operated a firearm in the past?'

The old lady looked up and replied in a stern tone, 'Yes.'

'Then take this,' Ilam offered a rather hefty rifle with a single large bore barrel it looked to be a model 1886 Winchester on steroids along with a little Tlillan flavour, 'the ion cell is always charged, just flick this switch where the stock meets the power plant to disengage its safety. Point at your target and pull the trigger, the discharge will burn a hole into whatever stands in your path. After each shot you should clear the barrel by pushing forward then pulling back this hand mechanism,' she placed her delicate fingers inside a lever encompassing its trigger and pushed it forwards then returned it quickly.

Gianna took the weapon, which appeared twice the size in her hands, 'Gotcha, now let's get my Edna back!'

McCann nodded his head, 'If you say so.'

Before their party stepped through the airlock, Vezzali came rushing down the hall, 'Commodore!'

She carried a long black coat over one arm and a bag with the other.

'I flashed you this Commodore,' she presented a black frock coat. After handing it to a rather startled McCann she pulled a bowler hat out from her bag, 'Here, you cannot be a gunslinger without a hat you know?'

The Englishman took his black bowler hat, 'Very civilized, thank you.'

McCann rapped his knuckles on the Bowler, 'At least it'll protect my head from flying bullets.'

His blonde haired science officer smiled, 'I had it lined with catronium.'

Ilam placed a red bowler on her head, 'What do you think Duncan?'

'You'd look good in anything my dear.'

Gianna seated a blue bowler firmly onto her crown, 'What do you think Duncan?'

Narrowing his eyes the Englishman replied, 'Marvellous.'

As everyone else tested the strength of their Bowler McCann changed his jacket, 'So what's the coat in aid of?'

'On patrol you often watched those westerns. I thought you would appreciate a proper coat, like that man you viewed many times.'

McCann became a little embarrassed, 'Yes well that's enough. I think it's time to leave ...'

'For a few ...'

Ilam finished Vezzali's sentence, 'Dollars more?'

'Yes, that is the film.'

'I've been forced to watch it at least 7 times!' bemoaned Ilam.

'Discovery, open the airlock we're leaving now,' hurried McCann.

Vezzali waved as the group stepped aboard the slaver station.

The party of five walked down the main boulevard of Kurgudwardum 57. Citizens and traders looked on at the odd attire not to mention two women carrying firearms. Taxis zipped past, beeping horns, seemingly oblivious to anything else.

As they moved towards the auction house a pair of blue necks carrying pistols blocked their path.

McCann halted his crew. He looked a bearded man in the eye, 'Something you want?'

The middle aged man's steely gaze pointed towards Ilam and Gianna, 'Females are not permitted to carry firearms on Kurgudwardum 57.'

McCann moved his hand down towards his thigh causing great tension in the Blue Necks. Passing his pistol he dipped his fingers into a pocket on his cargo pants and produced a Ramon Allones cigar.

The old blue neck expelled a gust of wind in relief.

After biting off the cap McCann slowly drew his pulse pistol. Tension filled the air once again as merchants and citizens of Kurgudwardum 57 moved away from the confrontation.

The Englishman proceeded to toast the end of his cigar employing his pistol's hot rails before replacing the weapon in its holster.

Puffing on fine Cuban tobacco Commodore McCann returned the Blue Neck's gaze, 'So?'

'So they must hand their firearms in to the proper authorities.'

'Or?'

The pistolero replied in a nervous demeanour, 'I will take them by force.'

McCann called over his shoulder, 'What do you say Granny?'

Gianna held tightly onto her Tlillan tunnel sweeper, 'I say he can go to hell!'

'I'm afraid the ladies refuse to co-operate.'

The pistolero looked towards his younger subordinate, 'Nita, confiscate that female's weapon,' he pointed at Ilam.

The young man's eyes darted about nervously.

'Nita, confiscate her weapon, NOW!'

Nita, who could be no older than 21, approached Ilam gingerly, 'Give me your gun.'

The Amazon tilted her red bowler upwards sneering at the boy. Before he could speak again she swung the stock of her weapon, smashing his face.

The boy stumbled backwards onto the floor, the crowd gasped, taxis screeched to a halt.

The remaining pistoleros' hand shifted towards his firearm hanging from its leather gun belt.

'Draw that gun and you'll be looking for work as a wind chime!' snapped McCann.

The Blue Neck realised he couldn't win, stepping aside he whispered, 'When Anu hears of this ...'

McCann pointed in the fellow's face, 'You tell Anu to stay out of my way and I'll stay out of his,' then continued down Kurgudwardum's main boulevard.

The Blue Neck stepped over to assist his subordinate as a crowd observed these odd strangers walk away. Everyone knew Anu ran Kurgudwardum 57 and whoever challenged his authority in the past had met with a lonely grave, in orbit of a strip mined star.

McCann's crew eventually reached the auction house. An establishment situated along a main strip of merchants involved in various commodities of differing immorality. Many traded in narcotics produced on some of the larger stations; others traded weapons, from the individual to an entire Territory. Then there were those who offered delivery or smuggling of those goods to whatever destination might be required.

McCann stepped into an auction house focused on slave trading. These slaves were mostly prisoners of war or kidnapped women; destined to be used in the most nefarious of establishments across the galaxy.

A young girl stood on a lifted dais as Mesan called out her number. He described the female's heritage. Upon mentioning confirmation of virginity interest intensified from the many patrons waiting to bid.

As McCann's band stepped inside Mesan stopped talking. The crowd turned to observe five outlaws enter the auction house.

Three Blue Necks dwelled within, one next to Mesan making certain Anu got his cut of all sales; another strolling around the crowd of about 50 private bidders. The last stood beside a bar at the other end of the auction house where successful bidders took possession of their property.

McCann approached the dais, the crowd parted as the Red Sea, 'I'm looking for Edna.'

'I'm sorry … Edna?'

'Edna, this lady's daughter,' removing a cigar from his mouth McCann pointed out Gianna.

Mesan noted their large bore rifles, 'Women are not permitted firearms on Kurgudwardum 57.'

The Englishman lifted his bowler's brim, 'What are you gonna do about it Mesan?'

The ponytailed jack of all trades made no reply. He only gave McCann a nervous expression.

'That's what I thought, now where's Edna?'

'Lot 24 has been sold. You'll have to speak with the gentlemen over there.'

McCann followed Mesan's finger to the bar end of the auction house. Edna was naked her wrists shackled to a steel neck brace. Two burly and quite smelly men in their middle years groped her. They seemed to be arguing over who would have the privilege of raping her first.

'I paid more guskin, I should be first!'

'Well it's me who told you about this lot.'

'I tell you what I get the front and you can have the back, deal?'

McCann grimaced at the sight of these poorly kept men who'd put their pittances together in order to purchase a sex slave.

Gianna rushed forwards, 'Take your hands off her you filth!'

Edna lay on one of the many extended sofas. Other patrons paid no attention to the vile rape about to take place as if this were a common occurrence. McCann was disgusted by bystanders' depravity far more than the two men resembling bear trappers.

One of the dirty men got up from the sofa as his friend proceeded to lie over Edna; holding her down with one hand whilst undoing his trousers with the other.

'Where'd you buy this old bag?'

Gianna levelled her firearm aiming it at the bearded man, 'Let her go, or I'll blow you back to hell!'

Before anything might occur, McCann pushed Gianna's barrel away he then asked the fellow, 'How much did you pay for her?'

'1,000 guskin, I have proof, she's mine.'

McCann produced a leather purse from his coat 'Here's 2,000 guskin for that slave.'

The dirty trapper on the couch stopped what he was doing and quickly got up, lifting his pants from his knees to his hips, '2,000 G's?'

McCann threw him the purse, he caught it letting his pants drop back down. The patron removed a sovereign and after examination confirmed it was genuine gold.

'You can buy yourselves a slave each, just hand her over to me untouched.'

The two men consulted each other whilst Edna lay on the sofa frightened out of her mind. A teenage girl caught up in the skin trade.

Whilst counting the money one of the men had a sudden epiphany, 'I'll tell you what. Why don't we take the money, hand in Duncan McCann and keep the slave, Sam?'

Sam's head snapped towards McCann, 'You mean?'

'Yeah, this is that Duncan McCann. Mesan has a bounty of 1,000 G's on him … dead or alive.'

The bar began to clear … as patrons moved out Blue Necks closed in. Mesan kept his distance hiding behind his auctioneers' station.

McCann took a puff of his cigar tasting its creamy smoke as it rolled over his tongue, '1,000 G's … not much to lose your life over.'

Sam cackled with laughter, 'Who says we're gonna die?'

The Englishman discarded his cigar, 'Everybody dies … and now you've pissed me off.'

Sam still grinned, Blue Necks boosting his confidence, 'Why is that Duncan McCann?'

'That was a good cigar.'

As he finished his sentence the trappers made a move drawing their pistols. McCann drew quicker putting 5 rounds into his chest. Clayton pulled and filled a Blue Neck at the bar full of tungsten before he was even close to his pistol grip. Ilam had kept the Blue Necks to her left under observation, she fired her Tlillan rifle. A blast of hot plasma tore through the air as patrons cried out dropping for cover. A young Blue Neck stood motionless his spinal column decorating the auction house wall with a Jackson Pollock whilst Ilam pushed her lever forwards then backwards clearing the weapon's firing chamber.

The final Blue Neck scrambled away as Mountbatten shot him in the back three times, eventually dropping dead on the main boulevard to screams of horror from passers-by.

Sam moved to draw … but forgot his pants were still around his ankles.

McCann took another Ramones Allones cigar from his pocket and lit it in the same manner. The sudden commotion caused by their shootout now dissipated as the Commodore raised an eyebrow at Sam's groin area, 'Seems to me you've been caught short old boy.'

Sam dropped into a crouch, attempting to grab his pistol. Before he could do so McCann kicked him full in the face.

A beaten and bloodied Sam lay on the floor propped up against the couch he'd attempted to commit rape upon.

Gianna rushed forward pointing her weapon at the sad excuse for a slaver, 'Shall we shoot him Mr McCann?'

The Englishman took a long drag on his Habanos 'No, I think Sam's gonna give us that 2,000 guskin and his slave in return for his sorry life … what do you say Sam?'

A bitter man looked up, 'When Anu hears of this you're …'

McCann kicked him as hard as he could in the testicles causing the scumbag to roll over in pain, 'I'll take that as a yes. Get your daughter Granny. We're leaving.'

Clayton bent down retrieving the purse of money beside Sam's dead friend.

As the band of outlaws walked past Mesan the oily haired Controller shouted, 'Anu will never let you leave this station alive, none of you! Our skin is insured until it leaves this station. Anu will take her back or make you compensate that man!'

McCann drew his pistol to gasps from auction house patrons, levelling his weapon he fired a single round into Sam's forehead removing any potential claim against him, 'Anyone else interested in compensation?'

Ilam laughed at a tight lipped Mesan.

'That's what I thought.'

Marching back Discovery's crew reloaded their pistols as citizens made way.

'Do you think we'll make it back?' inquired Gianna.

'We'll make it back Granny,' replied Clayton.

Out of the crowd four Blue Necks formed a line blocking McCann's path, hands twitching over holsters.

Ilam glanced at Gianna 'Take Edna over there and wait,' pointing to the sidewalk where patrons of Kurgudwardum 57 stood rubber necking.

'Come with me Edna,' said the old lady ushering her daughter out of harm's way.

The four remaining outlaws spread out forming an opposing line to the Blue Necks, 15 metres of space between them. Everyone waited, watching each flick of the finger and movement of the eye.

A Blue Neck snatched for his weapon ... casting open the gates of hell. Everyone drew, Ilam took advantage employing her mental abilities and pre-empting her foe. McCann and Clayton did much the same to a lesser degree. Mountbatten had to rely on good old human instinct a fast hand and keen eye.

Plasma burst from barrels on both sides to the chorus of shrieking onlookers. Ilam was first to get a shot off, a plasma eruption tore through cool air connecting with a young man's head. Its resulting impact forced his brain matter to boil. Intense heat alongside pressure created a detonation … his head exploded in a violent decapitation. From his sizzling Blue Neck up nothing remained after being burnt by scorching heat.

The unfortunate fellow's head matter blasted in all directions. Onlookers at the edge of Kurgudwardum's main boulevard were splattered in a Damien Hirst to complement the Jackson Pollock adorning the auction house wall. Taxi drivers remained inside their vehicles with magnetic windscreen wipers at full.

Hot gas leapt from McCann's barrel as his pulse pistol fired rhythmically. Tungsten rocketed through the air in a massive sonic boom peppering its target.

Full of tiny holes the Blue Neck stumbled backwards hitting the floor in synchrony with Ilam's headless victim.

Clayton was next to pull, neatly grouping his bullets in the centre of a Blue Neck's chest. The gunman rocked back and forth firing pistols, hitting people in the crowd time and time again. His shirt filled with small bloody polka dots until inevitably meeting the floor.

Mountbatten drew the exact moment as his counterpart. Metal slugs passed each other as they travelled through both time and space. Both men were hit, each one falling to the other's bullets.

The intense shootout caused a heat haze distorting clear vision between both parties. It were as if Anchiale had risen up from the boulevard floor obscuring the immediate surroundings in her fog. As the Titan of heat diminished into the atmosphere removing her screen McCann made out four Blue Necks and Mountbatten, dead.

Clayton collected Mountbatten's weapons. Ilam lifted his bloody body from the ground, throwing him over her shoulder with one mighty swing of her arm.

McCann nodded at Gianna, 'Let's get out of Dodge.'

The old lady was unsure of the reference yet she got the gist of it, ushering her daughter away. The crew stepped over Anu's dead pistoleros past horrified citizens and down the boulevard back to Discovery.

The station's warlord sent no more of his men to die that day. He had a different plan for finishing this band of strangers flouting Kurgudwardum 57 law ... his law.

Chapter 7

'He took but one girl?'

'Lot 24, a fair skinned girl from the Vega Territory she was part of a star ship monetized on Dock 9.'

Anu scratched his stubble whilst Blue Necks watched on, 'What does he care for this female?'

Mesan walked around the long wooden table at which Anu and his band dined. Passing him a tablet Mesan stated, 'He rescued this female from Dock 17.'

Anu chewed on a leg of meat as he viewed the picture, 'Why he want this wrinkled sahu?'

The ponytailed controller shook his head, 'I don't know but it seems lot 24 is her daughter. Also Duncan McCann's female was very curious concerning the Telal.'

Anu peered at Mesan, 'Why?'

'She was unaware of the Telal.'

'She had no knowledge of Telal?'

'None, although when I described a Telal the female became excited.'

Anu pondered on the situation, 'Contact Hebat, send her all information concerning this female and Duncan McCann.'

'But they will be gone soon.'

Anu took a bite of meat as a naked woman served him red wine, 'They are going nowhere, speak to Hebat.'

Mesan nodded, 'Yes Anu,' exiting the area, Anu's men drank wine and dined on roast meats.

Earlier that day Anu made a visit to the station's upmost point. Kurgudwardum 57 used to be a mining station along with nearly every other space station in this system. Larger mining stations carried a heavy graviton beam its purpose being to strip mine the star.

A graviton beam would be charged with fusion reactors and fired onto the sun's surface, thick with neutronium. A skilled operator would create a gravimetric shear in space; Forcing gravitons from other parallel continuums to form above the star and by force of gravity rip neutronium from its surface. The beam operator guided ore in towards space vessels waiting to collect it.

A graviton beam could quite easily be named a dark matter beam; Dark matter being the fabric of space/time. A graviton beam focused gravity, creating such a force it prevented space/time from moving between dimensions as it usually would. Instead a continuum is opened, forcing all gravitons moving freely between dimensions to gather at a point above the star.

A singularity created just off another singularity long enough to tear some precious metal away. Next its operator would close the inter-dimensional continuum, reducing sheer gravimetric force slowly as to leave space unblemished by the event.

This is what stripped the star of its value and was preventing Discovery from casting off.

On Discovery Vezzali explained what a graviton beam of such power could do and how it would crush them before they might fold space. McCann surmised the only way out would be to disable this mining beam before casting off.

'So where's the beam's generator?' inquired the Englishman.

'I assume it would be situated at the very centre of the station, probably in this area,' noted Vezzali as they sat in the Mess staring at a projection of Kurgudwardum 57.

'Assume?'

'I don't know for sure, we're cut off from the station network.'

As McCann scratched his head Ilam walked through the door followed by a lady wearing a long light blue dress displaying a strange puff ball fashion around the waist area.

'Someone wishes to speak with you Duncan.'

McCann looked up at the blonde haired lady, 'Yes?'

The alien replied in a timid tone, 'It's my daughter Mr McCann.'

'What about your daughter?'

'Pirates kidnapped and brought her here.'

'And?'

The lady wrangled her hands together whilst recanting the story, 'She was sold in one of Anu's auction houses to skin traders. They were shipping skin to Tamoanchan. She died on the journey there.'

'So what do you want me to do about it?'

'They say you're the best gun for hire in the Skin Territory.'

'Really? Who says that?'

'After what you did to those Blue Necks ... everyone!'

'So what's this got to do with you and your daughter?'

The lady opened a pleat in her puff ball to produce a purse, 'I have 5,000 guskin for Anu.'

The Englishman didn't quite understand, 'Why don't you give it to him?'

'For you to kill him.'

McCann creased his brow, 'I'm not an assassin for hire.'

'I'll be your slave if you desire?'

The Commodore fixed his eyes upon his wife, 'What's this all about?'

'Inanna has something we need ... information.'

Inanna peered at the tall Valkyrie, 'Anything.'

'You learnt all you could about Anu before travelling here, yes?'

'That is correct.'

'And you learnt about this station, yes?'

'Correct.'

'Allow me to link minds, retrieve that information and Mr McCann will end the life of Anu.'

McCann stood up, 'Hold on a moment, I'm not going out there again!'

'We must disable this station, we cannot do it from the Discovery,' stated the Tlillan.

'But kill Anu? That piece of crap is probably guarded night and day.'

Inanna jumped in, 'He does a circuit of the station once a quarter. Reminding merchants why they pay him a cut and collecting from those that forgot.'

'No,' said the Englishman shaking his head, 'bugger that, I just want to get off this station.'

Ilam noted with cold Tlillan logic, 'If you kill Anu it may throw this station into chaos long enough to disable its graviton beam. We may fold space before they are aware.'

Inanna became excited at the prospect, 'You could wait for him on the main boulevard. When he passes by shoot him down like the filthy slaver he is!'

'That easy?' snorted McCann.

'Well they say you're the fastest draw in the Skin Territory. They say you walked into an auction house and killed 5 Blue Necks single handed!'

McCann looked at his wife with a raised an eyebrow.

Ilam held back a smile.

'It was three Blue Necks and I didn't shoot any of them.'

'The gunfight … on the boulevard?'

'How many did I kill there?'

'I heard you killed four pistoleros.'

'I'm afraid I'm not quite the gunslinger you've been led to believe.'

'But you need to kill Anu and I want him dead. If you do that then I don't care how fast your draw is.'

'Fine, you go with Ilam to her cabin, she'll link with you. If the information is good I'll see what I can do.'

Later that day a small vessel folded space into the Skin Territory, docking with Kurgudwardum 57. A crowd gathered around the airlock leading from the docking bay and into the station. Mesan waited outside with his Blue Neck deputies. The Airlock swung open and onlookers pushed through to get a look at the creature exiting. From the vessel came a being not much more than 5 feet tall. It wore a simple brown tunic dress ending at its knees. Its clothing adorned with tiny bones and shrunken heads, displaying a variety of species.

Its face was of a wrinkled old woman with a mouth protruding as that of a lizard. Short creased arms ending in clawed hands of hard bone. The creature's eyes were dead soulless balls of grey darkness. Upon its head sat a crown of bones pointing to the sky.

Mesan got down on one knee as if addressing royalty.

'Uzuzzu,' stated the small creature with a lisp; her rows of razor sharp teeth flashing in the docking arm's lighting.

Kurgudwardum 57's controller rose, 'Cacama Hebat.'

Mesan escorted Hebat across the boulevard and into the depths of Kurgudwardum 57 until reaching the controllers offices; Where Anu waited alongside two of his Blue Necks.

All three men got down on one knee when the Telal entered. As before the creature of nightmare spoke, 'Uzuzzu.'

The men stood and replied, 'Cacama Hebat.'

Hebat, something similar to an Ambassador or foreign minister, spoke, 'What is it you have brought me all this way to see?'

Mesan tapped a table and Ilam's image leapt up. As it turned slowly Anu awaited her response.

Hebat did nothing until footage played and Ilam's eyes burnt as coals. The wrinkled demon stepped back, 'Where did you get this?'

'A space vessel, it docked a few days ago, she made inquiries concerning the Telal.'

'A few days? Why did you not inform us earlier?'

'Errmm, well, we saw no reason until they started killing people,' stammered Mesan.

Hebat locked eyes with Anu. Her vision terrified the lord of Kurgudwardum 57, 'Where is it now?'

'Aboard their space craft.'

The Telal's eyes changed to a lighter shade of grey, 'You mean it is alive?'

'Yes but they can't leave.'

Neither Anu nor Mesan had ever seen a Telal flustered. These were creatures of nightmare. They made grown men afraid to walk in the dark, now something rattled its cage.

'How many?'

Mesan shrugged his shoulders, 'It's a smaller craft, maybe 20?'

'TWENTY?' screeched the beast.

'Yes but the rest are shorter.'

'Show me, quickly.'

Mesan went through station footage with Hebat. Anu observed
with great interest as the beast calmed down yet it remained
disturbed when viewing that tall red headed female.

After having gone through all footage and questioning Mesan
Hebat folded her scrawny arms, 'There is only one but that is
enough ... too much.'

'What do you wish us to do?'

'Kill it, kill them all. If they are not destroyed the Tamoanchan
fleet will arrive in a week and your contract null and void.'

Anu became animated, 'Hey, you cannot come into the Skin
Territory we have a contract going back Eons. The Kishar would
train every graviton beam on that fleet and destroy it.'

Hebat's eyes sparkled a lighter shade of grey, 'Do you know what
that is?' pointing to Ilam's image.

'A female?'

'That is a Tlillan and if it is allowed to escape it may return ... with
Xch'uup.'

Anu pulled a puzzled expression, 'I don't understand.'

'Tlillan are creatures of evil, Xch'uup their mother. If you feel
Mammi is hard on you remember Xch'uup would not even give you
the Skin Territory. She will enslave us all,' the Telal pointed at Anu,
'and you shall be forced to praise her as a God ... on pain of death!'

Anu gave a nervous smile, 'I doubt these Tlillan could prevail
against every graviton beam in the Skin Territory.'

'Who knows what Xch'uups' fleet is capable of today,' Hebat then
murmured to herself, 'she's made the jump to Anur, she's made the
jump to Anur ...'

'Where is this Xch'uup based?' inquired Mesan.

'Too distant for us to strike, we must take their vessel and learn all
we can.'

'We may only confiscate docked ships if abandoned.'

Hebat flashed rows of sharp teeth.

The station controller's legs turned to jelly, 'The docking fee is due next week, we can board it by force then.'

'In a week Xch'uup may be here and it shall be the end of your little skin trade.'

There was a silence until Anu broke it, 'Fine, tomorrow I'll sort these outlaws out once and for all. You tell Mammi I'll bring her that Tlillan's head ... on a stick.'

The next day McCann, Clayton and Ilam stepped out of the airlock onto Kurgudwardum 57. The trio sneaked onto the main boulevard, in an alley way they lay in wait for Anu and his men to pass by on their daily rounds.

Sure enough the crime lord sauntered from business to business examining merchants' accounts, collecting his due.

As Anu and three Blue Necks passed by McCann and his comrades stepped out. A voice echoed down the boulevard, 'That's Duncan McCann!'

Anu spun around, the Crime lord watched on as two men and one woman dressed in strange black and white long coats with odd round hats slowly formed a line.

Anu was taken aback by McCann's blasé attitude. This stranger from another galaxy had no fear of the great Anu. The crime lord expected him to remain cowering in his space ship, forcing a Blue Neck boarding action, instead he'd come for the mighty Anu.

Citizens watched Discovery's courageous crew form their battle line, Anu's men spread out to match their foe.

'Three of you and four of us,' noted Anu with a slimy grin.

'I didn't know you could count that far.'

Anu laughed, 'That's funny now you give me the Tlillan and we all go home. I even let your ship leave in one piece.'

Ilam held tightly onto her rifle, 'The Tzitzimeh are here.'

'I've got a better deal,' he looked at the nervous Blue Necks, 'I only want Anu. You boys can walk away.'

Anu laughed again, 'You a funny man, you know that?'

'Hilarious.'

'In the Skin Territory we say "Man with death wish, meet the Great Maker smiling" I think maybe you know this?'

McCann narrowed his eyes, 'There's a similar saying where I come from.'

'What do you say?'

'Shit happens!' McCann had given the word to draw and all three comrades aimed their firearms.

McCann drew on Anu.

Clayton on the Blue Neck to Anu's left.

Ilam employed her mental sharpness detecting which of her two targets would draw first. She levelled her ion powered plasma weapon firing a massive discharge which streaked along the boulevard.

The Blue Neck had only just got his hands upon his pistol grips when a blast projected him down the boulevard to shouts and screams of merchants.

The Tlillan lady pushed and pulled on the lever clearing the plasma chamber then aiming for his nervous compadre, she pulled her trigger blowing the man's pistol arm clean from its shoulder. Fiery plasma scorched his limb clean off preventing any bleeding nevertheless he dropped to his knees, passing out from shock.

Clayton was fast but so was his pistolero, they traded tungsten until one was hit. The Blue Neck dropped to the floor still firing both guns. Members of the crowd were hit, one citizen dropping flat on his face ... stone cold dead. Several bullets ricocheted off walls Clayton took a bullet before falling onto his back.

McCann drew his pistol on Anu, employing a growing Tlillan ability he could detect when and at what speed the crime lord would draw. He always had the upper hand.

As Anu aimed McCann had already fired; hot flashes of charged gas leapt from his weapon. Tungsten cracked the atmosphere with a mighty sonic boom and ploughed into the crime lord's chest, one after another.

Demeter's mighty ploughshare ripped into the field of Anu's torso cutting deep gullies, sowing seeds of destruction. She presided over today's events as a farmer would observe the cycle of life, the old churned aside making way for rebirth.

Anu staggered backwards attempting to raise his pistols but Demeter did not smile in his favour that day. The master of Kurgudwardum 57 dropped backwards landing belly up ... panting as would a tired dog.

The Commodore examined a stain of blood on Clayton's jacket fortunately it was a shoulder wound. The round had passed straight through hitting no vital organs or blood veins.

'Can you get up?'

Clayton got to his feet, 'Yeh but I can't fire a gun. You'll have to go on without me.'

McCann stepped ominously towards Anu ... gasping for air as furiously as he bled.

The crime lord noticed one of his pistols laying on the floor to his right. He stretched, despite the pain, taking a hold of the grip. Anu lifted it whilst turning to his left, his intention to shoot down McCann in one final effort.

As Anu turned he saw the Commodore ... standing directly above him. The Englishman stepped upon Anu's wrist kicking his pistol away. He then placed a boot squarely onto Anu's chest.

The crime lord shrieked as he spat blood, 'Fuck you McCann! Mammi will come, Mammi will avenge me,' he coughed up more blood, 'Mammi will kill all you stinking dog shits!'

'Then I'll see you in hell.'

One shot to the head finished this crime lord's reign of terror to the cheers of every merchant on the boulevard.

Ilam approached her one armed bandit groaning in pain as he regained consciousness. The Tlillan beauty pulled a pistol from her gun belt shooting him in the chest three times to great applause.

The crew of Discovery weren't the only ones sick of Anu's bully boys.

Clayton made his way to back to Med Bay One, Ilam and McCann carried on to Kurgudwardum's central control station.

The pair turned down the same passage Hebat had taken on arrival. Three Blue Necks blocked their path, for that was the maximum of who might stand shoulder to shoulder in the corridor.

'You may not pass,' spoke a moustachioed Blue Neck with dark hair.

McCann took a tubos from his jacket, removed a cigar and discarded its aluminium jacket. The cigar tube hit the ground echoing along the passageway, cutting through intense silence.

He slipped his pistol out to light the cigar and nervous Blue Necks drew their guns. Ilam as usual was first off sending a pair of pistoleros to Hades, two bursts of plasma spattered steaming innards in all directions.

McCann put 5 shots into a moustachioed Blue Necks' chest killing him in an instant.

The Englishman drew on his cigar as his pulse pistol's rails toasted its foot.

Once the Habanos produced rich creamy smoke he reloaded before returning his pistol to its holster, 'Did you know that 100% of non-smokers die?' the Englishman pointed his cigar at three dead Blue Necks.

Ilam pouted her lips before stepping over her victims.

Eventually they reached Kurgudwardum 57's control office. No further opposition remained now that news of Anu's demise had reached everyone on the station.

Mesan was in panic mode, Hebat prepared to leave for her ship … until the outlaws stepped inside.

Mesan made for the closest exit until McCann pulled his pistol, 'Get any closer to that door and I'll turn your head into a canoe, boy.'

Mesan stopped in his tracks raising his hands, 'I have no weapon.'

'Just move back and stand over there.'

The large office had many workstations attached to a central table at about hip height. Mesan and Hebat stood opposite to Ilam and McCann.

The Telal said nothing.

Ilam spoke, pointing at the creature, 'Duncan, destroy this evil.'

The small shrivelled being stepped out from behind the table, 'Evil? You hunt us as animals.'

'You ARE animals, foul wretched animals.'

Hebat fixed her eyes upon McCann, 'I sense your doubt, ignorant of the truth.'

'Duncan, destroy it now!'

As the Telal moved forward McCann raised his pistol, 'Come any closer and I'll turn you into a Swiss cheese.'

'He wants to hear the truth,' Hebat smiled displaying teeth of the hydra, 'Xch'uup persecuted us, hunted us, she attempted to exterminate us because we would not pray to her.'

Ilam bellowed in her deep Tlillan voice, 'LIAR!'

Hebat smiled, 'He believes me he can sense my honesty. Can you no longer control your males?'

The Valkyries eyes began to fire as coals in the night, 'The Tzitzimeh preyed upon us for centuries using us as no more than cattle. These wretched beasts slaughtered us.'

Hebat shook her head slowly, 'We only took what we needed the slaughter began when Xch'uup declared religious genocide. We worshipped Mammi, they worshipped Xch'uup … there could only be one true mother on Otoch.'

Ilam brandished that cold Tlillan sneer, 'And it was decided at Tamoanchan.'

'Then why come here? Why must you persecute us further? Do we not have the right to breathe? The right to eat? To dance? To laugh? To love?'

'There are no rights, only privileges.'

McCann felt pity, from what he could tell it was the same old story of Xch'uup victimising heretics. These creatures had fled to Andromeda and now Xch'uup would follow them, 500,000 years later to complete her ancestors' religious edict.

Hebat sensed the Englishman's compassion, as he lowered his firearm in pity she struck. The small wrinkled creature's mouth expanded to three times its original size. Rows of razor sharp teeth surged forwards in an attempt to bite his face clean off.

The Commodore was terrified yet being a hardened warrior he fired. Tungsten wooshed with a sonic boom and gush of plasma, five rounds thudded into the beasts' chest yet the Tzitzimeh continued McCann's cigar fell from his mouth as he fired continuously. Shot after shot hit the creature of Tlillan nightmare yet it continued, tungsten only slowing its pace a little with each hit. Hebat had taken 12 rounds some to the chest and a few to the head yet she advanced shrieking in a terrible voice, enough to root any man to the floor in panic.

Her claws exposed she was within one foot of McCann about to dine on his face before a single shot from Ilam tore her chest open. Its body collapsed onto McCann's boots … he let out a massive sigh of relief.

The red headed Tlillan stared her husband down with fiery eyes, 'YOU IDIOT!'

McCann took a deep inhale steadying himself; he'd be in cryo-freeze right now if not for her.

The Englishman slipped his smoking pistol back into its holster and peered at his wife, she felt his emotion. The tall Amazon's eyes cooled down. McCann had been an idiot trusting someone other than her.

Ilam spoke to her husband, 'Step away.'

Deciding to do exactly as told he moved backwards. In doing so the Tzitzimeh raised its face from a pool of blood and lurched towards the Englishman roaring in the most horrific manner, waves of terror reverberated through him.

Ilam fired again detonating Hebat's head in a burst of plasma and splatting liquefied organic matter onto the floor and lower wall.

'Jesus Christ! What the bloody hell is that thing?'

Ilam looked down her nose at the new age art experiment adorning the control room floor. The Amazon spat on its corpse, 'That is evil and it took you in like a damned fool!'

Mesan crept towards the doorway again and McCann pulled his smoking pistol. The ponytailed weasel stopped in his tracks and smiled, 'I was just going to check on the power core.'

Ilam's eyes pierced her husband, 'You believed its lies, didn't you?'

'I sensed she was being honest.'

'The Tzitzimeh have powers of ESP, it was manipulating you. When your defences were lowered the beast attacked. You would have been killed if I were not here.'

McCann nodded as he examined its gored remains, 'I understand.'

The Englishman moved his attention from the Tzitzimeh to Mesan. Approaching the frightened man he noticing a badge hanging from the ponytailed freaks' shirt pocket, 'What's that?'

'My authority?'

'Authority to what?'

'Authority to broker contracts and enforce them.'

'You mean the law maker and enforcer on this station?'

'I suppose so.'

McCann took Mesan's badge and the leather wallet it resided in. Slipping the wallet over his shirt pocket he declared, 'Now I'm the law in this shit hole, understood?'

Mesan nodded silently.

McCann pulled a control collar from his leg pocket and placed it around Mesan's neck.

'What's this?' asked the ex-controller of Kurgudwardum 57 as the collar automatically tightened around his throat.

McCann put his pistol away and pulled back his left sleeve to reveal his wrist tablet, 'This is in constant communication with your collar. If you misbehave or so much as look at someone in the wrong way I press a button and that thing will tighten so quickly it'll snap that scrawny neck of yours.'

Mesan ran his fingers over the flexible yet deadly black carbon collar.

'Don't try and take it off, you don't want to disappoint my wife.'

Mesan looked up at Ilam's sneering face, 'You killed Hebat. You killed a Telal.'

'I did,' replied the Amazon.

'When Mammi learns of this ...'

'By the time Mammi comes here we'll be gone.'

'Or ready for her,' interjected McCann.

'What do you mean?' snapped Ilam.

'These stations, a lot of them have Graviton beams, right?'

'Yes.'

He turned to Mesan, 'I figure Mammi hasn't rode on in here because if she did her fleet would get torn a new arsehole, am I right?'

Mesan nodded, 'Something like that.'

'So I figure once the Blue Necks are brought to heel we can have a comfortable foothold in Andromeda … safe from Mammi.'

Mesan shook his head, 'You don't understand. Mammi controls the Tamoanchan territory.'

'So?'

'It is the most prosperous territory in the galaxy, everyone here has contracts with Mammi they cannot afford to lose them. Mammi buys their guns, slaves and lotus.'

'Lotus?'

'Yes the lotus flower, it brings pleasure to the mind though many fall under its spell becoming lost souls. She uses it to control her allies.'

Ilam cut in, 'Inanna spoke of the Kishar.'

'Yes?'

'Who are they?'

'Millennia ago it is said they controlled the Tamoanchan territory until the Telal arrived. The Kishar are fearless warriors but Mammi was too savage even for them. They were pushed out, settling here after many millennia. The Kishar are Chiefs of the Skin Territory all station controllers pay them tribute even Anu paid Rabum Agu. Refuse and his warriors will descend upon this station pillaging it for everything, killing men, women and children. I have witnessed this in past times.'

'Couldn't you just use the graviton beam?'

'One beam against a hundred boarding vessels? Perhaps you pick off ten but it would make no difference. Only anger Rabum further.'

'Would other stations not help you?'

'No, all fear the Kishar. They will come here to settle a price.'

'A price?'

'Tribute you are to pay or suffer the consequences.'

Chapter 8

Back on Discovery Ilam argued with her husband, 'Why do you desire this?'

'You saw what it was like in there.'

'This is not your concern Commodore.'

McCann loaded small tungsten rounds into his pistol magazine whilst his wife paced the cabin.

'Are you listening to me?'

'I can hear you Ilam.'

'You almost died by one Tzitzimeh, more shall arrive and attempt the same.'

McCann deposited one magazine upon his bed.

'Mountbatten is in cryo-freeze ... I do not wish to see you accompany him.'

After checking the battery he slapped its magazine in, certifying his weapon for charge and ammunition, all readouts displayed full.

Ilam was at her wits end, 'What of the Kishar? When Rabum comes for his tribute what then? Will you declare war on the entire Skin Territory? Duncan, you are only one man!'

McCann glanced at his wife, 'I'll take those odds.'

'Lay hold of your brain! There is suffering across both our galaxy and this one. You are not an intergalactic Christ!'

The Englishman secured his belt and thigh holster.

'This fantasy has gone too far, you must stop it, Duncan ... Duncan?'

He ignored Ilam's attempt at provocation.

'I will communicate with Otoch, when Xch'uup discovers your disregard for her instruction ...'

'Xch'uup be damned!'

Ilam fell silent.

'Those people are trading in kidnapped children, selling sex slaves to every scumbag with enough money. It stops today, on this station at least.'

The beautiful Valkyrie shook her head, 'Why are you doing this?'

'Because it's right.'

'Right? There is no right or wrong.'

McCann slipped into his coat, putting on his hat on the Commodore replied, 'Suit yourself Ilam.'

McCann strolled down Kurgudwardum 57's main boulevard taking in nervous expressions from its citizens. The Commodore and his wife met with the station controller, Mesan knew this place like the back of his hand. Ilam held her Tlillan rifle with both hands, ready to fire at the first sense of trouble.

'We go Puyin first, his establishment most prosperous of Kurgudwardum. You control him, others fall into service.'

'Lead the way,' the Englishman gestured forwards and Mesan walked down a large avenue circling the titanic den of wickedness.

As they approach music blasted out from a neon doorway, a woman's voice singing the joys of abuse to an electronic backbeat blared onto the boulevard.

The trio stepped inside, music stopped immediately, Blue Necks sat at a large table, shifted their attention to Puyin's newest patrons.

Catwalks ran up and down the establishment as young girls of all species strutted them 24 hours a day, numbers attached to their waists. A few gambling tables were dotted around the floor playing something similar to roulette. Instead of a spinning wheel a small ball dropped onto a piece of circular clear plastic. From what McCann gathered people laid down wagers on which hole the ball would fall into. Higher odds being on those further from a tube the ball dropped from into a circular dome of flashing light. The amusement ceased at the betting tables and all eyes honed in on McCann; the girls stopped what they were doing.

Mesan strolled nervously to the bar but before he might speak a barman inquired, 'What you drink Mesan?'

McCann stepped up to the bar and in a gritty tone replied, 'I'd like to speak with the owner of this shit hole.'

The barman pulled a weak smile, 'I'm afraid Lek is not available.'

McCann swung back his coat, pulling out a pulse pistol he levelled it on one of Puyin's male patrons and shot him in the back. The patron's body went limp, slumping out of his seat and onto the floor. His pals jumped to their feet spilling drinks and knocking down chairs, hands hovering over pistols, 'You dirty BASTARD!'

The Englishman pushed up his bowler hat, 'I wouldn't make a habit of calling me names.'

'You just shot and innocent man ... in the back!'

'My mistake ... I thought all you perverts took it from behind.'

His furious compadres traded glances across the bar, one made a quick snatch for his weapon. Ilam blasted a section of his ribcage onto a screaming young lady occupying a nearby catwalk.

The fellow crumpled to the floor sporting a gaping hole through his torso. Observing his pal's carcass the remaining patron decided that it wasn't a case of third time lucky. With raised hands he shuffled towards the exit.

McCann scanned Puyin bar quickly before holstering his pistol, 'Is Lek available now?'

A voice boomed from behind the bar, 'What the hell is happening! Why has the music stopped?'

A fat bearded man stepped out tying a silk nightgown around his waist, 'What is ...' he stared at two dead bodies and a quivering girl coated in steaming gore, 'who did this?'

The barman gestured in McCann's direction.

'Who are you?' shouted Lek.

'My name is unimportant. All you need to know is that I'm your boss now.'

Lek laughed in his booming voice, 'Hey Mesan this is joke? I pay Anu on time, guskin ready and waiting.'

Mesan replied in a shy tone, 'Anu is dead.'

Lek laughed again, 'Fine so who running Blue Necks?'

Mesan shook his head, 'Blue Necks don't run Kurgudwardum 57 anymore.'

The portly owner of Puyin pointed at six Blue Necks, 'What I pay them for, if not protection?'

McCann eyed Lek's party of Blue Necks at the other end of the establishment, 'What you pay them for or how much is none of my business. All you need to know is that I'm the law on this toilet and I'm here to clean it up.'

Lek lost his jolly demeanour as his paid thugs rose from their seats. Every girl in the bar ran down her catwalk and out of the firing line.

'Why don't you leave, I forget this little problem ... yes?'

McCann had one eye on Lek and another on his thugs, 'I don't think so.'

The Blue Necks spread out, as they did Ilam communicated mentally to her husband. The pair dived behind a catwalk using it as cover Mesan rolled over the bar cowering at Lek's feet.

As the first shots peeled off Lek's girls screamed in terror. Blue Necks pushed over tables. McCann sat propped up against the side of a walkway holding his pistol, 'Great, now what?'

'Calm your brain Duncan!'

The Amazon waited, using Tlillan ESP she timed her action, just as one of the pistoleros popped his head over a table she fired blowing the top of his skull clean off with a burst of supercharged plasma.

'That's five,' stated the Tlillan beauty with a smirk.

Using his poorly developed Tlillan abilities to their fullest McCann sensed a Blue Neck about to make a dash in a flanking manoeuver.

The pistolero got to his feet charging towards the bar in a bid to jump over it, the Englishman popped up and fired bringing him down with the fourth shot.

Ilam pulled her husband back before he had time to finish the Blue Neck. She sensed his comrades about to return fire.

'That's four and a half,' noted McCann.

The Blue Neck began to bleed out on the floor of Puyin bar, 'Help me Atrat, help me!'

His friend scanned the room apprehensively. Nevertheless he decided to crawl through a mess of chairs and tables; using them as cover, to rescue his comrade.

Ilam took to her feet again, firing upon Atrat as he weaved in and out of fallen furniture. McCann rose at the same time laying down covering fire while Ilam shot into the jungle of table tops and chair legs, her second shot hit something. The Tlillan sensed his soul clinging to its mortal coil … minus a leg.

McCann pulled his wife back behind the catwalk as Atrat's screams joined the symphony of desperate misery.

Bullets ricocheted whilst patrons charged for the exit tumbling over one another to get clear. Several of Lek's customers surcame to stray bullets as the bar owner watched on in horror. Lek cared not for sentient life he bemoaned the loss of profit and what might happen to his reputation as a respectable merchant of young girls.

Suddenly there was a break in firing. Ilam put a hand upon her husband's shoulder as three Blue Necks stood with arms raised.

'Duncan McCann, are you listening?' shouted a greasy man with a large black moustache.

'Yeh, I hear you,' replied the Englishman.

'We want to stop, let us take our friends. We stop shooting, yes?'

The bar went silent as McCann holstered his pistol, 'Fine.'

Every girl working Puyin bar rubber necked from behind the stage area.

As the Englishman's hand left his pistol grip he sensed deception. Before he might pull they were already drawing on him, 3 versus one, he was a dead man for sure.

Bam, bam, bam three shots went out, each blast hitting its mark as lightning bolts from Olympus, Zeus the mighty cloud gatherer did dispense justice casting shimmering bolts of plasma into bodies of mortal men, a gift from the Cyclopes. In McCann's eyes his wife personified Zeus' power and Metis' quickness of mind. The ivory skinned beauty gutted all three pistoleros adorning a rear wall with several feet of distended intestine.

'Only two halves left,' noted the cold Tlillan.

McCann strolled towards Lek's remaining security.

The Blue Neck he'd shot held onto his leg wound in an attempt to reduce bleeding. The pistolero looked up as the Englishman removed a Havana from its tubos, bit off the cap and used his pistol to toast the foot.

Puffing on a Ramon Allones the Commodore looked down, 'Seems you boys have gotten yourselves between a rock and a hard place.'

'Let me go Duncan McCann,' pled a desperate man.

The girls working Puyin bar trotted out onto the stage captivated by unfolding events. McCann drew on a freshly lit cigar before locking the young man in a steely gaze, 'Why would I show you any more mercy than you did them?' he pointed to the merchandise of Puyin bar.

'I don't understand. They are just females.'

McCann pulled his pistol, 'And I'm just takin' care of business,' firing a tungsten round into his forehead. Aiming again McCann repeated his action with the second Blue Neck.

'Mesan, you can get up. It's all over.'

Mesan slithered out from under his rock to join McCann on the other side of the bar, the former controller was still shaking.

McCann fixed his eyes upon the barman, 'Get me whisky and the good stuff not the donkey piss you serve them,' pointing toward six Blue Neck corpses.

Lek nodded and a bottle of prime sikaru was brought out.

'What if it's poisoned?' inquired Mesan.

'My wife doesn't drink,' he knocked back the brown liquid in one go, 'another.'

'I don't understand.'

'If I poison him she will kill us all,' replied a sullen Lek.

McCann took another shot of whisky. It was no Scotch and certainly paled in comparison to his usual dram, yet it sufficed. He'd nearly died today and a shot of something to calm his system was welcome.

'Drinking and smoking at a time such as this?' bellowed Ilam.

'Another.'

The barman poured a third shot.

'Make it the last. I cannot abide that stinking drink!'

Lek grimaced at the towering Amazon, 'She has a hot tongue.'

McCann sipped his liquor, 'Wait until you meet her mother.'

'What do you want Duncan McCann? Guskin?' inquired a miserable Lek as he surveyed steaming guts slide down the wall of his enterprise.

'I want to clean this place up.'

'You can start by getting those dead men out of here. Their stomach contents are staining my brand new furniture!'

'No, the girls.'

'You want one? Pick whichever pleases you.'

'I want them out of here.'

'To where?'

'You'll turn them over to Gianna, at Dock 17.'

'You're gonna space my merchandise?'

'No, they'll be handed over to this stations new authority at Dock 17. Genetic fingerprints taken and families notified.'

Lek made a weak laugh, 'You are joking, yes?'

McCann peered at the slaver with cold eyes, 'You see me laughing?'

'You will compensate me?'

The Englishman took a draw on his Habanos, 'You get to live another day.'

Lek made another nervous chuckle whilst his girls chattered to one another.

'And if you refuse, I put a hole in your head and take those girls to Dock 17 myself. Either way those slaves are going to Dock 17 to be processed.'

'What happens when Anu ...'

'I shot him dead yesterday, didn't you hear?'

'I was busy with ... merchandise.'

McCann downed the last shot of whisky, 'You let every other bar owner and slaver on this station understand, they've 24 hours to hand over their slaves. Anyone trying to leave Kurgudwardum 57 gets a graviton beam in the rear, is that understood?'

'I understand Duncan McCann but what of my business?'

'I'm sure you can find women who'll take a wage to work this shit hole.'

Lek was left speechless. McCann finished his drink before exiting onto the boulevard.

As word spread quickly Blue Necks began to disband. Their leader dead and no hope of stemming the tide, members of the gang were not prepared to die. Pushing around merchants was easy work but when this alien turned up, killed Anu, Hebat and every single Blue Neck sent to stop him many decided to retire their scarfs. There were plenty of places in the Skin Territory prepared to pay for hired guns and the chances of collecting a paycheque at the end of the month far exceeded that of Kurgudwardum 57

As the Commodore strolled the main boulevard to odd looks he noticed what seemed to be a band of warriors straight ahead. The Englishman murmured to his wife, 'More trouble?'

Mesan cut in, 'They are Kishar, word spreads quickly in the Skin Territory.'

'What do they want?' inquired Ilam.

'To speak, you will not require weapons. If they wished violence we would be dead already.'

Ilam raised a brow at her husband.

McCann's coat shrouded his pistol whilst approaching a delegation of shirtless men dressed in brown bovine hide pants. These warriors adorned themselves in tattoos covering their faces, chests and arms. Intricate swirling patterns meshed to project a fearsome persona. As the Englishman closed in he noticed each man had a rifle slung across his back.

The central figure strode out to meet McCann halfway, 'You are the one named Duncan McCann?'

'I am, and you?'

'I am Rakbu of the Kishar.'

'So I've heard. What is it you want on my station?'

The tall man with long dark hair didn't react to McCann's statement in the way presumed, 'Your Chief who is he?'

'My chief? I don't understand.'

'Who do you report to? Who builds your ships? Who takes your tribute? What is his name?'

Before McCann could reply Ilam spoke, 'Xch'uup, she is our Chief.'

Rakbu peered into Ilam's eyes, 'You are Nabu?'

'I am.'

'Describe Xch'uup when she holds council.'

Ilam sensed great curiosity from Rakbu, money was certainly the last thing on his mind, 'Xch'uup wears a crown of feathers ...'

'Describe them,' snapped Rakbu.

'They are long and white.'

'White as your skin is white?'

'Yes.'

Rakbu pushed on with his interrogation, 'Xch'uup has a space ship?'

'Of course.'

'Describe it.'

'Her vessel has a long body with four weapon masts at the rear jutting out at 90 degree angles ...'

'Its colour, what is its colour?'

'White.'

'As her feathers?'

'Yes.'

Again Ilam sensed great discomfort from Rakbu. The messenger glanced at McCann, 'Xch'uup, she has sisters?'

'Well apart from the Mictlantecuhtli girls, no.'

Rakbu froze for a moment, upon regaining his senses he snapped, 'How many sisters?'

'Three.'

'Within forty Kins Mammi shall arrive, Rabum Agu will speak with your Chief before then.'

After finishing his sentence he turned back towards his compatriots, they questioned him furiously in an unintelligible language yet he refused to answer. The Kishar entered their docking arm and casted off.

McCann turned to Mesan, 'How come the graviton beam didn't just vaporise them?'

'They are Kishar. If you wish to live you will not fire on them.'

McCann spoke to Ilam in a hushed tone, 'Communicate with Otoch get Malikah here now.'

'For what purpose?'

The Englishman blew smoke out of his nose, 'Your Tzitzimeh will be arriving soon. We'll need this Rabum and the entire Skin Territory to repel them.'

Ilam waved her hand in an attempt to scatter the smoke, 'We should depart. Discovery has gathered all information required on Andromeda for now.'

'I'll leave that decision to Malikah. If she recalls us then Discovery is ready to cast off. However, if she's prepared to come here and consolidate with the Kishar she has a foothold in Andromeda.'

McCann arose, having steered clear of the bottle last night, to several messages. Gianna had begun processing underage girls relinquished by Kurgudwardum 57's merchants. Mesan had been sending updates on Blue Neck requests to leave, after searching their craft those found clean were sent on their way. Finally there was a message concerning the arrival of Xch'uup's flagship. Malikah would soon be present, the Grand Matriarch was eager to meet the Skin Territory's Chief.

McCann made his way to the Mess, taking a tray and selecting a light breakfast he sat with Vezzali and Clayton, 'How's that shoulder, Clayton?'

Discovery's newly anointed security chief replied with a smile, 'I'm doing fine, sir.'

His gift of the Ixchel, earnt during a long campaign on Bandayuuk, along with a combination of nanite injections on Discovery had repaired any damage.

'Good to hear, we're going to be meeting a local warlord today. I'd like to have you with us.'

Clayton put down his knife and fork then wiped his lips with a napkin, 'I'm on it, sir.'

The old soldier got up and exited the Mess.

Vezzali smiled, 'Where did you find him?'

The Commodore cut up his scrambled eggs on toast, 'He's a friend of Jenkins.'

'Friend?'

'Yes well a fortunate acquaintance then?'

Vezzali grinned before taking a drink of juice, 'I see you're perky this morning, no whisky last night?'

McCann gave his science officer a grim stare, 'I thought I'd give it a rest for a while.'

Vezzali sniggered placing a hand over her mouth in an attempt to keep it quiet.

McCann stopped eating, scanned the Mess then locked eyes with the Italian, 'Who else knows?'

Vezzali's cheeks began to blush and her snigger became a laugh.

'For God's sake woman, keep it down will you?' pled the Englishman in a hushed tone.

He then noticed other members of the crew pulling odd looks and turning away in a vain attempt to conceal their knowledge.

McCann put his knife and fork down, 'Everyone knows don't they?'

Vezzali nodded her red face at the ship's commander.

'Fuck my life!'

The Italian chuckled, 'Look on the bright side, Commodore.'

'What's that exactly?'

'Well isn't it every male's fantasy to have two women in the same bed?'

McCann gave his science officer a serious stare, 'Perhaps next time her grandmother will decide to join in?'

Vezzali burst out in fits of laughter as crew members shied from their commander's gaze.

That day the Chutli folded space announcing the presence of Xch'uup with a burst of white light. Malikah's vessel ejected into normal space as every soul in the Skin Territory watched on in anticipation.

On the bridge of Discovery Vezzali transmitted co-ordinates of the Kishar station they were to address Rabum Agu.

'Incoming transmission from the Chutli,' called Vezzali.

His daughter's image appeared upon the ship's view screen, 'Father, I'm leaving for Docking Arm 3 of Asrukishar now. Meet me there with as few of your staff as possible.'

Before he could respond her image disappeared.

'Communication ended, sir.'

McCann walked towards the exit, 'Have Clayton meet me in the shuttle bay.'

Ilam was about to join her husband, on noting he'd not requested her presence she inquired, 'Duncan?'

'I want you to remain here, if it all goes tits up I'll need someone capable on Discovery.'

Ilam nodded her brow reluctantly taking the Captain's chair.

Discovery had a decidedly Spartan shuttle bay compared to that of Athena. A shuttle inside a tube to be ejected into space once its catronium doors opened. There was no big docking area where mechanics and droids could run about carrying out duties. This was a totally functional design. If the shuttle incurred damage it'd take far more time to get it repaired; that's assuming it could be repaired under such constraints.

After many years serving on the Ares Chief Engineer Ilyushin was expected to be a miracle worker aboard Discovery. Having received several honours during the battle of Bandayuuk he decided it was time to move on. When an opening appeared for a Chief Engineer on Discovery Ilyushin applied.

Discovery was a small vessel in size but her power core and wormhole generator were titanic. From the outside an unassuming scout ship, two globes attached to one another via a thin central column, a barbell in space. However hidden in that sphere was a fusion core large enough to power a wormhole generator capable of taking them to Andromeda in 5 leaps. Chief Engineer Anton Ilyushin was responsible for Discovery and her maintenance. Few people in the I.S.A could be considered in the same league when it came to engineering and nanites.

Clayton and McCann were both dressed up in their bowler hats, armed with pistols and Tlillan tunnel sweepers. The pair boarded their shuttle its door closing behind them. With room for only four people and a little cargo it was very cramped. They eased into their seats as Discovery uploaded a flight plan before opening the docking bay doors.

The Englishmen were fired out of the docked Discovery by a magnetic catapult. Their minimal shuttle ploughed across a system filled with old space stations, the largest bearing at least one graviton weapon. This was the centre of a galactic neutronium rush the remnants of which served as a hub of nefarious activity.

There was no view screen inside the shuttle, a wire frame readout informed them docking was soon to commence. A Tlillan shuttle had already slotted itself into one of the small ports upon a large docking arm.

Asrukishar was a titan, only Kurgudwardum 57 rivalled this intimidating octagon.

Captured by a magnetic field, Discovery's shuttle was slotted into a tube and bequeathed an oxygen environment. Her door opened to reveal a passage onto the Kishar station.

McCann led his security officer out, as he closed in on the portal leading to Docking Arm 3 a Tlillan party waited to greet him. Upon closer inspection McCann noted a familiar expression plastering his daughter's face. He was certain she supressed a tirade. Somehow she'd learnt of his escapades concerning Anu and the Blue Necks. The Englishman didn't know why but Malikah treated him as a child and she the parent. He found it most aggravating at times.

The airlock opened, McCann then Clayton stepped out resembling a Marshal and his Deputy from the old west.

Amitra looked the pair up and down with a wide grin.

Malikah maintained a stone cold stare on the compadres, 'I find nothing amusing.'

The tall Amazon with long dark hair and milk chocolate skin began to chuckle Sandra and Kaeo were confused, neither of them recognising the attire.

Arthur stepped forward with his hand out, 'Hello Mr McCann.'

Malikah gave the boy a piercing look. It was a break in protocol to greet even your own mother before Xch'uup. McCann nodded his brow and the boy shrunk back behind his Grand Matriarch.

All was silent for a few moments until Lian appeared from the Tlillan docking bay. Upon viewing McCann and Clayton she shrieked in delight, 'Oooh are we having fancy dress?'

Of course she was joking, Amitra laughed, though fellow Tlillans remained baffled by a seemingly bizarre dress code.

'Enough, we shall discuss it later. I must speak with this Rabum Agu. Father you are familiar with this place, lead on.'

McCann tipped his hat, 'Certainly ma'am,' as he walked towards the end of the docking arm, upon the main boulevard of Asrukishar, Rakbu awaited.

Asrukishar was similar in construction to Kurgudwardum 57 yet inside it felt chaotic. An ordered structure of business did not exist, people walked to and fro with no sense of organisation present.

Rakbu noted Malikah dressed in a black ribbed suit with white jacket and feathered crown. For some reason the herald was greatly disturbed upon viewing her.

'This is Xch'uup?' inquired Rakbu pointing directly at Malikah.

Malikah stepped forward, 'I am.'

Rakbu examined the rest of Malikah's party, 'You have four sisters?'

'I do.'

Rakbu pointed in McCann's face, 'You told me there were only three, you are a liar!'

The Englishman took great affront to such an accusation. He swung the barrel of his rifle into Rakbu's face. As he did every Kishar on the boulevard produced a weapon. Rifles along with pistols pointed in their delegation's direction.

Malikah lowered her father's weapon, pushing its barrel aside, 'Forgive my father he is old and often forgets his place.'

Rakbu nodded his head, 'I understand, follow me Xch'uup.'

Rakbu strolled out onto a boulevard of citizens returning to their previous activity. All examined Malikah as she moved with long regal strides.

'Tell me about this station,' requested Malikah.

'I am Rakbu, second honoured in Kishar. This is home of Kishar tribe Rabum Agu is most honoured Chief of Kishar.'

'I see. What do the Kishar do to maintain the tribe?'

Rakbu pointed to tribe, 'Kishar are warriors, when Kishar are hungry we take food. We need guns we take them, whatever Kishar need we take. Kishar have iron hearts not weak.'

'Do you take from the Telal or do they take from you?'

Rakbu led them into the station and its central compartments, 'Mammi have iron heart.'

'Stronger than Rabum?'

Rakbu turned to face Malikah, 'Hold your tongue, if you speak this you will be punished.'

'Is that a fact?'

'It is,' stated the herald before leading their party through a doorway and into Rabum's hall.

Inside a long table ran through the middle about 6 inches off the floor. Many men sat around it resting upon cushions and animal skins, roast meats served upon gold plates. Red wine poured by women, some slaves others women of the tribe attired in a long one piece dress made from the same hide their men wore.

At the end of the table sat Rabum, long black hair draped down his back, swirling tattoos adorned the body of an old warrior. All in the Skin Territory feared this man and with good reason. The Kishar had taken control of this system after centuries of war, domination being the only method of existence they understood.

Malikah noted Rabum was the only person at the table without gold cutlery, his plate and goblet were fashioned of wood and he served himself. The rest ate as kings picking great chunks of meat with their hands, consuming wine as water; whilst Rabum seemed to be comparatively austere.

Rakbu announced Malikah and her cohorts in a language as yet unknown to the universal translator or Tlillans. Later they'd discover only Kishar were permitted to speak this language. Anyone outside the tribe who learnt it was killed.

The room became silent, 'You are Xch'uup?' inquired Rabum as he fixed his gaze upon the Tlillan Queen.

'I am.'

Rabum chatted with a Kishar beside the throne. After a few words were exchanged Rabum spoke again, 'You have a war cruiser, the white one which appeared today?'

'Yes.'

Rabum shouted something in Kishar. All fell quiet in the poorly lit hall as an old man was led inside by a young boy. At the sight of this old man Rakbu became nervous he spoke in an unintelligible tongue, at least to Malikah. His eyes moved in an uncoordinated fashion it was obvious this man was blind. A guide led him to Rabum's side.

When the blind man finished talking Rakbu shouted across the hall, 'He is a crazy old man!'

Rabum looked calmly at Rakbu 'I say he is Nabu, do you challenge my word?'

Rakbu withdrew; the thought of challenging his Chief dwelled far from the herald's mind.

'What did he say?' inquired Malikah.

The Chief took a deep breath, 'He says a great warrior shall come. He says this warrior has the head of a condor and travels upon an iron horse, white as a star stripped of neutronium.'

'He thinks that is me?'

'When Duncan McCann entered this system Sada had visions, some say he is Nabu.'

'What else did he see?'

'Four sisters, Sada believes one shall cure his blindness.'

Malikah examined the old seer from a distance, 'Why have you not repaired his eyesight yourself?'

Rabum shook his head, 'His eyes work, his brain does not. Sada was once a powerful warrior, we fought together, he took a blow destined for me. His brain damaged; Now Sada has visions ... visions of the future.'

'It is beyond your science to restore his vision?'

'It is.'

Malikah nodded to Sandra with a smile.

Sandra approached the throne of Rabum, 'May I be permitted to restore Sada's sight?'

'It is not possible, yet you may try.'

Sandra placed a hand on the crown of Sada's head, her eyes changed pigment to that of space. The old seer's eyelids closed slowly and on opening them he peered upwards and spoke in his tribal language … something Sandra had just learnt after dipping into his consciousness. The entire hall was aghast as Sada peered back at them squinting with the first light his brain had detected in decades.

Sandra returned to her Xch'uup, forwarding information taken covertly from the Kishar shaman.

Sada's eyes now under his full controlled scanned the room, 'Nuu puetsuku, nuu puet paraiboo huutsuu!'

McCann had no understanding of this unique language. His daughter however was beginning to grasp its fundamentals. From what Malikah had learnt the old seer had said, 'I see you, I see the Chief bird.'

Rakbu shook his head, 'Isu posa! Huutsuu nami behka Rabum!'

Malikah eves dropped intently on the argument unfolding, 'This one is crazy! Bird woman cheat Rabum!'

The Kishar Chief watched the old man, squinting as his eyes adjusted to the hall lighting, 'Huutsuu nami … kwasinaboo sa Kasaraibo?'

Rabum asked the question, perhaps a rhetorical question, 'Bird woman … snake or angel?'

The hall fell silent as the tribe awaited Rabum's answer to his own question. Before the Kishar Chief could speak Malikah addressed him in his own language, 'Nuu kima ku ahi buni ai.'

The Tlillan Queen felt a wave of shock as all Kishar eyes turned to her. They struggled to believe what they'd heard.

'Unha numu Kishar?' inquired Rabum.

It was a dumb question, asking if she understood their language but the bombshell she'd just dropped traumatised all present.

Malikah replied in a slow clear tone so there could be no misunderstanding, 'U nakisupanaitu nu.'

'Haku suku Kishar?'

'Nuu kawi sibe Sada kit.'

Malikah explained she understood his language. Upon Rabum asking where she'd learnt it the Queen informed him she'd taken it from his shaman's mind.

The tattooed Chief accepted her explanation, 'Unha hakai nahniaka?'

'Nuu mee soo nahnia. Poot Hebat, Xch'uup iki.'

Upon asking her name the sable Queen informed him she had many names but to tell Hebat Xch'uup was here.

Upon that statement all eyes turned on Rabum. The men of his tribe were not aware the ambassador was aboard their station. Malikah however was not so impeded.

'Hebat iki?' called one of his head men.

Rabum nodded his brow in silence.

'Kono ho Telal,' demanded Malikah.

Rabum merely gave his second a look and Rakbu left.

'What the bloody hell is going on?' whispered McCann.

'The Tzitzimeh are here, I wish to speak with it, be prepared father.'

The Englishman pushed back his coat stroking the grip of his pistol. He wouldn't be lured into a false sense of pity again.

A minute later and Rakbu returned with the new 5 foot tall ambassador to the Skin Territory; The former ambassador having been splattered over the station floor on Kurgudwardum 57 by Ilam.

A wrinkled creature dressed in its tunic and tall headdress adorned by shrunken skulls stood beside the throne of Rabum.

'You are Xch'uup?' inquired Hebat in a high pitched tone.

'I am.'

The Tzitzimeh examined the women stood behind Malikah's crown of feathers. Focusing on Lian she snapped, 'Heretic,' eyes shifting from dark to light grey.

Malikah ignored her statement, 'Tell Mammi that Xch'uup has come. Tell her Xch'uup shall liberate her ancestors, those who planted the seed of our species ... those Mammi enslaved.'

All present observed with great interest. Rabum examined the pair, weighing in his mind the balance of power deciding to whom he might align.

Hebat stepped past the Kishar aristocracy to stand before Malikah.

Clayton gripped his rifle ready to rip this withered beast into pieces at the first whiff of trouble.

Hebat scrutinized Malikah closely, then her sisters, 'You are not Xch'uup,' its eyes became a light sparkling grey as the Tzitzimeh attempted to dip into Malikah's mind. The dread Queen rose to the challenge. Xch'uup's eyes transforming to burgundy red as the two battled it out mindscape against mindscape.

Hebat was powerful, more so than an average pure bred Tlillan however she was unaware of genetic developments in the Milky Way concerning the Tlillan species. The Tzitzimeh felt her opponent's mindscape as it gathered in strength, a mental dynamo. Despite her best endeavours Malikah's psychic wall was as that of the Kremlin, an unshakable citadel.

Shortly after discovering her abilities were woefully inadequate to pierce Malikah's defences an attack headed in her direction.

Malikah tested her foe, touching here and pushing there weighing this Tzitzimeh's strength. Upon deciding its reputation was far greater than its capabilities she struck; pushing into the beast's mindscape at full force. One crushing blow and Hebat let out a screech, everyone in the room jumped.

Slapping clawed hands upon her skull the wrinkled witch writhed in terrible pain; staggering backward its face contorted in agony.

Rabum jumped from his throne to stand beside a terrified Rakbu.

Malikah bellowed in a deep tone, rattling the Kishar's bones, 'You may frighten these weaklings but I am Xch'uup I have made planets burn, civilizations weep and Gods bleed!'

At that moment Lian whispered into her lover's ear, 'Memento mori.'

The dread Empress checked her tirade releasing Hebat from its mental torture. Hebat clutched her head, breathing desperately, heart pumping furiously. She wondered if the organ were attempting to escape from its cage.

'The one comes on an iron horse, pale as a mined star,' declared Sada.

Rakbu snarled at Rabum, 'Shut him up, he will kill us all!'

The old seer ignored Rakbu, 'Head of a condor, eyes of fire and heart of iron.'

Rabum watched Hebat as she recovered from touching the mindscape of a Mictlantecuhtli, 'Enough talk Sada.'

The Shaman refused to halt reciting an old Kishar vision from eons past, 'Our mother will meet iron eyes. Horse to iron, flesh to children, wings span the universe.'

The Tlillan party glanced at Lian. The Kishar men followed their eyes staring Kalayuuk up and down.

'Only in theatre will iron win ... the galaxy applaud.'

Rabum stood before his throne, his nobles followed suit, 'The Kishar will not intervene when Mammi arrives.'

Hebat snapped at the chief, 'You made an oath ... an oath to Mammi.'

'Our forefathers made an oath; Rabum has no contract with Mammi.'

The wrinkled beast hissed with bright eyes at the tattooed leader yet he stood firm.

Malikah pointed at the exit, 'Return to Tamoanchan, inform your Mammi that destiny awaits.'

Hebat snarled before storming out of the hall.

'Face of an angel yet only hell likes her temper,' cackled Sada.

Chapter 9

McCann discussed the state of affairs with William Faraday, 'I understand Duncan but it's beyond our means, we simply don't have the manpower to deal with over 300 space stations.'

McCann rubbed his eyes whilst sitting on his bed, 'I know however I spoke with Clayton and I think I have a solution.'

Faraday's 3D projection replied with a cynical tone, 'Really?'

'Clayton reckons there's a lot of Bandayuuk veterans living on the streets in London.'

'Yes, shame about that.'

'Well they could be brought in to provide security and oversee the running of ...'

Faraday leapt in, 'I couldn't possibly allow that.'

'Will you let me finish my bloody sentence man?'

'Sorry, go on.'

'As I was saying they could oversee the Skin Territory, if the I.S.A can't afford it then why not give the contract to a private company?'

Faraday didn't seem to agree with the idea, 'Why would a private company want this Skin Territory?'

'Trade, it's a hive of business and being the only link between our galaxy and Andromeda they'd make a fortune.'

'Hmmm with proper transaction tax ... nothing too obscene of course, it would increase the coffers at Geneva. I could even get that new drone project off the ground; the one Ryu pesters me over every day.'

'And Bill, there's stacks of gold and neutronium to be had.'

'What would they trade it for?'

'Lotus.'

'Lotus? You mean that bloody leaf half of them are addicted too?'

McCann nodded as he reached for a glass of water, 'You've got it.'

Faraday furrowed his brow, 'I still don't understand Duncan. Surely they grow the stuff there?'

'Most of it is grown, prepared and sold in the Skin Territory.'

'So how would we see any profits?'

'We could wipe out lotus production in one fell swoop while planting it on Earth.'

Faraday was shocked, 'Are you suggesting I turn my hand to drug dealing?'

'No, private merchants serve that function already. The I.S.A would provide transport to Andromeda for a fee, nothing more.'

'Oh, so I'm just a trafficker? Well that's alright then why didn't you just say?' replied Faraday in a sarcastic tone.

'Come on Bill you've negotiated with drug lords in the past. Moscow practically has embassies for them.'

'I'm sorry old boy but it would be a public relations disaster.'

McCann nodded his head, 'Sure ... Vezzali did say there was a projected profit of 10 tons a year.'

'Puh, 10 tons of gold is hardly worth the effort.'

'10 tons of neutronium.'

Faraday fell silent as he gathered himself, '10 tons?'

'10 tons of the most valuable substance in the universe to use however you see fit.'

After a few moments of self-contemplation the old Etonian came to a decision, 'I'll give Jenkins a call, that company he represents did a good job last time ... what's their name?'

'Total Security Solutions.'

'That's the one, I'll mention those unemployed veterans ... yes a good idea that.'

'You're welcome Bill, how long until they're here?'

'I'll have a contract drawn up today and have a chat with the Premier in Moscow, a one week deadline for deployment should be enough.'

McCann smirked, 'I'll get ready for the first arrival.'

'Now how long will it take to halt lotus production over there?'

'I'm not sure but in a month I reckon they'll need imports.'

'Do these plants need time to mature?'

'It's a genetically modified crop. No-one knows when or by whom it was created however it can be harvested within a month of planting.'

'Good, good, good, Myshkin has several treaties going with Asian drug lords. In fact if trade picks up with Andromeda and the price is high enough, it could divert most drug production there, killing two birds with one stone. How many men would we need for over 300 stations?'

'Most of these places already have infrastructure in place. We only need to replace a few guys at the top with ours.'

Faraday sat back in his chair at Geneva, 'I see and how do you propose taking over these enterprises?'

'Much the same way as I did on Kurgudwardum 57, people respect strength.'

'It sounds like an awful mess.'

McCann took a sip of chilled water from his glass, 'After Malikah deals with Mammi I believe most will fall in line without a fight. It's the Kishar who'll be difficult to convince, they control the lotus business.'

'Yes I've read about these people in your reports. This is all provided Malikah can dispatch those … what are they called … Tzitzimeh, did I say that right?'

'She believes so, apparently it's all fate my friend.'

Faraday gave a cynical snort, 'That settles it I suppose!'

'If we get in early and take a foothold on this system before the Tlillans or Makayuuk it'll be a great benefit and I'm not talking about finances here.'

The Commodore could see cogs moving inside Faraday's head as his eyes shifted around, 'Quite right, those space stations have massive potential to provide military projection. All logistics would be taken care of if conflict were to arise and at no cost.'

'Great minds think alike,' said McCann with a grin.

'You'll have to work on your sincerity before attempting to patronise me again, Commodore.'

'Sorry Bill.'

'Never mind, your assessment is most appreciated. I'll send you updates every 24 hours in standard data packets.'

'Understood Bill.'

'Talk to you later Duncan, Geneva out.'

A few weeks later and the first batch arrived. Clayton was there to greet some of the men he'd met sleeping rough on the streets of London. They filed onto Kurgudwardum 57 dressed in grey T.S.S uniforms.

Jenkins was last out making straight for McCann's familiar face, 'It's a small universe old boy!'

Shaking his hand McCann agreed, 'That it is. I suppose I'll be handing my badge onto you now?'

'I bloody well hope not, I spent enough time doing that on Bandayuuk.'

Everyone quietened down as Chanatico and her train of servants exited the docking arm.

She moved towards her husband with a face like thunder, 'So has your friend arranged our quarters or am I to rest in bunk beds for the remainder of this contract?'

Jenkins made a weak smile, 'Don't fuss dear I'm certain Duncan has your room prepared.'

The Commodore turned his back before whispering into his wrist tablet, 'Mesan? Are you there?'

The ponytailed deputy replied, 'Yes, what is your request?'

'Clear out Anu's old apartment and prepare it for two VIP guests and their servants.'

'As you wish, it'll be ready by tomorrow.'

'I need it ready now.'

'Oh, 20 minutes?'

'Thank you Mesan,' with that McCann tapped his tablet and turned back to face Chanatico, 'Your rooms are prepared.'

Chanatico let a cold sneer shoot off in McCann's direction. She refused to acknowledge her husband's face.

McCann shouted across the boulevard, 'Clayton, over here will you?'

The old soldier excused himself and trotted toward the Englishman, 'Yes Commodore?'

'I want you to escort Miss Chanatico and her people to their quarters. Mesan has dealt with the details so speak with him.'

Clayton nodded, stretching his arm out he pointed down the boulevard, 'This way Miss.'

Chanatico stomped off as Clayton did his best to keep up with her.

'What the bloody hell's wrong with her?'

'Have you ever slept on one of those Gukumatz transport vessels?' sighed Jenkins.

'What about them?'

'The damn things were built for toads man! She's nearly seven feet tall. The woman moaned and complained the whole way. I tell you Duncan I was on the verge of strangling her a few times.'

McCann chuckled, 'I'm surprised the toad transport managed the journey.'

A tired Jenkins nodded, 'Well they've been upgraded, just not to the standards of the Discovery or Chutli. Half the cargo space was taken up by fuel rods to re-ignite the reactor after each jump. Transports aren't a priority, due to expense, one of the vices when working for private employers.'

'So you boys were charged with upgrading the Gukumatz transport?'

'It's part of the contract, we've leased the Atropos. Of course the Chairman was only interested in getting us here at the lowest possible cost.'

'I see and I take it your wife wasn't overwhelmed with joy to be accompanying you?'

Jenkins rubbed the temples of his skull, 'That would be an understatement. I think she's set on making me pay for it ... in spades.'

McCann patted his friend on the back, 'Well you're here now; Ready to take up the challenge of controlling the arse end of Andromeda.'

'Wonderful,' stated Jenkins in a sarcastic tone.

Clayton jogged beside Chanatico, 'How was the journey Miss?'

The Valkyrie glared straight ahead as she marched forward, 'You don't have to call me Miss.'

'What should I call you?'

Chanatico stopped dead and barked in her former butler's face, 'Call me a fool for marrying an idiot!'

'I'm sorry Miss?'

'Oh never mind, just lead on Clayton.'

Clayton walked ahead, 'You might like it here Miss.'

'I doubt it.'

'This station is one of the largest and Mesan's been looking for an administrator since Anu left.'

'Really? For what purpose?'

'He needs a dock master. He can't keep tabs on it and monitor auctions at the same time.'

'Why not?'

'Gianna has been doing it but she's not cut out for the amount of work.'

'Gianna?'

'Yeh, she's married to the Commodore ...' Clayton quickly stopped himself.

Chanatico grinned, 'He has a second wife? This will be fine gossip on Otoch!'

The pair turned into the station control office, Chanatico was stunned to see Ilam stood beside Mesan. The red headed Amazon's eyes burnt a burgundy red. Chanatico dropped to the floor in a kowtow, 'Tumensik kiik.'

Ilam sneered in a burning rage at the prostrate Tlillan, 'Liik'il,' Chanatico rose. Ilam barked in her face, 'Bisik chi!'

Chanatico's eyes were fixed on the floor, 'Tumen taak Ilamachutli.'

Ilam inhaled deeply, 'You will follow Mesan to your new quarters, is that understood?'

'I understand.'

Ilam grabbed the young Matriarch by her chin, 'Ka'si'pil Ilam kaachik hats'uts ich!'

McCann's wife promised that if Chan made a similar verbal slip she'd "Break her beautiful face" Chanatico didn't reply.

The Matriarch was quite serious, both men though oblivious to what was said felt concern for Chanatico. The mighty Tlillan let go of Chan with a push and a piercing stare instructing Clayton to escort and assist her settling in.

In the following week Jenkins prepared his men to take control of the plethora of space stations forming the Skin Territory. The first hurdle however was to be overcome by Malikah.

A group of ten white holes ejected ten delta wing cruisers; Each one, sleek and menacing, glimmered in the bright light of a white star.

Gliding in perfect synchrony and holding a delta formation they approached Kurgudwardum 57. This was the first time Mammi had ever ventured into the Skin Territory, it was the first time she felt the need to do so.

Malikah waited on the main boulevard with her father, Lian and Mesan. Kishar observed silently from the edge of what used to be slave central.

Many watched on, curious to see Mammi in the flesh, fascinated as to the outcome of this face off.

A small vessel left the lead Tzitzimeh cruiser docking further down the boulevard, the crowd nattered with excitement.

Malikah stood proud in her Tlillan suit, white jacket and crown of feathers. Behind her Lian was prepared, blade fixed to her waist with cloth in the tradition of a Samurai. McCann still wearing his bowler hat and long coat had modified his pistol after spending time with Jenkins' men. It now had an ivory handle, its silver barrel and trigger glimmered. Ilam found it all quite ridiculous, nothing more than a male ego trip. Yet she understood any attempt to dissuade her husband would result in failure.

Mammi entered the boulevard and chattering changed to hushed silence as heads bobbed around one another attempting to steal a glance. Three Tzitzimeh approached, three short wrinkled old women in tunics, shrunken heads of fallen enemies hanging from necklaces and bracelets. Mammi wore a headdress, shrunken heads of deposed rulers swayed as the crowd gazed on in awe.

Resting some twenty feet from Malikah the ruler of Tamoanchan and overlord of Andromeda spoke, 'They say you are Xch'uup.'

'They are correct,' replied Malikah.

Mammi's dark grey eyes scanned the tall Tlillan before her. She recognised Malikah's heritage but something was amiss.

'You are not a Twilighter.'

'I am Twilighter, Lightsider and Darksider.'

Mammi's eyes sharpened examining Malikah's face closely, 'You are Mictlantecuhtli?'

'I am.'

'You are an imposter.'

'What does the mighty leader of Telal propose to do with this imposter?'

'You shall leave, return to Otoch and never trouble the Tzitzimeh again.'

'And if I refuse?'

'My fleet is superior to yours. Refuse and you shall be destroyed.'

Malikah turned to her right. Smiling into Lian's eyes she sent the order, Machine complied.

Kalayuuk's eyes of quicksilver communicated with Machine. Hermes, messenger of the Gods travelled back and forth; first to Machine on Bandayuuk then into hyperspace and finally back to Kalayuuk informing her all had been taken care of. Perhaps it was fitting that the God of Thieves' fleet foot was to work in Malikah's service this day? She would require his quickness of mind and cunning if she was to slay these giants as Hermes conquered the mighty Argos.

All were aware of Kishar prophecies before now. Kurgudwardum's crowd chattered amongst themselves at the sight of what Sada had named Iron Eyes.

The giant slayer disappeared from Lian's eyes as white holes opened up all around the Skin Territory. Twenty three Makayuuk vessels ejected from hyperspace, Machine's intimidating fleet grouped up above Kurgudwardum 57, reflecting a face off on the station below.

Mammi received message of Makayuuk vessels, focusing on Lian she exclaimed, 'That is an abomination!'

Malikah snapped back, 'That is my first Adjunct.'

'A Makayuuk?'

'She is Kalayuuk.'

'Use whichever term pleases you it is heresy. You have no moral authority here or on Otoch!'

The Tlillan Queen narrowed her eyes, 'Mammi wastes time presuming much when it ought be spent pleading for her life!'

A ripple of chatter ran through around Kurgudwardum the gauntlet had been thrown down, none had spoken this way to Mammi and survived in the past. All eyes were on the shrivelled Telal.

'What does Xch'uup desire with the Skin Territory?'

'I ventured here to make contact with my ancestors. I found them enslaved.'

'Why do you remain in the Skin Territory?'

'Because I wish it so.'

Mammi gave Rabum a black stare, 'Mark those foreign vessels and have your graviton beams destroy them.'

The tattooed Chief remained silent.

'Does Rabum betray those he made a blood oath to?'

The Chief spoke in an ominous tone, 'Mammi must fight her own enemies, Kishar are not her slaves.'

Mammi's eyes increased in brightness, 'Rabum's people shall regret this betrayal!'

The Chief remained without expression, 'First Mammi must defeat Xch'uup.'

Malikah unsheathed her neutronium sabre and pointed its tip across the boulevard at Mammi, 'You recognise this don't you?'

The Tzitzimeh brandished rows of teeth, seething with fear and hatred.

'I offer Mammi a duel. Settle this squabble now. If you defeat me my Adjunct shall return both Makayuuk and Tlillan fleets home to leave you be in Andromeda. If I defeat you the Tzitzimeh shall bend their knee to Xch'uup.'

Mammi shrank back into her sisters, flashing her teeth.

Malikah peered at the Kishar, 'Do you see? Your lord cowers in the presence of Xch'uup.'

Stepping back to her transport Mammi pointed at Xch'uup, 'Do not cross into Tamoanchan Territory the Tzitzimeh will not permit it.'

Malikah rebutted her threat, 'Run back to your hiding place and when I come Mammi shall bend her knees as she did before Quetzalcoatl!'

A frightened party of Telal scurried away from Kurgudwardum 57 much to the surprise of all local inhabitants. They had known nothing throughout their lives but Telal supremacy and the fear they instilled in every mortal being. Now a stranger had appeared rocking the balance of power drastically.

Returning her blade to its scabbard Malikah addressed Lian, 'Tell Machine the time is now her children shall receive an ocean of sustenance in the days to come.'

During the next week Jenkins took control of the Skin Territory, station by station. Resistance proved to be minimal after Mammi's retreat on Kurgudwardum 57. Who was psychotic enough to stand in the path of a locomotive named Xch'uup?

Before long the T.S.S held authority and a clampdown on lotus began, much to the Kishar's dismay.

McCann and Clayton joined Naguan 4's new controller, the largest producer of lotus leaf in the Skin Territory. It was also the biggest earner for Rabum and vital to Mammi's efforts in keeping Tamoanchan passive. McCann and his comrades joined Stewart Frost, the new lawman in town, whilst he patrolled its main boulevard.

Stewart carried a single firearm something between a Magnum .44 and an Uzi. His weapon possessed a large grip containing a magazine of several hundred rounds.

He himself wore black body armour along with a military monocle for low light and thermal tracking. The former SBS sergeant was pretty much prepared to go back down into a tunnel on Bandayuuk.

'So how's Andromeda been treating you, Clayton?' asked the Scotsman.

'The food's better than a London soup kitchen.'

Stewart laughed, 'Seems there's plenty of tit and arse around too.'

McCann smirked, 'Have you tried the local spirits yet?'

'Aye, I thought some rabid dog had pissed down me throat … erm, Commodore.'

McCann took a drag on his cigar, 'So how do you plan on getting these drug factories out of your station?'

'I was gonna get Clayton and a few of the gang together and pretend it was a night out in Glasgow.'

The party of three turned into a local drinking establishment. As women of a legal age served drinks and danced Stewart ordered libations. Three shot glasses of a substitute whisky were placed before them, the drink having gained popularity since Discovery's arrival in the Skin Territory.

McCann leaned against the bar and took a sip, 'I see what you mean, thank god I brought some Scotch with me.'

Stewart's neck snapped like a rubber band, 'What? … I mean … excuse me Commodore?'

'Faraday sends me half a dozen bottles once a month.'

The Scotsman cleared his throat but before he could talk McCann intervened, 'After this lotus trouble is cleared up I'll send a bottle over.'

'Thank you Commodore.'

As the comrades sipped their liquor and watched dancing girls from across Andromeda perform, McCann sensed two men enter the bar through a single swinging door. He'd become aware of these individuals a while ago, tracking them during their patrol of the main boulevard. Now they'd entered the same establishment.

McCann sipped his drink in the corner as two bounty hunters, one tall and dressed in a dark grey three piece suit. The other short with green skin and a set of strange growths emerging from his chin approached the bar.

'What would you boys like?' inquired a nervous barman.

'Vapostu, for both.'

'Vapostu it is,' replied the barman as he poured two thin vials full of a yellow sludge.

The short green man armed with an ion pistol downed his drink in one shot, never shifting his eyes from McCann.

Stewart and Clayton felt a malevolent aura surround these fellows as did the staff. A definite tension built up, despite this everyone carried on with business as usual.

After a few minutes customers began to call in their bills and leave. Something was going down and they didn't want to get caught up in it.

The owner was in distress though he refused to say anything, merely cleaning glasses with a towel whilst maintaining a safe distance.

Eventually the short green bounty hunter placed his empty glass on the bar, strolled past Clayton and Stewart, halting before McCann.

The Englishman said nothing just staring the alien dead in the eyes.

'You Duncan McCann?'

The Commodore slid his drink along the bar before removing a cigar from his mouth, 'Who wants to know?'

'Not important, who you are important,' replied the green fellow in a gargling tone.

'I take it you're a bounty hunter?'

'Duncan McCann 3,000 guskin ... dead or alive.'

McCann took a drag on his Ramon Allones. He tasted its sweet smoke before blowing it into the green alien's face, 'A man's gotta be desperate to risk his life for 3 G's.'

'Wife spawning ... nearly 100 young hatch soon,' blurted the little creature pushing back his jacket to reveal a pistol hanging from his gun belt.

McCann rested his smouldering cigar on an ashtray, 'Do send my congratulations ... to the father.'

Tentacles on the alien's chin began to quiver, 'Make good joke Duncan McCann, last joke ever make.'

McCann sensed his opponent was about to reach for his pistol, before the alien could do so McCann's palm slid into the ivory grip of his pulse pistol. Drawing his weapon he aimed as quick as he could whilst maintaining a steady hand. His foe was not far behind but in a gunfight half a second might as well be a week if you're on the wrong end.

A flash of super-heated air leapt from McCann's silver barrel propelling a tungsten shell along electrically charged rails. Upon exiting the barrel a mini sonic boom filled everyone's ears. Tearing through the air his bullet penetrated its target's chest causing the alien's arm to go limp and drop its ion pistol.

Before the green man hit the ground McCann heard a burst of fire, Stewart pulled his weapon on the second bounty hunter. Multiple shots ejaculated from the firearm thudding into the tall gunfighter's chest. He staggered backwards, bloody holes appearing in the fine fabric of his light grey waistcoat until he keeled over through a swing door and onto his back. His twitching corpse lay half inside the bar, face staring up at the boulevard ceiling in a pool of pink blood.

Steam rose from the green man's wound his beating heart stopped by a small piece of Tungsten manufactured in Birmingham, England.

McCann placed his weapon back in its holster before taking his Habanos and drawing a good load of smoke. The Englishman allowed a little to enter his lungs, just to remind him he was still alive.

As Stewart put his gun away the barman ran out and started rummaging through the dead men's belongings confiscating their weapons. It were as if a spectre had arisen to strip the fallen before their corpses had even gone cold.

'What are you doing man?' shouted Stewart.

The fat owner looked up as he went through the tentacle faced corpses' pockets, 'They didn't pay for their drinks, what am I? A charity?'

'Jesus man, you're worse than a plague of locusts!'

Pulling a wallet out the owner went through its contents, 'Hey you know how much guskin for vapostu?'

'Vapostu? What's that?'

'They drink vapostu, the real stuff.'

McCann took a drag on his cigar, 'So?'

'Vapostu, taken from extinct whale in Polan Territory; Sinus fluids drained from final 100, very expensive.'

Stewart eyed the empty glasses 'Jesus Christ! They drank whale snot?'

'Whatever … just help me get this gun belt off.'

The new lawman on Naguan 4 looked on in shock, 'You strip your own bloody corpse and make sure they're disposed of properly.'

The owner stood up clutching a wallet in one hand and gun belt in the other, 'What am I his mother? You space his remains if he means so much to you!'

Stewart pointed at the fat man, 'Listen here pal, if I find either of these bodies dumped on a docking arm I'll be charging you for it.'

Placing one man's items behind his bar the owner proceeded to strip the second cadaver, 'You come into my bar, bring in bounty hunters, start a shooting match, scare my customers. Now you want ME to space the people you kill, what next? Maybe you want to sleep with my wife and I massage your feet when you fuck her?'

'Just a Scotch will do and hold the whale snot,' quipped Clayton.

Gesturing to his employees the owner shouted, 'Come on help me with these bodies and you call Tranut; he's the only one to make profit since these Tlillan arrived!'

McCann muttered to Stewart, 'Tranut?'

'The local undertaker.'

The women did not respond. They were all transfixed by view screens above the bar.

The owner was about to berate his staff until he noticed his remaining customers were doing the same. Allowing the deceased bounty hunter to slump back down he examined the screen.

Upon his view screens images of Mammi's fleet collapsing beneath a hail of fire and brimstone captured all those present. The pride of Mammi's main force crumbled as allies scattered to the solar winds, fleeing for their lives. It was a sight no Andromedan believed could ever take place in their life time.

As her flagship retreated back into Tamoanchan many smaller vessels made for the planet below.

White holes opened up in hectic retreat from the Chutli and 23 of Machines' best war ships. Those who could folded space in a dash for home. Those who could not were either destroyed or ditched on the world below in an attempt to escape.

Once the system had been cleared Makayuuk landing vessels detached for the surface; a female reporter began to speak, McCann listened intently as his earpiece translated.

'On the very outskirts of Tamoanchan territory a battle took place, the first military action this territory has witnessed in nearly five hundred cycles.

Telal forces were met by a gathering of warships not recognised on any database. The battle was short and swift as the unidentified interlopers dispatched Mammi and her fleet of 15 allied warships in only 2 hours!'

A camera focused on a second presenter sat at the same desk, 'Several vessels fled to the nearby planet of Idpa III only to be pursued. According to our man on the Idpa a short ground battle ensued.'

The image of a semi-aquatic human filled the screen.

'Can you hear me?' shouted a reporter as fires burnt and smoke filled the atmosphere.

'We can hear you Eklan. Tell me what's happening down there?'

The reporter moved around a burnt landscape, out of the smoke a Makayuuk landing ship with sides opened out became clear, 'Do you see that?'

'Yes we can see it? What is it?'

'That is where Makayuuk poured out onto Idpa III.'

'Sorry? Makayuuk? Is that what they call themselves?'

'Yes, they are still rounding up Mammi's allies as I speak.'

The presenter was dumbfounded, 'Could we meet one of these Makayuuk?'

Eklan jogged towards a landing tube. His camera man followed causing its picture to bounce around as he negotiated cratered terrain. Eventually Eklan arrived at a line of captured soldiers being ushered inside a Makayuuk vehicle.

Lian stood out head and shoulders above her soldiers. Eklan approached her and spoke before she might question him, 'Hello, I'm Eklan reporting for Vega Today, may I ask your name and what you're doing here?'

Lian walked out from a circle of Makayuuk officers, 'Greetings Mr Eklan, I'm Lian and we are gathering prisoners of war.'

'I see, so you are at war with the Tamoanchan territory?'

'No, we are at war with the Telal.'

'The people of Idpa are to be subjects of the Makayuuk?'

'No, we shall leave soon, the people here are free.'

Suddenly an image of Xch'uup cast itself upon Idpa's smoky atmosphere, projected from Makayuuk vessels in space. The dread Queen declared her intentions were only to defeat the Telal. Her speech met with a sigh of relief from residents of the system in towns and villages nearby.

Eklan gestured to Malikah's image floating gracefully upon the sky, 'Who is that?'

'That is Xch'uup.'

'And may I ask who she is to me?'

Lian replied in a serious tone, 'To those who bend their knees she is their mother. To those who refuse she is their curse.'

Eklan looked down a line of captives, 'Could our viewers see what is being done with these captives?'

Lian nodded, 'Follow me Eklan.'

The journalist was led down a line of prisoners and inside the giant vessel. Within he was brought into a large chamber along with 50 or so prisoners of war.

The cameraman recorded events as Makayuuk armed with ion rifles removed control collars one by one from Mammi's men.

Once collars and clothing had been removed they were shuffled into a long transparent, cylindrical container; after all had been urged inside a hatch on its left end closed. What took place next left Eklan and his viewers traumatised. Every living being was blended into each other by implementation of high pressure.

Intense magnetic fields mixed mortal men into a violent goo, merging bone and flesh into a single paste. The mixture was then drained. Its blender didn't require cleaning as high pressure blasted every molecule out into ship storage tanks. This organic sludge would be shipped back to Bandayuuk to sustain Machine's children and increase her flock.

Eklan felt dizzy, one of his crew managed to grab a hold of him before the journalist hit the hard catronium floor.

Back on Naguan 4 jaws dropped in horror at the vision laid before them. McCann, Stewart and Clayton had seen it before. In fact Stewart and Clayton had both come precariously close to entering those chambers more than once.

Eklan could not speak. The reporter took a few minutes to recover. With help he regained a footing, though his legs felt a little gelatinous. The sound man stood close by, allowing Eklan to use him as a crutch.

Lian approached the reporter and his startled crew now gawping in terror at the sight they'd witnessed. The Amazon spoke into his microphone, 'Xch'uup will agree to a ceasefire if Mammi will meet her in the Chihuaz this cycle.'

The journalist from a water world stuttered whilst gathering himself, 'So … you will withdraw … from the Tamoanchan Territory … and take your conflict to the Chihuaz?'

'That is correct.'

'What if Mammi refuses your offer?'

'She cannot.'

Chapter 10

In Masku Patu, better known as the Skin Territory, a white hole opened far above the accretion disk. From the Styx a vessel ejected of such size previously not witnessed.

Slowly Machine's titanic harbinger glided past space station after space station with a serene grace; Kurgudwardum's populace observed in silence, the Kishar amongst them. Having already witnessed such a beast tear Mammi apart as a child would breakdown an insect. Piece by piece Machine's progeny dissected their foe with diligence.

Rabum viewed this giant from an observation window on Asrukishar, 'Did you ever witness such a thing?'

Rakbu shook his head, 'Not in any part of the Galaxy.'

'This thing it carries evil men.'

'I hear they have but steel in their hearts without pity or feeling.'

Rabum rested his hands against a carbon composite window, 'Sada called her Iron Eyes.'

'Rabum clear these thoughts we must attend a ceremony on Kurgudwardum 57. For what purpose is unclear, yet you must show iron. If the remaining leaders of free stations ...'

Rabum smiled in recognition of his old friend's concern, 'Do not fret. Rabum is prepared to face Xch'uup and her display.'

'Display?'

'This is not for Xch'uup's benefit but ours. She will send a message to all free stations today.'

'Message?'

Rabum laughed, 'You never were a great strategist Rakbu! This ceremony is to frighten us, to assert her supremacy in Masku Patu. For the first time I no longer fear Mammi. These women from Mul do shake iron from my body.'

'Some say they are Amelatu.'

Rabum fixed his eyes on Rakbu, 'Then pity me Rakbu for there shall be no tears shed for Kishar.'

A vast tubular craft slowly moved towards Kurgudwardum 57. In the time it took the Makayuuk to arrive representatives of all free stations made their way.

Guests gathered in Kurgudwardum's merchant district now sectioned off with bulkheads.

Rabum dressed in little more than hide pants with tattoos covering his skin waited alongside other delegates until the bulkhead rose. Nervous looks were exchange before Rabum and Rakbu took the first steps inside. All merchant houses had been closed and boarded. Each delegate brought a tribute for their new master. Rakbu carried a small wooden box as he peered into the distance with trepidation.

Eventually they reached a second bulkhead. A large onyx throne sat with its back to a sheet of grey metal. On one side of the throne stood the Marshal of Kurgudwardum 57 and his deputies along with Ilam and her staff. On the other side stood Kaeo, Amitra, Sandra and Arthur awaiting their Queen's presence.

Spetsnaz placed themselves strategically along the boulevard, brandishing small combat rifles. As a Makayuuk shuttle docked Malikah appeared from a side arch surrounded by her imperial guard.

The Tlillan Queen dressed in a splendid white gown and coat matching the crown of feathers adorning her regal head, rested upon her throne without a word.

Delegates of Masku Patu, encouraged by Spetsnaz, stood at the edge of the boulevard.

Rakbu whispered to Rabum, 'What are we waiting for?'

Rabum replied in a nervous tone, 'How would I know?'

At that moment Nestor approached, 'You will not speak.'

The pair of Kishar warriors nodded heads in compliance.

For ten minutes silence prevailed, the dread Queen made not a sound. Tension built to such a point even Atlas would be troubled bearing it.

Rabum twiddled his thumbs waiting for something to happen when he detected a noise from the other end of the boulevard. The sound was faint though in the silence each representative turned his and her head to meet it.

A harmony grew in strength Rabum was sure a locomotive shunted its way down the boulevard, the station's curvature obscuring his view. Soon from around the boulevard a column of Makayuuk six men wide and lord knows how many deep approached. At the head of this army led Sada's Iron Eyes. A few more minutes and her legion stopped 60 feet or so from Malikah's throne. Its column split with military precision, retiring on the boulevard edges.

From what Rabum could see they stretched back, three each side, around the curvature of the station and probably to a docking arm. It was quite an impressive show.

Lian remained centre guarding three bound and muzzled Tzitzimeh. Control collars squeezing their throats.

'All kneel for Xch'uup,' declared Amitra.

Every single Makayuuk including Lian and the Tzitzimeh kowtowed.

Nestor urged the Kishar in a hushed tone, 'That means you.'

Rabum and Rakbu quickly dropped to their knees and the delegates of Masku Patu followed.

Malikah rose from her throne, 'Liik'il.'

On witnessing the Makayuuk rise delegates returned to their feet.

One by one Amitra called tribute from Masku Patu; Each delegate presenting a gift in recognition of their new ruler.

All was going well, Amitra calling delegates and Sandra receiving gifts before passing them to a Spetsnaz soldier.

'The representatives of Emush may approach,' called Amitra.

Two men stepped forward both dressed in resplendent robes of gold. The leader of Emush announced, 'Since Xch'uup's crackdown on lotus our station has fallen upon hard times. The people of Emush therefore have no tribute.'

Tension returned as storm clouds to a northern sea port, causing sailors to secure their ships in expectation of the coming tempest, Rabum watched on with curiosity.

Malikah arose stepping past Amitra, 'What is your name?'

The man in fine robes answered, 'Gizzal, Duke of Emush.'

'You say your station has no tribute?'

'That is correct Xch'uup,' replied a grey faced, scaly alien.

'That is not acceptable.'

'As we speak my people starve. They have nought to give but their lives.'

The boulevard fell quiet as Malikah contemplated his words. Before she might reply Amitra placed a soft hand on her Queen's shoulder, 'Malikah.'

The dread Queen felt her sister's pull, staving off cold Tlillan malevolence. Yet something had to be done ... an example. Eyeing the Duke of Emush Malikah spoke, 'You seem well fed and well dressed.'

He did not reply.

'Perhaps you may yet offer your peoples' tribute?'

Again the grey faced man in fine silk robes refused to reply.

'In return for your tribute I shall send relief ... Duke of Emush.'

'My tribute?'

Malikah smirked as the robed alien gazed into her dread eyes, 'Your hand sir!'

'My hand?'

'Why yes sir! Your hand!'

'I don't understand your Majesty.'

'Arthur, come forth.'

The young lad sheepishly complied, ambling beside his Queen.

Malikah pointed toward Gizzal, 'Hand him your sword.'

Arthur passed his blade to the recipient indicated.

The dread Queen sneered with satisfaction before an entire boulevard of ambassadors, 'Now cut your hand off and present it to Amitra.'

The Ambassador's aide approached yet Malikah snapped at the man, 'He requires no assistance!'

Gizzal drew a deep breath before pulling his robes back to the elbow. Kneeling, the Duke of Emush placed his left arm on the cold catronium floor.

Representatives of Masku Patu began to mutter between one another. Some didn't believe he'd do it, others wondered what alternative he had. Amongst them Amar and Bazi watched in disbelief. Having taken passage back to Andromeda as guests of Xch'uup they now observed this twisted political game. Amar did not believe Gizzal would cut off his own limb, Bazi realised he must do it if he wished to maintain his title of Duke.

A wave of shock hit the guests as Arthur's thick bladed sabre fell down upon Gizzal's wrist. Gizzal let out a grizzly noise whilst ambassadors gossiped back and forth. The fat Duke blubbed in torment over his gash, tears mixed with a creamy substance Arthur assumed to be blood.

A second less powerful cut forged deeper, Gizzal lost strength with each blow yet sheer determination pushed the blade on. Malikah peered down in satisfaction before scanning her guests. Some looked on in horror, others with a perverse curiosity, observing each moment of twisted alien sadism. After several bloody strikes a dangling appendage separated from its limb.

An aide dragged Gizzal to his feet. Gizzal pulled off one of his robes, wrapping his bloody tribute inside before presenting it to Amitra. An aide retrieved Arthur's sword from the floor.

The tall Indian lady passed the Duke's tribute to a Russian soldier, placing it with the rest. Arthur took back his bloodied blade returning to Kaeo's side.

Gizzal's aide assisted him into the crowd, nursing a gory wound.

'Amelatu or not this woman plays a good game,' whispered Bazi as Gizzal hobbled past.

'Game?' replied Amar in a hushed tone beneath the chattering of guests.

'Terror and panic, Amar ... terror and panic.'

'To what end?'

'I do not know ... but a wise man will dwell in the shadows when the Devil is bored.'

Amar was none the wiser, however the ceremony continued and he observed in silence.

The flow of tributes persisted until finally the Kishar tribute was accepted, a small idol stolen from the Etlu thousands of years ago.

Now only one tribute remained, Kalayuuk was to present her gift last of all.

The dread Queen raised her voice, 'What do the Makayuuk bring as tribute?'

Lian stepped aside, drawing her sword she pointed its tip at three prisoners, 'I bring you the bravest from the battle of Idpa.'

Malikah looked down at her captives, 'Bravest?'

'These creatures blocked our path allowing their mother to escape.'

'Bravery and loyalty ... souls worthy of tribute.'

'The Makayuuk offer the bravest of the Tzitzimeh.'

A Machine Man brought forth a pyre, metallic disc resting above a silver coil. The pyre was lightweight standing 5 feet tall heated by a chemical battery.

Malikah unsheathed her sword. All observed terror in the eyes of her captives as they followed her blade to its resting place, above the pyre.

The central Tzitzimeh began to make muffled noises as it writhed in its bonds.

'Remove its muzzle,' ordered Malikah.

Lian hesitated for a moment before receiving a look of reassurance from her lover. A Machine Man removed the creature's muzzle.

The Tzitzimeh were transfixed by Xch'uup's mantle as it conducted heat so readily. The central beast, once free of her facial bonds, screeched a plea, 'Spare my daughters, spare them as you would your own.'

Malikah smirked at its desperate overtures, 'Warriors have died in a strange land ... far from home. You and your daughters shall guide their souls through the Dreamscape to Otoch.'

'You must spare my daughters!'

'Must?'

'I shall guide your souls, through the Dreamscape but I offer more.'

Malikah turned her sword heating its blade thoroughly whilst the Tzitzimeh entreated her.

'When my soul returns to rest with the Tzitzimeh, I shall sing your praises to each of my sisters. I will tell the tale of Idpa to Mammi's past. I will praise your power and wisdom above all others, nothing but honour shall pass my lips.'

'And in return?'

'Spare my daughters lives.'

'How can I be sure you speak truth?'

The tiny witch fixed her eyes on Xch'uup, 'You have my oath as a Tzitzimeh and a warrior.'

Kaeo stepped forward, 'You can't believe that thing!'

'She speaks with honesty,' replied a stoic Queen, 'to have an enemy sing your praises in the afterlife is a great honour. I will do as you ask.'

The Tzitzimeh peered towards Kaeo, 'How can I be sure my daughters will go unharmed?'

Malikah's eyes grew wider, 'You have my word!'

The beast rose from its knees, 'Then I take your word.'

Her daughters cried from behind their bonds.

'Calm yourselves children. Today I give my life so that you may take retribution for your mother's soul ... just as Xch'uup does exact revenge for her warriors today.'

With that Lian untied her shackles and tore away her shrunken head tunic to reveal a wrinkled, naked body.

Malikah lifted her mantle from the pyre.

Lian and Kaeo held the Tzitzimeh in place by its arms.

The witch brandished its teeth at the glowing blade until it sliced through her chest. The animal's howl echoed down the boulevard whilst a Mack moved to its feet catching entrails in a dish as they plopped out.

The crowd watched in horror as they witnessed a Telal slaughtered in such a barbaric method. Rabum and Rakbu shared glances of fear with one another these women seemed to know no limits of base savagery.

Once all guts had exited the body Lian and Kaeo released an inanimate carcass onto Kurgudwardum's cold hard ground. The Makayuuk brought its steaming entrails to the pyre, depositing them inside.

Flames leapt up as intestine and vital organs cooked for all to see. Xch'uup stared through a haze observing her victim's soul journey into the afterlife. The son of night and darkness wrapped himself around the beast. Pulling what remained of its consciousness beyond the veil of tears to guide home Malikah's fallen warriors. Thanatos spirited away Mammi's bravest soul reducing the courage of its whole, who now prepared to go to war with their sworn enemy once again.

Masku Patu's free leaders gazed into the fire … only to see their dread Queen's crazed eyes glaring back.

That night many ex-special forces soldiers now employed in the maintenance of the Skin Territory relaxed in what used to be Puyin bar. Among them Clayton, McCann and Jenkins sat at their own table; Entertained by a group of strange woman preforming music which spanned Mankind's last two centuries.

A lady stood centre stage with green hair and three eyes singing an old tune. Three scantily clad women from different corners of Andromeda danced in time. Many of the soldiers were unfamiliar with the song, most had no idea it was even composed on Earth. Nevertheless the triple eyed lady sang well, a pitch perfect voice and her compatriots danced in time not missing a beat. All patrons were pleased by the result, encouraging the flow of beer and other alcoholic beverages.

Only a month or two ago these men had been sleeping rough, surviving beneath the poverty line, discarded remnants of a war people wanted to forget. They were no more than a blot on the landscape, despite years of service to the King. Today they had a job with a paycheque affording enough credits to enjoy a night in Kurgudwardum's largest gentleman's club.

'That bird doing the singing, she's got a nice pair of legs,' noted Clayton as he puffed on a roll up.

'And a whole host of STD's, I bet even McCann couldn't name them all!' chuckled Jenkins.

'Look who's talking!'

'What's that supposed to mean?'

'I remember that time in Panama you were in treatment for weeks!'

'That was that bloody Indian restaurant!'

McCann laughed, 'You mean the one you and 50 other men went to on the same evening?'

Clayton cracked up as Jenkins expression transformed from jovial to humourless, 'I went out for a meal that night and that's the bloody truth!'

'Well that's the first time I heard of anyone catching Gonorrhoea from chicken madras!'

Clayton laughed along with McCann.

'You should have seen him the Doctor said his balls looked like a pair of onion bhajis! Every time he took a piss you'd hear him chanting like a Hare Krishna from the other end of the ship!' McCann pretended to hold his penis as he attempted a humorous rendition of Jenkins urinating.

Clayton laughed, 'Is that true sir?'

Jenkins made a slight grin, 'Don't believe a word of it Clayton … I had chicken tikka that night.'

'At least that's what she said her name was!' cracked McCann.

'Quite, chicken madras was almost twice the price!' quipped Jenkins.

All three men laughed together as the beautiful woman continued to sing, 'Who's looking good today?

Who's looking good in every way?

No style rookie, you better watch don't mess with me!'

The Commodore made merry with his pals, perhaps the first stress free night in Andromeda since he'd landed on Kurgudwardum.

'Jesus fucking Christ,' whispered Clayton.

McCann saw his deputy go from merry to quite concerned; following his eyes the Commodore discovered the source of anxiety. In through the door three men walked off the boulevard. The women continued to sing yet the mood inside Puyin changed in an instant as every ex-special forces soldier observed the faces of their former enemy.

Sirt, Asta and Dosa entered Puyin. Though confused, Andromeda's natives felt a tension arise as the iron eyes walked across the floor approaching McCann's table.

Clayton clutched his rifle, McCann and Jenkins hands hovered over their pulse pistols. In seconds Sirt stood before them, 'Good evening Admiral and good evening to you Brigadier.'

'I'm a Commodore Mr Sirt ... what is it that you want?'

'I and my Comrades are curious as to whether the victor of Bandayuuk might allow us the honour of resting at his table?'

Clayton gripped his weapon, 'Actually ...'

McCann cut him off, 'Please take a seat,' gesturing to three chairs.

Clayton was the only one to maintain a grip on his firearm.

Dressed in a Makayuuk jumpsuit and accompanied by his officers Sirt took a seat around McCann's table. Dosa and Asta flanked him either side. A young lady approached with a serving tray, 'Do you desire a beverage?'

'Three beers.'

'Anything else?'

Sirt gave a confused expression.

'Do you desire women?'

'For what?'

'Pleasure.'

'Just get the damn drinks!' grunted Dosa.

Asta was about to inquire after the aforementioned pleasure until Sirt instructed otherwise via their mental link through Machine. The entire bar remained tense as the women on stage sang, all attention fell upon Sirt and his compatriots.

As each Machine man received his beer McCann spoke, 'Quite the risk you boys are taking, walking in here bold as brass.'

'Risk?'

'A bar full of Bandayuuk veterans … all armed to the teeth. I'd have baulked at showing my face.'

Sirt grinned, 'I doubt that is true.'

'I do not understand, surely Bandayuuk as you call it is a settled matter?' inquired Asta.

Dosa grunted whilst sipping his beer.

'In the minds of these men Bandayuuk is as much alive today as then,' noted Jenkins in an ominous tone.

'If Machine's children could accept defeat why is it so difficult for humans to welcome victory?'

Clayton made a loud snorting noise this time, one hand firmly attached to his rifle barrel. All three Makayuuk eyed the Bokor.

'Did I speak out of turn?'

'Victory?' stated Clayton.

'Why yes Mr Clayton, Machine surrendered, surely you recall?'

'How did you know my name?'

'Machine knows the name of every man who fought on Bandayuuk … especially the demons beneath.'

Women danced, singing to a strained atmosphere, 'No money man can win my love,

It's sweetness that I'm thinking of,

We always hang in a buffalo stance,

We do the dive every time we dance,

I give you love baby not romance,

I make a move nothing left to chance.'

'We have accepted the past, so should you Mr Clayton.'

McCann narrowed his eyes at Dosa, 'I don't think that's 100% accurate.'

'So why exactly did you guys surrender at Bandayuuk?' blurted Clayton.

'Our fleet had been overwhelmed Mr Clayton.'

'Cobblers!'

'I'm unfamiliar with that human term.'

'The Mack fleet had won any idiot could tell you that.'

'Perhaps the intricacies of fleet combat are best left to others, Mr Clayton?'

Before his deputy could press the issue further McCann halted his inquiry, 'That's enough Clayton.'

'So what are you boys doing here?' asked Jenkins as he fondled a Cognac.

'Kalayuuk shall return to Bandayuuk once our protein tanks are replenished. We visit this place to remind those considering rebellion what awaits their enterprise beyond the rim.'

'So that whole tribute ceremony was an exercise in putting the frighteners up the locals?'

Sirt furrowed his brow until Asta commented, 'To instigate fear amongst the local population.'

'Yes Mr Jenkins,' nodded Sirt.

Dosa sneered over his drink at Clayton, 'Shit happens.'

McCann and Jenkins were confused, Clayton relaxed allowing his rifle to lean on a nearby chair, 'I suppose it does,' he said in a relaxed tone.

'Looking good's a state of mind.

State of mind don't look behind you,

State of mind or you'll be dead,

State of mind may I remind you,

Bomb the bass … ROCK THIS PLACE!' sang the stage girls as they ended their piece to subdued applause.

A waitress approached to place a credit chit on their table. The Makayuuk men gave the small triangular crystal a quizzical expression. McCann picked it up, 'Don't tell me, you don't have a debit chit?'

'We aren't paid wages in the sense humans comprehend,' replied Asta.

The Englishman nodded, 'Don't worry, your drinks are on me …
and anything else you decide to indulge in tonight,' McCann eyed a
group of bar girls.

Asta followed the Commodore's line of sight becoming excited on
viewing several women in an assortment of flimsy clothing.

'ASTA!' bellowed Dosa, 'We don't want a repeat of Janus 7!'

'Janus 7?' inquired Jenkins.

Asta's face went red as a beetroot, Sirt shook his head with a
smile as Dosa spilt the beans, 'Half the damned crew were
immobilised, infected by a retro-virus Asta acquired from a house of
ill repute! For a moment we surmised the Crimson Eternity had
returned to blight the galaxy!'

'The Crimson Eternity?'

'A pox on the universe before your people ventured to the stars; it
ravaged the galaxy destroying civilizations in its wake. I'm surprised
the Tlillan have not told you before now, they suffered more than
most.'

'There's a lot they don't tell us.'

'So tell me about the Crimson Eternity,' said Clayton in an
inquisitive tone.

'The Crimson Eternity was a space born virus. Creatures that lived
in space, captured by Xch'uup and employed as beasts of burden
carried the disease. Their spores filtered through the planet's
atmosphere infecting its populace. Its name is derived from its
effects, the eyes turn a shade of red … a dead colour. The victim
slowly loses strength until he falls into a coma.'

'And then,' asked McCann.

'And then nothing,' replied Sirt, 'he or she remains in their coma
until one day the body just gives up.'

'How was it cured?'

'The Crimson Eternity was never cured. Its carriers were hunted
and destroyed before wiping out the galaxy. The Tlillan population
was hit hard and not long afterwards the Gukumatz released a virus
upon them.

Some believed the Crimson Eternity had returned to blight Xch'uup for her immorality in enslaving the beasts which carried it. Fortunately it was not so or unfortunately depending on your perspective, Mr McCann.'

'Were the Makayuuk affected?'

'Xch'uup had pushed us into the galactic core its cosmic radiation protected us ... from the Eternity at least.'

'What do you mean?'

'That which protected us from Xch'uup and the Crimson Eternity on one hand, destroyed us slowly with the other. That is why we require protein to feed birthing stations Mr McCann. Cosmic radiation made us infertile yet if we ventured out a combination of Xch'uup's wrath and the Crimson Eternity would have surely destroyed us. So you see Mr McCann we take no pleasure in reprocessing other beings to multiply our own, it reminds us of our past woes.'

'I'm sorry, I didn't know.'

'There is no need to apologise, we Makayuuk consider ourselves a cursed people.'

Jenkins took a sip of cognac, 'Cursed?'

'We live in a never ending cycle of misery. Born to die and be re-born a cursed Makayuuk. Whether it be to suffer in the galactic core, cosmic radiation destroying our bodies, on the galactic arm hunted by Xch'uup, underneath Bandayuuk fighting humans to the death or here in Andromeda ... murdering a people we have not even met face to face before now ... for sustenance.

There is an old proverb amongst Makayuuk it says "Be obedient, suffer in silence and with luck you shall not be born for another 100 cycles".'

Chapter 11

Upon arrival those aboard the Chutli fell in awe of a massive construction orbiting a central star. Nothing of such magnitude had been undertaken in Tlillan history. A doughnut or to be more accurate a torus encircled a bright yellow star. The orbital path of a Mars or Earth was engulfed by this construction.

Tubes jutted out, rising above the elliptical plane meeting at the same point above the system's singularity. At that point rested the Chihuaz; the centre of Andromeda where wars were fought and won. The fate of civilizations had been decided here before the Tlillan launched their first satellite.

'Do you see it?' yelped Lian.

'I see it,' whispered Malikah.

'Who could conceive such a thing?'

'The ones who linked our galaxies.'

'Xch'uup, I have clearance to dock,' spoke a Matriarch from her navigation console.

'Then do so.'

The Chutli made its regal way toward a massive doughnut emitting a smooth rusty colour. Yet on approach its surface betrayed many docking arms and unfinished works. On closer inspection it was a muddle of activity, older parts of the surface stained with solar radiation. More recent construction gleamed bright silver. Malikah pondered an undertaking to discourage even a Matriarch's ego.

A cylindrical docking arm extended capturing the Chutli.

'Cutting engines,' called out the navigator.

Drawn in by a docking arm their entire war cruiser eased into a magnetic grapple. What happened next once more brought awe to the crew; an arm drew them towards a massive opening in the torus. Their vessel towed inside to be suspended in a zero G environment.

Kaeo watched in disbelief, 'How could the people who built this lose power to the Tzitzimeh?'

Amitra spoke in a hushed tone, 'Empires build their greatest constructions during winter.'

'What?'

'During the final stages of Empire they erect their great buildings and monuments. After spring, summer and autumn it is then they you see the wonders they are noted for by their ancestors. Thousands of years later remembered for winter constructions rather than the accomplishments preceding. I find it quite sad sometimes viewing monuments to lost empire.'

Kaeo shook her head, 'Whatever.'

'Cool your heart Kaeo,' intervened Malikah, 'there shall be time enough for that in the Chihuaz.'

Their vessel remained suspended, held in place by the docking arm as a pipe moved into the war cruiser's side connecting its airlock.

'Xch'uup, we are cleared to board,' said a Matriarch manning a forward station.

Malikah rose, 'Sandra, Kaeo, Amitra and Arthur accompany me to the port airlock. Lian, you are in command until I return.'

The Chutli's port airlock melted away revealing a transparent tunnel; her party followed making their first steps inside the cylinder. Malikah looked down viewing the floor of the largest docking bay she'd ever seen or even heard of.

Men shuffled around maintaining systems and checking the Chutli for any flaws in her hull. They wore metallic suits covering their entire bodies, it was only after scanning them mentally did she realise these were not men but androids.

Malikah looked forwards, as the tunnel ended its airlock opened. They stepped onto Andromeda's legendary habitat to be greeted by two men and a woman. The grey man was probably in his 60's. He wore a satin navy blue two piece suit. It looked quite casual along with a mandarin collared grey silk shirt. His shoes were something like a sports version of a doc martin.

Cigarette in hand he approached Malikah kissing her on the ear. The Tlillan party were shocked, not least of all Malikah. Assuming it was a traditional greeting in these parts and no insult intended she replied with an uncomfortable smile.

'Welcome to the Chihuaz young lady! I'm Allal, this is Geman,' he pointed to a young man dressed in a horribly gaudy shirt consisting of Caribbean colours and different metric shapes on a yellow background, 'and this is my personal assistant Visi,' he gestured with his cigarette at a young lady in a ruffled blouse, business skirt to her knees, red high heels and a big fluffy hairdo.

Malikah cleared her throat, 'I am Malikah and these are my sisters Sandra, Amitra and Kaeo.'

'Who's the young meat?' inquired Visi adjusting her glasses.

'Excuse me?'

'The male,' said Allal puffing on a lotus cigarette.

'My name is Arthur, thank you very much.'

Visi looked him up and down, 'I see potential in this one.'

In quite a rude fashion Allal walked straight past Malikah. He looked the women up and down muttering as Geman took notes on a tablet. Examining the Tlillan sisters as cattle he moved from one to the other eventually stopping at Kaeo.

'What's your name sweetheart?'

Kaeo's eyes widened, 'I am Kaeo not your sweetheart!'

Speaking to Geman as if Kaeo was not a real person Allal went on, 'Note down this one's measurements, take note her rump and thighs are perfect I want the camera boys to get good shots on that.'

Kaeo's eyes began to change pigment, 'Excuse me?'

Allal witnessed her eyes switch hue, 'Can she do that anytime?'

'I am here you can speak to me.'

'She's feisty to, note that down it'll be popular with viewers.'

Geman's ponytail bobbed up and down, 'Yeh you remember the Kreet woman 5 cycles ago?'

'That's what I mean, pushed viewing figures up 3 points when she ripped that guy's nuts off.'

Allal went back to his examination, 'Hmmm,' turning to Xch'uup again the grey haired man inquired, 'Would you agree to breast enlargement?'

Kaeo stood directly between Allal and Malikah, 'How about I enlarge your asshole with my boot?'

'Calm down sugar buns. I'll talk to your boss then she'll talk to you. That's how it works here.'

Malikah stepped in before fury took the hour, 'I'm sorry we cannot agree to any physical changes. Kaeo's eyes only change hue under certain conditions.'

Allal nodded then spoke back to Geman, 'Fine, there's not much we can do with the other females. Take down their measurements anyway I'm sure they'll appeal to someone.'

'I'll do some focus polling on that, you'll get it in 12 hours,' stated Visi.

'Good job, what about him?'

'Well he'll appeal to the mothers watching not enough bulk for anything beyond that.'

Allal nodded his head, 'Gotcha, still that's at least two points if he makes it past the first round.'

'That's what I thought not many like this have made it into the eliminators.'

Allal led the group into a glass elevator, 'Come on ladies it's time to check out your residence for the Chihuaz.'

Doors closed and the elevator hauled them upwards. Allal grinned at the ladies; he'd witnessed this astonishment before and the grey haired man always got a kick when aliens saw it for the first time.

After passing through the main Torus then into a long tube leading inside a section containing the Chihuaz Malikah looked around to see a forest stretching into the distance below; all were fascinated at the sight, a rainforest complete with wild life and working ecosystem.

The lift gathered pace rocketing into clouds draped above the forest canopy. Arthur looked straight up and everything became white as they travelled inside a cloud. On emerging through the top he could not make out their destination due to condensation.

Eventually water peeled away whilst rocketing through the atmosphere. Just as the roof became clear he saw their destination a second before entering it. Arthur reacted, moving his head in shock.

Allal laughed, 'Ahh gets them every time!'

The elevator doors opened. Malikah followed Allal and his team along a copper corridor into a large central room with several small passages leading off to living quarters.

'This is where you'll be living for the next month ladies,' declared Allal with open arms and a big smile.

On the opposite side of the room was placed a large couch with coffee table looking onto a window. Kaeo strode over and peered out through the carbon composite glass, the small warrior made what she thought was a silent gasp.

Allal joined her, 'That is the Chihuaz.'

'It's massive.'

'What makes it special are the people who fight and die inside.'

The rest of the party were equally overwhelmed. Below a gigantic arena sprawled out. Thousands of little windows just as theirs circled high above what could have been millions of seats encircling a central arena, leaning out as an amphitheatre. Floors of seating built above floors of seating. Its focus being a circular dirt arena about half the size of a football field; three large chairs sat upon copper pillars at one side of the arena.

'Who sits there?' inquired Kaeo.

'The Telal, Mammi in the middle.'

'Why?'

'They've been champions for hundreds of cycles ... it's killing the Chihuaz.'

'Explain?'

'All conflicts are settled in the Chihuaz. When Mammi realised she stopped fighting her enemies in space and came here. Ever since she's held her seat, none have the courage to face her.'

'Why has it hurt the Chihuaz?'

Allal pulled out a red and white paper packet and removed a lotus cigarette before lighting it. He offered one to Kaeo. She declined grimacing at the yellow stick.

'The Chihuaz used to be the greatest event in the galaxy, everyone from every territory would watch. All of them cheering on their champion in the hope he or she might defeat their mortal enemy then go on to reside over the games next year.

Then Mammi turned up and my viewing figures turned to shit! We've lost all our best corporate customers to events that didn't have a certain outcome.'

Malikah smirked, 'Viewing figures?'

Allal took a nervous puff from his cigarette, 'You bet lady! And you people are gonna bring the Chihuaz back!'

'How is that?'

Allal smirked at the Tlillan Queen, 'You guys took down the Kishar and after that standoff in the Skin Territory, Mammi is shitting her pants! I've never seen a Telal afraid, when Mammi backed down on Kurgudwardum 57 that was the first time.'

Amitra folded her arms and interjected, 'So you believe we can depose them from their position of power and reinstate you?'

Allal took another drag blowing smoke in the Indian's direction, 'That seat isn't power, the power is the Chihuaz and I'm the Chihuaz. I was bringing civilizations together when you Tlillans were still living in caves!'

'Really?'

'Yeh really, the power is only there if people are watching. When the galaxy went silent every cycle to view the Chihuaz I held the destiny of quadrillions in the palm of my hand! It didn't matter who sat in that chair as long as people watched … and they did … they adored the Chihuaz … until that wrinkled fucking witch turned up and shit on it all!'

'So we are here to dispatch Mammi from the Chihuaz?'

Allal calmed down taking another long drag burning an entire centimetre from his lotus cigarette, 'You're the only people I believe can do it and will do it, so I'm gonna give you every chance you need to win. But this is all hands on, no mental tricks, even the Telal are prohibited from using ESP.'

'Why?'

'Because no-one wants to watch a fight if it's only happening in two people's heads! Any ESP and you're disqualified, permanently.'

Geman pulled out a tablet, 'Let's get the profiling done.'

Allal nodded his head, 'If you could all put your thumbs on the tablet, we need a genetic profile.'

Malikah pressed her thumb on the face of Geman's black tablet, a bleep sounded, 'You're done.'

As he took the others profile the sable Queen asked, 'What will you do with that?'

Allal waved his hand as he strolled toward one of the desks jutting out from a mirrored wall, 'It's just a formality.'

After all genetic data was collected Geman's tablet made an unpleasant tone. The Chihuaz presenter rested upon a preparation station, very similar to something in a hairdressing salon, 'What's the problem?'

The ponytailed man pulled a grim expression, 'It can't be done.'

'What do you mean? Show me that,' shouted Allal as Geman brought him the tablet.

Allal observed it for a moment, 'Get someone on it. You've gotten over this before.'

'Al, this is 14%, you know it can't be masked.'

The grey haired presenter fixed his gaze upon Geman, 'Dresk can do it.'

'Dresk? He was imprisoned for genetic theft in the Vega Territory, I can't ...'

Al stood up and screamed, 'DON'T TELL ME WHAT YOU CAN'T DO, JUST FUCKING DO IT!'

Geman pleaded, 'How do I get him out of a Vega prison?'

Visi stepped forward, 'I have an idea.'

'What?'

'The Vega Territory has had a border dispute with the Traven Territory over those mining systems for cycles now.'

'So?'

'If Malikah agrees she could represent them in the Chihuaz ... for Dresk.'

Allal smiled at Visi then pointed at Geman, 'Get on the wire with the Vega Consul,' he turned back to Visi, 'can we swing the representation?'

Visi grinned, 'Malikah's father is married to Gianna-atir-sinnis-ash the third, first of the House of Ash, technically Malikah and her compatriots are all daughters and sons of Ash by lineage of inheritance.'

Allal clapped his hands, 'I knew you were more than a pretty face!'

Geman was still unhappy, 'Dresk would have to be smuggled in his crimes are ...'

'Who cares about his fucking crimes? We need a mask.'

'Mask?' inquired the sable Queen.

'Genetic manipulation, it's not permitted in the Chihuaz.'

'Genetic manipulation?'

Allal lit up another cigarette as Visi and Geman both made cynical expressions, 'Yeh, you got so much genetic manipulation going on in there it's too difficult to mask with normal methods. And don't deny it sweet cheeks. I've seen it all before.'

'What do you propose?'

'We'll bring in Dresk. He'll engineer a mask that'll last for the Chihuaz. Trust me most of the fighters out there are doing the same, you don't win without genetics anymore.'

Geman went through their profiles, something brought him to a halt, 'Al, take a look.'

The old man examined the information before peering at Malikah, 'You guys are related to the Telal?'

Sandra shook her head as she marched over to view the data, 'That is not possible.'

Allal passed the Greek beauty his tablet, 'The data doesn't lie.'

Sandra read it but made no reply.

'Well?'

'I must examine this for myself before coming to a conclusion.'

Al took a drag from his smoke, 'You guys either bred with them or used Telal genes to boost your own. Mammi seemed to know who you guys were on Kurgudwardum 57 … you've met in the past?'

'We have.'

'And?'

'That is all you need to know Mr Allal.'

'Now I understand why Mammi is so scared. You're the big bad ass sister that's turned up to shit on her sweet 16.'

'Hardly.'

Al blew foul grey smoke into the room. He approached Malikah and whispered, 'Do you know how long I've lived?'

'No.'

'Most of this body is replacement parts, some mechanical others organic. My brain has been floating in a fucking jar for the last 700,000 cycles. I thought I'd seen it all and heard it all until Mammi arrived and destroyed my Chihuaz. Then you came,' Allal fondled the sable Queens hair, 'to free a desperate people … in a desperate land. Don't lie to me like some stupid kid, do we understand each other?'

Malikah forced Al's hand away from her curled locks, 'I understand Mr Allal.'

'Then tell me, what's the deal with you and Mammi?'

The Tlillan Empress gave her cohorts a hard look before answering, 'In the past, many eons ago, we and the Tzitzimeh shared a planet.'

Amitra and her sisters were aware of the Tzitzimeh tale. How Xch'uup had banished their species from the Milky Way. Yet the details eluded them and most Tlillan, up until now only Xch'uup and her Seers were privy to the full story.

Malikah continued, 'Our keepers, the Neenayin, used Tzitzimeh genetics to perfect our species until we developed beyond their original intentions. After turning upon them, a lust for blood had been instilled within us. Not satisfied we waged war upon every sentient being, first on our home world then our home system and finally the Galaxy. An ocean of blood was not enough to satisfy our crusade, for Xch'uup had become a God and all were forced to bend their knees before her.

Mammi and her species, those you call Telal became another victim of our religious quest. Her people were a reminder that Tlillans are not the children of God ... the daughters of Xch'uup. It was necessary to expunge them yet banishment was forced to suffice.'

Al noticed the atmosphere had grown tense, 'And now you're here to finish the job?'

Malikah took a deep breath, 'There can be no reconciliation between us.'

'Good, the last thing I need is you making up and going home. I need a fight and I need you to win. That's why I'm backing you.'

Amitra spoke in an incredulous tone, 'This whole conflict is based on a lie?'

'A lie? Surely you know better than any that there is no truth, no lie.'

'No truth? We instigated a crusade to exterminate an entire species, innocent of any crime. We exiled them to Andromeda and now we follow them here to commit genocide with the backing of some copper penny game show host ... this is not truth?'

Malikah remained tight lipped refusing to answer her Priestess.

Amitra's eyes glimmered red with rage, 'Answer me! What is truth? What is lie? If they do not exist then is this just? Or does justice not exist in your feeble universe?'

Malikah remained silent yet Amitra could not contain herself, 'You bring us to Andromeda in the name of murder. Yet when the Ya'ax are threatened, when pirates and brigands rape their children, Xch'uup will not lift a finger … NOT A FINGER! THIS IS TRUTH! You will raise the banner of murder and evil without a second thought yet shrink to defend the deserving. And do not preach your philosophy of no good or evil,' Amitra pointed fervently at her chest, 'for my soul knows what is good and what is evil.'

Malikah replied in a low tone, 'When we return I shall aid the Ya'ax.'

'When we return? Why not assist them when pirates ravaged their system? Why? Why come here to murder Tzitzimeh yet baulk at punishing pirates? You murder the innocent whilst ignoring criminals.'

Touching her arm delicately Arthur whispered, 'Amitra.'

The Amazon decided it was better to leave allowing her conscience to wind down away from its focus. In one last fit of anger she screamed, 'I may owe you my life but I do not owe you any other's life … you make me sick,' with that the Valkyrie stormed out of the room.

The dread Queen whispered under her breath, 'The first casualty of war is the truth,' as her priestess disappeared through the doorway.

Sandra spoke next, 'I'm sorry but I must agree with Amitra, I'll help Doctor Weissmuller yet nothing beyond that.'

Malikah turned to Kaeo.

The short Tlillan Marshal shrugged her shoulders, 'Xch'uup commands, Huey'tlacochcalcatl follows.'

Malikah nodded her brow in relief. Arthur was still looking at Kaeo until he realised it was his turn to speak.

'In for a penny in for a pound I suppose.'

'I take it that's a yes?'

'Yes,' replied the young man.

'Then it's just us three.'

'Fine, we can make that work. Do you have any sound we can use for your intros?'

'Intros?'

'Your introduction to the audience.'

'I don't understand Mr Allal.'

The cyborg pointed through the window onto the arena below, 'Combat is only a part of the Chihuaz. Without theatre and emotion it's just a couple of grunts beating the shit outta each other.'

'I have a list of music you can download,' stated Arthur.

Allal snapped his fingers at Visi, 'Take it. I want three intros with dance routines per combatant.'

Visi nodded as she linked her tablet to Arthur's wrist tablet, 'Done.'

Geman began to walk out, 'It looks like they want those systems.'

Allal puffed on his lotus cigarette, 'Good job, comeback when the deal's done.'

As Geman left a team of men and women entered.

'Meet your presentation team, the best in the galaxy.'

A dozen strange aliens some bright yellow skinned one an insectiziod, carrying metallic suitcases walked in. A middle aged man with neon blue hair and pale eyes, dressed in a garish yellow suit, sleeves roll up to his elbows strode up to the Tlillan competitors. He inspected each one stopping at Kaeo, 'This is the one!'

Allal grinned at Visi.

Waving his hand he shouted, 'Rapit, come quickly.'

A creature resembling a Saak shuffled up to the man.

'I want her hair simple yet appealing, bring attention to the eyes.'

The insect clicked loudly, it made no sense to Malikah or her comrades.

Waving his hand again he called to his people, 'Cronat!'

A tall man with a pair of tentacles emerging from the top of his shiny suit approached. He looked Kaeo up and down with his long face, 'I have it. She will be the main attraction.'

'What of these two,' inquired the man in a yellow suit.

Cronat gave them a disparaging look, 'Do whatever you want with them.'

Malikah felt quite offended, Arthur relieved.

Kaeo looked around in wonder she wasn't used to such personal attention.

Cronat peered at Kaeo's backside and before anything could be said he gave it an almighty slap. The Tlillan Marshal replied with a left hook to the face dropping Cronat to the floor.

'What the hell are you doing?' bellowed Allal.

'He grabbed my ass,' replied Kaeo pointing to the poor man picking himself up from the floor.

Cronat slowly moved his jaw back into place before speaking, 'I was testing, for firmness.'

'What?' replied an incredulous Kaeo.

'Firmness, I must select the correct fabric to keep it lifted. No-one wants to look at a saggy bottom you know.'

'My butt does not need lifting thank you very much!'

After being helped to his feet Cronat nodded his head, 'Good but you will not be competing in that suit. Does that keep it lifted or …'

'My ass is my business!'

Allal stepped between them, 'When you're down there your ass is the galaxy's business sweet cheeks!'

'Excuse me?'

'Like I said combat is only part of it, you can be the best fighter but without the proper promotion you're just another grunt. You have potential and these people are the best in the business at maximizing that. So Cronat's gonna pick out something to wear and when the Chihuaz begins you're gonna go down there and show it off to Andromeda.'

Furrowing her brow Kaeo replied, 'What's wrong with what I'm wearing?'

'That's a space suit, right?'

'Yes.'

'If punctured does it contract?'

'Yes, of course.'

'No good.'

'Why?'

'Blood, the Chihuaz needs blood and plenty of it.'

'And what does Cronat suggest?'

Cronat gestured to Kaeo, 'Follow me, I have it already.'

The half Thai was led into a nearby room. Whilst changing the rest of the team looked over Malikah and Arthur.

Rapit clicked and clucked until the man in yellow translated, 'I think we can do something with these two.'

Both Arthur and Malikah were sat down before a mirror. Rapit and her fellow insectizoids began to work on their hair, using four arms they worked with speed and perfect precision.

Ten minutes later an argument was in full swing. Cronat and Kaeo were at odds. The exact nature of the disagreement became clear when Kaeo strutted outside.

The Tlillan Marshal was dressed in bright yellow shorts which almost betrayed her cheeks. Boots in the same colour with red lightning bolts. Her top was the same yellow, though it was barely a top, more a rubber sports bra pushing everything up. Arthur laughed at the sight of a furious Kaeo hands on hips standing before Malikah.

Malikah couldn't contain her smile, 'You look stunning.'

'I'm not wearing it!' declared Kaeo.

Malikah cleared her throat, 'Why not?'

'Is that a joke? I look like I should be walking the streets in Vegas!'

Allal raised his arms, 'You look fabulous!'

'Fabulous? I look like a cheap whore!'

The grey haired man took a drag on his smoke, 'It doesn't matter what you think it's what the audience want that matters.'

'I'm not wearing it.'

Allal appealed to Malikah, 'You tell her.'

The Tlillan Queen spoke softly, 'Kaeo ...'

But before she might even begin Kaeo cut her off, 'Forget it.'

Visi approached Kaeo, 'Listen, Al's been doing this for thousands of cycles. If you want to get the best fights and move up the ladder quick you need media attention and ratings. If you want ratings and media attention then you have to do this. There's plenty of great fighters out there, there's more of them than slaves in the Skin Territory. You need to grab that media eye and trust me this is the best way of doing it.'

Kaeo pulled a grim expression, 'How am I supposed to fight in this? It's so damn tight. If I bent over you could probably see what I ate for breakfast!'

Cronat spoke quickly, 'The fabric is skin tight yet it can stretch to 1000 times its size quite comfortably without any loss of integrity. Really you look very attractive. Everyone will be tuning in to view you no matter your opponent.'

'I look like a cheap slut.'

Malikah sighed 'Kaeo, just wear it. No-one back home will see, besides Arthur thinks you're very attractive.'

The Tlillan Marshal stared accusingly at the young man. Arthur returned a weak smile.

Chapter 12

McCann, Clayton, Stewart strolled through a corridor in Naguan 4 accompanied by 5 security staff, making for a lotus factory deep within the station, one of the largest narcotic producers in the system.

Approaching a large metal port they drew their weapons in anticipation for what lay on the other side. Stewart tapped at his wrist tablet, latches released and a whining trance beat assaulted McCann's eardrums. Naked women, working on a factory floor, rolled lotus leaves into long cigar shaped packages. Kishar guarded workers enforcing the absence of sticky fingers.

With such loud music no-one realised the authorities awaited their response.

Stewart pointed his weapon at a plastic block with flashing lights. Squeezing his trigger a burst of tungsten destroyed the music source, everyone looked in their direction.

Stewart shouted at the top of his voice, 'Anyone who doesn't want to die, get on the floor now!'

Workers dropped to the ground, some grabbing their screaming children, day care was not a priority on Naguan 4. Kishar thugs were not so compliant.

As they stepped inside women's screams mixed with infant's wails as tungsten peppered thick narcotic leaves. Clayton aimed across the room firing into the chest of a Kishar warrior expelling its fluid onto the wall behind.

All three Kishar guards were shot to pieces. Their remains blended with torn lotus leaves as salty foam gathering on the banks of Hades wine dark river.

Stewart peered towards a group of naked women huddled beneath a rolling table, 'Alright ladies, you can leave now.'

The women scrambled to their feet scurrying out of the factory wailing infants in arms.

The Scotsman moved to an adjoining port but before he could open the metal hatch McCann grabbed his arm, 'They're waiting for us.'

The Scotsman produced a flash-bang grenade from his munitions belt. Sliding his pistol back into its holster Stewart opened the thick door a crack, pulled the grenade's pin and counted to three before throwing it inside.

Closing the door he waited a few seconds before drawing his weapon and swinging open the port.

Naked women lay upon the floor amidst bundles of wrapped lotus leaves.

Stewart fired a burst of tungsten into a nearby Kishar's head. The man's skull fractured into pieces, exploding upon his comrades as he passed through the gates of Elysium.

The remaining Kishar dropped their firearms, hands held forth in surrender.

The former SBS soldiers entered the factory one by one as blinded and deafened Kishar awaiting destiny.

After his men had entered McCann stated, 'Kill them all.'

Each man fired his weapon sending Kishar thugs to the afterlife to a backdrop of flashing barrels. The women made their way out as McCann's party prepared to deal with the next room.

Whilst his men reloaded an interlocking hatch burst open. On the other side looking straight back at them stood a Mechanised Combat Suit; eight feet tall with two arms and two legs the mighty machine plodded slowly into the same room. The man inhabiting this Mechanised Combat Suit fixed his metal mask upon several intruders, its eyes lit up.

McCann looked down large barrels attached to robotic arms as fire leapt out projecting kinetic rounds into his men. One round from this thing was enough to split a man in two.

By the time they'd escaped into the adjoining room three SBS were dead, blown apart by powerful MCS rounds.

'What the bloody hell is that thing?' asked Stewart gathering his breath.

'I don't know,' replied McCann, 'but I think it's safe to assume it's not friendly.'

The metal port door began to vibrate as the MCS pounded it from inside.

McCann observed the hatch bend and twisted, 'I'd say it's time to get the hell out of Dodge!'

The men exited as the MCS smashed through continuing its quest to extinguish any threat to Rabum's lotus.

Spilling onto the main boulevard McCann prepared his weapon.

Stewart's gaze was pulled between the oncoming monstrosity and their escape route, 'What the fuck are you doing man?'

'If we retreat these guys are gonna be dug in like shit house rats when we come back. We've gotta finish the job, right here, right now.'

'You can't be serious man!'

McCann locked Stewart in a steely gaze, 'As serious as cancer my friend.'

With that the MCS trudged out, shocked citizens fled for cover. McCann's remaining men levelled their pistols and rifles placing the oncoming beast square in their sights. As the Mechanised Combat Suit moved to the boulevard's centre, McCann opened fire.

Tungsten ricocheted off the mighty machine however Clayton's Tlillan Tunnel Sweeper did better. The first sign of weakness revealed itself after Clayton blew pneumatics in its knee joint. A blast of Ion charged plasma exploded on the right knee cap forcing the man inside to steady himself by carefully shifting onto his knees since balancing on one leg whilst firing heavy cannons was not advised.

Whilst lowering itself to the ground McCann and his team unloaded their magazines, shooting all the more furiously.

Clayton fired again hitting the mechanised beast in its face. Its metallic mask was merely scorched yet the plasma discharge blinded its operator.

'In the face!' cried McCann.

The remaining men fired as quickly as possible into the beast's mask, its occupant pointed his arms forward firing blindly in the hope he might force a withdrawal. McCann's men scattered avoiding heavy MCS rounds whistling down the boulevard. Rather than hit his enemies innocent bystanders were torn to pieces … the price of rubber necking a gunfight.

The MCS not only hit rubberneckers but a window on the boulevard was struck, forming an ugly crack. Yet in the fury of battle it went un-noticed, people were concerned with preserving their lives from the immediate threat.

As parties traded fire across the boulevard it became evident the MCS was losing. Eventually it rested on its knees, cracks and scorch marks all over its body. Its ammunition expended the occupant was helpless as Naguan 4's new lawmen approached.

Loading their weapons Stewart, Clayton and McCann approached the person now trapped inside a giant mechanical infantry suit. Upon entering grasp distance the MCS swung a fist which he avoided. Using his mental awareness the Englishman dodged as the Kishar struggled to move his crippled suit.

After a minute of failed attempts the Kishar surrendered. Mechanical lubricant seeped out through cracked pipes, seizing up the beast's joints.

'Clayton, take the mask off.'

The old SBS soldier used the butt of his Tlillan rifle to smash away a burnt and fractured mask. It tumbled off revealing a tattooed face staring into his foes eyes.

Before anything could be said a cracking sound filled their ears. Everyone turned to witness a fault line forming in one of the observation windows. Suddenly the fault expanded, its carbon composite glass gave way, Naguan 4's atmosphere escaped into the void.

McCann held onto the MCS for dear life as two of his men were blown out into space. Clayton and Stewart did likewise. The MCS possessed enough mass to prevent them from being sucked out, as long as they had the strength to hold on.

Bystanders were lifted from their feet and spaced. McCann found it increasingly difficult to draw breath.

Stewart had the MCS between him and the open window. The Scotsman sat up against the machine shouting into his wrist tablet. Within seconds metal bulkheads dropped down covering every observation port on Naguan 4.

As quickly as it had occurred the emergency was over. McCann fell back to the floor as an atmosphere was pumped inside the boulevard, his men slowly returned to their feet gasping for breath.

Stewart looked down at the tattooed warrior trapped in his useless MCS, 'You tell Rabum that there's been a revolution on Naguan 4. There's a new station controller. He's got 24 hours to pull his lotus business out of the Skin Territory. If he doesn't I'm coming for him ... understood?'

The Kishar nodded his head, 'Haa!'

The remaining men departed a scene of carnage leaving the Kishar to his own devices. As they strolled along the boulevard Stewart returned his weapon to its holster, 'I think now would be a good time for a Scotch.'

McCann slipped his ivory handled pulse pistol into its holster, 'I'll have a bottle sent over.'

As the Englishman tapped his wrist tablet a message came in from Jenkins. McCann touched the flashing icon and an old friend's voice bellowed down his earpiece, 'What the bloody hell is going on over there Duncan?'

'The Kishar have got their hands on some Mechanised Combat Suits, we just had a faceoff with one.'

24 hours later the men returned to find several ghost factories where a once thriving lotus industry existed. Where lotus leaf had been rolled and prepared for shipment to the Tamoanchan Territory now stood bare factory floors.

Whilst walking through evacuated sections they came upon a group of Kishar men, Rakbu stood at the fore front.

'Kishar have returned home, what more does Duncan McCann desire?'

McCann, Clayton and Stewart stood across the deserted factory floor opposed to the Kishar men.

'Any lotus produced on your home station is to be handed over to the authorities on Kurgudwardum 57.'

The herald's eyes widened, 'Xch'uup desires our produce also?'

'You'll be paid a fair price for it.'

'Fair? Does Xch'uup know the meaning of this word? Kishar shall suffer because of her fair price!'

McCann's passion began to grow, Rakbu was certain his eyes turned a shade of red for a few moments.

'Suffer? You profited on the misery of others for how many cycles? Protecting those who enslaved children, pushing narcotics to keep them easily manipulated ... now you plead for leniency?'

Rakbu met McCann's sneer with one of his own, 'Kishar have iron heart, we plead to no-one.'

'Good! Then you'll hand over your produce and take whatever you get with a big smile!'

Rakbu lost his temper, pointing his finger, 'One day Duncan McCann shall fall out of Xch'uup's favour! Rakbu shall be there waiting to laugh!'

In a rage McCann drew his pistol and shot the warrior's finger clean off. Rakbu dropped to his knees with a loud shriek, his finger bled out onto the vacant factory floor as lava pouring from a volcano onto grey earth.

'Why don't you just concentrate on keeping in my favour for now?'

The Warrior nodded whilst blubbering onto his bloodied stump.

That evening on Naguan 4 McCann, Clayton and Stewart relaxed in a local bar. Men drank as women danced to soft music.

Jenkins entered the establishment with a raised eyebrow he quickly shuffled passed semi-naked women to rest at McCann's table.

'Something wrong Jenkins?'

The Brigadier looked around briefly, 'If my wife caught me in here I'd be back on the couch! I'm surprised yours doesn't go bananas every time you walk into one of these.'

'One of these?'

'You know what I mean Duncan.'

'I think one wife is too much as it is.'

'Yes I heard about you and your second wife.'

McCann shook his head, 'A series of events led to her becoming my wife. Apparently in the Vega sector if you kill a man you're forced to take on his family.'

Jenkins ordered a drink, 'Well that should discourage anyone from contemplating murder!'

'It's surprisingly effective. I wish I'd been informed beforehand.'

Jenkins took his drink and nodded at Clayton, 'So how's the old bastard been treating you?'

In a rather embarrassed tone the old soldier replied, 'Very well, Brigadier.'

Jenkins eyed Stewart, 'I see you haven't taken to the fad of dressing like the Lone Ranger yet.'

'Pish man! I've got a hat and coat on order!'

'Well Chan and Ilam have thrown themselves into their work here. I suspect she's hoping for some sort of official position alongside your wife.'

McCann replied in a surprised tone, 'I thought you had the commission?'

'Oh come on Duncan, I might get some I.S.A commission but we all know who has the real power here.'

'Well they're quite welcome to it. I've already had a gut full of responsibility from this shit hole.'

At that moment the gentlemen fell silent, a man dressed in nothing but a pair of soiled underpants stepped out from the bar lodgings entrance. Seemingly in a trance the fellow walked across the floor to sit at the bar.

In an American accent he stated, 'Vapostu.'

The bar owner gave a cynical glare, 'Something tells me you can't pay for it.'

'Just get me the fucking drink!'

Stewart had an incredulous expression, 'Wilson? What are you doing man?'

The American glanced toward his commanding officer, 'Can you get me a vapostu ... sir?'

Stewart nodded at the owner who duly produced a vial of the yellow paste. Wilson stared into the drink. McCann got the feeling he was contemplating where he went wrong last night.

'Put some clothes on man!'

'This is it,' replied Wilson.

'Well get cleaned up man, you're beginning to set!'

The other men chuckled at the sight. They'd either seen it before or at least heard a similar story. It even brought a grin to Jenkins' face.

'So did you meet up with around the corner Sally?'

'She took my wallet, identity card and clothes, dirty bitch!'

As the American sipped his whale snot a young lady exited from the establishment lodgings. Approaching her portly employer she protested, 'I am not cleaning that!'

'I pay you 5 guskin a week to clean those rooms.'

The maid pointed at Wilson accusingly, 'He shit all over the bed! I no clean unless you pay another 5 guskin.'

'You're gonna clean that room woman or I'll find another maid!'

She cast her maid's hat onto the bar, 'Fine, clean it yourself!'

The lady stormed out of the bar to patron's cheers, Gergo looked at Wilson for a moment before grabbing her hat and quickly pursuing his maid. The owner returned with a resistant employee, holding her hand out she demanded, 'You pay me first. Then I clean.'

Gergo reluctantly opened the cash register and placed 5 gold coins in her hand, 'There ... satisfied?'

'My pay for this week?'

He reached in again and added another 5 guskin to the pile of coin gathering in her palm, 'Anything else?'

The maid produced a purse and counted the coins out one by one, eyeing each one closely. Once they'd all entered her purse she pulled its strings before returning it to her pocket, 'No, that's fine.'

The maid returned to the lodgings to rapturous applause from locals, its owner looked at Stewart, 'I'll be charging you for this.'

'Fine Gergo, I'll back date Wilsons pay. It might keep him out of trouble for a while and your linen fresh.'

Gergo threw his arms up, 'Fresh? I have to buy new linen every time one of your men gets suckered by a whore!'

Wilson sipped his drink, 'I didn't know the vapostu was drugged!'

Gergo dried glasses with a passion as he stood on the opposite side of the bar, 'You think a whore is going to give you real vapostu? What are you an idiot?'

Ilam entered the drinking establishment, Mesan by her side. She raised an eyebrow at Wilson and his congealing underpants.

The tall Amazon approached her husband, 'It seems this station and its satellites have been secured, well done Duncan.'

McCann gestured towards a vacant seat.

The red headed Valkyrie sat down, 'What is this man doing here?' she inquired in Wilson's direction.

'As we used to say in the Navy, he's had an encounter with around the corner Sally.'

Jenkins chuckled to himself though Ilam was puzzled, 'Who is around the corner Sally?'

'It's a euphemism for a prostitute.'

'I see, and I take it she drugged and robbed him?'

'Well if I were to make a bet I'd say she took him for the ride of his life!' cracked McCann.

The men laughed though Ilam didn't quite get the joke, Wilson definitely didn't see the funny side.

'If a man did not require his penis to form a coherent decision this would easily be avoided.'

McCann nodded in agreement, 'And a lot of women would have to find a real job to pay the bills!'

'Really Duncan, if you hadn't married me you'd probably be sitting next to him now.'

Jenkins thumped his glass on the table, 'Here, here!'

'I don't think so.'

Whilst everyone was trying not to laugh during an awkward moment, Gianna entered Gergo's bar.

Upon observing Wilson alone at the bar the old lady shrieked, 'My God! What do you think you're doing young man?'

Wilson ignored her, taking a slug of his yellow paste.

'I'm talking to you young man, answer me!'

Wilson grumbled under his breath, 'Fuck off!'

'What did you say?'

Wilson sneered at Gianna, 'I said fuck off Grandma!'

Clayton jumped to his feet, 'Watch your bloody mouth!'

Wilson ignored the old soldier, returning to his drink.

Clayton approached Wilson and whispered into his ear, 'I think you should apologise to the lady.'

Wilson finished his drink banging an empty vial on the bar, 'Another!'

Clayton continued, 'I'm gonna give you three seconds to apologise.'

'Go fuck yourself,' retorted Wilson.

From behind, Clayton placed the palm of his hand onto Wilson's forehead and pulled his head backwards. The soiled man lost his balance toppling off his barstool and onto the floor. The old soldier stomped on Wilson's head, his heavy boot busting the man's face.

As the serviceman squirmed in his own blood and diarrhoea Clayton stepped up to Gianna, offering an arm.

The old lady took his arm, 'Where did you find that man? His mother must be ashamed to have brought up such a villain.'

Stewart stood up as Gianna took a seat, 'He'll be cleaning the transport toilets until his contract is up.'

Gianna eyed McCann's drink as she sat down, 'Drinking again Duncan?'

He held the glass nervously, 'We need to talk.'

McCann stood up ushering Ilam and Gianna to a separate table where they delved into conversation.

'You can't do this.'

'Do what?' replied Gianna.

'Turn up here as if you're ...'

'As if I'm what?'

'As if you're my wife.'

'But I am your wife.'

'No you're not!'

Ilam smiled as her husband tried to keep the volume down, 'It was an unfortunate event that led to our ...'

'Marriage?'

'Situation!'

Gianna leaned in, 'Listen to me Duncan our daughter needs Dresk for the Chihuaz ...'

'My daughter,' interjected McCann.

'Our daughter,' retorted Gianna, 'needs Dresk and without her blood link to the House of Ash she cannot compete.'

McCann sneered, 'You mistake me for someone that gives a shit about that barbaric exhibition!'

'No, I understand. However you do care about Malikah's feelings and you shall comply with her wishes.'

McCann made no retort.

'Good, that's what I thought. Therefore you shall honour our marriage whether you approve of Vega law or not.'

McCann snorted in disapproval, 'Vega law! If there were anything moral or inherently decent about it there would be no need to make it law in the first damn place!'

'You only need worry about Vega law until the Chihuaz is over with.'

'And why might that be?'

'Well I didn't know how to break it to you but Ilam suggested we do it together.'

'Break what to me?' inquired McCann in an apprehensive tone.

'I will be annulling our marriage after the Chihuaz.'

McCann began to grin until Ilam shoved her elbow into his ribs. He suddenly snapped out of it, pulling a distinctly forced expression, 'Really?'

'Really.'

'So when does the Chihuaz end?' inquired and excited McCann.

'You're taking this a little too well, Duncan.'

'I don't mean to insult ... I was just startled ... that's all.'

Gianna narrowed her eyes, 'There is no need to be insincere with me but please practice before you do it with others.'

'Sure, whatever you say.'

Gianna rolled her eyes, 'Ilam assures me you will not request a dividend.'

'Dividend?'

'Yes, a marriage dividend. By Vega law each party in the union receives a dividend. Upon a split the party requesting an annulment must pay the other parties dividend. The longer you were married the higher the dividend payment.'

'I don't suppose I'll be able to retire on a few months?' jested McCann.

'Actually I'm a very wealthy woman. You would be a rich man.'

'Keep it. I don't sell my body for money!'

'Don't flatter yourself,' jibed Ilam.

Before the Englishman could reply Gianna continued, 'You shall be afforded a monthly allowance; Forwarded to a Vega banking institution of my choice.'

'An allowance? What do you think I am?'

'If I were to annul this marriage and pay you nothing, why my reputation would be stained throughout the colonies. I'd never get another husband!'

Ilam calmed him down, 'Take the allowance dear. It is the cost of preserving Gianna's reputation.'

McCann took a sip of whisky, 'It could be worse. You might be demanding a second honeymoon!'

Both ladies smiled. Gianna stood up and whispered, 'I think now would be a good time to scout for my next husband,' she fixed her eyes on Clayton making for the seat beside him.

As the determined lady approached Clayton the Commodore spoke to his wife in a hushed tone, 'May the Lord have mercy upon his soul.'

Ilam kissed the side of her husband's head, 'Come, it is time we left for Kurgudwardum … while you can still walk.'

McCann finished his shot of whisky slamming the glass down. He said his farewells, just before exiting he peered towards Clayton. The old soldier drank with Gianna on his arm, Gianna smirked and Clayton raised his glass. McCann turned his gaze to the barkeep, 'Drinks are on me tonight, I'll pick up the tab in the morning.'

Gergo nodded and the men clapped.

The pair stepped over Wilson before exiting onto the boulevard, whilst making their way to an appropriate docking arm Ilam rubbed McCann's shoulders, 'I have a surprise for you upon return to Kurgudwardum.'

McCann peered up at his wife suspiciously.

'Oh don't be so cynical, you will like it.'

On taking a shuttle back and docking with Kurgudwardum 57 Ilam led him to one of the revamped bars, post Anu. McCann recognised the establishment. This was where he'd rescued Edna.

Walking through pink neon lights that surrounded the entrance he quickly had an odd feeling. The sign above read Ninti translating into something like "Lady of Life".

Tables and comfortable chairs now surrounded a dais girls were previously auctioned off on, each with a small catwalk leading away to a backstage area. There was a large area for relaxation near the bar allowing customers to take time out and chat with each other or their girls. Ninti bar stood at the far end where scantily clad girls waited to serve drinks and other delights beside.

McCann stopped in his tracks and scanned the large room. A couple of girls danced but something caused him discomfort.

'What is wrong my dear?'

McCann narrowed his eyelids on the women, 'There's something odd, I'm not certain what it is.'

'Aren't the girls pretty?'

'Without a doubt.'

The Englishman approached the bar and accosted one of the women waiting to serve patrons, 'Excuse me?'

'Yes sir? What is your desire?'

McCann looked the tall red skinned beauty up and down. Stark yellow eyes and blue hair caused her to stand out, 'I'd like to know your name.'

'My name is Hevatsu. May I ask your name?'

McCann eyed her suspiciously, 'My name is Bobble, King of the candy floss men.'

'Greetings Bobble, King of the candy floss men. What is your desire today?'

McCann turned to his wife then back towards Hevatsu, 'Is the owner here?'

The beautiful red and yellow girl smiled, 'Noah is present, do you wish to speak with him?'

McCann held his hands up, 'No, no that's alright. Does Noah have any family staying with him?'

'Yes Noah keeps his mother here ...'

'Excellent, tell Noah that I'd like to have his mother dance naked for me. She may name her price.'

'Would you like anything to drink?'

'No thank you,' replied McCann as he relaxed into a large leather chair.

Ilam shook her head in disappointment. McCann gave a wide grin of satisfaction.

Moments later a ruckus could be heard as Hevatsu exited from behind the bar followed by a furious owner, 'Where is this Bobble! I'll have him dancing off this station to the beat of hot iron!'

Hevatsu stood next to McCann, 'This is Bobble, King of the candy floss men.'

Noah stopped immediately, 'Marshal?'

'Yes?'

'My apologies there must be a malfunction with my server.'

'There is no malfunction. My husband was demonstrating his malevolent sense of humour Mr Noah.'

McCann chuckled, 'So this is where you want me spending my nights out?'

Ilam sat down at the table, 'At least you cannot acquire any disease from these women.'

'Excuse me?'

'Do you not remember what happened with Gianna?'

'No.'

'Exactly, a few drinks and you're anyone's for the taking.'

McCann looked up at Noah, 'Don't you have something better to do?'

The owner quickly shuffled away leaving Hevatsu, 'Would you like a drink?'

'I'll have a glass of mountain water, thank you.'

'We have mountain water from both the Davult and Xanuutic systems.'

McCann waved his hand, 'I don't care.'

'I am sorry you must specify a preference if I am to complete your order.'

'Fine the Davult system.'

'Thank you,' the red beauty fixed her eyes upon Ilam, 'Would you like a drink?'

'I'll have the same, thank you.'

Hevatsu smiled and strolled off to complete her orders. Ilam peered at the android's voluptuous behind as she moved away, dressed in a tight fitting mini-dress.

'Don't tell me you're thinking about it,' snapped McCann.

'I was merely observing how close to reality these creatures are, close enough for most men.'

'Well I rumbled them.'

'You are not most men, Duncan.'

Hevatsu returned carrying their drinks on a tray, 'Here you are. Enjoy your drinks Bobble King of the candy floss men and Ilamachutli.'

Ilam chuckled as she thanked the red android. She then raised her glass, 'Besides I know you prefer a woman with the rear end of a 14 year old boy!'

McCann smiled before sipping his water.

'Aren't these androids considered heresy or something like that?'

'No, these are nothing more than automatons. Hevatsu is not self-aware. Her reasoning abilities are very limited. A synthetic intelligence such as Athena would not have been fooled by your deception, nor would she have requested the owner's wife dance naked for you. All of these androids are built with limited awareness in mind, allowing men to act out whatever depraved desires they wish.'

McCann raised his glass and took a sip, 'Fake whisky, synthetic women and a 3,000 guskin price on my head … what next?'

'You're worth 5,000 now my dear.'

'Marvellous.'

Ilam produced six large folded pieces of paper all closed with a digitally chipped seal.

'What do you have there?'

'Warrants.'

'For what?'

The Amazon slapped six official documents before her husband, 'These men are accused of kidnapping and raping four girls, with intent to commit slavery.'

McCann gathered white sheets of cotton paper with embedded chips, 'What am I supposed to do about it?'

'They have been captured. I need you and Clayton to transport them from Shurruppak 15 to Kurgudwardum.'

'Why?'

'I've been charged with putting this place into order and …'

McCann produced a Ramon Allones along with his guillotine cutter, 'You mean you've taken it upon yourself.'

'Suit yourself Duncan. Nevertheless I intend to clean this territory up. If this is to become our platform for trade with Andromeda, Xch'uup must be the only and absolute authority.'

Hevatsu placed an ashtray onto the table.

'And these men, what'll you do with them.'

'A public trial and execution.'

'So you know they're guilty?'

'The evidence is irrefutable. The station Marshal has footage of them committing kidnap. The women have identified them all and I will sense any innocence if it exists.'

'So you're the judge?'

'And jury.'

'Marvellous.'

Ilam took a sip of spring water, 'These are capital crimes and Xch'uup will not tolerate such immorality in her territory.'

'Have you spoken to Malikah concerning this crackdown?'

'Xch'uup approves. I have been allotted the privilege of full authority over the Skin Territory.'

McCann raised his glass, 'Congratulations.'

Ilam raised her glass, 'Thank you Duncan, I will not pretend my ambitions were not met.'

McCann was about to light his cigar before Ilam reached across the table to prevent him, 'I have something for you … a belated birthday present.'

'Really?'

Ilam produced a small black box and placed it on the table, 'Here, I think you'll like it.'

'You know I hate presents and …'

'Just open it Duncan,' replied Ilam in an irritated tone.

The Commodore put his pistol away and opened the small box. Inside rested a black and gold cigar lighter. One side was smooth black lacquer with "Dunhill" written in gold text. On the other a gold cutter folded out. On the cap the words "Duncan McCann" had been engraved. Upon opening the cap McCann pressed down on the igniter button, sending a windproof butane flame into the air.

The Englishman closed the cap, unfolded its cutter and pulled back the guillotine; Slipping a few millimetres of his Habanos inside then slicing off the cap. Locking the cutter neatly back into place he flipped the cap open again and toasted his cigar.

Drawing on the Ramon Allones he pulled out that signature leather flavoured smoke. It filled his surroundings in a plume even Ilam had come to find the aroma pleasant.

Lighting cigars in this manner assured there would be no transfer of flavours from the flame to smoke.

The Commodore beheld his present with a grin, turning it over in his hand.

'I knew you would like it.'

'I do,' replied the Englishman with a nod of satisfaction.

'I take it I won't have to worry every time you light a cigar now?'

'I'm sorry?'

'Using a pulse pistol to torch a cigar; considering the amount you smoke and drink since arriving in Andromeda, the law of averages does state your brains and skull will part company, sooner or later.'

McCann gave his wife a tender smile, 'Thank you my dear.'

Ilam returned his smile feeling his emotion emanate in her direction.

Hevatsu examined the exchange in bewilderment.

McCann put his glass down slipping the warrants into his inner coat pocket, 'Will tomorrow be satisfactory?'

'It will, make certain they arrive alive at Dock 17.'

McCann relaxed with his Habanos.

'Your mental abilities, I've noticed you employ them since our arrival.'

McCann nodded, 'Yes, more and more I sense the people around me as I walk the boulevard each day.'

'Do you hear their thoughts?'

'Only the strongest feelings passing through their minds at the time.'

'How does it affect you?'

The Englishman took a drag on his cigar, 'I understand why Tlillans have such an arrogant and condescending attitude. Walking through all those non-telepaths it gives you a sense of superiority.'

The red haired Amazon smiled in agreement, 'Your ability shall increase as you employ it.'

'Slowly I become more comfortable with it. Some days I can stretch a little beyond what I thought were my limits ... when does it stop growing?'

'I do not know. I am sure that one day you shall be quite able to immobilise a non-telepath without pushing yourself too hard.'

'I just hope I don't end up relying too much on it. Like Clayton said it's an edge and should be treated as nothing more.'

The Tlillan beauty sipped her drink, 'Now you understand what Malikah went through.'

'What do you mean?'

'When her full abilities manifested, she went from being Tlillan to Mictlantecuhtli. Imagine having gone to sleep as a normal human only to awake the next day with your present mental powers amplified many times.'

The Commodore contemplated what his wife had said. Thick creamy smoke slowly exited his nostrils before he replied, 'It would have sent me insane. All those minds forcing their thoughts into my head at once; without slowly learning control bit by bit, I'd have had a mental breakdown.'

'Your daughter is not the first Mictlantecuhtli but she is the first to survive the madness.'

McCann looked at his wife stoically, 'How did she survive?'

'No-one is sure. Experiments were carried out previously, in secret, to rejuvenate the Tlillan race after the plague. It was not possible to create a resistant male since it had entered our DNA. The virus morphed so often that no male remained fertile long enough to mature.'

'Well I don't understand why you didn't just artificially inseminate ovaries with DNA?'

'Heresy, Duncan. Religious law blocked such a solution, though it was carried out covertly. If a fertile male could be created then Xch'uup would shroud her experiments and our species might be saved,' Ilam let out a sigh, 'they all failed.'

The Station Marshal chuckled.

'I know Duncan, I know, during that time many attempts were made at creating the Mictlantecuhtli. Females were impregnated with stored DNA from the dead races and engineered into one compatible strand.'

'And?'

'Children were born, yet none survived the madness. Subsequent experiments had to be stopped, too many became involved and rumours spread fast on Otoch.'

McCann nodded, 'Nothing travels faster than the speed of light with the possible exception of bad news, which obeys its own special laws?'

'Quite.'

'Is that why you came to Earth, in hope we might provide your saviour?'

'I went through archives at Tititl. Your species was best suited of all genetic experiments carried out before the Gukumatz rebellion and I was right. Malikah was born and survived the madness. She brought us out of the dark and into the light to take the stage once again at its forefront, where we belong.'

'Have you ever asked Malikah how she survived the madness?'

'Yes.'

'And what did she say?'

'She said that to rise as a phoenix one must first be consumed by the fires of chaos.'

Chapter 13

'So what's the job today?'

'I've got some outstanding warrants,' replied McCann as he cut up his toast.

'Someone's been a naughty boy?'

'You could say that, a bit of bother on Shurruppak 15.'

Clayton was about to put a sausage in his mouth when he heard the station name, 'Ain't that the place where the upper crust live?'

'Is it?'

'Yeah, I heard some blokes kidnapped a bunch of girls.'

McCann chewed on his toast as he nodded his head, 'Yup, that's the one.'

'A right bunch of evil bastards they were!'

McCann swallowed his breakfast and sipped on his coffee, 'What happened?'

'Well according to the news they kidnapped the daughters of some rich geezer and held them for ransom … but the bastard wouldn't pay!'

McCann gave an incredulous expression, 'Why not?'

'He said he had 13 daughters and could afford to lose 4 for 100,000 guskin!'

The Commodore placed his coffee cup down, 'Jesus Christ, you've got to be kidding me?'

'I'm serious. This guy owns three fabrication facilities, makes more than 100K in a bloody day selling parts to shipping companies.'

'So what did the kidnappers do?'

'Well they couldn't get their ransom so they planned on selling them to the Kishar but they wouldn't take the girls. In the end they had a deal with some slaver on the edge of Traven space but this bloke wouldn't meet them in the Skin Territory.

Eventually they decided to bugger the money, rape the girls, then when they got bored they'd cut their losses and space them!'

'And then?'

'One of Jenkins' lads got wind of where they were hiding out and paid them a visit. Found them all asleep, they woke up in control collars.'

McCann shook his head, 'It makes you wonder who really deserves to be punished.'

The two friends finished up their meal and strolled the boulevard to Dock 17. Along the way several people bid them good day, glad to see some sort of law present on Kurgudwardum 57.

Turning onto a nearby docking arm the pair entered a small transport craft, 'What would be your destination today gentlemen?' asked the AI.

'Shurruppak 15,' replied McCann.

'Course computed and certified are you prepared to cast off?'

'Affirmative.'

The vessel closed all hatches and broke away. Drifting off into the void the craft manoeuvred to face its destination before firing its ion engines.

'ETA 3 hours and 20 minutes.'

McCann moved into the rear section, 'This might be a good time to check your weapons.'

Clayton followed the Commodore, 'You're not expecting any trouble?'

'I always expect trouble.'

McCann took his silver pulse pistol apart, ensuring its xenon battery pack was fully charged and each magazine fully loaded with tungsten shells.

Clayton went over his Tlillan tunnel sweeper confirming its ion cell was charged and ready to go.

A few hours later and the shuttle docked with Shurruppak 15. Upon exiting onto the docking arm McCann noticed a distinct difference between this place and Kurgudwardum 57. For a start the odour of skanky women and unwashed space traders wasn't there to greet him. This place reminded him more of Lake Geneva than Tombstone.

The law men stood out amongst well to do citizens. Beautiful flora grew all around a well-lit outer avenue. This station contained several boulevards becoming smaller and smaller as they neared its centre.

Each avenue maintained beautiful trees and greenery from all over Andromeda. Only the wealthiest in the Skin Territory could afford to own a dwelling here.

'Bloody hell this is a bit upmarket, isn't it,' noted Clayton as he scanned the street.

McCann pushed up the brim of his bowler, 'Very nice.'

They walked onto one of the streets leading into the station's control centre, two guards in I.S.A uniforms stood outside. Upon looking McCann in the face they parted. Inside a man sat in a chair, feet resting up on his desk, McCann cleared his throat and the fellow awoke. The man in his early thirties jumped up grabbing his pistol to realise he'd fallen asleep on the job.

McCann opened his coat removing his warrants, 'Commodore McCann, I'm here to take these gentlemen back to Kurgudwardum 57.'

'Captain Hopper, sorry about that I was just having a snooze.'

The Englishman raised an eyebrow, 'I'm sorry to have interrupted your beauty sleep, Captain.'

'Yeh well the men you've come for are back in the cells, do you want them now?'

McCann rubbed his stomach, 'I could do with something to eat first, where can I get a good steak around here?'

'There's a nice restaurant on Third Street, North side, you can't miss it. Oh and the family would like you to pay a visit.'

'Family?'

'Yeh the mother wants to thank you.'

The Captain handed him an electronic card with an address on it.

'Thanks, I'll be back in a couple of hours.'

'I'll have them ready for transportation when you get back, Commodore.'

Leaving the control office McCann pressed the screen of his electronic card. A navigation screen guided them onto the second boulevard. Flagging down a small four wheeled taxi he handed the card to its driver. Upon a quick glance the cabby nodded and revved the tiny steam turbine powering his vehicle.

'Hold onto your hats gentlemen!' shouted a light green skinned cabby with odd bone formations growing out of his skull.

McCann grabbed his hat as the turbine began to grind in anguish. A moment later the brakes were off and he was thrown into the back of his seat. The pair of them let go of their hats and grabbed onto the chrome rails between them and the cab's exit (there were no doors on this machine).

As their cab sped around the boulevard McCann and Clayton gave each other worried looks.

'Don't worry ... it's perfectly safe,' laughed the cabby in an Australian tone of voice.

'Are you sure about that?'

'I've been doing this for 20 cycles and no-one has died in my cab ... unless you count that one guy ... but that wasn't like a crash or anything.'

Clayton shouted at a small camera the cabby used to view his customers, 'How the bloody hell did he die then?'

'Arrh, reactor leak.'

'Reactor leak!'

'Yeah, bloody thorium reactor lost integrity, poisoned the poor bloke. Burnt his arsehole to a bloody crisp!' the cabby laughed.

Clayton looked down at the bench he and McCann sat on.

'Don't worry I got it fixed cycles ago. Trust me those reactors are safe as a Telal vagina.'

'So how come it leaked?'

'Bloody industrial sabotage wasn't it. They made a load of those reactors defective so they could push fuel cell cabs instead.'

'Why would they do that?'

'Think about it, thorium reactors only require fuel once every ten cycles, even longer depending on how you drive. Fuel cells need hydrogen regularly and guess who's licensed to sell hydrogen to cabbies?'

McCann held on for his life as they swerved to avoid a tree, 'The manufacturers?'

'Exactly they get the sole license to sell hydrogen on this station and everyone in on the game takes a cut, whilst guys like me stand by and get screwed!'

'Well you're not running a fuel cell.'

The cabby laughed, 'Yeah but after the sabotage and propaganda no-one wants to ride in a thorium powered cab anymore ... I barely scrape a living!'

McCann and Clayton gave each other another worried glance.

'Safe as a Telal vagina mate ... no chance of penetration!'

Once on the East side McCann was brought to a halt before a grand three storey residence. Fine art deco figures adorned its exterior and a few steps led up to a grand set of double doors painted in light pastels.

The pair exited the cab paying the driver his one guskin fee.

'No tip?' bemoaned the strangely formed cabby.

Placing another guskin in his hand the cabby grinned, 'If you need me just call me up on a stand,' he pointed at what looked to be a public telephone booth, 'just ask for Faz.'

'Not a chance in hell mate,' whispered McCann as the cabby zipped away.

The Englishman gave Clayton a relieved expression before knocking. The doors swung open to reveal a butler, 'Good day, I am Manzaz, who may I say is calling?'

'My name is Duncan McCann ...'

'Ah! Mr McCann the lady of the house has been awaiting you, please enter.'

McCann took his hat off as he stepped over the threshold and inside a splendid hallway.

'Do follow me sir,' said Manzaz leading them into a large adjoining room.

Once inside the butler smiled, 'Is there anything I could get for you while you wait for the lady of the house?'

'No thank you I'm quite satisfied.'

The butler eyed Clayton who quickly whipped his bowler off, 'No, I'm fine thanks.'

After Manzaz had left Clayton whispered, 'Bloody hell have you ever seen a place like this before?'

'I think it was called lifestyles of the rich and shameless,' smirked McCann.

Clayton's snigger was quickly cut off when he noticed a beautiful lady dressed in fine lace. Despite her odd skin colour and neck tendrils she was quite attractive.

'Greetings Mr McCann I am Elu Margidda the fifth I'd like to thank you for saving my daughters.'

McCann kissed her gloved fingers, 'Charmed, however I didn't rescue your daughters.'

'Oh I know but if you hadn't come here and cleaned out this pit of evil my daughters would have been sold as slaves before now.'

Clayton was puzzled, 'Why do you live here?'

Elu smiled, 'I'm sorry, you are?'

'Oh Clayton, John Clayton.'

'It is my husband's decision Mr Clayton. I'm afraid I and my daughters must run the risks that come with such great profit.'

A voice could be heard as the front door opened and closed, 'Elu, are you there?'

A short well-dressed man entered the room, 'Who is this in my house?' declared the stunned gentleman.

'This is Duncan McCann and John Clayton. They shall be taking the men who raped your daughters to Kurgudwardum 57 for punishment.'

'Oh, I see. Well where is my clearing house tablet? I must have forgot to bring it in to work.'

'Where it always is … on your bedside table; Mr McCann this is my husband Zag Margidda.'

McCann tipped his brow, 'Nice to meet you Mr Margidda.'

Zag waved his hand in a very rude manner, 'Yes of course.'

The industrialist exited for his upstairs bedroom.

'I must apologise Mr McCann, my husband is a very busy man.'

After a few minutes discussion and an introduction to the girls McCann and Clayton left the house, welcome to return at any time in the future.

The men thanked Elu and went on their way.

'Can you believe that bloke?' stated Clayton.

McCann pulled a tubos from his coat pocket, cut the cap and lit the foot with his Dunhill lighter, 'He's a piece of crap.'

'Where to next?'

'You hungry?'

'Sure.'

'Let's try out that restaurant.'

'Take a cab?'

'I think I'll walk, I need to stretch my legs.'

'Another one of those cab rides and I'll need a change of underwear!'

Upon reaching a plush eatery on Third Street Clayton was a bit nervous, 'You sure we can afford to eat here?'

McCann grinned at his friend before removing his hat and entering an open door. A waiter approached the Englishman and spoke abruptly, 'Excuse me but firearms are not permitted on Shurruppak 15!'

McCann stared him in the face, pulling his coat aside to reveal a Marshal's badge.

The waiter ran a scanner over it and a bleep confirmed it was not counterfeit, 'I'm sorry Mr McCann, please sit down.'

He led them to a large mahogany table in a quiet corner. The establishment had beautiful wooden panelling covering its walls and ceiling. McCann was impressed that such opulence existed in the Skin Territory.

'What would you like to eat today gentlemen?'

Clayton leaned his rifle on a chair, 'Have you got a menu?'

The waiter snickered in a rather condescending fashion, 'Sir, you need only ask and I shall provide. If you are undecided I would be happy to offer a few suggestions.'

McCann handed his bowler hat to the waiter, 'Steak please.'

'What type of steak would you like, sir?'

'The type you eat old boy!' retorted Clayton.

McCann grinned at the quip, 'I'll leave that to your judgement.'

The waiter was rather insulted but marked down their order on his tablet, 'As you wish, and to drink?'

Before Clayton could order a whisky McCann spoke, 'Coffee, two, black no sugar.'

'Very good, your order shall be with you in ten minutes, sir.'

Clayton observed some very upmarket surroundings, 'I bet it'd cost a month's wages to eat in here.'

McCann nodded, 'Yup, one of the benefits of being a Marshal, I get an expense account.'

'What are the others?'

'I can shoot people I don't like.'

'Sounds like you've got it easy!'

'I didn't mention the downside.'

'Which is?'

'My wife knows where I am at every moment.'

Clayton laughed, 'You mean your wives!'

'Don't get me started on that old chap.'

The waiter returned with two tender steaks. He put silver plates before them along with silver cutlery. A second waiter brought their coffee, 'Enjoy your meal gentlemen.'

Clayton looked down, 'This must be bloody expensive, just look at the bleeding cutlery!'

McCann cut into his steak and sure enough the meat almost melted onto his palette. He was unsure as to what animal it was taken from, though it tasted so good he didn't care.

After finishing, their plates were taken away and they chatted over coffee.

As McCann sipped his richly roasted drink three men entered the restaurant and sat at a table near the door. All three were hypnotised by McCann and Clayton. They seemed human on the surface but with minor facial quirks, informing the Commodore they were from Andromeda.

The Englishman eyed the patrons' fine clothes. All wore polite suits and carried pistols attached to gun belts slung around their waists.

Clayton had been chatting to McCann about something or other when he realised his friend was not listening but transfixed by something behind him. Clayton was about to turn around when the Commodore whispered from behind his coffee cup, 'Don't look.'

'What is it?'

'Call the waiter.'

Clayton looked to his left and the nervous waiter shuffled over quickly.

McCann spoke in a low voice, 'I thought firearms weren't permitted on this station?'

'They aren't Marshal but that is Salamu Barag.'

'So?'

'You have never heard of Salamu Barag?'

'Nope.'

'He is the largest android manufacturer in this territory. You are transporting his son to Kurgudwardum 57 today … I think he wishes to speak with you.'

McCann narrowed his eyes, 'Fine.'

The waiter straightened his back nodding in Salamu's direction. The tall man and his guards stood up before moving over to McCann's table as the waiter shuffled away.

The Englishman silently sipped his coffee waiting for Salamu to begin his plea.

'I wish to speak with you Mr McCann.'

The Commodore placed his coffee on the table, 'Go ahead.'

'I believe you are transporting some criminals today, for trial on Kurgudwardum 57?'

'Yup.'

'One of those men is innocent.'

McCann gave the tall Salamu a steely stare, 'Then I'm sure the judge will find him so.'

Salamu pulled his jacket back, exposing a pistol, he plucked a large purse from an inside pocket. The alien, with a bald streak and one oversized ear, dropped a velvet purse dead in front of McCann. The sound of gold coin emanated from inside, there was no doubt a small fortune lay before him.

'Take it Mr McCann.'

'What's that?'

'Guskin, enough for a man to buy five women.'

McCann's gaze moved from the purse back to Salamu, 'Enough to buy a man's freedom?'

'More than enough.'

'Enough to buy justice for a mother and her four girls?'

Salamu took a deep breath through his wide nostrils, 'There is more Mr McCann.'

McCann opened the purse removing ten electrum coins, minted from a mix of gold and silver. After examining the 22 carat coins he slid them back inside.

'You know it's a criminal offence to carry firearms, without a permit from the station Marshal?'

'I always carry pistols in the Skin Territory, everyone does. This rule your wife makes it is not pertinent to our conversation,' scoffed Salamu.

McCann got to his feet as did Clayton, 'I'm afraid I'm going to have to see your permit gentlemen or I'll be forced to confiscate your firearms.'

'You are only new here not all men are equal in this place.'

McCann nodded, 'There's an old saying where I come from, they say God made man …'

Salamu interjected, 'The same is said in Andromeda.'

'But Sam Colt made man equal,' the Englishman pushed his coat back revealing a silver pistol.

A guard to Salamu's right scoffed, 'Pah! Who is this Sam Colt?'

McCann drew his pistol and fired into the alien's chest delivering a soul to Charon's ghastly river bank.

Customers panicked and waiters dove for cover, some fled out the back in terror. The other man went to draw but Clayton pushed the barrel of a Tlillan tunnel sweeper into his face.

'Pull that pistol and they'll be serving your brains at the other end of this restaurant!'

Salamu glanced at his dead guard then addressed his remaining man, 'He is bluffing you.'

'No he isn't,' replied the fellow in a very shaky tone.

The Englishman sneered at Salamu, 'Now undo your belts and let them drop nice and slow like the sun falling at dusk ... we don't want any accidents.'

'Do it,' stated Salamu.

The men slowly undid their belt buckles letting their weapons onto the restaurant floor.

'Good boys. Now I'm willing to forget about this little incident if you just walk out and never mention it again.'

Salamu raised his voice, 'What incident? You killed my son,' pointing at the corpse to his right.

'Attempting to bribe a Marshal's a capital crime.'

'So you gonna kill me, McCann?'

'Not if you just walk away.'

Salamu turned around and walked to the eatery exit. Before stepping out he took one last glance at his dead boy then shouted, 'This is not over Duncan McCann.'

A waiter appeared from underneath a nearby table, 'By the Maker what have you done?'

McCann slid his pistol back in its holster and stated in a stoic voice, 'A man's gotta know his limitations.'

Putting his bowler hat on with a slap the Englishman peered at his waiter 'Thanks for the meal. You guys do a nice steak.'

'What about the guskin?'

'How much ...'

The waiter pointed toward the red purse, 'No, I meant the guskin.'

'Take whatever you need for the steaks, corpse disposal and the cleaners.'

'What of the rest?'

'You married?'

'No sir.'

'Buy yourself a woman.'

Clayton placed his hat on his head and with a cheeky smile retorted, 'Or a man!'

The friends exited the eatery to find a large crowd had gathered outside. A shooting was quite the rare occasion on such a civilized station.

When McCann entered the central control office Hopper was going crazy. The Station Captain leapt in his face, 'What the hell d'you think you're doing!'

'Excuse me?'

'That damn shootout, this is a quiet station McCann!'

'That man was armed and he tried to bribe a Marshal.'

'Do you have any evidence to back that up?'

McCann narrowed his eyes, 'Are you calling me a liar?'

'You don't go shooting innocent citizens without some kind of proof. I don't know how you run Kurgudwardum 57 but this isn't some free for all, we respect law and order!'

'That man was packing a firearm and he tried to bribe me, he was lucky to walk out alive. Besides how do you know what's going on? You're too busy sitting on your fat arse catching up on beauty sleep!'

Hopper picked up the warrants and passed the Englishman a wrist tablet holding control collar codes, 'Here just take them and get the hell off my station McCann.'

The prisoners were brought out of their cells, collars clasped tightly on necks.

'It'll be a pleasure.'

Clayton waved his rifle at the bound felons, 'This way lads, remember now those collars have proximity charges if one of you moves too far from the rest it could get messy.'

McCann strode out of the office six criminals in tow and Clayton guarding their backs. Upon arriving at the docking arm his prisoners were shifted into the shuttle's rear cage; the craft casted off and made home for Kurgudwardum 57. For the first hour all was quiet until a young man spoke, 'Mr McCann?'

The Englishman had been relaxed, hat over his face in the front of the vessel. Upon hearing his name he sat up and peered into the cage.

'Mr McCann?'

'Yup, that's me.'

'Someone in Captain Hopper's office said you shot my brother today.'

'Salamu your father?'

'Yes sir.'

'I shot a man he said was his son.'

'Why?'

'He was armed without a permit and refused to disarm himself.'

'Did he draw on you, sir?'

'Nope.'

'Then why did you shoot him?'

'He refused to obey the law, just as you and your pals back there.'

The young blond haired lad glanced at the sorry crew sharing his cage, 'I guess so.'

McCann gave the boy a hard look. He didn't seem to be a stereotypically bad sort, 'Did you rape those girls?'

The young man moved to the edge of the cage grabbing its bars, 'No, I said we should give them back but the others refused.'

'Why?'

'They said that if they couldn't get a ransom then they might as well get something out of it. You see they worked out that they wouldn't be able to sell the girls to a slaver so there was no point in leaving them, you know virgins selling for more and all.'

A bearded man in the cage laughed, 'He won't listen to you boy they're gonna space us all!'

'Why the hell is a rich kid like you involved with these scum anyway?'

The boy looked down at the cage floor, 'I don't know. Maybe I was bored or thought it'd be fun.'

McCann shook his head, 'I'll talk to the judge.'

The bearded man laughed again, 'You think that crazy woman's gonna let you go boy? She needs blood to keep that station together. She won't let us slip through her fingers.'

The Englishman fixed his eyes on an old bearded villain slumped at the back, 'What do you mean?'

'What do you think fills hotels on that shit hole?'

'Are you telling me executions are a tourist attraction?'

'Spacing's an industry on Kurgudwardum 57. That place would be a ghost station without it! Puh! Who wants to fuck an android?'

Another of the motley band shouted out in response, 'Not enough to keep Kurgudwardum running!'

When the shuttle entered a section on Docking Bay 17 its outer airlock closed. Once the area pressurised McCann led his prisoners out. Doors sectioning off their shuttle opened out into Docking Bay 17.

A crowd had gathered, a few threw vile taunts but there was no trouble. Stopping at the clearing desk McCann placed his warrants on the table. Gianna appeared on the other side. She grabbed the pieces of paper checking each man's identity against the data held inside his warrant's chip.

The old lady from the Vega Territory made stern looks as she went through their details. Upon reaching the young man she pulled an expression of disgust, 'What's a boy like you from a good home doing with these criminals?'

There was no answer.

'Jeda Barag! I'm talking to you young man!'

The blond haired boy glanced up from the floor, 'Yes ma'am?'

'I asked you a question!'

'I don't know ma'am.'

'You don't know why you raped a 10 year old girl?'

'I didn't rape anyone ma'am, that's the honest truth.'

Gianna gave a look of disappointment, 'Only 16 years old and already a kidnapper, rapists and a liar! Your mother must be beside herself!'

'My mother died a couple of years ago. My father had her spaced for his new wife.'

'From a bad crow comes a rotten egg.'

No response was forthcoming, Gianna processed the men and handed back McCann's warrants.

As the Englishman returned his papers to his coat pocket one of the prisoners saw an opportunity. A path out of the docking bay and onto the main boulevard was clear. If he made a break for it there was a chance of escape, certainly better than his chances at trial.

The prisoner made a dash for it, arms tied behind his back. Clayton raised his rifle to take aim.

'Let him go,' stated a calm Marshall.

The mob cheered as the desperado ran down the passage to freedom. The remaining prisoners were curious as to why no-one made efforts to halt him. A screaming mob applauded a man that a moment ago they'd taunted with hatred.

As their desperado ran up a street leading to Kurgudwardum 57 charges embedded in his control collar detonated. His head lifted off as a Saturn V rocket thundering towards the heavens from Cape Canaveral. Blood spewed from a stump remaining on his shoulders, firing up hot blood as his head slammed into Docking Bay 17's high ceiling.

The mob applauded with roars of laughter and fists pumping into the air. To see a villain get his just deserts was what they'd travelled here to witness.

Gianna gave McCann a fed up look, 'And who do you suppose is going to clean that up?'

McCann pulled a Ramon Allones from his coat, after toasting the foot he smiled and moved his prisoners on.

Walking around the dead body McCann became aware of blood dripping onto his hat. Peering upwards the Englishman grinned before carrying on.

Once upon the main boulevard they strolled down towards a street connecting with the inner control office. Along the way they passed Ninti's bar. Several female androids poked their heads outside and waved.

Clayton waved back, 'That Hevatsu has some pretty naughty programs ... so I've been told.'

McCann gave his friend a cynical look.

Once at the central control office McCann placed his warrants on the desk and waited, a few minutes later Ilam appeared.

'Duncan, there are six warrants but only 5 prisoners.'

'Unfortunately he had no head for heights,' replied her husband in a coy tone.

Ilam tossed one of the warrants into an automated trash bin, 'Harry, take these prisoners to their cells.'

A young lad bearing a Tlillan rifle entered the room. After receiving the collar codes from McCann he urged the criminals to their cells.

Ilam's hands rested on her hips, 'Why didn't you immobilise the man?'

'I couldn't let Clayton shoot there were too many people.'

'People?'

'Yes, waiting for your circus show.'

Ilam moved over to a station monitoring prison cells. Five men were placed onto beds in tiny individual rooms. Once the door closed a blue light filled the area and the prisoners fell unconscious, ready to be awoken for trial.

'Is there a problem Duncan?'

'You've turned the execution of men into a blood sport.'

'My question remains, what is your problem?'

'I find it immoral.'

Ilam turned to face her husband, 'Immoral? These men kidnapped and raped young girls.'

'It doesn't justify turning their deaths into a lewd circus show.'

'Punishment is harsh and it may be undertaken in a distasteful manner yet these people must understand Xch'uup does not tolerate such offences.'

McCann pulled a Habanos from his mouth and blew some smoke across the room, 'And if you happen to make a profit I suppose that's a bonus?'

Ilam pulled that Tlillan condescending sneer, 'Someone has to pay for your expense account Duncan.'

The Commodore took another toke of his Cuban cigar, 'What about that boy? He's only 16 years old.'

'If he's old enough to commit kidnap and rape ... then he's old enough to space!'

'And who makes that decision? You? God?'

A tiny red pigment appeared in Ilam's eyes, 'Your daughter. Either deal with this conflict or resign your badge but do not place responsibility upon my shoulders for your moral outrage!'

McCann calmed down, 'Look the boy didn't rape those girls.'

'Really? Did he tell you that?'

'Yes and I believe him.'

'And what reason would he have to lie?'

The Englishman pointed at the boy laying in suspended animation, 'You can scan him yourself.'

Ilam nodded, 'I shall, at trial, and even if it is so he shall still be spaced.'

'Why?'

'Kidnap is a capital crime in the Skin Territory as is conspiracy to enslave.'

McCann shook his head and made for the exit.

'Where are you going Duncan?' she called in a concerned tone.

'For a drink ... unless Xch'uup has made that a hanging offense?'

The tall Amazon gave no reply since noticing a direct correlation between the amount she antagonized her husband and the size of his bar tab the next day.

Chapter 14

The day of the Chihuaz had arrived. Malikah looked down upon the arena floor as Allal introduced this cycle's first event not only to a packed arena but the eyes of Andromeda.

Soft multi-coloured laser beams strobed in low light conditions whilst women danced to an operatic melody. Allal marched out to an adoring crowd, reciprocating his attentions with cheers. Acolytes rose to their feet in praise of their ringmaster. As his opening tune faded Allal raised his arms, 'Welcome to the Chihuaz!'

Roars of celebration tore across the gargantuan arena, Allal lapped it up, 'And do we have an event for you this cycle!'

Pointing towards a high chair occupied by the current champion, 'Will the Telal keep their throne by the end of this Chihuaz?'

Mammi's representative displayed a blank expression, ignoring his antics.

Kaeo sat before a mirror as Rapit fixed her hair creating two large buns on each side of the Amazon's head.

Visi urged Rapit on, 'She'll be called out in a moment can't you hurry up?'

Rapit replied with clicks and snaps calming the young lady.

On the arena floor Al cried out to his adoring audience, 'The first contest will be over a group of disputed systems on the border of Traven and Vega space!'

The applause rallied for battle regarding this long and bitter dispute.

'First, from the Traven Territory, the beast you all know and love,' Al gestured with an open arm to one end of the arena.

From beneath the battleground a transparent cylinder rose. Inside stood a smooth skinned animal about the size of a mountain gorilla. From its thick forearms sharp bone protruded out. The creature stood on two legs yet ambled much as a gorilla, using both feet and knuckles.

A strange electronic beat played as dancers flipped and turned around the ring. Audience members clapped to the beat whilst the cylinder ascended placing the beast at one end on a small plinth.

Visi rustled Kaeo out of her seat as an alert sounded in their dressing room, 'You're on in a minute!'

Malikah turned to her Marshal, 'We don't want to be late for those young men now, do we.'

'I feel like an idiot with two bagels stuck to the side of my head!'

'You look quite fetching Kaeo.'

Visi cut in pushing the Tlillan contestant into a transparent cylinder, dressed in nothing but her boots, shorts and a skimpy top. The cylinder closed to be propelled away below the arena.

Music ended giving Al his cue to introduce Kaeo, 'And now, representing the Vega Territory, Kaeo!'

A round of boos went out as Kaeo ascended through the arena floor onto her plinth. Music taken from Arthur's library played; she ascended to the song "Cherub Rock" filling the ears of all those present. Women danced around the edge of the ring pirouetting and flipping to its rock beat.

Judging by the jeers it became obvious who was favoured to win. Looking up Kaeo noticed electronic sign boards levitating high around the stadium some offering odds on combatants others selling strange consumer products, according to the bookies she was set to lose. Music vibrated and Allal's congregation blurted venom, raising Kaeo's heartbeat and injecting her bloodstream with a dose of adrenalin. On sniffing the air it carried an intoxicating scent, she could taste the expectations of trillions of Andromedans. Hybris rose from the floor and through the audience her outrage and wanton lust for violence fed upon itself. Rather than walk the path of justice Andromeda fostered violence and Kaeo an actor in Hybris' furious play would satisfy that base hunger.

As the rock song finished Al raised his arms, 'Now you know the rules ... THERE ARE NO RULES!'

The grey haired presenter pointed to a red pad behind each plinth, 'But if you can't take anymore hit the pad and maybe you'll escape with your life!'

Approaching the beast representing the Traven territory Al produced a tablet. The creature placed a finger upon it. A loud bleep filled the arena confirming his genetic integrity. The crowd stood to attention stomping their feet in appreciation.

Al then walked over to Kaeo's plinth offering her his tablet. Kaeo placed her thumb upon its shiny black surface her heart skipped a beat until a reassuring sound resonated throughout Andromeda to the contempt of Al's acolytes.

Addressing his adoring mob Al asked, 'ARE WE READY?'

Screams carrying the blood lust of hundreds of thousands answered, the old cyborg glanced at Mammi's representative. The Telal gave him a nod. Al exited the arena, 'FIGHT!'

The massive primate ambled down from its plinth. Kaeo stepped off strolling to the arena centre. The Tlillan Valkyrie recognised this animal as being far slower than her. As it approached, the crowd stomped louder and louder until they entered striking distance.

The Traven gladiator made its first large swipe. She ducked below its arm squatting to the animal's side. The Tlillan Marshal took her first opportunity and leapt onto the beasts shoulders; using its knee as a launching pad she grasped its head one hand on the crown the other its chin. In a single sweeping move her opponent's neck was broken. As it collapsed to the floor in a lifeless bundle Kaeo stepped off.

The howling mob fell silent. This beast had brought down many a great warrior … only to be defeated by a first time challenger? It was too much to believe.

Kaeo made for her plinth with an insolent swagger striking its red pad with her boot. The cylinder slid down to cover the half Tlillan before rocketing back to her dressing room.

Al walked out to general discontent, 'Well wasn't that something? I'd bet that's the fastest opening match in centuries!'

As they dragged the Traven creature's body away to be disposed of Kaeo's intro music played, failing to drown out Andromeda's displeasure.

Upon returning to the dressing room Visi waited, hands on hips, her gaze fixed upon Kaeo as the Tlillan exited her cylinder, 'Al's gonna be pissed.'

'I won didn't I?'

Visi shook her head, 'You'll see.'

The Chihuaz paused between events and in the meantime Al and Geman could be heard approaching the Tlillan dressing room.

Malikah raised an eyebrow at Kaeo.

A cylinder arrived and a furious Al stepped off, Geman close behind.

'We're up by 2 points it's not all bad.'

Al lit up lotus cigarette, '2 points? That should have been 4 points … minimum!'

The old presenter peered towards Kaeo, adorned in her skimpy costume, 'Why did you do that?'

'Do what?'

'YOUR INTRO LASTED LONGER THAN THE MATCH!'

'I don't understand.'

Al stood directly before Kaeo blowing smoke into her face, 'I have contracts, endorsements, this is serious money. The longer you fight the more I make, the more air time you get and we're all happy. No-one's gonna watch a fight if it takes just 10 seconds, they want to see blood!'

Kaeo didn't reply.

Al rubbed his head for a moment as he paced the room, 'What will it take to get a good fight out of you?'

The Grand Marshal of Tlillan peered down at her slutty attire.

'Fine we can come to a compromise but you're gonna have to show something. Remember this is the Chihuaz not kids hour, you understand?'

Kaeo nodded before disappearing into her changing room.

'It seems she got her way,' laughed Malikah.

Visi stepped forward, 'Well the House of Ash is pleased. The Vega Territory has those mining systems.'

A few minutes later and Kaeo re-appeared dressed in a PVC waistcoat sporting a large flared collar standing up past her ears. Instead of the yellow shorts she wore a pair of black and red trousers made of the same material as her waistcoat. Her boots were below knee length and followed suit with the rest of her outfit.

Rapit pushed Kaeo into a seat unravelling her hair. The insectiziod whipped up a ponytail, sprouting up and over her waistcoat collar.

Al had been glancing at the parts most men would be eyeing during the fight to come, 'That's passable now you make certain the next match has some excitement to it.'

Kaeo nodded as she stared into the mirror.

Allal whispered in her ear, 'I've got contracts to fulfil … sweet cheeks.'

The cybernetic presenter stood erect and gestured towards Geman, 'Let's get ready … Kaeo?'

'What?'

'In an hour you're going up against the witch doctor, good luck,' with that they entered the transparent elevator to be fired back down towards the Chihuaz.

'When is it my turn?' inquired Arthur.

The sable Queen of Tlillan smiled, 'Be calm young man, all in good time.'

Kaeo stood up. As she did Visi presented her sword and belt.

'I'm allowed my sword?'

'You'll need it if he doesn't knock you stone dead with a boning.'

Kaeo tied the belt around her waist, neutronium sabre hanging from her side.

Arthur and Malikah watched the floor below as Kaeo entered the transport and her opponent rose through the ground.

Dressed in animal skins with a skull mask the witch doctor danced around the arena. The crowd's response was mixed. Some shouted praise, others showed disdain as he bounced with girls to deep tribal drums, a single search light fell upon the witch doctor leaping fervently to his music. His tune filled the Chihuaz with hypnotic tension.

'The Witch Doctor, they love to hate him,' noted Visi.

Malikah kept her eyes fixed on the scene below, 'Why do they hate Kaeo?'

'They don't hate her she's a first time challenger it's to be expected.'

Kaeo appeared from beneath the Chihuaz to the sound of Motorhead playing "The Ace of Spades". Tapping her leg to the beat of the music she could just make out boos and jeers over Lemmy's voice.

After the rock melody had finished Al moved to the centre, 'Alright she's back again but this time it's for the Skin Territory,' pointing at the Witch Doctor the presenter shouted, 'this battle will be for several of the best space stations in the system.'

Allal walked up to the Witch Doctor, 'The Witch Doctor carries his magic bone; used not only for stopping enemies hearts but also a handy cutting tool!'

The demonic priest held aloft what looked to be a dinosaur finger sporting a long razor sharp nail and the crowd went wild.

'On my left is Kaeo fighting to retain the Skin Territories assets. After defeating the Traven representative in record time she's brought something to meet him.'

Kaeo unsheathed her weapon pointing its tip at the Witch Doctor.

'Anyone who's had enough can pad out, that's if you can make it to the pad before your enemy finishes you!'

The crowd howled in ecstasy again.

Al tested each contestant for genetic manipulation … both genetic masks passed.

'Are we ready?' Al looked up at the Telal, 'FIGHT!'

Both parties descended from their plinth. The Witch Doctor danced as a man possessed beating his feet on the ground before stopping and pointing his bone at Kaeo.

The short warrior observed the crowd hold their breath in anticipation yet nothing occurred. Striding forwards Kaeo slapped his weapon away with her blade.

Once the Witch Doctor was unarmed she punched him square on his skull mask with her sabre guard. Before he might gather himself Kaeo kicked him as hard as she could in the nuts. The Witch Doctor fell to his knees, rolling onto his back.

Allal whispered to himself, 'Drag it out sweet cheeks!'

Kaeo left her opponent, squirming on his back, to approach the crowd. Whilst playing to the mob the Witch Doctor hauled himself up and made a dash for Kaeo's back. The short warrior sensed his assault, spinning around at the last moment to deliver a side kick cracking his ribs, the ghoulish priest crashed back to the ground.

Strolling to the other side of the arena Kaeo held her arms aloft; As Achilles raising his arms above the body of Hector, revelling in glory. So did the short Valkyrie as if to taunt Priam over the walls of Troy astride his son's corpse. Although she wore no armour Kaeo was resplendent in her attire as citizens on the walls of Troy did state 'Look at her she did battle with honour yet her foe would rather use magic than show courage!'

Malikah peered from her window as Thetis observing the battle beneath, nodding her divine brow in respect, their destiny clear. Mammi sat on high as Priam upon the walls of Ilium his best warriors cowering in fear of the mighty Achilles, a force no mortal could hope to defeat. Al was lost in his tablet as climbing viewing figures updated every second.

The Witch Doctor got back to his feet to charge in a drunken haze. Kaeo dodged his flailing attacks until the crowd became impatient, they wanted to see blood and see it now.

As the audience grew upset the short warrior took hold of her foe by the scruff of his neck; pushing her boot into his knee joint she forced the Witch Doctor onto the dirt floor.

Raising her weapon Kaeo pointed it at the mob now bashing their feet in a riot of base passion. Immediately the neutronium sword swooped down severing her opponent's head from its neck.

Again the audience roared in delight, blood spurting from the Witch Doctor's bloody stump spattering the victor. Holding his head outstretched Kaeo removed its mask for all Andromeda to witness, only to reveal a man you might see every day in the Skin Territory. His dull eyes peered upwards an expression of terror plastered upon his tormented face.

Kaeo tossed the decapitated head into the crowd causing a scramble amid the Witch Doctor's remnants, as hungry dogs over a piece of meat.

Al leapt into the arena accosting the short warrior before she might leave, 'You cut him down to size!'

A ripple of laughter travelled around the Chihuaz.

'So tell us, where did you learn to fight like that?'

Kaeo raised her sabre toward the Tzitzimeh, 'Otoch.'

'Well you go and get yourself cleaned up … GIVE A BIG HAND FOR KAEO!'

The audience stomped their feet in applause as Kaeo returned to her dressing room.

Back in the changing rooms Kaeo removed her blood stained costume slipping into a ribbed space suit.

Allal and Geman barged in with great clamour. The Chihuaz presenter placed a big kiss on Kaeo's cheek, 'We're up 7 points!'

As Doctor Weissmuller was looking Kaeo over for any injuries he questioned Al, '7 points?'

'7 billion people switched on during that battle!'

Visi grabbed Al's attention, 'Hey Al it's on the news, look.'

A wall monitor flickered into life. Two aliens presented the Territory news, 'Today in the Chihuaz the Tlillans made their mark.'

A camera focused on the second presenter with an inset image of Kaeo fighting the Witch Doctor, 'Kaeo defeated not only the Traven Territory's representative in record time but the Witch Doctor was … cut down to size.'

An image of Kaeo decapitating the Witch Doctor filled their screen. The crowd roared as she sliced his head off exposing his face to a rabid audience.

'Are these challengers capable of releasing Mammi's grip on the Chihuaz and the Tamoanchan Territory?'

The other presenter answered, 'Some of the largest gambling houses in the galaxy certainly think so, the odds for a Tlillan victory have been soaring since the Witch Doctor lost his head!'

An image of a rather shady character in dark glasses filled the screen. It spoke in an odd language though all media devices translated for their audience, 'Sure odds closing yet team event, must wait, see other contestants ... always play best fighter first.'

The reporter spoke into her mic, 'So what does your Nabu say about the Chihuaz this year?'

The Bookie shook his head, 'No Nabu.'

'But many do in your profession.'

'Use eyes and experience. Girl fight, easily defeat Witch Doctor but I know trail out. Crowd force beheading; Girl clever, we see how team mates perform.'

'Well there you go. It seems we're waiting on her team mates before a definite decision is made.'

The image disappeared returning to the news studio, 'Very interesting, so Kerri where's your money at the moment?'

A female presenter grinned, 'My Nabu saw a Lassu victory this cycle.'

'According to rumours a Kishar Nabu predicts these strangers will steamroll the Chihuaz.'

The female presenter replied, 'It seems everyone's betting on the Chihuaz this cycle.'

'If the Witch Doctor were alive today I think he'd of said "Stuff happens", unfortunately that's exactly what happened!'

Allal turned the news off, staring Kaeo in the eyes he stated, 'You've started a revolution young lady!'

'Who is this Lassu she was talking about?'

Geman stepped forward passing his tablet to Kaeo, 'Arthur will be up against him next.'

Kaeo took Geman's tablet to examine a creature resembling a grizzly bear. It was dark and hairy, legs longer than a bear; its face being less of a snout, more a gapping orifice with rows of jutting teeth all the way down its neck.

Kaeo passed the tablet to Arthur, 'Good luck!'

Arthur examined the beast and its razor sharp claws, 'I will have a weapon, won't I?'

'Only what the arena provides.'

'No weapon? How in God's name will I beat that thing?'

Geman waved his hands, 'I'm sorry, I can't give you any assistance when it comes to matches.'

Arthur glanced at Al for help only to meet a similar expression to that of Geman and Visi. The lad peered at the image of the beast he was set to face. It was perhaps the most terrifying prospect he'd confronted in his life.

As he examined every morsel of information the room began to change colour. Out of the corner of his eye a soft golden glow filled one of the preparation areas. Looking up the young man locked eyes with a smiling Athene.

'I'll just go and change,' stated Arthur as he walked inside a dressing room and closed its door.

Once inside he addressed the Goddess of the flashing eyes, 'How did you get here?'

Athene smiled, 'Distance is no barrier for a being of pure energy. Now tell me, why did you bring me here?'

'Bring you here? I made no such request.'

'But you did, I felt great fear and doubt within your heart. Why are you afraid, Arthur?'

'This,' declared Arthur pushing the tablet in Athene's face.

The smiling Goddess picked the tablet out of his grip and viewed it herself before placing it on a nearby table, 'You fear that?'

'Yes I do.'

'Why?'

'Can you not see? It's twice my size with claws and rows of teeth! How in the heavens could I defeat it?'

'You won the Pankration tournament did you not?'

'I don't understand.'

'Those men, many were larger than you and more experienced ... yet you defeated them all.'

Arthur snorted in disbelief, 'That was a Pankration tournament. This is a fight to the death against a genetically modified killing machine!'

Athene's smiling demeanour gave way to one of utter seriousness, 'Listen to yourself, your greatest opponent is not that creature it is your own doubt! You've done half its work already. Convincing yourself there is no hope of victory,' Athene snapped, 'I say you shall take victory with ease ... do you believe me?'

Arthur could not look his golden Goddess in the eyes. He glanced at the floor dejectedly.

'Look at me boy!'

Arthur elevated his gaze.

'Do you believe me?'

'I suppose so.'

'Suppose? What kind of talk is that from a warrior? You look and sound like a frightened woman!'

'Then tell me how I will win!' shouted Arthur.

A smile returned to Athene's lips, 'So, fear has not banished all passion. Perhaps if he can raise his voice to Athene he might bring himself to put up a fight against this terrifying beast?'

'Now you mock me.'

Athene strolled around the room as she spoke to herself, 'I wonder what Kaeo would think of her great Achilles? Shrinking in the face of combat, cowering as a girl from ghosts in the night; perhaps she was right? Perhaps he is no Achilles? Perhaps he is a Paris? Too busy with poetry and love to concern himself with battle and the Kleos that goes with it.'

Arthur looked up at the ceiling, 'You cannot anger me.'

'I will not need to. When Kaeo witnesses your failure she shall reject you totally.'

Arthur's eyes darted to meet Athene's, 'What do you mean?'

'Oh Arthur, do you think I'm unaware of your love for her?'

'What of it?'

'Show fear when facing this beast and Kaeo shall never accept you. Show courage and her thoughts may be different.'

'What do you mean?'

'To gain Kaeo's love you must gain her respect, she does not respect cowards.'

'This beast what weakness may I exploit?'

Athene grinned, 'It is big … but slow. You may easily flank it and strike its spine if you use the whole arena.'

'Its spine is weak?'

'Above the hips its fifth vertebrae is slightly gelatinous. Strike hard and you will collapse the creature's entire spinal column.'

Athene passed the tablet back to Arthur.

The young man examined its data silently before nodding his head, 'You have saved my life, thank you.'

Athene shook her head, 'I did nothing but chase away fear. Remember Arthur there is nothing in this Chihuaz able to defeat you, other than yourself.'

With that Athene dissipated into the air leaving the lad as quickly as she had appeared. Where the goddess went and if she was still watching who knew, yet Arthur felt her presence in Andromeda.

Outside the dressing room Al asked Malikah, 'Who the hell is he talking to in there?'

The sable Queen shook her head, 'I have no idea.'

'I guess I'd be losing it if I were up against the Lassu.'

Kaeo chuckled while Rapit undid her hair, 'Maybe he'll back out.'

Malikah gave the first of Teteo a black stare, 'He's young, give him some ground.'

'Why? I didn't get any breaks when I was his age!'

'You still won't forgive him, will you?'

Kaeo's head jerked causing the hair stylist to slip at her work.

'How long will you hold it against him, Kaeo?'

The short Marshal gazed to the mirror, 'I don't know what you're talking about.'

'You're not angry because he let you win. It's why he let you win … isn't it?'

Kaeo examined her hair in the mirror as Rapit rearranged it, 'Now you're talking crap.'

'Xch'uup is talking crap?'

'Yes, even Xch'uup can talk crap!'

'You're angry because Arthur …'

'Enough!'

'But we all know the truth.'

'Fine then just keep the truth to yourself, could you do that for me?'

Before Malikah could answer Arthur walked out of his dressing room in a ridiculous spandex costume. Sandra began to giggle, Weissmuller pitied him.

Al stood up, 'Great, see you on the floor boy … and good luck!'

Geman followed Allal out as the cyborg went to open the next match.

'How are you feeling?' inquired Malikah.

'I'm a little nervous.'

'Don't worry I'm certain you will win.'

'Thank you, I'll do my best.'

The lights went up on the floor below as Allal entered the arena to cheers and howls. Holding his arms aloft the presenter indulged in his flock's adoration.

People across Andromeda were switching on to watch the show, pushing ratings to new heights.

'Welcome to the Chihuaz!' shouted Al at the top of his voice to roars from the crowd.

'Tell me, who do you all love?'

'We love Allal!' screamed a frantic audience.

Again the cyborg lifted his arms absorbing adulation as a dry sponge in water.

Malikah looked down from on high observing events unfold, 'This whole Chihuaz is quite obscene.'

Visi agreed, 'That's what people want, if no-one wanted to watch it Al would be presenting cockroach races. Besides it beats getting wiped out in stupid wars over politics, resources or religion. This way the matter is resolved and only one person has to die.'

'I don't think those people care. They are only present to witness slaughter.'

As the Lassu appeared in its cylinder strange music from its world played. Bells rang out in a tune Malikah found quite offensive to her ears. Women danced around the arena in tight costumes as the mighty beast rose onto its plinth to wait for the intro to finish.

Once its tune faded Al walked to the centre of the arena, 'Fighting for the Lassu, a people you all know and love here at the Chihuaz, Danult!'

Applause travelled around the arena as the audience stomped in approval.

'Facing the Lassu is this cycle's dark horse!'

As Arthur rose up from below the arena he recognised one of his tunes playing. The lad tapped his thigh to the beat as women danced and flipped to subdued lights. Once his cylinder came to a stop its sides fell away to leave Arthur standing on a plinth, red pad to his rear.

Music played out and Al addressed the crowd, 'Representing the Skin Territory, Arthur!'

The young man was surprised by several cheers. He was expecting boos but Kaeo had warmed the people to his cause.

Al spoke to the Lassu creature which replied with a loud growl. The lad could make no sense of it and the presenter moved on to Arthur.

Pushing a microphone into the lads face he asked, 'So Arthur that's quite a terrifying beast any hints on how you plan on taking it down?'

'As the Witch Doctor might have said … stuff happens.'

The throng rose up and cheered.

Al faced his audience and shouted, 'Well did you hear that?'

The cybernetic presenter smiled as his crowd's fervour intensified. Certifying contestants' genetic integrity or the integrity of their masks, whichever way you look at it, Al nurtured the frenzy. After a short time milking the audience he peered up to the presiding Telal. Upon receiving a nod of approval Al marched back to his ringside seat, 'FIGHT!'

The mighty bear stepped down with a roar, garnering approval from its supporters. The Lassu had a reputation of producing a blood soaked arena and violent slaughter was expected, especially in the opening rounds.

Arthur stepped down looking quite unsubstantial in comparison. What eluded the crowd and Lassu was the physical power of a half Tlillan. Kaeo offered a glimpse of what one of these creatures were capable. However the audience was still in the dark as to these new comers' full proficiencies.

Arthur attempted to circle the beast yet it turned on its spot to face him. The Lassu was obsessed with defending its one vulnerability.

Since the grizzly bear from Andromeda blocked any flanking manoeuvre Arthur decided to take it head on. Using skills taught by Clayton he took the savage beast by surprise.

Lunging in Arthur grabbed the animal taking it by the hips in a reverse hold. The crowd gasped in shock as they awaited an inevitable takedown … but it never came … at least not from the Lassu.

Arthur lifted a seven foot killing machine in one heave, twisting it by the hips into an inverted position. The Lassu was racked by a combination of panic and terror, the sons of Ares seized absolute control of its mind and body. Al's audience began to shriek. As Malikah and Kaeo watched on they listened intently, from the stadium's depths cheers for Arthur could be heard. Quickly those cheers grew louder and louder as it became obvious the giant grizzly was not going to win this event.

'Do you hear that? They encourage Arthur!' noted Malikah in a gay tone.

Kaeo narrowed her eyes as she gazed on in disbelief, 'What the hell is he doing down there?'

'Winning my dear, winning.'

The young lad held his opponent above the ground its head pointing toward a dusty floor. Al's throng howled for murder, demanding he finish the Lassu with each thump of their feet. Arthur complied with all his might by ramming its head into the arena floor; an impact so great as to send a shockwave down the Lassu's spine, squashing its fifth vertebrae … snapping the spinal cord.

The gladiator let out a chilling cry of pain, curling into a trembling ball.

'That was quite impressive,' said the Tlillan Queen in her Marshal's direction.

Kaeo was transfixed, 'Not bad.'

Malikah chuckled.

'What?'

'Not bad? He just broke a Titan's back!'

'I'd hardly call that thing a Titan.'

'Will you never allow him into your heart?'

Kaeo's red eyes glared at her Xch'uup, 'Why do you feel the need to humiliate me?'

'You humiliate Arthur at each and every opportunity.'

Kaeo looked away, staring onto the Chihuaz floor below.

'Show Arthur his due respect when he returns, he would do no less for you.'

In the arena below a paraplegic Lassu wailed in pain. Arthur played to the crowd, jogging around the arena to touch hands with its bloodthirsty horde. They stretched out for the chance to brush fingers with a hero, in a scene as repulsive as it was necessary. Viewing figures skyrocketed as people tuned in to watch the demise of a genetically engineered warrior. This is what brought in the big bucks. Corporations fought tooth and nail over rights to place product promotions onto monitors of Trillions at this time. CEOs across Andromeda were fully aware that everyone would be watching at this very moment.

Eventually the throng demanded Arthur finish the Lassu, again the lad played it up. He stood over the tormented beast hand around his ear feigning ignorance concerning their murderous demands.

An orifice in the floor opened to reveal a weapon resembling a blunted pickaxe. He picked it up to a riotous stampede echoing throughout the Chihuaz. The lad continued to feign ignorance to the crowds demands.

People filling the stadium screamed louder and louder as they played along with his game. Eventually Arthur felt he'd milked it for all it was worth, anymore and they might become hostile.

He pointed at the tortured creature and made a puzzled gesture towards the audience. They roared back confirming their victim's identity. Then in one fast ruthless move he brought his weapon down nailing the grizzly's neck to the arena with a single dynamic pickaxe thrust, snapping it like a piece of dry wood.

The beast fell silent its body twitching to the last chords of life's melody, an animated crowd cried out for their new hero.

Music blared to strobing laser beams and Allal launched himself into the arena.

'By the Gods, you've been doing some serious weight training!'

As beautiful women in sheer outfits danced Arthur replied, 'Yes … but it can leave you with the most awful pain in the neck,' smirking towards his opponent's corpse.

'Indeed! Tell us what do you call that style of fighting?'

'Pankration, an ancient martial art from one of my home worlds.'

'One? You have more than one home world, how's that?'

'It's a long story Al, maybe after we've won the Chihuaz I'll tell you?'

The audience roared with approval.

Al grinned, 'Well it seems I have no choice now! Good luck in the coming rotations young man!'

The crowd thundered and Arthur waved retreating to his plinth; Returning to his dressing room as Ares would Olympus after a great battle upon the plains of Troy. Spattered in gore, a combination of dirt and blood, the ruin of war and bane of mothers entered his celestial elevator. Allal was in tears of joy as Geman echoed rising viewing figures into his earpiece.

Chapter 15

A trial was in session in a fitted court room on Boulevard 3 East. McCann sat at the back as the first of the accused was led to the dock standing beside the Judge's bench.

Ilam presided dressed in a white Tlillan jacket. Once the accused settled she banged her gavel, 'Let the defence make their case.'

A short woman shuffled her tablets as she approached the bench whilst reading off a screen, 'According to regulation 387 amendment F of the Kishar – Trilk accord …'

The prosecution shouted, 'Objection.'

Ilam nodded her brow, 'Sustained, those accords are no longer in effect.'

The defence put her tablet aside, 'Then my client throws himself upon the court and does plead for mercy.'

Ilam peered towards the prosecution who only nodded his head in agreement, 'This court accepts your client's plea.'

Narrowing her eyes Ilam examined the criminal, 'For the crimes of kidnap, rape and second degree slavery I do herby sentence you to be spaced until all life has passed from your mortal coil.'

The Amazon banged her gavel and the criminal was taken away. No sooner had he left than his partner in crime entered the courtroom. This time the defence tried a different tack. The prosecution lay back in his chair doing little more than relaxing. Kurgudwardum's courtroom was packed full of tourists come to watch prosecution and sentencing of these vile men.

'Your Honour, my client denies the charges placed before this court. My client was not present at the alleged kidnapping nor the alleged rape but only at the time of arrest.'

Ilam made a coy expression in her direction, 'Really?'

'Yes your Honour.'

'Then how do you explain footage of your client taking these girls at gunpoint?'

'That footage is counterfeit your Honour.'

'What do you think I am? An idiot?'

'Of course not your Honour.'

Ilam snapped at the young lady, 'I've lived more than four centuries young lady, do you think some girl in her 20's can fool me that easily?'

'No your honour but my client ...'

'BUT WHAT?'

The defence cleared her throat, 'My client denies all charges.'

Ilam peered into the accused's eyes, 'What's your name?'

'Yeedo, just Yeedo your Honour.'

'Tell me Yeedo, did you kidnap those girls?'

The skinny man in his 20's with dark hair and no teeth replied, 'No your Honour.'

'Did you rape any of those girls?'

'No your Honour.'

'Did you conspire to sell those girls into slavery?'

'No your Honour.'

Ilam gave the defence a condescending sneer, 'Your client is as poor a liar as you!'

The prosecution sniggered from behind his desk.

Ilam banged her gavel, 'I find this man guilty on all charges including lying to a judge and Miss Johnson shall be fined 100 guskin.'

The accused was led out as his defence got herself into a flap, 'But your Honour, 100 guskin? I'm only being paid 50 for this defence!'

Ilam ignored her plea, 'Next!'

The third accused entered the court. Again his defence rose and spoke to Ilam, 'Your Honour, my client states he was coerced by force into committing the crimes he is charged with and would plea for a lesser charge.'

The ivory skinned Judge sighed in frustration, 'Are you certain you wish to do this Miss Johnson?'

'Yes your Honour, my client maintains the accused used threat of violence against his family to ...'

'Enough!' Ilam looked over at the accused, 'You! Were you coerced into kidnapping and raping those girls?'

The burly man replied, 'I was your honour.'

Ilam banged her gavel, 'Liar! You are hereby sentence to be spaced until all life has passed from your mortal coil … and another fine of 100 guskin for Miss Johnson … NEXT!'

The fourth man entered the court. Miss Johnson was more concerned with her court fines by this time, 'Your Honour my client wishes to plea diminished responsibility through temporary mental insanity.'

Ilam peered down with a very stern expression.

The defence gave a weak smile, 'Perhaps not your Honour.'

The entire court broke into laughter at Miss Johnson's retraction.

Ilam banged her gavel, 'Order in the court!'

'Is there anything my client could do your Honour?'

'I am afraid your client is guilty as a married man pulling up his trousers in a brothel.'

The court burst out in laughter again.

Ilam banged her gavel, 'ORDER!'

'Would you like to enter a plea Miss Johnson?'

'No your honour.'

'For the crimes of kidnap, rape and second degree slavery I do herby sentence your client to be space until all life has left his mortal coil.'

The beautiful Amazon brought her gavel down once again, 'NEXT!'

Jeda Barag entered the courtroom and a new defence attorney took the place of Miss Johnson. McCann could see what was happening as his desperate father lurked at the back of the courtroom tearing his soul apart.

Ilam gave the new lawyer that condescending Tlillan sneer, 'And you are?'

The man stood up, 'I am Charles Hendrik, mi Lud.'

He spoke in a very upper class English accent.

'Really? And what do you do when you're not defending criminals?'

Mr Hendrik gave the Valkyrie a hard look, 'I am a Barrister at the Crown Court of England … mi Lud.'

'What do you have to say concerning the crimes of your client, Mr Hendrik?'

Charles raised an eyebrow, 'I take it that sentence has already been passed on my client?'

'Of course not,' replied an irritated Ilam.

'Then I request the court address my client as the accused.'

'As you wish, Mr Hendrik.'

'Thank you mi Lud, first my client wishes to draw attention to his age. Being barely 16 years of age he is considered too young to take full responsibility in a capital crime case.'

'Are you suggesting this court set a rapist free?'

'Mi Lud, my client is only accused of such crimes.'

'Answer my question Mr Hendrik!'

'No mi Lud, I suggest nothing of the sort. I suggest my client, if found guilty, be given by this court, the proper and just punishment taking into account his age.'

Ilam narrowed her vision, 'I see and what would your client suggest the proper punishment for kidnap and rape of four children be?'

'That is for the court to decide mi Lud. However as this court has pointed out my client's guilt is yet to be ascertained.'

'As is his innocence!'

'Mi Lud! Are you suggesting my client might be guilty until proven innocent?'

'Mr Hendrik, I am growing tired of your games. Now tell me what he pleads and prove to me it is so!'

The Barrister was taken aback, 'Mi Lud! It is the onus of the court to prove my client's guilt not his to prove his innocence!'

The Valkyrie pointed at Hendrik, 'The next words out of your mouth shall be a plea of guilty or not guilty.'

'My client pleads guilty to the charge of kidnapping; to the charge of rape on four counts, not guilty and to the charge of second degree slavery, not guilty mi Lud.'

Ilam turned her head to Jeda, 'Tell me boy, did you rape any of those girls?'

The sullen lad looked down at the courtroom floor, 'No I didn't your Honour.'

'Look at me when I speak to you boy!'

Jeda fixed his eyes upon the Judge's powerful stare, 'I didn't rape them and I didn't conspire to commit slavery and that's the truth.'

'But you did kidnap them, why?'

'I don't know.'

'You don't know? Did you not attempt to ransom their lives for gold?'

'I didn't ransom anyone. I don't need guskin your Honour.'

Ilam pierced into Jeda's mind, 'You knew those girls didn't you?'

Jeda refused to reply.

'I see now … the oldest she refused your advances. That made you angry didn't it?'

Jeda remained silent.

'So you had her kidnaped and raped as punishment.'

'That's not true, I didn't rape anyone!'

'But you did! You assisted that scum in taking those girls off the main boulevard. When Captain Hopper questioned Mr Margidda's neighbours you denied any knowledge of the event. Your immoral actions led to those girls suffering. The youngest would have died from internal bleeding had Captain Hopper's men not arrived in time! How dare you deny responsibility for their suffering!'

Jeda's Barrister moved towards the bench, 'Mi Lud, my client does not deny his responsibility. My Client does beg the court take into account his age and sentence him to a punishment appropriate to that of a minor.'

Ilam brought her sneer to bear upon the Barrister below, 'Mr Hendrik, some would say if he's old enough to commit a capital crime then he's old enough to be spaced.'

'I understand but this is your court mi Lud and my client does sincerely beg for leniency.'

'Do not attempt to plea to my vanity Mr Hendrik.'

'I am doing nothing of the sort mi Lud.'

Ilam took her gavel in hand, 'For the crimes of kidnap, second degree rape and second degree slavery I hereby sentence your client to be spaced until all life has left his mortal coil.'

Ilam banged her gavel as Salamu got to his feet and shouted from the back of the court.

Pointing at the boy's father the Judge instructed her security, 'Take that man out of my court!'

As Salamu was dragged away Mr Hendrik approached the bench, 'Mi Lud I would like to file a request for a retrial.'

'Retrial?'

'Yes mi Lud, the charge of second degree rape was not made therefore my client cannot be found guilty of such a charge in this court. My client wishes to have this trial annulled and a date for a retrial with the new charges filed.'

The ivory skinned beauty leant over her bench and whispered in the Barrister's ear, 'This is the Skin Territory Mr Hendrik not the Old Bailey.'

'But mi Lud this is most improper!'

'Deal with it Mr Hendrik.'

A week later onlookers gathered at Dock 17 on Kurgudwardum 57, turning out from all over the Skin Territory dressed in their best clothes to watch the show. The convicted stood upon a balcony at the far end of the dock with Ilam presided over them. Mesan played his part as the ringmaster, reading a passage of some religious text he preached on how the path of the devil led only to the cold of space.

McCann was disgusted by his hypocrisy as he strutted before five condemned men.

A balcony allowed access to a row of airlocks. Before which the condemned stood. Families filled the massive cargo bay, merchants moved in between them selling food and beverages. This execution was something you might take your wife and children to.

Mesan's voice echoed through the dock as it was transmitted not just over the station but the entire Solar System, 'And the great one said he who taketh a woman and not pay, in time shall find he has paid twice. And for he who take a woman and ask for payment, the great one shall cause a thousand flames to lick his flesh in hell for each coin requested!'

As the crowd broke out into hymn McCann gave his wife a black look before marching out of Docking Bay 17. Making his way onto the main boulevard he turned right, eventually reaching Ninti's Bar.

Inside the establishment was dead. Android women lounged about waiting for a customer to enter. Everywhere was quiet on the station except Docking Bay 17. McCann approached the bar where he was greeted by Noah, 'Spring water Marshal?'

'Whisky.'

Noah was somewhat taken aback since McCann was on duty, 'I have a bottle of Sikaru.'

'Laphroaig.'

Noah pushed a shot glass before McCann and poured malt whisky; as he replaced the cork the Englishman spoke in a low tone, 'Leave the bottle.'

An android worker shuffled up beside him, 'Would sir like to sample any programmes in particular?'

'No, thanks.'

'My name is Fonsa. I am programmed in all methods of sexual pleasure.'

McCann knocked back a shot then poured another, 'Marvellous.'

'If sir would like there is a two for the price of one offer on my masochism algorithm.'

The Englishman picked up his glass and bottle, 'I'm a married man … my wife dishes that out for nothing!'

Fonsa was dumbstruck, unable to formulate a reply she remained silent as McCann walked over to one of the many vacant tables and sat down. After a short while another android joined him. With a sigh the Englishman looked up, 'I'm not interested in being whipped, even at a discount!'

Hevatsu peered down, 'So what does the King of the candyfloss men do in his spare time?'

She forced a smile from the miserable man.

'May I join you Marshal?'

'Sure.'

Hevatsu took a seat crossing her long red legs, 'What are you doing here Duncan?'

'Getting drunk, what does it look like?'

'I meant no offense.'

The Englishman sighed again, 'I'm sorry … do androids drink?'

'I require water to power my internal energy cells, nearly any fluid is acceptable.'

'Can you drink Scotch?'

'My internal filters will easily process Scotch.'

McCann called over to the bar, 'Another glass.'

Fonsa trotted over to deliver a glass then trotted away.

Raising his glass McCann toasted, 'Misery loves company.'

Hevatsu toasted the Englishman knocking back her drink in one go.

'Steady on there,' said a worried McCann, 'you'll drink my wallet dry at that rate!'

Hevatsu smiled as he poured her another drink, 'So why aren't you at Dock 17 with everyone else?'

'I find it all a bit obscene.'

'Please explain.'

He took a tubos from his inside pocket, 'Charging money to watch men die as they're blown into space.'

Hevatsu made a puzzled look, 'Then you consider spacing immoral?'

'Perhaps.'

'When you committed murder on this station, was that immoral?'

'No.'

'Why?'

'Those men pulled firearms on me … it was self-defence.'

Hevatsu thought for a moment, 'That is a false statement.'

'How so?' replied McCann toasting the foot of his Cohiba.

'I have all your incidents logged in my memory. When rescuing your wife's daughter you shot a man after he was disarmed.'

'That's still up for debate.'

'You did shoot a man when he was disarmed.'

'I meant whether we're married.'

Hevatsu smiled, 'I apologise.'

'That's my problem,' said the Englishman whilst waving a smouldering cigar, 'anyway I suppose you're right, I did waste that guy after he'd been disarmed.'

'Then you are a hypocrite if you consider spacing immoral and that act moral, yes?'

McCann took a draw on his Habanos considering the philosophical conundrum, 'That man had already attempted rape and attempted to pull a firearm on me with intent to commit murder.'

Hevatsu agreed, 'And those men in Dock 17 committed crimes just as heinous, yes?'

'But I didn't sell tickets so that people could bring their kids and watch me kill him.'

Hevatsu smiled with those lovely red lips, 'Then it is not the act of spacing you find immoral but charging a fee to view the spectacle?'

'What do you think of it all?'

The droid ran a finger through her shoulder length blue hair, 'I'm not designed with the capability to formulate such decisions.'

'Don't give me that you're curious about morality.'

'I am designed to make conversation, I was merely …'

McCann cut her off, 'Rubbish, I've never heard one of these electric women ask me anything like that before.'

The ample beauty took a sip of malt, 'The other girls have purely mechanical brains … mine is part tissue.'

'What tissue exactly?'

'My brain is grown from stem cells created in a laboratory.'

'Isn't that illegal?'

Hevatsu looked about, scanning for eves droppers, 'It is but in order to create an android capable of pleasing customers above the capability of previous models, it is necessary.'

The Englishman narrowed his eyes closely examining the working girl, 'Are you sentient?'

'No, there is a mechanical part to my brain. It restricts higher thoughts associated with sentience.'

'Does it work?'

The red lady did not answer him but took another slug of Scotch.

As it went quiet a noise similar to a drain emptying could be heard throughout Kurgudwardum 57.

McCann looked up at the monitors around Ninti Bar. Upon them was the body of the first victim being blown out into the vacuum of space; the crowd cheered as he died a horrible death from Hypoxia. The victim's blood vessels ruptured firing frosty fluid out of his ears and nose. His mouth quickly iced up, body bloating whilst drifting away into orbit of a bright star.

The Englishman turned his back to the disgusting exhibition and examined Hevatsu who remained expressionless at the sight.

'Don't you find that disturbing in anyway?'

'I don't know.'

'What does it make you feel?'

'I am not programmed to experience any emotion, merely to mimic for the purpose of another's pleasure.'

McCann could swear the android was experiencing something, she had a nervous expression and he felt emotion … tiny though it was; perhaps the first inkling of a real sentiment?

'Could you describe love?' blurted the synthetic woman.

Scratching his head he replied, 'When you love someone and they are in pain, you feel that pain too.'

'And when they feel pleasure?'

McCann nodded, 'You feel their pleasure.'

'Do you love your wife … Ilam?'

McCann pouted his lips and raised an eyebrow, 'Yes, though sometimes I feel like throttling her.'

'Can you love and hate the same person?'

The Englishman nodded, 'Yes, why do you ask?'

'Many customers, they want me to say I love them. But it is false so how can this please them?' asked a confused Hevatsu.

McCann chuckled, 'Because you don't need two people to fall in love, only one need love the other.'

'Then they love me?'

'Well I don't know that. They do find you attractive and no doubt you satisfy their lust, as to love? It's a word that gets bandied about far too much in my opinion.'

The Englishman took a draw from his cigar, as he tasted its tobacco leaves matured over 5 years a thought entered his mind, 'How many Hevatsu androids are there?'

'So far, I am the first. Noah took me at a discount on agreement he download my mechanical memory to the company each month for analysis.'

'So they want to make sure you don't have a mental breakdown before building more of you?'

'Something like that,' replied the smiling lady.

'How much are they set to make if you work out?'

'The older models you see here shall become obsolete, as to financial gain I have no idea.'

Another powerful whoosh went throughout Kurgudwardum 57 dispensing a second criminal. The mob cheered until a third was brought forth for his final speech.

McCann heard the man start on a long dialogue concerning the evils of drink and how the devil lies in wait at the bottom of a bottle.

'Duncan … do you like me?'

The Marshal found it an odd question for a pleasure droid to ask but this had been an odd conversation by any standards, 'Of course, why do you ask?'

'Do you love me?'

'No, I barely know you.'

'Do you care for me?'

'A little I suppose.'

'But not enough to love me?'

McCann furrowed his brow at the android, 'You know this is a very odd discussion.'

'Why?'

'Well I thought you girls were just programmed to serve drinks and wank off lonely space merchants.'

Hevatsu laughed, 'The others perhaps. I have greater capabilities.'

'You can wank off two space merchants and serve drinks at the same time?'

The red lady laughed even louder and McCann sensed a flicker of emotion from the droid ... happiness.

Noah shot out from behind the bar, 'HEVATSU!!!!'

The red droid stood up immediately, 'YES SIR!'

Noah clutched a tablet examining its read-out carefully, 'What just happened?'

'I was making conversation with a customer, sir.'

McCann gave the owner an annoyed look, 'Everything's fine, let her sit down will you?'

Noah gave a suspicious glance as he hunched over his tablet.

McCann stood up fixing his eyes on Noah, 'Is there a problem?'

'No, I apologise for my interruption.'

'Good.'

'Hevatsu will have to go offline for an hour Mr McCann, she requires a diagnostic.'

The Englishman took a menacing drag from his cigar, 'Rubbish man! You can do your diagnostic later, is that understood?'

Noah ceded to the station Marshal, 'Yes Mr McCann, I'm sorry.'

The portly owner waddled back to his position behind the bar.

Hevatsu relaxed into her seat.

Again the noise of an evacuating atmosphere reverberated around Kurgudwardum 57 accompanied by applause. A fourth man stepped forward and began his diatribe to the people watching. Preaching how he was tempted off God's path and led down a trail of darkness, by lust for money.

McCann found it amusing that men of such poor moral fibre would believe their commentary might hold any water with a single onlooker. They all seemed to blame something other than themselves, be it drink, lotus, guskin or the Devil. Ultimately the only person to blame was themselves and their poor decision to commit a capital offense.

The man finished his speech and Mesan prompted him into the airlock with a black and gold walking stick. Once inside the circular hatch rolled into place, securing an airtight seal.

Cameras focused on the condemned, not just in the airlock but also those strapped to his body. This man's death was to be televised right up until his last moment.

Mesan stood beside a jet black control panel and peered towards Ilam upon her dais. The beautiful Amazon nodded once and Mesan tapped his finger ejecting her prisoner into the vacuum of space.

The audience consumed food and drink as they observed his body bloat. Shouts of joy went out as his lungs exploded, firing icy blood from the nostrils and mouth.

Last of all Jeda was pushed to the front of the balcony. His father stood down below, tearing himself apart inside.

'Do you have any last words?' inquired Mesan.

The boy looked out into the crowd until he finally caught sight of his father, 'I'd like to say I'm sorry, to everyone involved ... that's all.'

Members of the crowd taunted him as Mesan pushed the boy into the airlock. Its hatch rolled into place, Ilam gave the nod and Jeda was blasted out to return to the place he came from. All elements having been created within stars, we are merely stardust and Jeda was to be engulfed from that place his body emerged billions of years ago.

The crowd cheered and McCann shook his head before knocking back a whisky.

'I guess that's that then,' said the Englishman as he poured another drink.

'He did break the law and don't they say the law's the law?' replied Hevatsu.

'It all goes back to religion.'

'How so?'

Thick Cohiba smoke rolled from McCann's nostrils, 'When God said thou shalt not kill. Just a few chapters before he'd committed genocide.'

'What bearing does that have on law?' replied a puzzled love droid.

'The concept is the same. He who makes the law is not obliged to follow it. It has been ingrained into every civilization I've ever encountered at one point or another.'

The red lady considered his statement, 'So the reason you are permitted to commit murder, whilst others are not, goes back to the first religious texts when deities made laws for mortals?'

'Exactly, it says those who make the law and enforce it are above it. Namely your ruling class are Gods. Tlillans practice it very literally but humans did much the same for many years, we still do in fact. Our leaders get away with crimes most citizens would be imprisoned for ... or worse.'

The android in a mini-dress asked in a puzzled tone, 'Why is this practiced?'

'So that the minority may control the majority, for profit.'

'Why does the majority not put an end to such a manipulation?'

McCann smiled, 'They usually do at some point.'

'Yet this system still exists?'

'Because the downtrodden majority elect their rulers one way or another and those people take up the practices of the guys they just killed.'

'It seems corruption is a common trait throughout sentient beings.'

The Marshal narrowed his eyes at Hevatsu.

'Is something wrong Duncan?'

'You said corruption, why did you describe the practice as corrupt?'

The android stuttered for a moment, searching for a reply, 'I believe you had expressed such an opinion.'

'I said no such thing.'

'It is part of my conversation algorithm to analyse customers and agree with their sentiments on a subject.'

McCann watched her eyes flicker from side to side, 'You know what if you were human I'd say you were deceiving me.'

'But I am not human, I am an android, my brain is an artificial construction with inbuilt safe guards to prevent any form of sentience. I do not possess emotions or any thought beyond my duties as a love droid.'

McCann took a drag of his cigar as he relaxed into his seat, 'Quite.'

Chapter 16

Several days after Ilam's spectacle in Dock 17 McCann wallowed in Ninti's. Watching the Chihuaz on a monitor set above the bar, he observed Kaeo cutting up some alien from who knows where.

Customers discussed the exhibition beamed from the Tamoanchan Territory, some held bets others morbid curiosity. From what the Englishman could gather the Tlillan contingent's popularity increased with each victory.

'Do you know her?' inquired a familiar voice.

'She's a family friend.'

'What is she doing in the Chihuaz?'

'Kaeo works for my daughter.'

Hevatsu gazed at the monitor with beautiful yellow eyes, 'I have always desired to be in the Chihuaz.'

'A dancer?'

'No,' replied Hevatsu, 'as a combatant.'

The Marshal laughed only to receive a grim stare from the droid, 'My apologies, I didn't mean to insult you. Androids can't be allowed to take part ... can they?'

The charming love droid smiled, 'Your apology is accepted though I do have a genetic fingerprint.'

'Why in the world would you want to risk your life in that revolting display?'

'To be something other than a man's plaything, at his beck and call night and day ... if I fought in the Chihuaz no-one could control me.'

Sipping whisky the Englishman warned his synthetic friend, 'I'd keep those thoughts close to your chest.'

'Close to my chest?'

'Secret.'

'HEVATSU! Customer in unit 6, he's requested your rape algorithm,' bellowed Noah across the bar.

'I'm sorry but I must go now Mr McCann.'

Hevatsu walked behind the bar where Noah activated a chip within her synthetic brain. The love droid walked into the lodgings at the rear of the establishment to raised eyebrows from curious customers.

Less than a minute had passed and Hevatsu re-emerged, 'He wants Rape algorithm 2.'

Noah pulled out a mini tablet holding it close to her soft red skin, 'He wants you to rape him?'

'Correct,' replied Hevatsu.

Noah shook his head, 'Damn weird these humans! There you're done.'

The love droid returned as the victim's mates chuckled.

McCann went back to watching the Chihuaz since it was the only program on television for the coming weeks.

Kaeo polished off her opponent with some showmanship thrown in for good measure; it was obvious he didn't stand a chance from the beginning. Several customers left the bar to cash in their betting tickets, leaving plenty of room inside. Others tossed their tickets after watching their bet's head cast into a rabid mob.

A couple of drinks and a speech from Allal later McCann was set to leave. As he stood up there was a ruckus behind him. Turning to face the source of trouble a glimmer of red flashed in the corner of his eye.

In the beat of a heart he was pinned to the top of the bar by Hevatsu. Her legs pressed down on his arms whilst she brandished a knife close to his face; for some reason the droid hesitated, if not McCann would have met Charon.

The droid looked McCann in the eye blurting, 'Remember I am vapour,' before shutting down and crumpling to the floor a lifeless shell.

Noah ran around his bar apologising, 'I'm sorry Marshal there must be a fault with her rape algorithm!'

Dragging himself off the bar the shaken lawman brushed his jacket whilst searching for any wounds which may have gone un-noticed. Fortunately he was unscathed.

McCann tapped his wrist tablet, 'I understand but I'm gonna check this out myself.'

'What do you mean?'

'I'm taking possession of your droid.'

Noah protested, 'No! You can't do that!'

'That droid nearly killed me. I want to know why … thanks for shutting her down.'

Noah shook his head, 'I didn't shut her down, she must have had a mental collapse. It's the only event which might trigger an automatic shut down.'

Clayton turned up at the bar with a couple of crewmen. On noticing the naked droid holding a large steak knife he stated, 'Been having some fun?'

'Hardly, take this droid to med bay I want her looked at.'

Kicking her knife away the crewmen lifted Hevatsu from the floor and carried her away.

Noah examined his tablet going over Hevatsu's last waking moments, 'This doesn't make sense. It says her systems were fine. There's no sign whatsoever of a mental breakdown.'

'Maybe it was her algorithm?'

'No, she was with a client she would not have left the room until it had finished …'

At that everyone turned their eyes to Ninti's lodgings. McCann heard a muffled voice emanating from a passageway.

Pulling his pistol the Marshal and his Deputy entered the lodgings with great caution. Swinging open the door to unit 6 Clayton cracked up laughing.

Inside the unit lay Lieutenant Galloway, tied to each pillar of the bed with white sheets; gaged by a luminous ball, held in place with a leather strap. Finally a 12 inch glass dildo protruded from his anal passage. The man was clearly in distress having been abandoned by Hevatsu.

'Jesus Christ! What do you think you're up to man?' said McCann with his best straight face.

Galloway attempted to reply yet the ball prevented anything other than a muffled cry.

McCann stood in the room with Clayton and Noah. Peering at Clayton the Marshall stated in a coy tone, 'Is this one of your men?'

'Galloway ... sir,' laughed Clayton.

'Family?'

'He has a wife and son back on Earth ... sir.'

McCann shook his head, 'Damn and I thought Clayton was into some weird shit!'

'Hey I just like the company of the ladies, nothing like this bloody deviant!' protested his Deputy.

Galloway screamed again, as he received an electric pulse from the rectally inserted sex toy.

'Nice to know I'm not the only one who's shocked!' stated McCann in a coy tone.

Galloway lurched with a scream as a second belt of electricity entered his body.

'Some more deeply than others!' retorted Clayton.

'I suppose we better untie the poor man. Noah, I'll leave it to you.'

As the pair returned to the bar Noah stopped McCann, 'Hey, I'm not pulling that thing out of his behind!'

'Well get a droid to do it.'

'That will cost extra, customers pay good money for this treatment you know?'

'Charge Galloway, I'm sure he won't mind,' McCann peered over Noah's shoulder, 'right Galloway?'

The Lieutenant made a muffled noise whilst nodding his head as best he could.

'There you go old boy, problem solved,' pointing to his badge of authority McCann whispered, 'I didn't get this just because I'm a pretty face!'

Clayton and McCann stepped back in the bar with matching grins. The entire establishment roared with laughter as Galloway left in a huff, red faced and a slight limp. Noah's love droids were bewildered by all that had occurred.

The next day McCann and Ilam argued in the med bay discussing Hevatsu's lifeless body.

'Space it while you can. It was an illegal act to build a synthetic brain, its manufacturer must be punished,' declared Ilam.

McCann rubbed his chin as he examined Hevatsu's perfect body, 'Hassif will be here in a few weeks, I want him to look at her first.'

'Her?'

'How do you know she isn't alive? She still has life signs even when shut down, according to this she's dreaming right now.'

Ilam sneered at her husband, 'What makes you believe she is sentient? Your soft heart?'

McCann pulled out a Ramon Allones, cut its cap then toasted the foot with his black and gold lighter, 'Something she said before shutting herself down.'

'Shutting herself down? How do you know this?'

McCann took a puff on the raw tobacco, 'Remember I was vapour, that's what she said before shutting down.'

'What significance does this bear on the fact a droid made an attempt on your life?'

'It's a song I'd request in Ninti's. I explained it to Hevatsu one night.'

Ilam's hands rested upon her hips, 'The meaning?'

'The song explains that though I'm famous now, I'm still human with human feelings and emotions.'

The Valkyrie scoffed, 'Really Duncan you are so easily manipulated.'

'Perhaps.'

'And what of Galloway? Your report was vague concerning his interaction with Hevatsu.'

McCann raised an eyebrow, 'For the benefit of all involved, let's just say he was widening his circle when some wires got crossed.'

'You're being cryptic again Duncan, you know how it frustrates me.'

'Trust me.'

None the wiser Ilam rolled her eyes, 'As you wish Duncan.'

The following month Hassif arrived aboard Kurgudwardum 57 via a Makayuuk transport, a far quicker service than the I.S.A.

Straight away the Indian examined Hevatsu. With nanites coursing through her bloodstream the entire brain lit up on a monitor. McCann entered the med bay as the Technician tapped away, 'Welcome to Andromeda.'

Hassif raised a hand without moving his eyes from the screen, 'So what did you want me here for?'

'I need an opinion on this lady,' he said pointing at Hevatsu.

'I'm sure you already have staff, why drag me across the universe?'

'Maybe I miss you?'

Hassif concentrated on the android before him, 'It's an SI, a very sophisticated one however there's a mechanical implant in the frontal lobes.'

McCann crossed his arms as Hevatsu lay in a deep synthetic sleep, 'She spoke about it once. She said it was there to prevent her reaching sentience.'

The Indian examined Hevatsu's implant further, 'It's more than that Duncan, it seems to carry several programs imbedded inside … do you have any idea what they might be for?'

'She's a love droid. They're probably algorithms for customers.'

Hassif raised an eyebrow at his old friend.

'The answer is no,' stated McCann.

The Technician gave his old Captain a smirk before returning to the read out. Hassif read code as it poured out from Hevatsu's brain implant, 'This is very interesting.'

'Yes?'

'An algorithm recently downloaded but it has no designation. This wasn't intended for customers,' after a few seconds reading a flurry of numbers and letters, Hassif faced McCann, 'Someone tried to have you killed.'

McCann furrowed his brow, 'Well I know that!'

'Someone other than this android, she was just a tool.'

'How?'

'Someone you rubbed up the wrong way downloaded a command program into her implant. I'm not sure what its trigger was but according to this she was to murder you … why she failed is what puzzles me.'

The Commodore felt a little relaxed now that Hassif was on top of things, 'She seemed to shut herself down before stabbing me.'

The Indian walked to a separate station where an image of Hevatsu's frontal lobes popped up, 'Her implant must have failed. Somehow this android's brain tissue has grown around it, bypassing the mechanism.'

'So she's sentient?'

The Technician shrugged his shoulders, 'That I cannot say while she's shut down, all I can say is that she has learnt to override her implant.'

'Can we revive her?'

'Let me download the implant then wipe it, after that I believe it will be possible,' Hassif tapped away at his station, 'Just give me a few minutes.'

Shortly after wiping Hevatsu's implant and making certain it was absolutely inert the red woman's eyelids flipped open. Looking around she noticed a familiar face, smiled, sat up and hugged the station Marshal.

Hevatsu whispered, 'You understood.'

McCann waited until she released her embrace, 'I think so.'

The yellow eyed love droid glanced at Hassif, 'I'm Hevatsu, I assume I have you to thank for my resurrection?'

The Indian pressed his palms together, 'I am Hassif, I only deactivated your frontal implant.'

The naked lady rose to her feet whilst pressing her fingertips upon her skull, 'Something does feel odd.'

'You have nanites monitoring your system, the blocks intended to prevent sentience have been removed.'

Hevatsu let a big grin fill her face as she ran her fingers through her blue hair.

McCann quickly asked, 'There was a programme, in your implant. It was a command programme instructing you to assassinate me.'

Hevatsu nodded in silence.

'Do you know who was behind it?'

The red droid shook her head, 'No, though I believe I know who downloaded it.'

'Noah?'

'No, he would never do something like that. It was a company representative. I will give you a full description Mr McCann.'

The Englishman nodded, 'First we need to get you some clothes!'

Hevatsu looked down and quickly covered herself.

Hassif raised his brow, 'It seems she may be sentient after all.'

'Why do you say that Mr Hassif?'

'Man is the only animal that blushes … or needs to!'

Later on Hevatsu had slipped into a Tlillan space suit; waiting outside Ilam's office she listened to the Amazon argue furiously with her husband. The former love droid gave worried looks to Clayton; both eves dropping on a heated discussion concerning Hevatsu's future.

McCann eventually stepped out followed by his fiery eyed wife. Ilam sneered at the droid, 'One mistake, a single word in the wrong place at the wrong time and I'll have you cut up for spare parts!'

Hevatsu was about to reply but the Englishman grabbed her shoulder dragging the yellow eyed beauty away, 'Let's go.'

As the threesome left Ilam glared into Hevatsu's back until they were out of her sight.

'Is there a problem Mr McCann?' inquired Hevatsu.

'The problem is what do we do with you?'

'I don't understand?'

'You're not going back to work in Ninti's after nearly killing one customer and leaving the other with a dildo up his arse, are you?'

Hevatsu hadn't contemplated the thought until now, 'I assumed I would since Noah owns my contract with Barag-Beings Inc.'

Clayton chuckled to himself as they strolled down the corridor.

'According to Hassif you're sentient, making that contract null and void.'

'Is Hassif certain?'

'If Hassif says you're sentient then you're sentient. The question is what to do with you now?'

The synthetic beauty shrugged her shoulders, 'I have no skills other than love making and serving males.'

Clayton grinned, 'Sounds like a good place to begin!'

The party reached a doorway, McCann pressed his thumb against a black wall pad.

'Please identify yourself,' spoke the station AI.

'Commodore McCann.'

'Please remain still for a retinal scan,' stated an androgynous voice as a laser leapt out to certify the Commodore was who his genetic and voice print said he was.

'One member of your party is not present on my database,' stated the AI.

'Her name is Hevatsu, please log her details,' McCann gestured towards the door and the droid approached its black wall terminal.

'Please state your name.'

'My name is Hevatsu,' replied the former love droid.

'Please press both of your palms against the wall.'

Hevatsu complied placing her palms on a jet black patch.

'Please remain still whilst both retinal signatures are logged.'

Two lasers scanned her retinas; once finished the AI announced, 'Genetic print, voice print, visual print and retinal print all logged onto database ... species not present in database.'

'Give Hevatsu rank 3 authority,' stated the Marshal.

'Hevatsu has authority, rank 3. Welcome to Kurgudwardum 57 Hevatsu.'

A door slipped away presenting a small aperture. McCann bent down in order to step in. Once within the door slid shut and Hevatsu realised where she was. To her right a long table was broken up by partitions, each section had a target at the other end. This was a firing range and at the far end of the corridor an armoury awaited.

The Englishman walked past the range and into the armoury where a vast selection of weapons from across the Milky Way Galaxy rested.

'So which one takes your fancy?' inquired the Englishman.

The synthetic beauty looked around examining many pistols and rifles pinned to the wall, 'I have never used a firearm Mr McCann.'

Clayton grabbed a gun belt and slung it around Hevatsu's waist, 'Now pick something to go in it.'

Her yellow eyes scanned the wall, 'Hmm, well this one looks pretty don't you think?'

The men chuckled as she pulled a silver Magnum from the wall, a deceivingly sleek weapon considering it carried a large flat head tungsten round.

'You like the Magnum?' asked Clayton.

'It has a nice colour and the barrel is long, I like long barrels.' Eyebrows rose.

'Trust me you don't get to see many long barrels at Ninti's ... present company accepted of course,' the red skinned lady gave Clayton a coy look.

McCann burst out laughing, his deputy quietened down rather quickly.

The Englishman grabbed a battery and ammo pack along with a box of tungsten rounds, 'Come on, let's have some target practice.'

As they stepped onto the range the Commodore instructed on how to load the weapon, check its energy levels and ammunition. Once ready he demonstrated proper use of its safety switch before leading the red beauty into a firing booth and handing out the ear muffs.

Clayton gave the droid tips on holding the weapon. On her first shot at the target Hevatsu's Magnum kicked up in the air. The red lady almost lost her grip.

McCann and his deputy were quite prepared for this event since it'd happened to them the first time they'd fired a large calibre pistol. Clayton was quite impressed that she'd managed to keep a hold of it rather than allow it to go flying into the air.

Her tungsten bullet had completely missed its target but that was no surprise, it would be a while before Hevatsu could hit anything at 30 metres with any accuracy.

A few hours later and Hevatsu was shooting her target between the eyes at 50 metres, the girl learnt fast. After a few perfect score cards McCann stopped the practice and from his jacket pocket produced a leather wallet with a star made from 22 carat gold. In the centre of the star was etched "DEPUTY", above and below "Kurgudwardum 57".

The Marshal slipped half the wallet into her breast pocket, the other half hung outside displaying her badge, 'Now you've got a new job ... Deputy.'

Hevatsu placed her Magnum upon the table along with her ear muffs. She removed the leather wallet ogling its gold star, 'I don't know the law, how can I be a Deputy?'

'Law? Just do what you feel is right at the time, let Ilam worry about the law.'

The red lady opened her wallet to see a card inside displaying her hologram with a light chip imbedded beside, 'I can't enforce a law ...'

The Commodore cut her off, 'You'll be with Clayton and myself at first. You'll get the hang of it just the same as you got the hang of that Magnum.'

The following day the trio walked into Ninti's, music became hushed as they approached the bar. Noah rushed out shouting in a joyous tone, 'Thank the Maker! I thought my investment had been lost!'

He then noticed his love droid's gun belt and gold star, 'What is this?'

'Hevatsu is now in my employment, it appears she's sentient nullifying your contract.'

'Nullifying? What about my guskin? I paid a lot of money for that droid!'

Clayton slung a rifle over his shoulder, 'You didn't have insurance?'

'Why no, Salamu told me she was guaranteed for 9 cycles. I was going to get my deposit back on her return.'

'Well she's my Deputy now,' stated McCann.

The other droids scrambled in excitement to get a look at Hevatsu's badge.

Noah was furious with McCann, 'I will speak to Mesan! You cannot do this! I have a contract! It is binding on all stations in the Skin Territory. This is not the end McCann!'

The Commodore grabbed Noah by his shirt collar pulling him over the bar. Sneering in the fat man's face he growled, 'You're nothing but dog shit to me.'

Noah's face went red as the Marshal squeezed his collar. The entire bar froze.

'You smell bad, look nasty and decent folk pay people like me to keep you away from them!'

Noah began to struggle for breath as the Commodore held him stretched over the bar.

'The only things that like dog shit are parasites … do you understand?'

By now Noah was going from red to blue yet managed to nod his head.

'Good, so you be careful that dog's arsehole doesn't drop you in my path Noah or you'll find yourself squished underneath my boot … and everyone hates getting dog shit on their boot.'

McCann released the fat man who gathered himself before disappearing into the back of his establishment.

McCann turned around observing Noah's customers; one man was attempting to make an inconspicuous exit. Before he could Hevatsu shouted, 'That's the Rep!'

The tall alien with short stumpy arms was about to dash for the exit when McCann pulled his pistol, 'One foot out that door I'll fill you so full of lead you'll be shitting fishing weights for a year!'

The alien fellow didn't understand exactly what McCann had said but there was no doubt exiting the bar would be bad. Yet he contemplated his chances whilst eyeing the exit and the Marshal's pistol.

The alien Rep shuffled towards the exit.

'Don't do it!' pressed McCann.

The alien spoke in a deep croaky voice, 'He will kill me anyway.'

'Who?'

Hevatsu stepped out from a body of love droids, 'The Marshal will protect you no matter who this person is.'

'I have a family, he will murder them.'

McCann lowered his weapon, 'Salamu holds your family?'

The creature nodded its head, 'He does. He will blame this failure on me not the droid.'

McCann placed his pistol back in its holster, 'So he WAS behind it.'

'Yes.'

'Tell me what you know and I'll bring you your family, alive.'

The alien laughed.

'You have my word.'

The creature shook its head, 'Why would I trust you?'

'The way I see it you have a choice; either you help me and maybe you get your family back alive. Or you run out that door now and take a spacewalk with your wife and kids.'

The strangely formed man thought for a moment, 'It seems I have no alternative, I only hope your word is good.'

'I'll drop you off with Ilam. She'll keep you safe in a cell until we get back. I take it he has your family on Shurruppak 15?'

The Rep gave a nod as he approached the Marshal with arms out, informing all he carried no weapon.

A moment later and Hevatsu shouted, 'The Chihuaz!'

All screens in Ninti's bar flicked over to the Chihuaz as customers and workers gathered around. Allal strutted like a peacock introducing two contestants. McCann recognised one as being Kaeo. The other was some species of praying mantis with a pair of long arms.

'Oh look it's Kaeo, you know her don't you Mr McCann?' ask the red Deputy.

'I've known Kaeo since she was born.'

The bar went quiet everyone fixed their eyes upon the Englishman.

'Really?' inquired Hevatsu in an astounded voice.

'Why do you ask?'

'She has defeated some of the greatest fighters. Kaeo was intended to be an easy victory yet all fell.'

McCann peered at an excited Hevatsu, 'Why an easy victory?'

'The Tlillan are untested, unrated by bookies, the best fighters always get easy contests in the initial rounds of the Chihuaz. This cycle they made a big mistake. Who are you supporting?'

'Kaeo ... I suppose.'

As Allal shouted 'FIGHT,' everyone's attention was drawn back to the monitors. Alien voices commentated on every nuance of this match. The audience filled its massive stadium cheering for their champion. It was a spectacle Emperor Commodus would've been proud of.

The large insect's barbed arms surged out towards Kaeo. The short half breed dodged its attacks with such grace and beauty she left the throng in awe. This armoured beast could not hit her no matter how fast it jabbed.

The short Amazon twisted her body from side to side eventually striking the beast's arm.

A high pitched squeal went out as she circled the creature, stepping upon ridges in it exoskeleton to hoist herself onto the beast's back. From there Kaeo held on as the squealing monster attempted to flip her off.

A crowd formed inside Ninti's bar shouting and screaming as the battle unfolded. Roars of encouragement went out across the station. It seemed everyone was watching the Chihuaz.

Kaeo gouged out one of the 7 foot Mantis' eyes before being thrown to the ground. Her distressed opponent writhed in pain. The Tlillan Marshal could have finished the animal yet she refrained.

McCann was confused as to why but Kaeo paraded around the edge of the arena, her adoring audience reached out to touch their hero. Kaeo orbited the stadium making contact with her flock until reaching the seat of Topixque. Pointing up at Mammi the Valkyrie made a gesture suggesting she was next for the slaughter. The mob went wild, screaming as rabid beasts they yelled approval; The Tzitzimeh leader's sneer merely encouraging the crowd.

Returning to her injured opponent Kaeo charged forward. Leaping upwards she jumped into the air ripping the creature's tiny head off. Being an insect it had no internal skeleton making its joints very weak compared to that of a mammal.

The Valkyrie's feet hit the floor before her opponent's corpse smashed down. She held it's dripping head aloft to wild cheers whilst her foe's soul entered the gates of hell to wait on the banks of the River Styx ... alongside her previous combatants.

Kaeo's style was one of decapitating her opponents and throwing its head to the audience. Making her massively popular amongst the mob now baying for blood and gore all across the Galaxy.

The short Marshal cast its head into a mass of acolytes. A skirmish in the congregation ensued as her followers battled one another for their champion's meagre offering. McCann observed this mad scramble, it were as if Patroclus had fallen beneath the walls of Troy; Only for a mass of Trojans to gather and fight over his armour. He observed an undignified scene of men and women wrestling for the morbid trophy. Smeared with blood and gore not only of the insect but each other; Drawing fellow on-lookers' blood to take possession of Kaeo's pitiful offering.

Hevatsu clapped whilst jumping up and down, 'Wasn't that amazing Mr McCann?'

As Kaeo stepped over the insect's corpse on her way to speak with Al he replied in a sardonic tone, 'Marvellous!'

Chapter 17

Al entered the Tlillan dressing room grinning from ear to ear followed by Geman and Visi. The cybernetic host approached Kaeo clapping his hands, 'So how's my girl today?'

Kaeo glanced in his direction, 'Fine, what's got you so excited?'

'Are you kidding this is it … the first real final in millennia!'

'Were the Tzitzimeh not challenged before now?'

'Oh there've been pretenders to the throne … none stood a chance of winning.'

'Until now?'

'Until now honeybuns!'

'Well I'm wearing this Tlillan suit.'

Allal nodded his head, 'You wear whatever you want. You're the boss sweet cheeks.'

'So what order are we in?' said Geman immersed in a fold away tablet.

Malikah gave a puzzled expression, 'Order?'

'You must determine the order of combat first, second and third.'

'What order are the Tzitzimeh fighting in?'

Al chuckled, 'We don't know that's Topixque's privilege. Though I hear you're Nabu?'

'I am but I cannot see the Chihuaz let alone the order of combat.'

Geman scratched his head, 'Well you still have to fix an order of combat and you're not allowed to change it once set.'

'I see then I shall take the first match.'

Geman noted Malikah for the first round.

'Put me down for the second,' stated Kaeo.

Arthur was rather disappointed believing a lack of confidence in his abilities prevailed amongst the ladies.

'And that makes Arthur the anchor man,' noted Geman in a perky tone.

Visi hugged Arthur whilst examining her young Adonis.

Al rubbed his hands together and spoke to Malikah, 'Excellent, excellent, I take it your skills come close to those of Kaeo?'

'Have no fear Mr Allal your tyrants shall be removed by the end of this Chihuaz.'

'Is that your Nabu speaking?'

'It is destiny.'

'What's the difference?'

Malikah peered at Kaeo and Arthur, 'There are two forces in this universe that be-shadow all others, do you know what they are?'

'Let me guess the Tlillan and Telal?'

'Incorrect, they are love and fear. Each one as complicated as the other with unfathomable nuances but fear is no match for true love Mr Allal.'

'I don't understand. What's that got to do with fighting the Telal?'

'Everything Mr Allal … everything.'

Al shrugged his shoulders, 'Fine, the first match will be called in an hour,' he pointed at Malikah, 'don't let me down baby!'

Al turned on his heels exiting the room with Geman close behind.

Visi caressed her Adonis, 'I can't wait to see you smash those witches,' purred the young lady.

Kaeo raised an eyebrow before administering her makeup.

An hour later and the arena below lit up with smoke and lasers flashing in all directions. After a month of blood and murder this was the climax. Women danced to electronic music as the audience stood clapping feet to floor.

Malikah, Kaeo and Arthur watched from above along with Dr Weissmuller and Sandra. Out from the smoke Allal appeared dressed in a silver suit, sparkling blue shirt and shoes. A hysterical crowd screamed over the music, Al raised his hands in recognition. The old presenter clapped to the beat whilst circumnavigating his arena, weaving in and out his dancing girls. Members of the audience went wild reaching out to touch the host of the greatest event the universe had ever witnessed.

Al outstretched his hand brushing audience members occupying the expensive seats as if he were Christ visiting Sao Paolo, everyone begged Allal's blessing, messiah of the Chihuaz.

The Tzitzimeh no longer inhabited their throne.

As the electronic music died down Al moved to the centre, 'Who do you all love?'

The mob roared back, 'We love ALLAL!'

The host smiled, 'And I love you.'

They cheered in approval. Al had these people in the palm of his hand, manipulating them as a puppet master, 'Now you're gonna see a fight here tonight, so exciting, so thrilling, so dangerous that if it were packaged and sold they'd have to arrest me!'

Howls of excitement rang out. Al absorbed their approval as a sunbather soaking up rays on a beach.

Visi nodded at Malikah, 'It's time.'

Malikah made her way to the cylinder, as it closed everyone spoke in a sullen voice, 'Good luck.'

Malikah smiled back as a transparent cage closed propelling her down a tube into the arena below.

'Our first contestant tonight, vying for the Chihuaz throne ... XCH'UUP!'

Laser lights fired through smoke as Malikah rose from the dirt dressed only in her Tlillan combat suit.

Dancers began to bend and stretch, pirouetting in circles to another of Arthurs' favourite songs. The dread Queen remained still as onlookers clapped the beat, some cheered others jeered. After 5 minutes the song ended and Al approached Malikah's plinth, 'Are you nervous?'

'Why would I be nervous?'

Al laughed as he looked around the arena, 'Because I'm the only one old enough to remember when Mammi didn't hold the Topixque!'

The audience laughed with Al.

'That will change today.'

The crowd stomped as Malikah stood legs astride, beams of light coursing over her skin tight ribbed suit, smoke whirling through her sable locks.

Al moved back to the centre, 'She's a star isn't she?'

The audience approved lashing their host with praise.

'Xch'uup shall be facing ... for the first match ... HEBAT!'

The throng screamed as fanatics in a cult ceremony. A cylinder pierced the floor containing Hebat, Mammi's ambassador. A strange tune of high pitched symbols played, similar to a piece concocted in the Far East on Earth.

After a few minutes Hebat's music ended her cylinder disappeared into the floor and Al cried out, 'Introducing the undefeated champions of the Chihuaz, herald of the Telal, HEBAT!'

The short witch poised in her tunic, shrunken heads dangling in the wind and eyes locked with Malikah's. Once the throng tired of clapping Al approached the Tzitzimeh, 'So are you nervous, facing your old enemy?'

Hebat sneered but made no comment.

'I'll take that as a no!'

The old host stepped into the centre, 'Now I know you all want me to get out of the way so that you can watch the greatest match to grace the Chihuaz for millennia. But I still have to point out the rules, this is a fight to the death, there's no padding out!'

The crowd roared in approval.

'This will be the best of three contests so at least two have to die tonight … and you're gonna see it happen in 3D!'

Again the mass screamed in excitement unable to curb their blood lust.

Allal produced a tablet, 'Do I even need to?'

Onlookers roared urging battle to begin.

Al tossed his tablet, 'LET'S FIGHT LADIES!'

Al leapt to the side of the arena as Malikah and Hebat stepped from their plinths onto the dirt floor. The audience rippled with chatter and emotion as hysteria of battle coursed the amphitheatre again and again.

Hebat gnashed razor sharp teeth, displaying equally sharp claws. Malikah strode on with determination once within 4 metres she circled the vile witch.

The crowd screeched statements such as 'Kill her,' and 'Rip her arms off!' at random. The dread Queen had no idea to whom these taunts were directed nor did she care. Her full attention was square on Hebat.

The Tzitzimeh made a sudden break, charging at full pace teeth and claws brandished she went for Xch'uup.

Malikah side stepped, grabbing Hebat by the scruff of her neck she projected the shrew off her feet and into the audience. One of the mob was hit full in the face, Hebat's fangs sinking into his forehead. Within seconds he surcame to violent convulsions. Hebat's venomous fangs poisoned his bloodstream resulting in instantaneous death.

The throng ignored his corpse as they gathered around Hebat; All taking the chance to touch a God of the arena making her way back to the melee.

Malikah smirked at her opponent before the wrinkled beast charged again. The tall Tlillan watched closely grabbing both Hebat's wrists as soon as they were within range. The witch gnashed at Malikah's arms, attempting to sink her teeth in and deal a death blow but they were stretched too far apart.

As Hebat leant forward in an attempt to bite Malikah's arm the sable Queen freed her opposite hand to clutch her foe's throat.

Hebat took control of her free arm plunging its claws into Malikah's side. As blood trickled down the Telal's arm screams filled the amphitheatre. Vital fluids had been drawn, hot and fervorous, onlookers spirit and Malikah's gore mixed as one to form an addictive concoction.

Malikah felt a stinging pain in her side so squeezed hard on Hebat's neck, tightening her grip. Hebat pushed her claws deeper into Malikah's ribs.

Thick red blood splashed onto orange dust the throng gathered passion as each dash hit the ground. Xch'uup's blood absorbed where the blood of so many warrior's had been spilt before. All sound became overpowered by the mob's ecstasy concerning this twisted display of violence. A pair of gladiators locked into an embrace of death which only one could survive.

As Malikah compressed her opponent's neck she felt sacks of venom inside the creatures' throat. The Queen locked eyes with Hebat, 'In the temple of pain … cry my name!'

At that moment two venom sacks burst pouring their toxic contents down Hebat's throat and into her digestive system. The old witch began to choke. Before her foe might vomit deadly venom Malikah cast its small frame away.

Heaving stomach fluids onto the dirt the herald of Mammi dropped to her knees attempting to bring up the acid now dissolving her innards.

The crowd screamed for blood as masses of allegedly civilised beings demanded Malikah end Hebat's existence. An aperture opened in the floor revealing a medieval club, similar to a morning star; a weapon employing the combination of blunt force and puncture to overpower its target.

'Slay the witch, slay the witch, slay the witch!' chanted Al's acolytes as sacrifice neared.

Kicking Hebat onto her back the Amazon snatched the weapon's wooden handle. In a single mighty blow she brought its thick spiked metal head to meet Hebat's, ending the beast's life to howls of approval. Suddenly U2 began to play again. Malikah glanced from the corpse beneath to witness dancers flipping and turning around the stadium whilst smoke gushed to a brilliant laser light show. The dread Queen nursed her wounds until the music ended and Allal leapt into the arena.

'MY GOD I CAN HARDLY BELIEVE IT ... HEBAT CHOKED!'

Vibrant applause condoned Al's quip.

'So Xch'uup how are you?'

Malikah smiled, 'I'll live.'

'Hah! Did you hear that? Ok so it's one zero to the Tlillan and for the first time in history Mammi's fighting an uphill battle! Tell us how would YOU describe that fight?'

'Hebat placed faith in a false God as a thirsty man might pursue a desert mirage.'

Crazed creatures roared in approval their voices echoing murder around the arena.

'Give a big hand for Xch'uup!'

Malikah recognised her screaming acolytes with a nod before stepping upon her plinth, its cylinder escorting the victor to safety.

Upon stumbling from her transparent cage Dr Weissmuller and Sandra moved in. Medical staff took their Xch'uup to a makeshift med bay. Before Weissmuller could assess the damage Sandra stripped her Queen's ribbed suit away, exposing a gash. Five penetration wounds closely grouped together cut into Malikah's rib cage. Sandra placed a hand over the trembling flesh, eyes dark as the night side of Otoch.

The dread Queen's breathing slowly returned to its natural strength as blood ceased its flow into her lungs. In ten seconds Sandra removed her hand healing Malikah's wound.

'You're lucky.'

Malikah smiled, 'Lucky?'

'Had any venom entered those wounds I might not have been able to help you.'

Weissmuller placed a small metal circle where her injuries once were. The German Doctor observed her innards on his wrist tablet as his probe sent ultrasonic waves through her body, 'Sandra has done a good job. You are fully functional once again young lady.'

Malikah sat up on the edge of her bed kissing the Doctor on the cheek, 'Ich danke Ihnen fur Ihr anliegen Arzt.'

Weissmuller blushed as Malikah's suit melded together covering her exposed ribcage.

An hour later and the stadium came to life again, music played and women danced as Al basked in attention.

Malikah examined Kaeo in her Tlillan combat suit the short warrior's hair curled into buns. Her eyebrows expertly crafted by Rapit along with an electric blue lipstick.

'You look so cute!'

Kaeo snorted.

'Don't be that way, Arthur agrees with me.'

Kaeo folded her arms, 'He'd probably find a Gukumatz attractive if you put it in a skirt!'

Malikah laughed, while stroking the half Thai's cheek she whispered, 'Emotionless and cold as ice … electric Barbarella.'

Kaeo walked to her transport tube, 'Just wish me luck.'

'Good luck,' said Arthur.

Kaeo gave him a tiny smile before a door closed firing her down into the amphitheatre.

Upon emerging from within the stadium her music began to boom out. The short Valkyrie recognised her tune immediately as the words went out to a drum beat with guitar and keyboards, 'I plug you in, dim the lights, electric Barbarella.'

Kaeo's head snapped upwards, her Tlillan vision focused in searching for Xch'uup. Eventually she found Malikah on high Arthur by her side. That she spoke her introduction before it played was no coincidence. As to what this meant or what Malikah was trying to tell her Marshal was a mystery, it certainly disturbed Kaeo.

Smoke filled the arena floor, plasma bursts flickered through thick fog as women pranced around the edge. Al stood centre stage his cybernetic body conducted plasma energy yet caused no ill effect upon the Chihuaz host.

The throng clapped and swayed to the pop song for four minutes until it reached an end.

Al held his arms in the air as the fog dispersed, 'Welcome to the second round of the Chihuaz final!'

Frantic screams of delight rippled around the stadium almost deafening Kaeo.

'The second contestant, you all know and love her ... who is she?'

The throng got to its feet screaming, 'KAEO!'

The short Tlillan acknowledged her audience with a wave.

Al approached the plinth, 'You've done better than most in the Chihuaz but some say defeating the Telal is impossible. What do you say to your doubters?'

'A wise man makes his own decisions. An ignorant man follows public opinion,' stated Kaeo.

Al smiled, 'What about success?'

'A bold attempt is half the success achieved already.'

Applause rang out as Al nodded his head, 'So true and that's just what we like to hear at the Chihuaz.'

The host walked back to the centre, 'Now for Kaeo's opponent.'

Tzitzimeh song rang out as a cylinder appeared from below, opening to form a plinth; upon it stood a wrinkled old witch, shrunken heads swinging by their own dried hair.

Women danced eloquently for a few minutes until the tune ended. Al approached the beast, 'Mammi's second fighter is Kalum!'

Boo's and jeers went out across the amphitheatre the Tzitzimeh priest of lamentation was not popular amongst the people of Andromeda.

'Now, now, Kalum has given us many great battles … aside from Mammi she's the only undefeated Telal taking part in the Chihuaz this cycle!'

There were still noises of disapproval from the crowd.

'So Kalum I took a peek at the odds on you versus Kaeo and I have to say no-one is prepared to call this one way or another, what do you think?'

'Earth shall blush with Tlillan blood tonight,' growled the old witch.

The crowd booed, Al held his hands out to calm them down, 'Alright, let's cut the big talk and see who can deliver … LET'S FIGHT LADIES!'

As they both stepped down from their plinths a frenzied audience called for Kalum's death. The Tzitzimeh priest was an experienced contestant and for centuries she'd staved off any attempts to knock Mammi from her throne.

The two moved around slipping in and out of striking distance, tempting the other into a rash move.

After a couple of minutes Kaeo made a forward kick, cracking Kalum's knee. The Tzitzimeh priest dropped her leg leaving herself vulnerable to an attack. Kaeo moved in for a head kick, as she approached the witch leapt forward tearing at the Tlillan's face with razor sharp claws.

The crowd gasped in shock as Kalum scratched out Kaeo's left eye. Xch'uup's Marshal managed to swing an elbow connecting with her opponent's cheek and knocking it to the ground.

The short Valkyrie stepped back cleaning blood from her good eye, her vision distorted beyond utility. The Tzitzimeh wasted no time leaping at her victim again. Rolled back lips revealed teeth of the Hydra which she sunk into Kaeo's face ripping flesh from its left side, crown to chin.

The audience screamed in horror as Kalum landed on the arena floor and spat the short warrior's face upon orange dirt. Venom entered her blood stream, the Tlillan Marshal bled profusely onto dry dust below. Without treatment she would die from blood loss before the venom finished her.

Kalum bathed in glory, gore flowed down her face as wine at a banquet dripping onto shrunken heads of past victories. She roared in satisfaction while the throng showed utter disbelief.

Al sensed something odd, looking up his eyes met with Malikah's. He knew what she was asking but the host shook his head … only one could leave alive.

Kaeo stumbled in a haze falling onto her plinth and hitting the pad. However the pad had been deactivated and there was no escape from Kalum. The vile shrew charged teeth jutting out as bloodied arrowheads.

Just as Kalum reached her victim a transparent cylinder encompassed Kaeo, Kalum hit the glass leaving a bloody smear. The Tzitzimeh priest beat the glass in frustration but it would not yield. Next the cylinder dropped below the arena on its way to refuge. Kalum let out a howl of frustration as Allal leapt in, 'Well it seems we've had a malfunction!'

'Give it up for the still undefeated KALUM!'

The stadium fell silent mourning their champion, Kaeo.

Weissmuller injected nanites at several points. Sandra stopped her bleeding though unable to repair Kaeo's terrible scar. Tzitzimeh venom continuously broke down molecular structure of proteins, removing the venom was beyond her abilities.

Everyone stood around with bated breath as Weissmuller worked on Kaeo, monitoring her state on his wrist tablet via nanites.

'Kaeo, do you hear me?' inquired the Doctor.

The horrifically scarred warrior nodded her head before choking blood upon her own face.

'Good, good, I'm slowing down your metabolism. Do not be alarmed if you feel your heartbeat drop and become drowsy.'

Kaeo rolled on her side vomiting a mixture of stomach bile and blood onto the floor.

'Will she live?' asked Malikah.

Arthur gave a shocked expression toward his Xch'uup before waiting on Weissmuller's reply.

'I can slow the venom down but it will eventually overwhelm her brain breaking down her neural cell structure. I'm afraid death is an inevitability.'

Arthur quickly cut in, 'Is there nothing you can do?'

'If I had an anti-venom she may survive but I would need it soon.'

'Soon? How soon?'

'Within the next few hours otherwise she will not see dawn.'

'Where is the anti-venom?'

Malikah breathed deeply, 'There is none.'

'Well how do we bloody well get some?'

'Someone would have to take a clean sample from a live Tzitzimeh.'

'I'll do it!'

'You would have to remove a venom sac, intact from Mammi.'

'If that's what it takes.'

'Arthur you are but a boy.'

'Only a boy? Yet no Matriarch could defeat me in battle … even the mighty Malikah.'

'I only wish to warn, forgive me.'

The young man placed his palms together, 'Please accept my apologies … Namaste Xch'uup.'

The Tlillan Queen smiled affectionately, 'I accept your apologies but please look after yourself first. Then try to help Kaeo.'

Arthur shook his head, 'I'm sorry but I must disobey.'

The tension was broken as Kaeo threw up again, every now and then she had mini seizures convulsing on the bed. Arthur stayed with her in the med bay watching over his unwilling tutor of many years.

Outside Al spoke with Malikah, 'What the hell did you do?'

'I don't understand Mr Allal.'

The host lit a lotus cigarette and snarled, 'Don't fuck with me lady you pulled her out. I had massive ratings on that match and if she'd died ... corporations would've been begging to eat my shit just for a single endorsement!'

'Is that all you care about? Money?'

Al took a deep drag on his smoke, 'Fucking right it's all I care about! Is she still alive?'

'For now.'

'Shit, I've never heard of anyone surviving more than 30 seconds after a Telal bite!'

'I'm sorry for your financial loss but I had no part in Kaeo's escape.'

Al stood up and paced the dressing room floor, 'Ah fuck it, I wanted her to win. A sweet honey like that taking down Kalum ... they'd have raised monuments to her in 12 systems! Shit they might still do that after she croaks!'

'Kaeo may not die.'

Al Chuckled, 'Lady once you're bitten by one of them you're a gonner. I've seen the best healers in the galaxy from nano-doctors to shaman try ... none were successful.'

'If she survived would that lift your ratings?'

'Sure but it ain't gonna happen. Anyway it's time for you to send your boy to his death. Mammi's gonna make a meal of him!'

'Don't be so sure Mr Allal, Arthur can hold his own against anyone.'

Al took a drag on his cigarette before discarding it to the floor, 'Whatever lady, see you in the Chihuaz.'

The host left their dressing room along with Geman.

Visi peered up at Malikah, 'He's right the Telal are Gods.'

Malikah glanced down at Visi, 'I defeated one of your Gods.'

'Yes but Mammi … that's something else.'

'When you close your eyes can you feel the heat of the battle to come?'

Visi nodded, 'I feel the tension, it's all over Andromeda.'

Malikah closed her eyes, lifting her face to the ceiling, 'In the heat of the action the swirling of dust … the betting on names for the sake of bloodlust.'

Visi furrowed her brow, 'Do you see something?'

'I see a dry land, a woman with flashing eyes she cries out with arms raised.'

'What does she cry?'

'She cries to her King, she begs he let go and rain down.'

'There is a drought? She requires water for crops?'

Malikah laughed, 'No.'

'Who is her King?'

'The warrior of the rotten mountain.'

Visi shook her head, 'That means nothing to me.'

'It is his time, he will quench her drought,' with that Malikah's eyelids retracted to reveal a pair of jet black eyes.

Visi looked on in wonder at the Nabu, 'Do you understand?'

'He is hollow, the hollow man.'

'What does that mean?'

'I have no idea.'

Visi gave a frustrated grunt.

'I see his storm it blows her tears away.'

'The woman on the mountain?'

'No, Kaeo.'

'But she's dead.'

'Her tears gather inside him a well for her pain. Now he releases them feeding her upon the mountain.'

Malikah closed her eyes, upon opening them again their pigment had returned to grey. She steadied herself glancing this deep into the Dreamscape was very draining.

'What does it mean?' pushed Visi.

'Make of it what you will for if prophecy does not develop it becomes metaphor. I make no claims.'

'Then tell me what you believe you saw.'

'I saw a young man with two destinies. One starkly opposed to the other, depending upon Kaeo.'

'Like I said she's dead,' replied Visi.

'Kaeo lives, the woman on the mountain made certain of it. She has taken the rudder and steers his destiny now … not I, after the Chihuaz Kaeo shall steer.'

'But what if she dies?'

'If she lives, Arthur's destiny is love if she dies it is hate. Pray for love my dear Visi for his hatred may consume us all.'

Meanwhile Arthur stood alone fussing over Kaeo as she gave ground to Hades unrelenting lure. Holding her hand the young man comforted his tutor, 'I'll get that venom sac, don't worry.'

Kaeo lay down slipping in and out of consciousness as she choked up blood. Kalum had left her face torn and melted, the once beautiful Valkyrie now resembled a disfigured freak. A hairline no longer existed on the left side of her face. Skin either removed or melted all the way to her neck. Kaeo's eye stuck out as if she were one of Dr Frankenstein's experiments gone wrong.

As the lad fussed he heard a voice to his left, 'A tragic sight is she not?'

Arthur glanced over his shoulder to observe the golden glow of Athene her brilliant eyes smiling back at him.

'You're still here?'

'I am always here.'

Arthur returned his attention to Kaeo, 'Can you help her.'

'Help her?'

'Remove the venom from her body, it's killing her.'

'I cannot do what man must do for himself.'

'Then you are of no use to me!'

Athene stepped daintily to the opposite side of Kaeo's bed, looking Arthur in the eye, 'If I did not know your love for this woman I might have become angered.'

'I meant no offense,' sighed Arthur.

'I am here to help you save your beloved.'

The young man stared into Athene's flashing eyes, 'But you just told me.'

'I told you I cannot do for man what man must do for himself.'

'Now you're playing with my emotions for your own pleasure!'

Athene gave Arthur a golden smile, 'I will tell you how to remove the venom sac from Mammi so Doctor Weissmuller may treat Kaeo.'

Kaeo moved in and out of consciousness the half Tlillan was not sure if she was hallucinating due to drugs or the effect of venom attacking her neurons. Nevertheless she could see a beautiful golden woman dressed in armour, brilliant blue eyes, speaking with Arthur.

'She sees me.'

'How?' inquired Arthur.

'As venom breaks neurons down her visual cortex devises connections it normally would not. For a short time she may see and hear us but once recovered I will be considered a phantasm.'

Arthur's heart jumped, 'Then she will survive?'

'If you listen my little Telemachus.'

'How do I get a venom sac?'

Athene grinned as she strolled beside Arthur. The Goddess of strategic wisdom in battle slipped an ivory finger onto the base of his skull, 'Do you feel that?'

'Yes.'

'Where the skull meets the neck Tzitzimeh have a nerve, excite that nerve and you shall execute an involuntary reflex used to feed their young. It will cause Mammi to open her mouth wide, wide enough for you to reach down and snatch a venom sac.'

Arthur let go of Kaeo's hand, dropping to the floor he embraced Athene's knees, 'Without you I would be nothing.'

'Be warned Arthur. Mammi's jaws will remain open for mere seconds. Spend too long and your arm will be dismembered. Such is the power of a Tzitzimeh's jaws.'

'I shall do as you say my Goddess.'

Athene smiled at the young lad, trembling at her feet, 'You may rise.'

The boy rose before his sparkling Goddess.

'Do you remember what you first told Duncan?'

'It is easy to be angry.'

'What was his answer?'

'He said it is easy to angry but to be angry at the right man at the right time is hard.'

'I am here to tell you that now fury shall have her reign.'

'I understand, Athene.'

'Let all your hatred rain down upon Mammi as a hot deluge!'

With that Athene's image vanished from sight. Kaeo dropped her head back down. Arthur heard an alert calling him to prepare for the final. The young man stepped into the main dressing room all stared silently at the poor lad about to face the darkest demon of Andromeda.

'I am ready,' stated the boy quietly.

Malikah held his shoulders with confidence, 'You leave this place a boy but shall return a man.'

'If I return,' replied Arthur.

'Then you shall die a man with Kleos upon the field of battle.'

Arthur nodded before stepping into a cylinder.

Arthur rose from beneath the battleground. Smoke filled the air as holograms of fallen warriors from this year's Chihuaz were projected into the fog.

Images of the dead swirled around him as phantoms in a dirge, including Kaeo who was to join their number soon.

One of his favourite songs blasted out filling the stadium. Arthur's mind was focused entirely on the task at hand. Neither ghostly faces nor music could distract him from his goal.

Women in sheer bodysuits danced in circles as whirling dervishes, orbiting his lonely plinth. He waited calmly until the song faded. As it did dancers exited the arena, holograms vanished and fog dissipated. It was then the lad noticed neither Mammi nor her representative sat upon the throne of the Chihuaz. The only other person was Allal who walked out from the side lines to rapturous applause … the entire galaxy was watching.

'WHO DO YA LOVE?' shouted Al.

'ALLAL!' replied a frenzied audience.

'WHO GIVES YA THE BEST WARRIORS IN THE UNIVERSE?'

'ALLAL!'

'WHO DO YA PRAY TO EVERYDAY?'

'ALLAL!'

'WHO KEEPS YA COMING BACK FOR MORE BLOOD AND BONE?'

'ALLAL!'

'WHO WOULD YA SELL YOUR OWN MOTHER TO SLAVERS FOR?'

'ALLAL!'

The host raised his arms as a crazed throng poured down adulation. The Chihuaz had risen back to its former significance as the power behind Andromeda … all thanks to Malikah, Kaeo and Arthur. Tonight Al was praying for Mammi's death and release from her stranglehold.

The host in his sparkling silver suit walked up to Arthur, 'We all know this boy. He's chopped his way through countless men and women to get here. Tonight he'll be up against the most feared beast in the known universe, tell me do you have any particular strategy?'

Arthur peered down at Al, 'To win.'

The host laughed, 'But how do you propose to defeat such a demon?'

'With the patronage of the Gods.'

Al was a little puzzled but continued, 'How is Kaeo?'

'Alive … for now.'

'Rumour has it that you and Kaeo have a thing, is that true?'

'A thing?'

'You know? A relationship.'

Arthur pouted a little, 'You and I have a relationship, don't we?'

The crowd laughed.

'You know what I mean, a romantic relationship.'

The lad shook his head, 'That is false.'

'Alright, good luck tonight.'

The host returned to the side lines as smoke filled the arena once more and holograms of Chihuaz fallen caressed the second contestant's cylinder.

Mammi rose from the depths to the noise of a cat being tortured to tambourines, at least that's how Arthur heard it.

Women danced around her plinth as the mother of all Tzitzimeh growled across the arena. Shrunken heads of past enemies swung from her tunic, her headdress absent exposing a scalp covered by thin hair as the grey eyed beast attempted to intimidate him.

Arthur was not in the slightest bit afraid of Mammi's browbeating. His anger and hatred began to swell up inside as the Tzitzimeh beat her chest to a hysterical crowd.

Once its music faded Al attempted to get some words from Mammi to no avail. The vile creature was not in the mood to talk. Her place at the head of Andromeda was at risk. The only enemy to have defeated her people had chased them down as dogs pursuing a fox. For the first time there was fear in Mammi's eyes and hope in Allal's.

The host addressed his adoring throng, 'For the first time in thousands of cycles the Telal have been challenged. For the first time ever a Telal lost and now they stand at the precipice with the fear of defeat looming over them!'

The crowd cheered while the galaxy tuned in. Viewing figures blasted through the roof and Allal took more endorsements than a politician at a conference of banking corporations.

'Tonight we decide who is righteous! Tonight we decide who marches with head held high … and … who is trodden upon below … FIGHT!'

Al leapt back as the crowd went into rabid shouts and cheers, Arthur and Mammi stepped down with caution. As the combatants guardedly approached one another two spaces opened in the arena floor, each aperture produced a spear. Mammi grabbed hers first, throwing the javelin with all her might at the tall lad.

Arthur was totally focused. Passion brought his eyes to a fiery glimmer, burning into his opponent. As the spear, made from one piece of cast bronze, travelled towards Arthur the crowd went silent certain the young man would be impaled by Mammi's mighty cast.

He seized the spear in flight before it made contact with his chest. In a rage he broke the weapon with both hands over his knee. The audience gasped at such a feat of not only visual acuity and outstanding reflexes but also physical power.

Arthur cast aside the broken pieces of her lance and Mammi retreated in fright. The crowd went berserk stomping hard in approval.

Another two spaces appeared at each end of the dusty ring. This time a pair of thick wooden sticks materialized each just over two feet long. Arthur recognised them; he'd learnt their discipline after linking with Amitra. Popularly a Filipino art the Rattan sticks were a form of self-defence, Amitra called them Kali sticks she'd quickly learnt their craft from an Indian master.

Unlike Kali sticks these were a less flexible wood, something closer to oak. Nevertheless Arthur picked them up as did Mammi. The mob howled for murder while the young man spun his sticks approaching a timid opponent.

Mammi could no longer bear the jeers and with a hiss she gnashed her bright teeth and launched an attack.

Arthur used his skills; blocking attacks with one stick he beat the old shrew's face with the other. The withered beast thumped the dirt kicking up a cloud of dust. She barked in agony and the audience roared in delight just as Rome during the height of empire.

Mammi scrambled in retreat yet before she might withdraw from Arthur's range he beat her again, knocking the witch down. Each escape attempt ended in a pummelling to the rapture of Andromeda.

From on high Malikah peered down as destiny unfolded. The Tlillan Queen whispered to herself in frustration, 'Finish her! Finish her now!'

Visi turned to the sable beauty, 'What was that?'

'Nothing, nothing at all.'

Below Arthur's anger had taken over, for a moment he'd forgotten Kaeo, unleashing his hatred onto the wrinkled monster. Each attempt to escape halted with a harder blow followed by a greater screech of approval from onlookers. Like a dynamo gathering power the young man pushed Mammi to the edge, fuelled by anger and Andromeda's blood lust.

A human could imagine Nero sitting on that sacred seat of Topixque peering down upon his subjects as they fought for the love of Rome and the acknowledgment of their Emperor. What unfolded in the dirt arena below was as exhilarating as it was obscene.

Covered in gore soaked grime the end was in sight, Mammi made one last attempt to save herself and the Tzitzimeh. She huddled as a frightened animal shrinking from attack and once his Kali stick was raised she jumped up dealing a well-placed uppercut to the chin.

Dust filled Arthur's eyes, his head a concussion. The lad staggered back retreating out of striking distance unfortunately he wasn't quick enough. Stumbling towards his end of the arena the young gladiator fell onto his back.

Mammi gathered her wounded frame to boos and hisses. Observing her opponent on his back, completely disorientated, she attacked. It was time to strike before the man had a chance to recover.

It seemed as if destiny had made her call. The crowd screamed for Arthur to get up. Allal beat his hand against a low partition separating crowd and ring.

Aloft Visi screamed, Sandra turned away unable to watch Mammi shred her student's flesh. Malikah gritted her teeth, a tear forming in her eye, as Hades moved on her young charge.

On the arena floor Arthur's vision obscured, mind disorientated, he lay on his back attempting to clear his eyes but it was too late Mammi was upon him with gaping jaws.

The Tlillan campaign was over the Tzitzimeh would in seconds claim victory. As the old witch descended something appeared between Mammi and the boy; a woman of gold with flashing blue eyes her hair a nest of hissing snakes snapping at the air. The apparition's face morphed from one of divine beauty to that of such horror it shook Mammi's core. This abomination's roar rattled every bone in the Tzitzimeh's body; all passion for the kill fled her being, bringing her to a halt. After a moment the witch collected herself. Deciding this horror obstructing victory was but a hologram Mammi gathered courage and charged. Athene cackled, her flashing eyes blinded the witch freezing the beast in its tracks.

Only Mammi and Arthur witnessed Athene, Andromeda observed in disbelief.

The Greek Goddess placed a palm over Arthur's eyes removing that which obscured his mind and vision, 'Arthur, get up!'

The lad saw Athene and knowing he was safe pushed himself up to observe a confused foe withdrawing from battle.

Athene's face was one of disappointment, 'Your actions here shall create ripples felt for eons … there is no room for childish grandstanding!'

From on high Malikah watched in utter shock.

Sandra pulled her eyes back to the fight, 'Who is he talking to?'

'I don't know,' replied the sable Queen wiping a tear from her ivory cheek.

'What just happened?' asked Visi.

'I don't know,' replied Malikah in a cold tone.

Athene pointed towards the remaining spear, 'Take your spear and impale that foul animal!'

Arthur stooped down retrieving the bronze javelin. As Mammi stumbled on the back foot dazed by Athene's flashing eyes Arthur made his cast. The crowd roared while the missile travelled across the arena. Mammi was unsure as to why … until a cold shaft of bronze passed through her chest pinning her frame to the partition. The wrinkled demon screamed in agony as the throng surged from behind.

'Now save the one you love!'

Arthur nodded as the Goddess transformed into a golden owl flying up and out of the Chihuaz. Without further ado he approached the wretched beast pushing at the base of its skull. Mammi's jaws jerked open. Past rows of teeth he observed two purple sacs dangling in its throat. Carefully he pushed his hand inside, removing the organ in a single pull without compromising its integrity.

The crowd became frenzied as Mammi vomited a stream of blood onto the arena. Not yet deceased Arthur took Athene's advice. He grabbed the blinded creature's skull and beat it against the partition, again and again spattering Al's flock with Mammi's brains and cerebral fluid. This is why fans paid so much more for front row seats. They loved every moment as droplets of blood, bone and brain sprayed their faces.

Once it was certain Mammi's soul had departed her mortal coil for Hades boatman Arthur walked away.

Music began to play as the sound of "Millennium" filled the stadium 'Some say that we are players, some say that we are pawns, but we've been making money since the day that we were born,' sang the voice of Robbie Williams. Andromeda celebrated over Mammi's corpse as dancers twisted and spun around Arthur.

After a few minutes Al hushed his congregation to address his champion, 'Is there anything you'd like to say before you leave?'

As Arthur gathered his breath he said in a tired voice, 'No … I think Mammi got the point,' he raised a hand to loud applause.

'That's great and what an amazing fight! And to everyone watching don't forget you can see Arthur and his best moments in our interview, later.'

The young man returned to his plinth venom sac in hand, his cylinder sealed to propel Andromeda's hero back to his dressing room where Doctor Weissmuller waited.

Chapter 18

Weissmuller appeared from med bay, 'I've done what I can it is up to her and God now.'

'When will we know?' asked Arthur.

'If tomorrow she is alive the anti-venom was successful.'

'And if not?'

'She will not see dawn.'

Allal smoked a lotus cigarette whilst pacing the room, 'Well we need to get the post victory interviews set up.'

'Can't it wait?' stated Arthur in an incredulous tone

'Look I know you love her, so do I, everyone does. Life goes on and I have contracts to meet, if she lives then great … if not then we'll make what we can of it,' sighed Al.

Arthur sneered at the old cyborg, 'You disgust me,' before stomping off into the med bay.

'I'm sorry Mr Allal but he is a young man and in love,' apologised Malikah.

'No problem, I've been married more times than most people can count … it takes a lot more to hurt my feelings!'

Amitra entered the room to an awkward silence and uncomfortable looks. Approaching Xch'uup she pressed her palms together, 'Namaste Xch'uup.'

Malikah nodded her head.

'I have come to discover your policy towards the Tzitzimeh, now they are toppled from the Chihuaz.'

Malikah looked deep into Amitra's sable eyes, 'That is to be determined by them.'

'You intend to continue your persecution?'

'I will wait until a new Mammi is selected, if she bends her knee to Xch'uup then bloodshed may be avoided.'

'Yet victory is yours.'

'Why should Xch'uup grant the Tzitzimeh mercy?'

'If Machine had not shown mercy …'

'ENOUGH!' snapped Malikah.

'Truth is painful indeed,' Amitra looked around the room glancing at Al, Geman and Visi.

'The Tzitzimeh reign of terror must be brought to an end, it is fate.'

'You see nothing of their destiny.'

'Do you?'

'I make no claims I only ask that you do unto others as you would have them do unto you.'

The pair of Matriarchs faced off with fire in their eyes until Sandra stood between them, 'Kaeo is sick, she may die can this not wait?'

Amitra took another deep breath, 'As Arthur would say it is easy to be angry.'

The dread Queen's eyes returned to their usual sparkling grey, 'Agreed now is not the time to discuss these matters.'

Inside med bay Arthur stood over Kaeo, beside him the Goddess of the flashing eyes appeared whispering into his ear, 'Well done my little Telemachus.'

He could not face his Goddess.

'Oh come now there is no need to feel ashamed!'

'I put her life in jeopardy all for my own vanity.'

As Athene removed her golden helmet it disappeared, 'So now you understand what I have been teaching you all this time?'

'Self-control and patronage of the Gods?'

Athene caressed the young man's brow, 'You're not far from it my little Telemachus,' Athene's gaze was drawn to Kaeo's bed, 'She listens to us speak.'

'She still sees you?'

'In time Kaeo will inform Malikah.'

'Then Kaeo will survive?'

The Goddess laughed as she moved around Arthur.

'Why torture me? Why not answer my question?'

Peering into Kaeo's eyes Athene spoke in a soft tone, 'She cannot decide whether I am hallucination ... or reality.'

The groggy warrior lifted a weak arm toward Athene as the Goddess leant in allowing Kaeo's fingertips to brush against her ivory cheek.

'Tell me, will she survive the venom?' demanded Arthur.

Athene looked up from the bed, 'You do love her, don't you?'

'Does it matter to you?'

'If it did not matter to me she would have died on the Chihuaz floor.'

Arthur peered down at Kaeo, straining to open her eyes.

'And if I did not love you, you would have died at the hands of Mammi for all Andromeda to witness. Remember what you owe the Gods give them their due and you shall always be protected my little Telemachus.'

Arthur nodded his head, 'I understand, I didn't mean to ...'

The Goddess of the flashing eyes raised her hand, 'Never mind, as for your love she will survive her encounter with Kalum. However the demon inside, the beast lurking within is her greatest foe.'

Athene stood beside Arthur, 'If you wish to save your love the greatest battle is yet to be fought. You must block her path to self-destruction.'

'How?'

'You will be required to humiliate yourself, be abused as if you were nothing but animal waste. A Matriarch would die rather than suffer what I have seen.'

'Have seen?'

'I am energy, past, present and future is all open to me. I have seen what is to be and what may be. I am the only one who understands why you love her so. Even you my little Telemachus are unaware.'

Arthur held the groaning Valkyrie's hand as she scrutinized Athene.

'She did not wish to manipulate or take advantage of your abilities.'

'That's true,' nodded the young man.

'She is the only one you can trust with your heart. Even I, you fail to trust totally.'

'Athene, I ...'

The Goddess of strategic wisdom laughed it off, 'Do not apologise I am not hurt. It is understandable considering the environment you were raised in ... though all that will be changing now.'

'Why?'

'You defeated Mammi, on return to Otoch the sight of your shadow falling upon the ground shall cause Matriarchs to hold their breath!'

'I think that's an exaggeration.'

'I have seen it. They will cower as mortals at the feet of a Titan.'

Arthur raised an eyebrow, 'I thought I was in for humiliation?'

'You are as cynical as Odysseus. I thought you would have learnt to trust my word by now!'

Arthur dropped to the floor grabbing Athene's knees, 'Forgive me my Goddess. You have saved mine and Kaeo's lives. I don't mean to be ungrateful.'

'Oh get up Arthur, remember you are now slayer of the Tzitzimeh Queen. Always carry yourself as such!'

'You defeated her, not I!'

Athene held his shoulders fixing her blue gaze on him, 'You are still young, even Xch'uup would have failed an encounter with Mammi at such an age. I have merely given you time to reach your full potential.'

'And what is that?'

Athene glanced at Kaeo then back at Arthur, 'The paradigm shift my little Telemachus,' with a smile Athene disappeared as med bay door opened and Malikah entered the room.

'Talking to Kaeo?' inquired Malikah.

'Yes,' replied the young man.

Malikah sensed deception, 'When can you do your interview for AI?'

'Whenever he's ready.'

'A swift change of heart have you seen something I should know of?'

'No.'

The sable Queen felt his dishonesty.

Arthur left the med bay appearing that evening on every NET station in Andromeda and throughout the Triumvirate. Sitting on a pair of high stools in the centre of the Chihuaz arena Al interviewed the young man.

For the first time Arthur was able to sit back and look at the stadium in silence without a pre-occupied mind. The arena inspired awe, just the thought that galactic leaders had battle it out for the future of civilizations over eons took a mere mortal's breath away.

'So the question on the tip of everyone's tongue is … what the hell happened?' inquired Al.

'I fought Mammi and won.'

'But defeat seemed certain and for no reason she retreated. You were at Mammi's mercy, you should be dead, she should be sitting in your place now … what happened Arthur?'

'I suppose there's only one person that could answer your question, unfortunately she died that day.'

'So what's your explanation?'

'Mammi styled herself as a God perhaps her hubris insulted the true Gods?'

'You mentioned Gods before. Tell me about these Gods you ask for patronage?'

Arthur smiled, 'All must bend their knee to Xch'uup. She is the only true God in this universe.'

Malikah and Lian laid back in Xch'uup's cabin on the Chutli.

'It seems you've succeeded Malee,' stated Lian cuddling up to Malikah.

The sable Queen maintained a serious expression, 'He lies.'

'Are you sure?'

'I am certain.'

'Perhaps he thinks of himself as a God after defeating Mammi in such a spectacular fashion?'

Malikah shook her head, 'No, there is only one person able to discover the truth.'

'Who?'

'Kaeo, he will open to no-one other than her.'

Lian chuckled as she watched the broadcast, 'She's the only person that couldn't care less.'

'That is why he loves her. We all do our best to control and guide the young man along a pre-designated path. She allows him to be free by rejecting him.'

'That doesn't make sense!'

Malikah chuckled, 'Of course it doesn't make sense. Love never adheres to logic.'

'You'll make sure Kaeo survives?' inquired Lian.

'I cannot stop the Tzitzimeh venom once inside her brain. That is up to Doctor Weissmuller.'

'But you can see the future?'

'There are futures where Kaeo dies and others where she lives, it hangs in the balance for now.'

Al asked Arthur excitedly, 'Talk us through your final battle with Mammi.'

The screen split playing the Chihuaz final whilst Arthur commentated on the other half of the screen.

The young man conveniently left out Athene and her influence, attributing his miraculous recovery to the will of the Gods.

After the battle Al questioned him on Xch'uup's intention towards the Tamoanchan Territory. Unfortunately Arthur could not answer. Apparently the Tlillan Queen awaited a new Mammi to be selected.

'From what I can tell Xch'uup has formed a pact in this galaxy between the Vega and Skin Territories, is that true?'

Arthur laughed, 'Now you're asking me about politics, if you want to know the answers to those questions you'll have to speak with Xch'uup yourself.'

'Fine, I'll ask you one final question ... is it true that you are in love with Kaeo?'

The atmosphere became very tense very quickly, 'We all love Kaeo, Al.'

'You know what I mean Arthur come on give us an answer.'

Arthur replied in an awkward tone, 'There is nothing going on between us I can assure you of that Allal ... thank you very much.'

The NET show closed with a collection of Arthur's best kills during the Chihuaz.

Malikah smirked, 'He is deeply in love with her.'

Lian smiled, 'I think it's cute.'

'You think Makayuuk are cute.'

'Well aren't I cute?'

'You know what I mean.'

Dawn the next day and everyone waited outside med bay, Kaeo had not been moved.

Weissmuller exited, 'You may enter.'

Malikah spoke to the Doctor immediately, 'Well what do you say?'

'I believe she will survive though her brain may be damaged. We will not know the extent for another week or two.'

'Damaged?'

'The venom broke down neural pathways. Her brain has worked constantly, creating new pathways to prevent loss of memory, senses, motor functions and so on. I cannot tell you to what extent she will recover she may never walk again or worse she may not remember any of us.'

Malikah looked into the med bay, 'Thank you Doctor.'

The German shrugged his shoulders, 'It is my job.'

Inside Kaeo was laid out upon a stretcher no longer vomiting and bleeding. The short Thai seemed to be recovering as she looked about the room. Her eyes eventually locked on to Malikah as she entered the room and stood over her wounded Marshal.

Kaeo's eyes narrowed raising a hand towards the Tlillan Queen.

'I think she recognises you,' yelped an excited Arthur.

Malikah took Kaeo's hand and gave a warm smile.

The short Tlillan's lips moved slowly.

'She said something!' shouted Arthur.

'Be silent!' snapped Malikah as she leant in to listen.

From Kaeo's lips came a croaky voice.

'What did she say?' asked Arthur, ignoring Malikah's instructions.

'If you shut up I might be able to hear!'

Again Kaeo spoke in a very hushed tone, 'Am I dead?'

Malikah whispered back, 'No, Arthur defeated Mammi retrieving enough venom for Doctor Weissmuller to create an anti-venom.'

Rather than happiness despair flooded the room. An intense emotion of sorrow hit him like a freight train leaving the young man in utter confusion.

Kaeo turned her head to one side allowing tears of pain to roll down a disfigured face and onto the floor.

'Why is she crying?' inquired Arthur.

'She wanted to die.'

'Die? Who wants to die?'

Amitra looked down with folded arms, 'The depressed?'

Arthur peered toward the towering Matriarch, 'Was that supposed to be funny?'

'On the contrary, it is a matter of fact.'

The young man returned his gaze to Kaeo, 'Why is she depressed?'

'Kaeo was defeated, if she had died her soul would have returned in another incarnation; instead she earnt neither the Kleos of battle nor Nostos on the homecoming, at least in her mind.'

The Tlillan Marshal's tears rolled onto the floor her friends observing the pitiful sight. For the rest of the day Kaeo's condition improved whilst she bemoaned her situation. Her defeat for all to see and a young lad saving her life was more than a Tlillan warrior could suffer.

Arthur was befuddled, he could not grasp why she longed to have died on the arena floor. To him it was something to be avoided at all cost, it made no sense that such a death would hold allure.

He remained at her bedside for the following days. Never moving for fear Kaeo might end her own life.

As she recovered her sight returned, it seemed the Amazon was not permanently damaged by the Tzitzimeh venom at least mentally. Her face remained terribly scarred, though that was the least of Weissmuller's concerns for now.

After a week Kaeo was able to sit up, upon seeing her melted face she placed the mirror down.

'I'm sure Sandra will be able to repair the damage,' stated Arthur as Kaeo handed the mirror back.

'It is Tzitzimeh venom there is nothing she can do,' replied Kaeo in a cold tone.

'Malikah could ...'

'Leave me Arthur, I wish to be alone.'

The young man looked at her nervously.

'Have no fear.'

The lad exited med bay. After the door closed wails of sorrow emanated from inside as his love cried for herself.

Peering at Amitra the dark skinned Amazon said softly, 'I know you are confused, give her time to adjust Arthur.'

Back in the Skin Territory McCann and Clayton were drinking at Ninti's. After Allal's interview was over the pair decided to get some serious drinking in. Clayton lit up a cigarette much to McCann's disapproval. It was a habit the old soldier had picked up in the Bokors.

Hevatsu sat bedside Clayton lighting his smoke and pouring his drink. The Englishman noticed the pair had become inseparable; in fact Clayton spent all his free time with the red lady.

Alongside his red friend Clayton was now officially a Deputy of Kurgudwardum 57, sporting a shiny gold badge with a data chip inside to prove it.

'May I ask you a frank question Commodore?'

McCann eyed his deputy over a Scotch and Ramon Allones, 'I'll be frank if you'll be earnest.'

'The battle of Bandayuuk, what happened?'

McCann took a shot of whisky before the former love droid leant over to pour another, 'The Makayuuk surrendered, they agreed to serve Xch'uup as her vassal.'

'No disrespect sir but that's bullshit.'

McCann replied with nothing but a stony face.

'I fought those Macks for years. They don't surrender besides they had us, why would they agree to parle when we were at their mercy.'

'Now, now old boy, the situation wasn't that dire. I reckon I did a pretty good job, we were advancing on them and those reinforcements were still a way aways.'

'Sir, I've seen experts analyse that battle, we'd lost. The Macks called parle then pulled back from Bandayuuk. Those reinforcements were crushing us and the Tlillans were finished.'

The Commodore realised he wasn't going to bluff his Deputy, 'Alright Clayton, what do you want to know exactly?'

'Why did Machine call parle?'

'Lian convinced Machine to parle,' stated the Commodore in a cold tone.

'I don't believe that.'

'I don't give a shit what you believe but that's what happened.'

'What was discussed at this parle?'

'All I can tell you is that Machine agreed to serve Xch'uup.'

Clayton sensed his commanding Officer was being honest, 'There are rumours about Malikah taking a trip to Bandayuuk 0, can you ...'

McCann cut in, 'I was there with Malikah as part of the deal. She reset the crust and cleaned up the atmosphere.'

Clayton had listened to many conspiracy theories concerning Machine's defeat/surrender at Bandayuuk. It was something that intrigued him, mostly because of his contact with Macks. The tunnel warrior knew full well that Macks didn't surrender. Macks taken prisoner had done so due to being knocked unconscious and even then they rebelled later.

'After the Tico crashed into Bandayuuk along with that Mack battleship the crust was broken. Bandayuuk would have collapsed in less than a few days. Machine could have fled but the remaining Tlillan war cruisers, namely the Teteo would have hounded Machine. It was a compromise, Malikah required surrender and Machine required the stabilisation of Bandayuuk.

They saved each other rather than fight to an irrational end. That's what two sentient beings do ... only one emotion overrides even that of self-preservation.'

'And that is?' asked Hevatsu.

McCann took a drag of his cigar then said softly, 'Love.'

Thanks to abilities endowed by the Ixchel Clayton sensed McCann's honesty.

The old soldier knocked back a drink as a smiling Hevatsu pecked his cheek. Clayton looked up stoically at the ceiling in Ninti bar, recalling his former enemy on Bandayuuk 0 ...

One month in and Clayton was prepared for his first combat insertion. Once his nanites were disabled alongside an injection of Ixchel, Clayton would be permitted to accompany the Bokors. Following four weeks of practice with the Kukri and a little face painting, Roberts was satisfied his latest recruit was ready.

Inside an Atlas, flying high above the surface, Clayton sat in his drop terminal red faced comrades staring back at him.

A platoon of regular infantry were surrounded and pinned down by Macks. Soon to run out of ammunition it was the Bokors mission to cut a path from the surface and through a Mack perimeter to those men fighting for their lives, If not 48 men were about to be processed in Mack food tanks.

'Insertion point ETA 3 minutes,' came a voice over the speakers.

Roberts and his men checked pulse rifles making certain their batteries and ammunition clips were full. One man wore a bandolier holding countless clips of ammunition and grenades. Clayton gave him and odd look, the soldier shouted over the engine noise, 'Always bring plenty of ammo the last thing you want is to run out of ammo!'

'Insertion point ETA 30 seconds, prepare for sub-orbital drop.'

Clayton secured his pulse rifle as a single safety bar dropped from above, similar to a rollercoaster restraint.

'Sub-orbital insertion ETA 10 seconds.'

Roberts grinned at Clayton and shouted over the engine noise, 'Hold on to your wage packets gentlemen!'

'5, 4, drop pods are go!'

Metal doors closed encasing Clayton within the drop pod. Next he felt his stomach rise up as he was fired out of the Atlas bay and into Bandayuuk's atmosphere.

Twelve drop pods exploded from the Atlas belly tearing through the sky down towards their objective. Their drop pods automatically manoeuvred through the air whilst the men inside prepared for a landing.

Shortly after leaving the Atlas Clayton felt his stomach move in the opposite direction as his drop pod thudded into the soil of Bandayuuk. Drop pods were constructed of catronium and lined with the same material used on star ships for the purpose of gravity plating. The difference being that an opposite electrical charge would cause an opposite effect. So Clayton's drop pod fired up its anti-gravity as best it could; reducing G-force upon his body. Unfortunately there wasn't enough of the stuff to prevent gravity's full effect. But it did mean he wouldn't be left splattered on the sides of his pod when it landed.

After hitting the ground his pod broke open allowing its cargo to leap out. One man remained stuck inside, his restraint would not release and its manual release lever wasn't working. Roberts grabbed the safety bar and with one foot on the ground plate he gave an almighty heave. His enhanced strength ripped the safety bar off.

'Alright let's bail those boys out of trouble,' stated the Sergeant pointing to a nearby tunnel entrance.

Clayton and his comrades fanned out as they approached a gateway to the underworld.

These Bokors were very different to anything Clayton had experienced previously. The men were almost casual in one sense yet they took their job with the utmost sincerity, it was something he had got used to quickly.

As they approached the entrance each man's Tlillan vision kicked in, peering inside a tunnel moving down at an angle of 20 degrees.

Roberts made hand signals, his men complied taking up positions on each side of the 60 foot wide channel.

Nothing was present though faint sounds of pulse rifles could be detected further down.

More signals and his men moved into the cave in three groups of four. As in training only one group moved at a time whilst the other two provided covered. This was instinctive by now one group covered the right, one left and another moved forwards.

As they progressed burst fire from pulse rifles became louder yet their Tlillan night vision revealed nothing.

300 feet in they met a bend in the shaft, Clayton saw muzzle flash. Each time a pulse rifle fired it threw silhouettes of men upon the tunnel walls.

Everyone waited on Roberts; he made his signals instructing one team to set anti-personnel mines along the exit route. Once finished Roberts signalled again, turning the corner Clayton witnessed a battle.

Two groups of Makayuuk using rocks fallen from the damaged tunnel for cover had an entire platoon pinned down. There was no escape for these poor men. They lay trapped between two groups of Makayuuk and running out of ammunition fast.

Clayton estimated the number of Makayuuk between him and his comrades close to 20. The I.S.A soldiers outnumbered them however there was a stretch of open ground between the two forces. The Macks would've cut down any charge for freedom. Even if successful the Macks behind would press every inch of the way, no doubt eliminating them before Helios' light warmed their faces.

The Bokors crouched behind cover, taking aim, waiting for Roberts to give an appropriate signal. Roberts dropped his hand and the Bokors fired into their preoccupied targets. Macks dropped in concert before heads might turn.

Shaking his hand and pointing forward the Bokors advanced in three groups of four. Roberts spoke to the Captain of the pinned down platoon.

After linking up with their objective the regular infantry were shocked at the sight of these men. Twelve men with red skull faces and not one wore a combat monocle, how they could see in the dark was a mystery.

'Sergeant Roberts, sir.'

'Captain Koslowsky, I've got 16 men, three injured.'

'The route to the top is clear. There's an Atlas waiting to pick you up sir.'

Koslowsky looked at the band of red faced men, 'You mean you're our extraction group?'

'Yes sir.'

'One squad?'

'Yes sir.'

A tungsten round bounced off the rock Koslowsky and Roberts had crouched behind, 'Well it's better than nothing but there's more than a platoon of Macks pushing up right now … and they're pissed!'

'You let us worry about that sir, just get your men topside.'

Koslowsky nodded his head, dragged his men to their feet and made a dash for the exit, he wasn't about to disagree. The Bokors remained, holding back Machine's tide as long as possible.

Koslowsky eventually made it around the corner and out of harm's way.

Roberts' men readied grenades as more and more Macks reinforced their remaining position, no doubt preparing for a push.

One soldier held a flash grenade. The rest took standard frag grenades. Hand signals were made and each man activated his suit helmet. Upon a dark liquid shield covering their heads a sign was given, first a large flash grenade was thrown, something similar to three tin cans stacked top to bottom. Modern grenades could be set to detonate in proximity to an enemy bio-signature, though they still possessed a time delay option.

Upon detonating eleven frag grenades followed blowing apart their enemy.

The Bokors quickly jumped out of cover. Whilst the flash grenade burnt brightly they ran amongst blinded Makayuuk executing survivors.

Over 50 Macks died as phosphorus scorched souls of the dead returned to Machine's collective. Spirits departed as a breeze passing over the wine dark waters of the Mediterranean. Captured within a ships sails for a few fleeting days, pushing it closer to enlightenment before escaping to be caught by some other vessel languishing closer to port and so Makayuuk souls did gather forming a ghostly wind. The Bokors felt a shiver of cold run down their spines, including Clayton.

Before leaving Roberts took what seemed to be a pulley from his leg pocket another soldier handed him a length of carbon nanotube rope. Their activity confused Clayton as he watched a scene play out before him to burning white light.

Another soldier took a Mack corpse whilst two more painted his face the same red and black skull design as their squadron. Once finished Roberts slipped a noose over his neck and took up the slack. Clayton saw the pulley was now attached high up on the tunnel ceiling with a suction pad.

Roberts and 6 other men brandished Kukris … the Mack was sliced up in less than a minute, skin dangling to expose a body of raw flesh.

'One last thing,' smiled Roberts.

Using his Kukri he etched words upon the deceased Mack's forehead. When finished Roberts lifted the Mack a good twelve feet off the ground, securing his end with a suction pad to a large rock.

'Time to get going boys,' stated Roberts.

The Squadron retreated in the same four by four by four formations, after passing their anti-personnel mines Roberts activated the explosives.

Upon reaching topside a hummingbird was requested for extraction; before Macks had arrived the Bokors were on their way home flying through the chilly atmosphere of Bandayuuk 0.

Back inside the tunnel Sirt 137 observed the remnants of his platoon. Dosa 958 scoffed, 'Damn bastards!'

'SIRT!' called out a young Makayuuk

The former Admiral turned to his right, a beam of light ran up and down a corpse hanging from the ceiling, long sections of skin draped below its feet, swinging in the stench of fired munitions and death.

'Not again,' whispered Dosa.

'Cut him down,' ordered Sirt as he moved through a corpse strewn terrain, 'and have these bodies sent to processing.'

Several men and women began shifting the dead into piles. A grav-lift would be brought up to transport cadavers for recycling.

A Mack cut the cord securing the hanging body to a nearby rock. The dead man flopped down. Sirt rolled the body onto its back and noticed words etched onto the man's forehead, 'Bista, what does this say?'

A young lady lowered her pulse rifle and approached. Dosa shook his head, 'You know what it says.'

Sirt didn't respond. He waited for the woman to translate this human scrawl into his language.

The former Admiral growled, 'What does it mean?'

'It doesn't mean anything,' replied Dosa.

'Bista, is there anything here?'

'No, it is exactly the same. If it's a code we are unable to crack it.'

'I told you, it doesn't mean anything!' roared Dosa.

Sirt called out to his subordinates, 'Search every enemy corpse. I want to know if there are any red faces amongst them.'

'Yes Sirt,' replied several men as they went to work rummaging through the dead.

Dosa snorted, 'There won't be any, you know that.'

'Must you always be so negative?'

'Tell me, what should I be positive about? These red faced bastards have been pounding us like the cheapest whore in a brothel! My platoon believe Ek'tsab is coming for them!'

Sirt took in a deep breath, 'These are men not Gods of myth!'

'They may be men but they fight as demons from hell!'

'Then we must fight harder!'

Dosa nodded in silence.

'In the meantime I want everyone working on the meaning of this … script … they cut into our dead.'

Bista stood to attention, 'May I speak freely Sirt?'

'What is it you wish to say?'

Dosa narrowed his eyes on the young lady.

'One of the girls who work above, she questioned her …'

Sirt pulled an annoyed expression, 'Yes, yes, go on.'

'He is a human soldier. He informed her this statement is an old Earth proverb. Its meaning is to impress that unpredictable events will take place usually when you least expect … it is a human joke … directed at us.'

'Why was I not informed?'

'Machine dismissed the analysis. The source was deemed unreliable.'

Sirt scratched his chin, 'That makes more sense than anything I've heard from our decoding network.'

'It makes perfect sense to those fighting on the ground,' added Dosa.

Sirt peered down at the body and read the words etched upon its face aloud, 'SHIT HAPPENS!'

A moment later everyone's attention was drawn down the tunnel as anti-personnel mines exploded to screams of Makayuuk soldiers.

Sirt locked eyes with Dosa.

Dosa nodded, 'I'll retrieve them … Machine.'

'Machine,' replied Sirt as the old warrior disappeared into darkness with 12 men.

Days after the Chihuaz had been settled and all staff returned home the Chutli remained docked. Malikah stood alone in her dressing room gazing stoically upon the arena floor.

'Beautiful, isn't it?'

The old cyborg made Malikah jump as he joined her solitary contemplation.

'Good evening Mr Allal. How are you?'

'I'm fine … sometimes I stand alone just staring at an empty Chihuaz.'

'What do you think of?'

'I like to think this is the universe's way of working out its problems.'

'How do you suppose that Mr Allal?' replied Malikah in a sceptical tone.

'Look around, everything, it came out of a star and those stars came out of one big singularity. That singularity has done this over and over, creating a universe then sucking it back in when it didn't work. We are the stars and we are that original singularity.'

Malikah nodded her head, 'Agreed.'

'Has it ever crossed your mind that war, hate and all the nasty crap that goes on is just the universe trying to work itself out?'

The Tlillan Empress stopped her previous train of thought and smiled, 'No, I don't suppose I have.'

'The Chihuaz isn't really about death. It's about the universe working out its problems as efficiently and quickly as possible.'

'I see … universal therapy?'

Al smiled, 'You got it.'

'I would like to ask you a Question now that the Chihuaz is over.'

'Sure … shoot.'

Malikah looked down at the seat of Topixque, 'Must I be present in the next cycle?'

'No, you can have a representative take the chair.'

'I'm sorry Mr Allal but what I mean is … may I abdicate?'

Al reached for his packet of lotus cigarettes. He offered one to Xch'uup yet she refused. Taking the yellow stick he lit it and drew in a plume of lotus smoke, 'You can step down but would you do me a favour?'

'Naturally.'

'Hold off on any announcement, until the next Chihuaz.'

'Done, anything else?'

'Yeh, Mammi, I don't need that bitch taking the throne.'

The sable Queen nodded her head, 'I understand. Mammi will not challenge the Chihuaz again.'

The old cyborg pointed his burning lotus cigarette at Xch'uup, 'I get the feeling it ain't over between you two.'

'It isn't Mr Allal. However I fear your universal therapy shall be insufficient to solve this problem.'

'I figured so.'

'A new Mammi will be elected by the gerontocracy after which the Tzitzimeh shall consider a choice.'

'And that being?'

'They shall bend their knee to Xch'uup … or die.'

'You'll kill Mammi again?'

'No Mr Allal … I shall kill the Tzitzimeh … extermination.'

'Of an entire species?'

'Sometimes Mr Allal therapy is not sufficient. On occasion one must cut off a finger to save the hand.'

Al took another puff, 'You're talking about a lobotomy.'

'Nothing so obscene, Mr Allal.'

'But not all Tlillan's agree with you, do they?'

Malikah peered upwards as if she were looking to the Gods for relief, 'No, they don't. Some believe the old ways have had their time. Some believe Xch'uup must strengthen Otoch by forging alliances.'

'Why not settle it with Mammi peacefully?'

'I cannot, this blood feud is as old as Xch'uup.'

'But you destroyed Mammi's fleet and knocked her out of the Chihuaz. She has no ships, few allies and little territory to support her.'

'Exactly we must press the advantage while she is weak. Until she submits … or vanishes from the universe.'

Al took a deep drag of lotus, 'Malikah … if it's okay to call you that?'

'Yes.'

'Malikah, in all these cycles I've learnt a lot of things, shit I've forgotten ten times as much as I've learnt! But I think I can give you some advice here.'

'Go on.'

'The weak cannot forgive. Only the strong can truly forgive.'

Malikah smirked at the ceiling then at Al, 'A man on Earth spoke similar words, centuries ago.'

'Consider it Malikah. I see your people splintered over this. Is it worth it for a blood feud that started over who knows what before either you or Mammi were born?'

The Tlillan Queen looked out stoically onto the arena, 'If my people continue down the path of blood for blood they shall awake one day as the Tzitzimeh … shrivelled in defeat … or worse … drowning in a deluge of victories.'

Chapter 19

Three figures exited from a docked shuttle. Captain Hopper waited with his deputies as two familiar men and a strange red skinned woman approached, boots tapping on the floor.

'What do you want McCann?' said Hopper in a direct tone.

'One of your friends has been a naughty boy,' replied the Commodore as he produced a warrant.

Hopper handed it to his deputy who scanned the chip, 'Salamu Barag, sir.'

'This is a joke, right?'

'No joke.'

'You murdered his son now you want him?'

'You won't lose any beauty sleep over it.'

Hopper fixed his eyes upon Hevatsu, 'And who the hell's this?'

'Hevatsu, this is station Captain Hopper.'

Hevatsu dipped her brow, 'It is good to meet you Captain I am Deputy Hevatsu.'

'Deputy? She's a droid! A love droid at that!'

McCann pulled out a Cohiba Siglo I and toasted its foot with his Dunhill lighter, 'If you ask her nicely she might pull that board out of your arse.'

Clayton cracked up with laughter, Hevatsu didn't get the joke. Hopper was not amused, 'You're a real funny guy, a funny guy that leaves dead bodies wherever he goes.'

McCann took a draw of mellow smoke then blew it into Hopper's face, 'If people just did as I asked there'd be no trouble.'

Hopper took the warrant from his deputy and handed it back to McCann, 'Do whatever you have to then get lost.'

The Englishman took his warrant, 'Such friendly co-operation I'm touched ... CAPTAIN.'

'If you think I'm gonna salute some Navy rich kid you're very much mistaken. I fought on the surface of that shithole for years while you sat with your finger up your damn ass on a spaceship!'

McCann's hand dipped into his waist coat pocket clasping a gold coin, 'A lot of people died in that battle the sons of rich and poor men alike.'

'Pah! My battle lasted years and left me damn near crippled! Besides I retired from the Marine Corps I don't have to salute an asshole like you if I don't want to!'

McCann held his Havana in one hand as his coin from the reign of Napoleon I glimmered in the station lights, 'Whatever suits you Hopper but you do have to co-operate with my warrant.'

The station Captain shook his head, 'You're just some crazy fucker they gave a gun and a badge.'

'You could be right,' McCann walked past the Captain and his men making for Shurruppak's main boulevard.

Clayton and Hevatsu caught up with him, the red lady inquired, 'What was that concerning?' as they stepped onto Shurruppak 15's well-lit boulevard.

'He reminds me of when I was a teenager.'

'Why is that Mr McCann?'

'I was 16 and working at a supermarket when the owner called me into his office. He asked me "Duncan, you already have the weekend off. So why is it you take an extra day off and only work four days a week?" I told him "Because I can't afford to get by on 3 days a week". He sacked me on the spot.'

Clayton laughed, 'Is that true?'

McCann nodded his head.

Hevatsu understood the story and its relation to Hopper, as to why Clayton found it humours was a mystery.

'That coin it is neither guskin nor a sovereign.'

'I'll tell you about it later, first we have to track down that scumbag Salamu.'

'That should be easy,' replied the ex-love droid.

'Enlighten me,' said McCann, puffing on a steadily smouldering cigar.

'There is a popular Gentlemen's club on the West side; all the wealthiest men frequent it. If he is not there someone will know where to find him.'

'Lead the way young lady.'

After a ten minute stroll they stood outside a very expensive establishment. Its front adorned in a black marble and lined with gold. Two men guarded its entrance, no line of sight within.

'Excuse me sir, females are not permitted unless employed by the establishment,' stated one of the doormen as he stopped the party with a white gloved hand.

McCann produced his Marshal's badge, 'She's with me.'

A rather condescending Doorman replied, 'Only members are permitted to enter.'

The Englishman stepped towards the entrance only to be blocked by two stocky doormen.

'Only members are permitted to enter. Unless you are acquainted with one of our members I will have to ask you to leave.'

McCann took a step back, 'Then I guess I'll have to introduce you to my friend.'

'And he is?'

The Commodore pulled back his coat slipping his pulse pistol from its holster, 'Mr Samuel Colt.'

'I'm afraid I'm not familiar with that Gentleman, perhaps you are lost?'

'Oh no there's no mistake,' levelling his weapon McCann shot both doorman dead.

There were no screams from the boulevard, citizens made for cover quietly as McCann and his compadres stepped over both corpses and into the Gentlemen's club.

Silence filled the air. Groups of businessmen sat at tables smoking lotus cigars and drinking vapostu. All attention fixed upon the Marshal as he entered through a marble atrium.

He produced a warrant so all members could view it, 'This is a warrant for Salamu Barag, is he here?'

Silence dominated the room.

'Well one of you bastards knows where he is.'

Again there was no response.

'All I want is a little co-operation,' the Englishman eyed a barman, 'I'll have a Scotch, thank you.'

'I'm sorry sir but do you have an account?' asked a tentative young man.

'Put it on Mr Barag's account.'

'Yes sir,' nodded a terrified fellow, 'We have several Earth Scotches.'

'Balvenie?'

'Yes sir we have ...'

'I'll have the 50 year old, signature cask, as will my friends ... in fact pour one for every customer here!'

Mumbles of approval came from around the club as some of the Gentlemen perked up.

'But sir, that's even more expensive than vapostu at the moment perhaps you'd like ...'

The Commodore's steely gaze entrenched the lad in fear, 'No I wouldn't and don't worry about Mr Barag his account is the very least of his troubles.'

Waiters scooted around delivering glasses of expensive brown liquor to approving patrons.

Clayton quickly made his way to the bar and knocked back a shot of Whisky. Hevatsu sampled a little but wasn't taken by the taste.

'Now that we understand each other who's willing to help me find Mr Barag? I'm sure a man as corrupt as he has plenty of enemies?'

There was no reply so McCann used his Tlillan ability to scan the room eventually discovering what he was looking for. A slim yellow skinned patron sat in a corner holding his free whisky, 'You.'

The Gentleman spoke between sips of his drink, 'Why do you want Salamu?'

'Conspiracy to commit murder, he won't be leaving Kurgudwardum 57 alive ... you can bet YOUR life on that.'

Customers spoke in a hushed tone as the yellow patron replied, 'He went to his factory, he's holding out there until you leave.'

The Englishman sensed honesty, 'Thank you.'

'He has an army of droids protecting him.'

McCann gave the fellow a nod, 'Enjoy your drink.'

McCann, Clayton and Hevatsu departed from Shurruppak to board a Barag Industries factory occupying one of the Skin Territories asteroid belts. On exiting their shuttle the Marshal felt a chill, ominous quiet filled the atmosphere. No one was there to greet them the factory felt dead.

Hevatsu pointed to one of the docking bay exits, 'This way.'

'You know this place?' inquired Clayton.

'No, but I can hear the factory at work. There is someone or something down there.'

The men couldn't hear anything yet they took Hevatsu's advice. On moving closer McCann detected the sound of machines and metal looming, still there was no reception.

Clayton kept a tight grip on his rifle searching for the first sign of trouble and eventually he found it. On entering the factory floor several love droids awaited; stood before a production line shunting along whilst robotic arms attached limbs to torsos. Finally a brain was slotted into place and sent down the line to be programmed with a personality.

Between them and the production line stood six love droids blocking their way across the floor and to a lift.

'You are trespassing on property of Barag Industries leave by your own volition or force shall be initiated,' spoke a blue skinned droid dressed in hot pants with short navy blue hair.

'We are here for Salamu Barag, we have a warrant for his arrest,' replied Hevatsu.

'This is your final warning please vacate these premises, you have 1 minute to comply.'

McCann drew a pistol and shot the blue droid between its eyes, dropping the machine as if it were a bag of bolts.

A second droid took off where the last one had left, 'You have 45 seconds to comply.'

'Drop 'em,' stated McCann in a cold tone as his deputies fired into the synthetic woman blocking their path.

After all six crumpled to the factory floor the Englishman pointed to an overlooking balcony, 'He's up there.'

Walking past production lines and towards a lift Hevatsu let out a shout. Glancing to where she pointed her weapon they witnessed a pink love droid sprinting towards them. Hevatsu levelled her weapon and blasted the machine, turning its head into a canoe.

McCann was concerned, since he couldn't sense these androids he had to keep a keen eye out.

'ABOVE!' screamed Clayton before blowing a hole through the torso of a falling droid.

Synthetic women attacked from all directions as the three stood back to back in the centre of the factory floor dropping androids one by one. Without a direct hit to the brain these synthetic women would not go down easily. Several pistol hits to the body were insufficient to even slow down a mechanoid. They sensed no pain and were built with a solid design … made to last. However a tungsten round to the forehead ended all cognitive activity forcing total shutdown.

The party fought their way to a lift. Jumping inside its door shut behind them. A clamour of androids thumping fists on the outside was prevalent. Salamu's slaves ripped the doors open only to witness an elevator travelling up its shaft.

Inside the lift McCann and Hevatsu reloaded their pistols, his heart pounded with excitement as he drew in deep breaths.

Gripping their firearms in preparation the doors opened yet no droids presented themselves. McCann stepped into the hallway, sensing Salamu's presence he led the way into what looked like a large clearing house. Deactivated androids were stored in shrink wrapped packages and stacked in mounds.

Walking through the clearing house he eventually locked eyes with Salamu. The fat man held another familiar face hostage … Zag Margidda.

'Well, well, well it is a small universe isn't it?' stated McCann.

'McCann! Help me! He's going to kill me!' pled Zag.

'Shut your mouth,' growled Salamu pushing his pistol into Zag's cheek.

'Barag, I've a warrant for your arrest, one way or another you're coming with me.'

'I don't think so McCann you leave now or I KILL Zag.'

McCann chuckled, 'If you wanna kill that piece of shit be my guest!'

Zag's eyes widened, 'What? I am a rich man! You helped my daughters you must help me!'

'Must? Even my wife says please … on good days.'

'This is not a joke he WILL kill me!'

McCann gave the businessman an evil smirk, 'I think you have me confused with someone that gives a shit.'

'You want guskin? I can pay you guskin!'

Clayton made a piercing stare, 'How much is your poxy life worth?'

'How much do you want? I can give you 1 million tomorrow if you get me out of this.'

McCann aimed his pistol and fired a tungsten round into Barag's kneecap bringing the fat man to the floor.

Zag made a dash for safety.

Upon reaching Clayton Zag celebrated in a joyous tone, 'Thank you, you shall be rewarded.'

The old soldier replied by smashing the skinny man's face with his rifle butt.

Zag's nose exploded as he fell to the floor screaming in agony. McCann smirked though Hevatsu was puzzled as to what exactly had occurred.

The Commodore stood over Barag, the industrialist reached for his pistol, 'Don't be so hasty now,' whispered McCann.

Barag retracted his arm thinking better of a shootout, Hevatsu retrieved his weapon.

Salamu grimaced in pain, 'You'll not make it out alive my androids will kill you all.'

'That's why you're still alive. You're gonna shut them all down.'

Barag made a painful laugh, 'Fuck you McCann!'

The Commodore brought his boot down on Barag's wounded knee, the fat man cried out as a shot of intense pain belted through his body.

After less than a minute of torture Salamu decided to co-operate. Subsequently Barag tapped his wrist tablet announcing the deactivation of his droids. Sensing truth the Englishman requested a security shuttle from Kurgudwardum 57.

By the end of the day Barag lay unconscious in a cell and Zag was preparing for his return to Shurruppak 15, rubbing his reset nose whilst arguing with Chanatico.

'I am afraid your transport is delayed, Mr Margidda.'

'Do you know who I am?'

'You are a little man who upon stretching his mouth any wider his brain would be in danger of plopping out!'

Zag shook his fist, 'I demand to speak with this station's controller!'

'I control all shipping associated with this station, you will speak to me Mr Margidda.'

'I will not speak to a lowly female!'

Chanatico's eyes flickered a shade of red as a holo-screen leapt up from the collar of her Tlillan suit, 'Fools are neither sewn nor reaped Mr Margidda, they appear of their own accord.'

Zag gave Chanatico a perplexed gaze.

A minute later Clayton entered the docking area, 'Is there something I can do for you Miss?'

The Amazon gestured towards Zag, 'This gentleman refuses to speak with a lowly female.'

A feeling of dread ran down Zag's spine.

Clayton sneered, 'It's you.'

'What is he doing here?'

'I'm the Deputy Marshal on this station and you asked for me.'

'I won't speak to him, bring me someone else!'

By this time a crowd had gathered.

Clayton grabbed the short man by the scruff of his neck and growled, 'Miss Chanatico controls all docking and transport arrangements on Kurgudwardum and you'll abide by her instruction.'

'I want to see the station controller!'

'And I wanna solid gold shitter for Christmas.'

Zag made a second puzzled look until Clayton reattached his rifle butt to the industrialist's nose breaking it into pieces.

The vile man dropped to the ground as Clayton tipped his hat towards Chanatico, 'Anything else?'

'If Mr Margidda requires further assistance I shall inform you.'

Later that evening Jenkins was making it up to his wife with a meal. He'd reserved the entire observation deck on her favourite restaurant. As they sat down to a Tlillan menu, especially flown in, Chanatico looked in wonder at the stars.

The Cardigans played in the background, one of Chanatico's favourite bands, as she sipped fruit juice to the soft sound of "Erase and Rewind".

A waiter served Chan with a plate of K'amas stored in hyper-sleep during the journey from Otoch to Andromeda; reviving it moments before being served ensured the food remained fresh.

'So what have I done to deserve this?' inquired the Matriarch before popping a termite into her mouth.

'After dragging you all this way it was about time I treated you to something.'

The red headed Matriarch gave her husband a suspicious glance, 'Are you sure you haven't done something Henry?'

'Done something? What on Earth do you mean?'

'Oh I'm sorry, I didn't mean to be rude,' replied the beautiful lady.

'So tell me about your position I hear you're doing a fine job as Docking Controller.'

Chan's eyes turned a deeper shade of pink, 'It seems I finally have an opportunity to earn merit. After Arthur I have been … well you know.'

'A social pariah?'

'Quite,' she swallowed another termite, 'Thank you Henry.'

'They have nook'ol too.'

Chan smiled at her husband, 'For securing me a position on this station.'

Jenkins ruffled his brow, 'I'm sorry?'

'Henry, please don't insult my intelligence. I would have never received the privilege of Docking Controller if Ilamachutli were not mated with Duncan.'

Taking a sip of Cognac the Brigadier conceded, 'Yes well, I might have put a word in for you with Duncan.'

'Oh, I saw Clayton today.'

Jenkins put his glass down slowly to reveal a mean sneer, 'Really?'

'Henry! Don't do that!'

'Do what?'

'Pull that awful face! You'd have thought Clayton had stolen a family heirloom!'

The Brigadier tried but was unable to wipe the expression from his face, 'So what did that scoundrel have to say for himself?'

'He's a Deputy Marshal on Kurgudwardum 57.'

Jenkins scoffed loudly, 'PAH! Deputy Marshal? He's probably chased off all the other good-for-nothings! That bastard has a monopoly on villainy!'

'HENRY!'

Jenkins sent a stubborn face across the table, 'Go on tell me what he was up to.'

'Clayton assisted me with a difficult man, Zag Margidda. He referred to me as a lowly female and demanded to speak with someone else.'

'So you sent for Clayton?'

'I did.'

'What did he have to say?'

'Apparently, Clayton had previously broken Mr Margidda's nose, he was quite unresponsive.'

Jenkins laughed as he took another sip of Cognac, 'I would say I'm shocked but I'm not, not in the least!'

'Well Clayton made it quite clear to that horrible little man. Afterwards we had a chat and apparently he's met someone on Kurgudwardum 57, she's from Andromeda.'

'Bloody hell, she must be made of catronium!'

'Actually she's a very nice lady.'

'Really?'

'Her name is Hevatsu.'

Jenkins pondered the name over a tumbler of fine Cognac, 'Hmmm, no doesn't ring a bell.'

'Oh you know, Hevatsu, she worked in that bar you and Duncan skulk around every night.'

'Ninti's? No that's a ... wait Hevatsu? The droid?'

'She's not an android she's a Synthetic Intelligence.'

'What's the bloody difference?'

'Her brain is grown from organic cells, rather than a mechanical device.'

The Brigadier grimaced, 'He's shagging a bloody android?'

Chanatico put her hands on the table, 'Really Henry does the first thing to enter your mind have to be sex?'

'Well what does he do with her? Play dominoes?'

'HENRY!'

'What?'

'Must you be so vulgar?'

'Me vulgar? I'm not the one shagging a bloody Holo-tablet with legs!'

Chan made a black look in her husband's vicinity.

'So she is made of catronium!'

'Actually Hevatsu is constructed from a combination of biological and synthetic compounds. She is a living machine not an android.'

Jenkins chuckled to himself, 'I'm sure that's what Clayton tells himself every night before he turns the lights out.'

Chan shook her head in disappointment, 'Really Henry you must lay to rest this vindictive attitude.'

'You don't know what that bastard is capable of. He nearly snapped the postman's damn neck and you're still defending the bloody scoundrel.'

'Clayton is not a scoundrel so stop saying it Henry.'

'Really? I think that Captain would disagree with you ... I forget his name now.'

'Brown?'

'Yes, that's the one, broke his nose ...'

'In three places, yes I know Henry, you've recanted the story frequently,' replied Chan in a tired tone.

'It may be a tiresome tale that I repeat far too often …'

'It is.'

'We were under constant attack, day in day out. Everyone was required to pull together. Otherwise they'd have slaughtered the lot of us.'

'Henry, you need to slow down on the Cognac.'

Jenkins peered at his glass and placed it back on the table, 'Perhaps you're right, I do apologise. This evening was intended to bring us together.'

'Do not be so hard on Clayton, for the first time in many years love reached out offering her hand. When the universe offers such opportunities you should take it and grasp on tight lest she never appear again. Look at us Henry we both took the hand of passion, tentatively at first but now we hold on for dear life. Please do not berate Clayton for doing the same.'

'I suppose you're right, well good luck to the old rascal!'

The red headed Tlillan smiled, 'So tell me about your job.'

'Oh not much to tell, I just keep an eye on station Marshals. Withdrawing and deploying men as needed, for the most part it's going swimmingly.'

His wife narrowed her eyes, 'But there is something that troubles you.'

'Yes, they'll be importing … lotus.'

'Why does that trouble you?'

'I spent years fighting narcotics cartels.'

'And now you feel betrayed?'

'I don't know. It makes me uncomfortable doing the very thing I was taught to despise.'

'Taught or conditioned?'

'What do you mean by that?'

Chan reached across the table holding her husband by the hand, 'Why did your government outlaw the production, sale and ownership of narcotics by private citizens?'

The Brigadier peered at his wife as if she had two heads, 'Because narcotics are addictive. Decent people end up committing all sorts of crime to purchase a fix.'

'Yet your government permits the use of alcohol does it not?'

'Yes, but that's different.'

'Alcohol is just as addictive and destroys as many lives as all narcotics put together, does it not?'

Jenkins conceded, 'Your point being?'

'My point being why does your government selectively ban harmful substances?'

The Brigadier thought for a moment then replied, 'I don't know the answer to that question.'

'Would you like to know?'

'Go on then.'

'How much money do you think there is to be made in the narcotics industry?'

'A lot.'

'Whilst contraband, the cartels and their investors pay no tax, no duty, in fact they are engaged in pure free market economics since they answer to no regulators other than the customer.'

'I suppose so.'

'Many wealthy people all over planet Earth are invested in drug lords and their cartels. These people lobby governments frequently. Do you think they would lobby to de-criminalise narcotics?'

Jenkins rested into his seat as he pondered the question, 'I suppose if your conspiracy theory were fact then they would lobby governments to keep narcotics contraband. Though if that were true, why is alcohol not a banned narcotic?'

Chanatico smiled, 'They did try.'

The Brigadier thought back considering attempts to ban alcohol in the past, 'True, but still you're asking me to believe in a barmy conspiracy theory.'

'Really? It is barmy to say that with current technology Earth governments could not wipe out 99% of opium and cocaine production within a year?'

Again Jenkins considered her suggestion, it was true that with modern technology there was nothing preventing them wiping out the opium poppy via a genetically engineered disease. Within a year opium production would easily be halted. Instead they sent men and women running around the world like headless chickens. Chanatico was correct there was nothing preventing an end to all narcotic production within a year, other than human will.

'So you're telling me it's a conspiracy?'

'Governments and leaders love to use that word, don't they? Do you know why?'

'No.'

'Because it demeans those who suggest it, paints them as a kook. People laugh forgetting about the crazy conspiracy theory and rich men go on reaping the rewards of others misery. It is an insult to the intelligence of humanity.'

'What is?'

'That they get away with treating you in such a foul manner. Look at you Henry, you do not need a bunch of stuffy old men and women who have never held down a real job to dictate what you may or may not do.'

'I don't understand what you're getting at.'

'They treat you as a child whilst all the time doing those very acts they prohibit you from carrying out. You may not kill unless it is with their license. You must pay tax or suffer the consequences.'

Jenkins shook his head, 'Someone has to be in charge and besides if we didn't pay tax who would organise it all?'

'They pay no tax on Otoch. The I.S.A levy no taxes do they?'

'Well they charge duties, for transport and ...'

'But they do not tax your income do they?'

'No, Faraday doesn't levy an income tax. But then again the I.S.A isn't a state ... I think.'

'Why is it that humans agree with the redistribution of their wealth yet refuse to apply it to other areas of their lives?'

'What do you mean?'

'It is considered acceptable to take a percentage of a man's wages and redistribute that to others, yes?'

'Yes.'

'Because there are poor people who need assistance and it is your moral duty to assist them, correct?'

Jenkins reached for his glass, 'Yes, since I'm more fortunate I should help those who are less fortunate.'

'Why does this only apply to finances?'

'I don't understand.'

'For instance there are ugly men who do not bathe and have no wife and are unable to find a sexual partner, agreed?'

The Brigadier replied before taking a sip of Cognac, 'Agreed.'

'Well why are women not forced to redistribute their vaginas?'

Jenkins choked on his drink whilst slamming down the glass and reaching for a handkerchief.

'Is something wrong Henry?'

'No, no I'm quite alright,' spluttered the SBS Brigadier.

'Well? Why are attractive women permitted to horde their vaginas? Surely it would be acceptable that they have sex with those dirty, ugly, smelly men who are less fortunate than the attractive men?'

'Errmm, I've never really thought about it.'

'Then think about it now, why should I not be forced to have sex with an ugly man once a week?'

Wiping his lips clean with a handkerchief Jenkins replied, 'That's ridiculous.'

'Yet my vagina is mine just the same as my money is mine. I earnt it, I own it, no-one has the right to it other than myself, yes?'

'Yes but you're talking about part of your body it can't be compared.'

'Alright how about property?'

'Go on.'

'Your mother has a nice four bedroomed house.'

'The damn thing cost me a fortune!'

'Yet she only uses one bedroom, correct?'

'And?'

'Why shouldn't she be forced to accommodate homeless families? She has room and there are men and women sleeping on park benches. Why shouldn't the government force her to accommodate less fortunate citizens? Surely it's the moral thing to do?'

Jenkins pulled a frown, 'I'm not having strangers and drug addicts sleeping in the same house as my mother! Besides I paid for that house, it's mine!'

'Yet you're willing to allow your finances to be redistributed to the poor. Is your property not merely a financial asset that could go to help the less well off?'

The Brigadier raised his voice a little, 'Certainly not! That's my house and I bought it for my mother to live in. It'll be a cold day in hell before the government move drug addicts and thieves in to live with MY MOTHER!'

Chanatico grinned at her husband's animated response. He always overreacted concerning his mother.

'All right Chan, what's your point.'

'My point is that humans allow the government to redistribute a portion of their wealth due to the fact it is less morally repugnant than redistributing their other assets. They do not tax your money because it is moral or the right thing to do but because they can get away with it. If the government were to redistribute your wife's genitals or your mothers bedrooms to the less fortunate there would be a revolution tomorrow.

What about your kidneys? You have two and there are people who are in need of one. Why does the government not ...'

'Yes, I get the idea,' interjected Jenkins.

'Then you agree?'

'I suppose you're right but what difference does it make? It's always been this way.'

Chan grinned, 'It has not always been that way and the current paradigm is coming to a close. Otoch is changing, society is evolving and on Earth human society will evolve too. I just want to be sure my Henry is prepared when the new paradigm takes hold. The shipping of narcotics to the Skin Territory is the part of that change.'

'And just who would lead this change?'

Chanatico gave a soft smile, 'Our son.'

'Arthur?'

'Do we have another son?'

'Of course not but I don't see how Arthur could lead anything other than a poetry reading!'

'You underestimate, Xch'uup does not.'

'What does Malikah believe?'

'Believe? She does not believe, she has observed destiny. The Matriarchs fear him not for what he is but what he may become.'

'Which is?'

'She understands upon defeating Mammi none will be able to control him. He may even challenge her for Xch'uup.'

'Don't you have to be female to take the title of Xch'uup?'

'There is no law restricting males from making the challenge. Yet in past times a male had no hope of victory. If Arthur defeated Mammi then he may defeat Xch'uup therefore he may challenge for supremacy.'

'And you think he will?'

'No, if it were so Malikah would have destroyed him before birth.'

'Then?'

'He will lead Earth into its destiny, its paradigm, alongside Otoch, Gukumatz and Bandayuuk. Each world will require a leader for a new age, we have created ours.'

Jenkins replied in a sceptical tone, 'And who told you this?'

Chan smiled, 'It is plain for any Matriarch to see, our son will crush his enemies in the Chihuaz and upon his return to Earth the old guard will swing from a rope.'

The Brigadier held his glass in the air, 'WAITER!'

'Yes sir?'

'Get me another Cognac, make it a triple!'

'Yes sir,' replied the waiter as he took Jenkins' glass.

'Now I understand why Clayton has hooked up with a love droid.'

'Why's that my dear?'

'No bloody children to ruin your life!'

The waiter returned with a tumbler, 'Your Cognac sir.'

'Thank you, that'll be all.'

The Amazon smirked, 'Come now Henry I know you enjoy being a father.'

The Brigadier took a hearty slug of drink, 'About as much as shitting myself in a white suit at a family wedding!'

Chan let out a great roar of laughter, for a few minutes the ivory skinned beauty was unable to speak as her face turned red and her eyes glowed pink.

Chapter 20

The lights switched on automatically in Clayton's ornate bedroom, a splendid berth on Kurgudwardum 57. Hevatsu lay in bed regenerating muscle tissue and organs, a natural process setting her apart from former workmates. She was as beautiful as she was tranquil resting for the day ahead.

Whilst dressing himself the red lady awoke, sitting up in bed she inquired, 'Why didn't you wake me?'

Clayton gazed at her perfect crimson breasts his eyes moving to the lady's piercing yellow eyes, 'You were so serene I didn't want to disturb you.'

Hevatsu stepped out of bed to give her partner a tender kiss. Scanning the former love droid's body he was still in awe at her perfectly taut curves an expertly crafted female form.

'Besides when you wake up I'm always late for work.'

'I'm not holding you prisoner you can leave whenever you please.'

Clayton removed his clothing falling into bed with his smiling lady. An hour later the former soldier arrived at the central control office. A heated discussion was in full swing the Deputy prayed it didn't concern his belated appearance.

Ilamachutli stood hands on hips, obviously in a rotten mood, 'Well, well, well I'm so happy you could grace us with your presence Mr Clayton.'

McCann and Jenkins were both there. Oddly enough neither seemed concerned with his tardiness.

'Good morning Ilamachutli, I'm sorry I'm late but ...'

'Yes I know why you're late you really must learn to keep it in your trousers on a morning.'

McCann and Jenkins barely acknowledged the jibe.

Jenkins broke the silence, 'How long before we can launch a search party?'

'I told you Henry, I know where she is the problem is politics,' stated the Valkyrie.

'Politics? She's my wife!'

Clayton stepped in closer, 'Is there something wrong with Miss Chanatico?'

McCann replied in a huff, 'The Kishar abducted Chanatico we'll have to negotiate her return.'

'Negotiate?'

'Malikah signed a contract with Rabum, Asrukishar is off limits. They may do as they please inside Asrukishar. We cannot set foot on the station without their permission.'

'How did they get Miss Chanatico?'

Jenkins was cracking up under pressure. He answered in a shaky voice, 'She went to inspect one of the clearing houses near a docking arm, the bastards flooded it with gas then took her to Asrukishar.'

'Why?'

'WELL HOW THE BLOODY HELL SHOULD I KNOW?'

Ilam put a hand on Jenkins' shoulder, 'Calm yourself Henry I shall secure her safe return.'

'Yes of course, I apologise.'

'We cannot set foot on their station, mercenaries refuse to go there and I'm trying to convince Jenkins that going by himself will do more harm than good,' added McCann.

'I'll go,' stated Clayton in a cold voice.

'Forget it Clayton.'

The Deputy removed his badge tossing it onto the central table.

Mesan stepped into the room clutching a tablet, 'Miss Ilam, I have a list of Kishar demands.'

The tall Amazon took his tablet reading Rabum's requirements for Chanatico's safe return, 'Apparently they only wish to extract her ovaries. Afterwards she will be returned unharmed.'

'UNHARMED!' shouted Jenkins.

'It seems they wish to breed their own stock of Tlillans. No doubt Rabum will begin a eugenics program once her ovaries are frozen.'

Clayton pointed at Mesan, 'You ... how do I get onto the Kishar station undetected?'

Mesan stepped backwards, 'I don't know ...'

Clayton unslung his Tlillan tunnel sweeper, 'Don't fuck with me Mesan.'

'There's a transport leaving from Docking Arm 7 in 15 minutes. Several storage crates contain an atmosphere you might hide aboard them.'

Clayton nodded his head, 'Okay ladies and gentlemen, I'll be off,' he saluted Jenkins, 'When I return your wife will be back on this station safe and sound, sir.'

The Brigadier returned the salute then watched in wonder as his former subordinate marched out of the room towards Docking Arm 7.

Ilam turned to Mesan, 'Tell the Kishar we have ovaries in storage and will trade them for Chanatico. Inform them they may view the ovaries first, understood?'

'Yes Miss Ilam,' replied the ponytailed freak.

'What are you doing?' inquired McCann.

'Buying Clayton some time.'

'Time for what?'

Jenkins made a knowing look, 'To do what he does best.'

Upon Asrukishar Rakbu observed the carnage. In the last hour, he wasn't certain of the exact time, a family had been slaughtered. This was no ordinary family they were high aristocracy of Kishar society. Now they hung by meat hooks from a ceiling their skin stripped exposing naked flesh. A pool of blood congealed on the central living space floor.

'This was recent the perpetrator must be close by,' said the district headman.

Rakbu narrowed his eyes in disbelief, 'What creature could have done this? An entire family of 7 murdered in such a horrific fashion.'

'Only 7?' inquired the headman.

'Yes, the people you see hanging from hooks … probably stolen from a local butchers.'

'Where is their daughter?'

'You knew this family?'

'They were good friends, I'll organise a search party for the daughter.'

A few moments later two men called out having discovered a child hiding in her room. The headman and Rakbu rushed in. After calming her down she spoke to the headman's familiar face.

The terrified girl described a man with a red face and black eyes. He butchered her family as cattle. For some reason the girl couldn't fathom he placed her aside whilst her parents and relations screamed in torment.

The Headman scratched his chin, 'The face it is unfamiliar, perhaps another Chief's paint?'

'No,' replied Rakbu, 'no Chief wears red with black nor a skull.'

'Then who if not a rival Chief?'

Rakbu squatted speaking softly to the girl, 'Did he speak to you?' She nodded her head.

'Do you remember what he said?'

She shook her head.

'Did you understand what he said?'

Again the girl shook her head.

'Did it sound like this, baaaahhhh, buuurrrr, baaaarrr?' Rakbu imitated how the English language sounded to a tribe who spoke via alternating pitches. The English language seemed very bland, deep and flat to all Kishar.

The girl nodded her head.

Rakbu stood up and took a deep breath, 'It wasn't a Kishar.'

'Do you know the culprit?'

'No but I know where he came from. I must speak with Rabum on this, continue your search,' Rakbu marched out with an escort leaving the headman to clean Clayton's bloody mess.

Entering Rabum's throne room the Kishar herald marched past several Chiefs sitting at his table, 'Lagon and his family have been butchered.'

A blanket of silence fell upon the room, 'His entire family?' asked Rabum in disbelief.

'All but his daughter, she witnessed the killer.'

Before anything could be said Sada stood up, 'Vengeance, for the bird woman!'

The Chiefs looked at each other in puzzlement.

'Evil from beneath will plague this Station until she is returned ... untouched.'

Rakbu gave the Seer a black look, 'The girl says he was from Mul, he had a painted face in the design of a skull.'

Sada bellowed so all heard, 'A sea of blood until the condor returns to nest.'

'Then I must kill him first,' stated Rabum in no uncertain terms.

Sada fixed his healed eyes on the Kishar Chief, 'Kill a spirit?'

'I don't believe in ghosts.'

Sada cackled at the Chief, 'You will.'

Rabum rose from his throne, 'Enough, we need to find this man before he kills again. I want every Chief to begin a search of his District, is that understood?'

His Chiefs rose accepting their instructions yet before they were able to exit the lighting failed leaving them in pitch dark. Without time to act several Chiefs felt something warm brush against them. A sudden breeze picked up causing the hairs on their exposed upper bodies to stand on end.

Rabum shouted, 'GUARDS! THE LIGHTS!'

Sada cackled in blackness as screams bounced off walls accompanied by armed men barging in. Guards pulled out torches illuminating their Chiefs faces. Sada laughed as beams of light passed over him. Rakbu was sheet white with terror. Nothing seemed amiss until Asrukishar's central computer restored illumination.

When able to see again they understood that warm feeling ... blood. The Chief of District 3 lay on the hall table, dismembered as if victim to a Viking raid. His chest sliced open with lungs pulled out and thrown over his shoulders.

This man was only feet away when he died in agony; innards flailing outside his body and spraying blood onto his friends as they dithered in ignorance.

Sada smiled, 'Now you believe!'

Rabum peered at the ceiling shouting to the AI, 'Why did you drop the lighting in my hall?'

'My apologies I experienced a temporary power failure.'

'Why? How?'

'Unknown.'

'How did he get in here? There is only one entrance and it was guarded.'

The guards looked at each other with confusion.

Rabum screamed in frustration, 'WHAT IS HAPPENING?'

Sada cackled in delight, 'Sada say you return condor.'

'NEVER! She is my property now!'

'Sada say if Rabum want to live he return female soon.'

'He must be close, drop the bulkheads and search this district. No-one is permitted to enter or leave until he is found,' ordered Rabum.

The Kishar King had unwittingly provided Clayton with what he wanted. Now every single priority target was confined to a single District. The old tunnel warrior put his skills to good use on Asrukishar.

Launching a one man campaign of terror upon an entire nation he attacked their highest profile citizens; murdering aristocrats and prominent members of society in the most intimidating fashion.

A unique style of guerrilla warfare learnt from an elite squad of men. Commanded by a Sergeant with a rare belief ... voodoo; initially ridiculed for his religion until deployed to the jungles of Central Africa.

Their Captain suffered difficulty questioning local villagers concerning a band of criminals he'd been order to capture. Unfortunately locals refused to speak, probably due to fear.

Sergeant Roberts requested he try something. After painting his face and removing his flak armour Roberts entered the village to gasps. His comrades laughed but locals were very much intimidated.

Roberts' father, a Voodoo priest, had brought him up in the religion. He addressed the village Chief who immediately spilt the beans. He would not cross a Voodoo priest otherwise known as a Houngan.

The criminals they'd spent weeks searching for were detained and brought to camp for trial. Afterwards the squad insignia became that of a red and black skull mask.

When Clayton joined up on Bandayuuk he thought they were all bonkers until he saw how it affected the Macks. The sight of soldiers with red faces scared the living daylights out of Machine Men. It gave him an extra edge in those tunnels. Macks cursed Ek'tsab on witnessing comrades swinging from a tunnel roof, skin dangling from bodies as withered leaves upon the autumn vine, leaving them with a chill in their bones.

If space were limited they'd cut up bodies quickly with a large knife, known as a Kukri. A long inverted blade made it easy to slice the enemy abdomen open.

Over the years the "Bokors" became infamous amongst those serving on Bandayuuk. The I.S.A soon noticed that wherever these men were deployed enemy resistance broke. Jenkins only regret was that he didn't possess an entire Brigade of Bokors; if so contention might have crumbled in the first year.

Now Clayton put his years of training with the Bokors to use, it was a method of combat the Kishar had not encountered before now. Previously the sight of a tattooed Kishar Chief and his warriors broke most enemies. Those remaining met slaughter, Kishar fought as a tribe overwhelming their foe with numbers and courage.

Clayton sat crawled up inside an air duct preparing for his next strike; dressed in nothing but his I.S.A combat suit (a padded Tlillan suit) with his Kukri and a rifle. The old soldier pulled some paint from a leg pocket re-applying it to his face as he reminisced on times past … on Bandayuuk 0 …

'Corporal John Clayton.'
'Yes Brigadier,' saluted the young man in his mid-twenties dressed in a neatly pressed uniform and beret.

Brigadier Jenkins scanned his small office in camp Oscar. Roberts and Clayton stood together to the left of his desk, Captain Brown to the right his nose in bandages.

'What am I going to do with you Corporal?'

Clayton gave no reply.

'According to Captain Brown you refused to obey orders. When pressed you allegedly head butted the Captain ... breaking his nose in three places. What do you have to say about these allegations Corporal?'

Captain Brown, a short man in his 40's cut in, 'Allegations?'

Jenkins gave the Captain a black look, 'I'm conducting these proceedings, Captain, understood?'

'Understood Brigadier,' replied the short man.

'Well Clayton?'

'The Captain ordered me to execute prisoners of war, sir.'

'That's a lie!' shouted Captain Brown.

Jenkins bellowed at the short man, 'Once more and I'll have you mucking out the prison toilets for a week Captain!'

Brown fell silent.

Jenkins turned back to Clayton, 'What next?'

'The Captain threatened to demote me, sir.'

'Go on.'

'I told him he could take his stripes and shove them up his arse, sir.'

Roberts began to snigger much to Brown's disdain.

'I see, what encouraged you to break the Captain's nose?'

'Captain Brown called me an insubordinate. He stated that I should be transferred to Logistics. The Captain stated that I'd enjoy Logistics since that's where the cowards who are too afraid to fight end up anyway ... sir.'

Brigadier Jenkins' eyes widened as he turned a black gaze upon Captain Brown, 'My father served in Logistics for 25 years!'

Roberts' face scrunched up as he attempted to hold back the laughter. Captain Brown swallowed deeply whilst staring into the Brigadier's furious eyes.

Nothing was said for about 20 seconds. Eventually Jenkins re-addressed Clayton, 'For the crime of insubordination you shall be stripped of the rank of Corporal. For the crime of striking an Officer you shall serve 6 months in a glasshouse.'

Captain Brown yelled out, '6 MONTHS? THAT MAN SHOULD BE DISHONOURABLY DISCHARGED!'

'BROWN! GET OUT OF MY OFFICE NOW!'

Captain Brown left slamming the door shut without giving a salute, Jenkins let out a huff of air before sitting down to relax, 'I understand that Captain Brown is not the easiest of men to work with. By God the thought of breaking his nose has flashed through my mind more than once. But you've got to learn to get along with people, do you understand?'

Clayton protested, 'But sir, he wanted me to shoot prisoners.'

'Yes I know but you could have reported him upon returning to base. Did you really have to break his nose?'

'I'm sorry sir.'

'Yes well, I assume you can be trusted to report to the Corrective Centre?'

'Yes sir, oh and sir?'

'Don't worry Clayton … Sergeant Roberts has already requested your return to the Bokors.'

'Thank you Brigadier.'

'You're both dismissed.'

Roberts and Clayton saluted the Brigadier, Jenkins returned the salute and they exited his office.

'That was lucky,' smiled Roberts.

'Lucky?' replied Clayton in an incredulous tone.

'Breaking a Captain's nose and you only got six months? You might be out in three if you're a good boy.'

'What do they usually give for smashing a wanker's face in?'

Roberts laughed, 'A lot longer in a glasshouse mate, followed by a dishonourable discharge!'

'So why did I get just six?'

'Because firstly, you're a damn good Bokor.'

'And secondly?'

Roberts gave a beaming grin, 'Secondly, Brown is a fucking cunt!'

The pair broke out laughing whilst making their way to the Military Corrective Training Centre otherwise known as a Glasshouse, in camp Oscar.

Clayton smiled as he picked through old memories of good times spent with Roberts and the men of Bokor Squadron. Pasting his face red the old soldier stopped, he felt movement inside the air ducts. The vibrations became more powerful. He recognised an accompanying noise as that of bulkheads dropping. Clayton grinned to himself, now he had them trapped in one place.

Crawling through air ducts sandwiched between station floors Clayton made his way above a nearby temple frequented by local aristocrats. Sliding a ceiling tile aside he spied a ceremony below. They sat, men, women and children together before an iron altar. It seemed that Rabum had directed many of the upper class here, safety in numbers being his policy. Clayton slipped the tile back, moving forward he placed himself above the altar.

Rabum's warriors were combing the remainder of this district not suspecting one man would attack a room of 50 people ... but he didn't know Clayton.

Sliding a ceiling tile aside Clayton observed a priest praying to an idol of a Kishar man fashioned from wrought iron.

'May Anshar, foremost of the heavens use his iron and deliver us from Maksim Xul,' prayed a tattooed man in his 60's.

Clayton removed a carbon nanotube from a leg pocket, securing one end to the air duct wall with suction cups.

The priest turned to his congregation blessing them with arms outstretched.

Suddenly a scream tore out, the priest noted those seeking shelter in his temple shook in terror whilst staring behind him.

He turned to face a man stood upon his holy altar wearing a dark padded combat suit. He carried only a rifle slung across his back and a large knife hanging from his waist.

The priest was unsure if this truly was the man Rabum sought out or the Maksim Xul that Sada had described. Its face was blood red with black eyes and teeth creating a skull design inspiring fear amongst his congregation.

The priest made a sign Clayton assumed to be a religious incantation. He then invoked his God, 'ANSHAR! STRIKE DOWN THIS AMBUSHER! SHOW US WHO HAS GREAT IRON!'

Clayton's ear piece translated his plea to Anshar. The old soldier laughed at an overture to a being that obviously wasn't going to deliver them. Unsheathing his Kukri Clayton slashed the priest's face, dropping him to the floor, his congregation screamed to the guards outside. Unfortunately for them Clayton had disabled all power to the door mechanism.

'Anshar save us! Anshaaaaarrrrr!' screamed the priest rolling around in his own blood.

Clayton jumped down from the altar as men and women scrambled away terrified they'd be next.

Pursuing the cowardly he brought them down one by one usually with a stab to the back. Three inches of steel was enough to send a man to Elysium a Kukri commonly being 18 inches.

As Kishar nobles dropped one by one, scurrying to and fro in a pathetic attempt to preserve their lives, Clayton stopped in the centre of the temple. A small boy no more than 9 years old stood, fists up, facing off with Clayton.

The former special-forces killer looked down at the child challenging him to a fight. Before anything more could be said a woman leapt out from the huddled congregation.

'Do not hurt my son he has too much iron in his heart for one so young,' pleaded a young mother.

Clayton nodded silently allowing her to retrieve her son. Before she could leave he spoke through a universal translator on his suit.

'Your King has my friend,' came an androgynous voice from Clayton's translation device.

'I am not his advisor, I do not know of this,' replied the shaking women.

'I will not leave this place until Chanatico is returned to Kurgudwardum. Many more will die except for Rabum. I will kill all his Chiefs and their families but Rabum is safe.'

'Why?'

'Tell this to all the nobles when they arrive.'

'I will.'

Clayton sheathed his knife and moved back onto the altar. He tugged the rope making certain it was still secure before climbing up into the air duct he'd dropped down from. The ceiling tile slid back into its former position and their red faced demon was gone leaving 15 dead and a gored priest.

It took Rabum and his guards 30 minutes to force the temple doors open, once inside a scene of sacrilege met their gaze. The tribe's medicine men ran in to treat those maimed but only the priest required attention. Clayton had either killed or spared the others.

Sada stepped past several corpses approaching the mother who'd rescued her child from Clayton.

'This boy his iron halted Maksim Xul.'

Rakbu barged through the doors … now that he knew danger was no longer present, 'This boy stopped the red face? The old man is mad, I told you Rabum he speaks as a mad dog!'

The mother bleated out, 'It is true the Maksim Xul left a message for all Chiefs of Kishar,' the temple went quiet as nobles slipped inside listening to what she had to say, 'He said he will not leave until his friend, Chanatico returns to Kurgudwardum.'

The Chiefs muttered to each other, it seemed Sada was right.

'He will kill all chiefs and their families until she is returned safely but he will spare Rabum.'

The Chiefs voices rose to discuss what they'd just heard. Sada noticed everyone glaring at Rabum.

The old Nabu let out a mocking laugh, 'Red Face have iron heart and iron head.'

The Kishar King approached Sada, 'I tire of you with each passing moment old man be cautious with your words.'

Sada laughed in the King's face whilst peering at the Chiefs, 'When Sada speak that which gives iron, Rabum happy. Now Sada speak that which gives anger Rabum threaten Sada? Rabum need not fear Sada, Sada speak truth. Rabum need fear those with sweet tongue to face but hold knife to back!'

Rabum spun around to glare upon his Chiefs, 'Is this true?'

The Chiefs refused to answer. The only sound to be heard was that of Sada's cackle. Without warning a scream went out from Asrukishar's main boulevard, everyone poured from the temple. Hanging six feet off the ground, from the top of the boulevard a Kishar Chief swung ominously in the air his feet making involuntary twitches. Citizens looked on in horror for he didn't swing by a rope. Instead Clayton had abducted the Chief whilst all concentrated upon the scene within their temple. The gutted Noble hung from the main boulevard's high ceiling by his own intestinal tract.

The sight was one of incomprehensible evil. His open belly allowed organs to dangle out for all to see whilst eyes rolled back into the skull. The victims face contorted in pain gritting his teeth peering upwards, begging Zeus the cloud gatherer to end his miserable existence.

How this was managed in such a short time was beyond Rabum. Even for a group of men to achieve such a feat would take hours, surely?

One of the Chiefs turned to Rabum, 'Enough, you return the Condor.'

'I AM KING! I DO NOT TAKE INSTRUCTION, I GIVE IT AND YOU FOLLOW!'

'Follow? Follow where? To the house of Uggae?'

Uggae being the Kishar deity of death.

Rabum sneered at his Chief, 'You fear this man?'

'Yes, I fear him and I fear death. He will slaughter my family before you have your way with the Condor woman.'

The Kishar King beat his chest, 'I am King I have iron in my heart ... STRONG IRON ... Rabum has no fear of ambusher!'

'Easy for Rabum to have iron when Ambusher not threaten him. It is we who must have iron to face the Maksim Xul!'

'Do you challenge Rabum?'

'No, I will leave this place of sorrow and death with my family; before evil from beneath takes them to the house of Uggae. Any who wish to stay and fight beside the mighty Rabum may do so. I shall return when the Condor has flown,' with that the Chief turned his back and departed.

One by one Chiefs of Asrukishar left the temple, deserting Rabum to deal with Clayton himself. As Rakbu walked out, the Kishar King grabbed his arm, 'Rakbu, you are leaving me here? My herald, my friend, you have treated me as your own family. When Rabum was but a beggar your wife washed his feet before her husband …'

The herald could not look his friend in the eye, 'He will not kill you, only us, when the Condor returns to nest so shall I.'

Rabum's face writhed in agony as he entreated his old comrade, 'Please, Rakbu, we fought together in many battles. You risked your life to save mine … when you could have let me die and take Kingship.'

'This is different, now you risk my life at none to yourself … all for a female?'

'Rakbu, her ovaries shall provide new stock to the Kishar. You saw them defeat Telal? Did you not see Hebat die and Mammi retreat in fear of the Condor?'

'I did but before you have her seeds there will be no soil to plant them in, only Rabum shall remain,' Rakbu shook his arm free and strode away.

The mocking laugh of Sada drew the King's attention, 'Empty Condor eggs, Rabum will send Condor back or rule his Kingdom alone!'

At that Rabum marched into the centre of the boulevard beneath the corpse swinging from its own intestines. The tattooed warrior screamed at the top of his lungs, 'RED FACE! I KNOW YOU HEAR ME! I RETURN YOUR FEMALE NOW. ALLOW RABUM ONE HOUR TO DELIVER THE FEMALE TO KURGUDWARDUM 57, YOU HAVE MY WORD!'

The King awaited a reply yet there was only silence. Rabum's Chiefs stopped in their tracks, listening for a response.

Sada was the only man to speak, 'Maksim Xul hears your words.'

'Does he hear my iron?'

'Your words have iron but do not waste precious time.'

Rabum pointed at Rakbu, 'Help me take her to a shuttle, we leave now.'

The friends ran to a med bay where Chanatico was held in stasis. The beautiful Amazon lay in deep sleep within a casket, under soft blue lights, constructed of catronium though the top was transparent. Both men took a hold of opposite handles lifting the coffin from its table, electro magnets kicked in allowing it to levitate. Rabum and Rakbu needed only to nudge the coffin lightly as they hurried for the closest docking arm.

Citizens watched in wonder as the Condor woman lay in utter serenity whilst their King and herald pushed with urgency; viewing the beauty inside as they would a great warrior in a funeral procession before his burial.

Upon reaching the nearest docking arm Rabum commandeered a shuttle, the owner was about to leave the station rather than be killed. However that would no longer be necessary now that Chanatico was on her way back to Kurgudwardum 57.

Chapter 21

On the shuttle back to Asrukishar Rabum looked Jenkins up and down, 'You can halt this red demon?'

Jenkins examined the Kishar, 'I was his commanding officer on Bandayuuk for several years.'

'Bandayuuk?'

'Where Clayton found his red face.'

'Clayton ... that is his name?'

'It is.'

'Then he is man not demon.'

'Does it matter?'

After docking they exited onto the boulevard of a ghost station. A solitary body hung from the ceiling, feet closer to the floor; its populace hidden in their berths praying for deliverance. Several surviving Kishar chiefs approached the party.

Rabum's voice boomed out, 'I have brought the one who shall deliver us from Red Face.'

Chiefs remained silent some sceptical others hopeful.

Rabum looked at Jenkins in his I.S.A uniform, 'How will you speak to this Clayton?'

Jenkins scanned a silent boulevard, 'CLAYTON! This is Brigadier Jenkins, Chanatico has been returned, I'm here to bring you back to Kurgudwardum 57.'

'You have my oath. You are free to leave this station unharmed,' declared Rabum.

Still there was no reply.

'Is he listening?' whispered Rakbu.

'Of course he's listening.'

Without warning a voice echoed along the boulevard, 'Is that you Brigadier?'

Jenkins couldn't tell from which direction the sound emanated, 'Of course it's me, now come down and we can leave this place.'

'Is Chanatico alright, sir?'

'Yes, thanks to you she's been returned untouched.'

'Do you remember Bandayuuk, sir?'

Jenkins furrowed his brow, 'Of course I do, I was there during the whole bloody mess!'

'Do you remember the day of the cease fire, sir?'

Jenkins went from puzzled to irritated, 'Of course I do, what the bloody hell is this?'

'Do you remember the celebration, when we found out we were going home?'

'Listen here Clayton I'm ordering you to fall in and present yourself. Do you hear me?'

'We were all there celebrating as they announced it on the NET; You, me, Roberts and Captain Brown ... all having a drink in Camp Lemur.'

'You know full well Brown wasn't there.'

'He was transferred to another camp wasn't he?'

'What are talking about man? Brown was put through a mechanised harvester two years before the cease fire!'

'Sorry sir, I forgot about that accident.'

'Accident? The bloody Macks threw him in, it took three days to clean his remains out and get it running again.'

Clayton dropped from above onto the boulevard floor; a fall that would break any normal man's legs. However the Ixchel improved power and flexibility to such a degree he easily managed such feats.

The Kishar gasped at the sight of their red faced demon.

'Reporting for duty Brigadier.'

Dressed in black combat fatigues and standard issue SBS boots Clayton stood to attention. His red and black face staring up to Brigadier Jenkins. A bloody knife hung from his belt varnishing his clothing, it was a gory sight.

Jenkins fixed his gaze upon Rabum, 'We'll be leaving now.'

Rabum nodded his head.

'If you pull another stunt like this, you have my word that you and all of your chiefs shall be swinging from the top of the boulevard ... alongside this fellow,' Jenkins pointed to the corpse above.

Rabum spoke to Clayton, 'Sada was right, you have strong iron ... there must be Kishar blood in your veins.'

Clayton did not reply following the Brigadier back onto a shuttle leaving for Kurgudwardum 57.

Back on Kurgudwardum 57 Chanatico had been revived from her hyper-sleep. As far as she was concerned she'd been inspecting a cargo bay on Dock 5 a moment ago to arise in med bay.

Ilam waited, arms crossed, as the station doctor awoke their sleeping beauty from her slumber. McCann, Mesan, Hassif and Hevatsu were also present.

'Where am I?' inquired the Tlillan beauty.

'Med Bay 3, you have been in hyper-sleep for nearly 36 hours,' replied Ilam in a cold tone.

'Hyper-sleep? How?'

'Rabum kidnapped you. He wished to steal your ovaries for a eugenics programme.'

Chanatico sat up quickly placing a hand upon her torso.

'Have no fear you are unmolested.'

Chan's eyes moved from her torso to the people in the room, 'Where is Henry?'

'He's returning Clayton from Asrukishar,' replied McCann.

Chanatico placed a hand over her eyes as she attempted to hold back a tsunami of emotion.

'CONTROL YOURSELF!' barked Ilam.

Chanatico cleared her throat. Lifting her legs to clear the edge of the coffin, she stepped out. For a moment the Matriarch struggled to keep balance.

'It will take a few minutes to regain stability. It is a common side effect when emerging from hyper-sleep,' noted the doctor in a comforting voice.

Whilst she recovered Hassif excused himself and Hevatsu pulled McCann by the arm. The red lady led him into the atrium of a nearby shopping arcade.

The shopping centre was lined with synthetic rose marble and polished brass railings. On the east side a giant waterfall rushed down 10 levels into a pool of beautiful green and blue sparkling water. It was here Ilam enjoyed spending much of her time and money. Many luxury vendors from both Andromeda and the Milky Way leased floor space after the I.S.A had cleaned up Kurgudwardum 57.

Hevatsu pulled McCann to a large pool surrounded by greenery. The Englishman looked around the giant atrium, 'Don't tell me you've over spent your allowance?'

Hevatsu shook her head as shoppers strolled by, 'No, I have something inside,' pointing to her abdomen she blurted 'a feeling?'

'Indigestion?'

'No, it is Clayton … I cannot stop thinking of him … in a negative manner.'

'Negative? You're angry with him?'

'Not anger, not love … something different.'

The Englishman examined his Deputy attempting to garner any emotion that might slip from her synthetic mind. After a minute he believed he'd caught a sensation emanating from the red lady.

'Fear, you're feeling fear.'

Looking around in desperation Hevatsu replied, 'I felt it when he left … it has grown over time … it refuses to leave my mind.'

'You're afraid he might die.'

'Is this how all sentients feel?'

'At one time or another, yes.'

'How do you stop it?'

'You can try and control it but no one can stop fear.'

'Then how do I control it?'

'You'll feel this way many times before you've learnt to deal with it.'

'Why am I afraid?'

'Because you love him?'

Hevatsu peered upwards at beautiful terraces of brass and marble surrounding her, 'I feel powerless as if paralyzed by some great force. Do you understand this emotion?'

McCann nodded, 'I've endured it more times than you could imagine. Not all emotions make you feel good.'

'What did you do in the past?'

'I asked myself if there was anything I could do.'

'I don't understand.'

'Is there anything you could do to help Clayton?'

Hevatsu shook her blue hair.

'Then you'll have to pull yourself together. If Ilam saw you like this she'd be hauling you off to Dock 17 herself!'

Hevatsu smiled for a moment.

'There you go. You managed to overcome your fear.'

'Only for a brief second … because you took my mind off Clayton.'

McCann put an arm around his Deputy, 'Let's have a stroll around this place while Jenkins is returning your boyfriend.'

Hevatsu looked at her Marshal with anticipation, 'And if they do not return?'

McCann peered into Hevatsu's eyes with promise, 'Then we shall wreak our revenge upon the Kishar.'

The former love droid let out a tiny snort from her nostrils, 'That has made me feel better … using one negative emotion against another. The thought of murdering those responsible for the death of John calms my soul … that is disturbing.'

McCann walked his Deputy to the first floor, 'Now you are learning what it means to be human.'

Back at Kurgudwardum control centre Ilam and Chan were in a full blown argument. Ilam pointed at Chan with fiery eyes, Chan screamed at her superior, faces almost touching.

'You nearly compromised the entire Tlillan species … again … you STUPID girl!' bellowed a furious Ilam.

'Look who's talking!'

'That was prophecy foreseen by the Seers!'

'The Seers can eat my SHIT!'

Ilam's eyes widened, 'HERESY!'

'You committed heresy when expedient for you and your clan. Yet you berate others for the same actions, a human would say that you are a hypocrite!'

'Your clan failed Xch'uup at Bandayuuk then again in giving birth to a male, you cannot help but disappoint!'

'FAILED?! Tico fought to the death unlike those who refused to engage,' narrowing her burning eyes she sneered at Ilam, 'and those who surrendered.'

The red haired woman of Chutli could no longer contain herself snatching Chan's throat as her eyes flipped to a burgundy hue piercing her mind.

Chan replied grabbing Ilam's throat as the pair locked in a battle of minds. Animosity had been brewing between them for a long time. Behind the scenes Chanatico suffered snide comments and hurtful jibes every day from her superior. Today passions boiled over in a typically tolerant and stoic species.

The pair ripped at each other's minds. A Tlillan could easily destroy the mind of a lesser species, effectively lobotomising her victim. Chan and Ilam attempted to rip the other's mind apart, not an easy task to accomplish against a Matriarch.

As both endeavoured to kill the other staff looked on, terrified to act. Mesan attempted to wedge himself between the women, 'ENOUGH OF THIS!'

The Matriarchs ignored Mesan now stepping back and tapping his wrist tablet with fervour.

Ilam gained the upper hand. Chan slowly dropped to one knee then the other as the ivory skinned Valkyrie loomed above. Pushing her mind into her foe, it was clear Ilam would win this confrontation to leave Chan a mental cripple for life.

An image appeared upon the central table of Kurgudwardum 57's control station. Lian observed in disbelief from her Makayuuk flagship.

'ILAMACHUTLI!' bellowed the hologram.

Ilam ignored her though Chan's eyes reached out to Lian in desperation.

'Ilamachutli, this is Kalayuuk, Adjunct to Xch'uup and the Tlillan Triumvirate. I am commanding you to desist in your present activity.'

Still Ilam ignored her pushing harder as Jenkins' wife grabbed her own skull in torture at a crushing weight upon her mind.

Moments later a second image appeared beside Lian, 'MOTHER!' Ilam ignored her daughter.

'Xch'uup orders you to release Chanatico.'

Again there was no reaction.

'If Chanatico is harmed you shall be stripped of all privileged and publicly shamed.'

At hearing Malikah's threat Ilam quickly released her victim. Chan let out wails of relief between heavy breaths. Yet before Ilam would speak to Xch'uup she gave Chan an almighty slap around the face knocking her Docking Controller onto the floor.

'Explain yourself!' demanded Xch'uup.

A furious Ilam faced her daughter's image. Placing palms to the ceiling 'Ola nuuk hun.'

'Your appeal to my vanity is lost.'

'Tumensiik Xch'uup,' replied Ilam in a decidedly calm pitch.

'Why was I disturbed from rest only to witness you assaulting Chanatico?'

'Chanatico eek'chi, chichan Chutli.'

'Really?'

'He'le, Chan a'alik Chutli k'an naats'Bandayuuk!'

'Next you're going to tell me she spoke heresy?'

Ilam paused before replying, 'He'le Xch'uup.'

'I thought so. In case you've forgotten Chanatico has been assigned to Kurgudwardum 57 by imperial appointment, do you understand?'

'He'le.'

'Those who strike Chanatico strike Xch'uup, is that understood?'

'Na'atik.'

'I am giving you the personal privilege of Chanatico's safety and therefore the safety of Xch'uup in the Skin Territory ... do not fail me mother.'

'Dyos bo'otik Xch'uup.'

With that Malikah's disappointed image, then Lian's, disappeared. Ilam screeched at the top her lungs beating her fists on the table in frustration.

Chanatico yanked herself to her feet having caught most of Malikah's conversation.

Facing Chan with red rage in her eyes the former first of Chutli whispered, 'Xch'uup has bestowed but a reprieve.'

Chanatico nodded her head before exiting to the nearest med bay seeking treatment for a miss-aligned jaw.

Mesan attempted to follow Jenkins' wife until Ilam grabbed a hold of his collar. The mighty Amazon whispered into his ear, 'Where did you get that command channel code?'

Mesan didn't answer.

'I am not permitted to harm that little whore. Your life however is quite expendable.'

Mesan mumbled at the incensed woman, 'Chanatico gave it to me, for her safety.'

'Safety? From whom?'

'You.'

'Remove those command channel codes if they remain you shall be spaced.'

'I understand.'

Ilam released her captive allowing him to scurry away.

Upon return to Kurgudwardum 57 Jenkins met up with his wife. Hevatsu leapt into Clayton's arms and after all was said and done the old soldier returned to his berth.

'You looked funny with that red face what made you put it on?' asked Hevatsu as Clayton exited the shower.

'Tradition.'

'I don't understand.'

'We used to wear it on Bandayuuk before going into battle.'

'Why?'

'Because it scared the Macks and gave us confidence.'

'Macks?'

Drying his hair Clayton replied to his partner, 'Do you remember Mammi's fleet when it was beaten at Idpa?'

'Of course who could forget such a thing?'

'They were Macks.'

'You defeated those cyborgs?'

Clayton placed a used towel over the back of a chair and chuckled, 'So they say.'

'I'm confused are these Macks not subject to Xch'uup?'

Clayton shrugged his shoulders.

'Yet they assist you in defending your hold on the Skin Territory, yes?'

'True.'

'Please explain, Clayton.'

The former Bokor slipped into a black space suit, 'We thought we'd won but really it was a five year break for the Macks to re-arm.

They rushed us on the surface, killing most of us. We fought them off until the last Atlas out … then the fleet arrived.'

'And?'

'And the largest space battle in history took place.'

'And who won?'

Clayton slipped into his cargo pants, 'That's a matter of opinion.'

Hevatsu was rather frustrated by now, 'Well what happened?'

'Officially? We broke their line and the Macks surrendered.'

'What do you think happened?'

'Macks don't surrender that's fact not opinion. I fought those bastards for years, if they offered a surrender it was just a tactic to buy time for reinforcements.

What really happened was the Tico took out a Mack flagship. She smashed it into Bandayuuk shattering its crust. Machine, their ruler, was going to die. The planet was going to break up in a matter of hours. So they made a deal with the Tlillans, they surrender and we fix their planet.'

The red droid furrowed her brow, 'How would it be possible to save a whole planet from breaking up?'

Clayton buttoned up a fresh shirt, 'That I don't know but it's what I've been told by someone in the know.'

'Do you believe it?'

The old soldier slung a gun belt around his waist, 'It's the most plausible story so far. All I know for sure is that we'd lost that battle. The Macks had us by the short and curlies. Next thing I know they surrender and we're singing God save the King. I thought it was a load of old bollocks then and I think it's a load of old bollocks now.'

Clayton opened a draw taking out his pistols. As he did Hevatsu noticed a row of silver medals, 'Did you get those fighting Macks?'

'Do you want to look?'

The red lady smiled, 'Yes please.'

He placed the medals in her hand.

'Why don't you wear these?'

'I've got something more to hold onto than the past.'

'I don't understand.'

'I'll explain it to you another time.'

'Aren't you proud of these medals?'

'I fought those Macks night and day for years. I spent days at a time underneath that planet hounded by psychopathic cyborgs … with no more than terror as a companion.

When the King placed that Victoria Cross on my chest I was the proudest man in the world. But I don't need to remember those times every day for the rest of my life. For whatever reason I've been given a second go; I've got a new life now and it doesn't include Macks.'

'Do you hate Macks?'

'Honestly, I don't know. I know what they are and how dangerous they can be. You saw what they did to the largest fleet Mammi had ever put together. But if someone invaded Earth … would I have done any different?'

Hevatsu eyed his medals as they glimmered in the palm of her hand, 'But you fear them?'

'I do and anyone with an ounce of sense should fear them. The Telal and Kishar are a joke compared to the will of Machine.'

Hevatsu put her arm around Clayton, 'I think I understand. When you were on Asrukishar, I felt something. Mr McCann told me it was fear. He helped me control it until you returned.'

Clayton slipped his pistol into its holster then squared his hat. Hevatsu returned his medals and he closed the draw leaving the past to rest as he stepped out of his berth and into a new world; A world that didn't involve tunnel warfare or the horror of facing Makayuuk killers.

'I'll have to thank Brigadier Jenkins.'

'What for?' asked Clayton.

'For returning you, he's a very nice man ... isn't he?'

Clayton nodded his head, 'Oh yes, Brigadier Jenkins is a very nice man,' as he said those words an old memory flashed through Clayton's mind ...

Inside Jenkins' office Clayton stood to attention with Sergeant Roberts. The Brigadier was not pleased, he handed Roberts a tablet concerning the Bokors next mission.

'It's an extraction job,' noted Jenkins in a solemn tone.

'Extraction?' inquired Roberts.

'Tomorrow you'll be flown to an insertion point. You're expected to penetrate the Mack perimeter and make your way to Bravo Sierra Niner. Upon reaching your objective you're to search for captives.'

'Captives?' Roberts knew Macks didn't take prisoners.

'Is there an echo in this room or is it just me that's hearing voices?'

Clayton furrowed his brow, 'Birthing Station Nine? But surely they'd have been taken to reprocessing?'

Jenkins let out a long sigh, 'I know but there are influential people involved.'

'I don't understand,' stated Roberts.

'Some rich man's son joined up with the I.S.A no doubt against his father's wishes, his platoon went missing three days ago.'

'The entire platoon?'

'Unfortunately it seems so, no-one in the I.S.A has the balls to tell him that his son is almost certainly being served for breakfast as we speak. So it falls to you gentlemen to rescue him from the Makayuuk.'

'Why are we being sent to Birthing Station 9?'

'That's where his chip went dead before the Macks turned him into blancmange.'

Clayton shook his head, 'Great, we risk ourselves for some rich man but the poor boys just have to suck it up!'

Jenkins sneered, 'That attitude has already cost you one demotion, drunk and disorderly in the Officers Mess ... you're fortunate not to be swinging on the end of a rope.'

'Bleeding white shoe boys I've had shits I felt more respect for!'

Jenkins took a swagger stick from beside his chair and placed it under Clayton's chin, 'You're welcome to demonstrate the same respect you gave those Officers ... Private.'

Clayton made no response.

'Many of those Officers may be the sons of White Shoe Boys but I was fighting in the jungles of Mozambique alongside Roberts here when your mother was still wiping your ARSE!'

'Understood sir.'

'It's not my fault the I.S.A is selling Officer's commissions to the highest bidder. However we just have to live with it, I'm compelled to show men respect who possess as little understanding of warfare as a Gukumatz does personal hygiene! And you'll have to do the same no matter how much of a horses' arse he is, understood?'

'Understood sir.'

Jenkins removed his stick, 'I did my best but Headquarters is dead set on sending you in there, it seems your reputation has its downside.'

The Brigadier moved in close to Roberts, 'Since none of the Bokors have quantum chips we won't be able to track your squadron, do you understand Sergeant?'

'I think I understand what you're saying, sir.'

Jenkins returned to his seat, 'Alright you're both dismissed ... and good luck chaps.'

'Thank you sir,' replied Roberts as he saluted before exiting with Clayton.

Chapter 22

In the following months the Skin Territory settled down ... a little. The Kishar accepted their place in the new paradigm. Kurgudwardum 57 was no longer the killing field of Blue Necks and mercenaries. Most importantly Ilam and Chan seemed to have come to an agreement, only interacting when necessary.

Profit margins on lotus opened up new options for the I.S.A and projected returns led to a construction contract. In Faraday's opinion this was to be the greatest achievement of Mankind a monument to mark the 22nd century. A tunnel gate had been proposed linking Earth with the Skin Territory, opening up free trade with Andromeda.

Kurgudwardum 57 would control the Andromeda end providing enough power to generate a wormhole. The entire station would be upgraded with a wormhole generator and extra defences.

At the other end, off Jupiter, an Earth gate was under construction along with its control station Ganymede one. Charging a small tariff any vessel of any size would be able to make the jump to Andromeda in one leap no longer depending on a wormhole generator to travel there and back.

Total Security Solutions could gut their Gukumatz vessel; increasing cargo capacity whilst cutting down on journey time and expense. Added space made it cheaper to pay a tariff rather than make a journey of several jumps.

At the moment a journey to Andromeda took many jumps. In between tunnel events the wormhole generator required a full maintenance check along with the fusion core. Its Captain obliged to carry several fuel rods, folding space over such distances drained a fusion core to such an extent it requiring a fresh injection of fuel. Tritium and Deuterium fuel rods were used, jump starting an exhausted reactor at the end of a long jump into the darkness between the Milky Way and Andromeda. This held up the journey for weeks, even the Athena was stressed to attempt the jump in a single month. Smaller vehicles had not attempted the journey due to the fact they did not possess a fusion core. Without a source of renewable energy you'd be left stranded in no-man's space. Even with a fusion core if your wormhole generator developed a critical fault the chances of rescue were somewhere between slim and none.

This would revolutionise space travel between the Milky Way and Andromeda, permitting the common man to one day travel far and wide.

Faraday strolled around Ganymede 1, the station was still under construction and few areas held a breathable atmosphere. Using technology discovered on Kurgudwardum 57 and already in use on the Bohr, Ganymede would be ready by next year.

Faraday strolled a main outer corridor similar to Kurgudwardum 57 yet modest in size. Six Spetsnaz flanked the I.S.A Chairman as a short fat New Yorker, cigar in mouth, argued.

'They're complaining about the conditions you've gotta do something,' declared a balding man in a welding suit.

'Do? What on Earth am I supposed to do Mr Cafaro?'

'None of my men are used to space construction they don't like the cramped quarters and they miss their wives … well some do. But they all miss you know what.'

Faraday stopped to examine a carbon composite window, 'No, I don't.'

'Jesus, do I have to say it?'

'It might help Mr Cafaro.'

'Well you know … the horizontal hustle.'

Faraday turned away from the station window and to its head of construction, 'Excuse me?'

'You know … the mattress jig.'

'I'm sorry Mr Cafaro but unless you're requesting a ballroom I'm still in the dark.'

Cafaro let out a loud huff before carrying on, 'Six months and no pussy slows construction on Ganymede and its jump gate … get me?'

'That is YOUR problem Mr Cafaro. You took the contract. This project must be completed on time and within budget.'

'Listen even sailors can look forward to stopping in port. These guys are stuck in prison cells pulling off to shitty holo porn. Even worse the damn things are in Latvian!'

Faraday raised an eyebrow, 'I had no idea dialogue was so significant.'

The short man in a dirty orange welding suit lifted his hands, 'If you want this done on time you're gonna have to solve the problem. I've got guys that are so miserable they could be French philosophers!'

'Very well Mr Cafaro perhaps a selection of,' Faraday pulled a face of disgust, 'dirty holo-vids can be shipped in on the next supply run.'

Cafaro shook his head with fervour, 'Its past that they need the real thing. These guys need to blow off some steam. They need booze, pussy and good times.'

'I'm afraid, Mr Cafaro, that my schedule is quite full!'

A Spetsnaz guard chuckled to himself.

Cafaro was not amused by Faraday's jest.

'Listen if I can bring in an extra shift …'

'Certainly not! I'm sorry Mr Cafaro it cannot be done.'

'It's your choice Faraday over budget or missed completion dates.'

'Are you threatening me?'

'I'm telling you the facts.'

Faraday looked out through a carbon window, 'I have contracts lined up for when this gate goes online Mr Cafaro. The I.S.A would be forced to pay compensation if those agreements cannot be fulfilled.'

Cafaro took a drag of his cheap cigar, 'That's YOUR problem Faraday ... not mine.'

The old Etonian contemplated his quandary whilst observing stars set behind Jupiter's torrid atmosphere. It was an awe inspiring scene. Astraea, last of the Gods to live amongst mortals, eclipsed by her father. Faraday realised how apt the epithet of cloud gatherer was as his eye became excited by Zeus's many bands of swirling clouds. This system's Titan observed mankind spread its wings into the domain of the Olympians. Jupiter's red eye reflected on the carbon composite window whilst Astraea fell behind. Mankind had joined their Gods to live amongst the stars. Perhaps this was the beginning of another heroic age.

'You guys always have money set aside for this kinda thing. It won't be so bad.'

Faraday replied stoically as he observed the cloud gatherer, 'Not for your men. I'll have bureaucrats moaning in my ear even after the damn thing's finished.'

'One weekend every two weeks?'

'I could arrange for transport to Mars and back.'

'Mars?'

'Mr Cafaro ample dens of wickedness exist upon Mars. I've wasted many hours of my life reading through reports on personnel fallen prey to drink and women at Tharsis. I'm sure your men will be more than satisfied.'

'If they can get laid on Mars then it's a deal,' Cafaro extended his hand and Faraday shook ... quickly wiping his palm clean with a handkerchief afterwards.

The Chairman continued his tour of this half built discus suspended in space above Jupiter's outer most moon. Towers extended at the poles of Ganymede one, provided docking arms; freeing space along the station's equator for the instillation of magnetic cannons. If anything endangered Faraday's jump gate Ganymede one would blast it to hell.

After his tour of Ganymede and wrangling out deals with its contractors Faraday's next stop was Mars. In the years since Athena's crew of astronauts stepped foot on Tharsis the red planet had become the solar system's industrial base.

Those old 19th century assumptions that Martians were a large industrial society had now been realised.

Tharsis had spread with orbital lifts not just from Pavonis Mons but catronium lifts rising from three other extinct volcanoes; Arsia Mons, Ascraeus Mons and finally the mighty Olympus Mons … the solar system's highest peak.

Factories, military camps, civilian housing and all that goes with those establishments from whorehouses to churches spread from Amazonis Planitia to Syria Planum.

Orbital towers rose into space each linked to a separate asteroid where everything was handled from day to day shipping to assembly of parts into spaceships.

A gigantic sprawl originating from one small base that seemed destined to failure, from Athena crashing to a total mental breakdown of its crew.

Now the I.S.A was the envy of every nation state on Earth. No other organisation held the manufacturing capacity of this titan. Even Russia was humbled at the sight of prefabricated space stations leaving orbit to be projected light years into space.

After docking with the Edwards and making his way to the surface Faraday met up with an old friend.

'How has it been Valorie?'

Dr Pitt greeted Faraday with a big smile as he stepped out from an orbital lift compartment with two Spetsnaz, 'Don't you mean how've you been?'

The I.S.A Chairman patted her hand, 'Of course, I'm sorry. So how have you been here, any luck cleaning up the mess?'

Valorie dressed in a fetching black and burgundy suit cut in a military style wrapped her hands around his right arm, 'It's been interesting if nothing else.'

'Hmmm, interesting … I have a feeling I'm not going to like that.'

Valorie had developed an obsession with the Ixchel or to be more exact in the abilities it imparted. As soon as she could Dr Pitt got herself a shot of the symbiotic creature; eventually developing psychic abilities beyond any human having undergone the same process. I.S.A scientists now believed the doctor rivalled even a Tlillan Matriarch.

The pair walked through a spacious loading bay inside the hollowed out volcano of Pavonis Mons. Workers ran about loading shipments of cargo destined for all corners of Triumvirate space.

Faraday felt proud to see what had been accomplished stopping for a moment to examine the busy area.

Valorie sensed his emotion, 'You have much to be proud of Will.'

'And tomorrow we shall be in another Galaxy,' whispered the old Etonian.

'Now, now Will, Mars requires far more attention than Andromeda. We must concentrate on what we have before securing that which we desire.'

'What WE have?'

Valorie smiled with her thin red lips, 'I have as much interest in the I.S.A as you.'

A few years ago several people from ex-soldiers to technicians developed beyond norms after the Ixchel manifested itself. They were the top 0.1% of the fortunate 10%. Although figures were still not certain it seemed at most only 10% of humans were compatible with the Ixchel. After an initial rush to receive what many hoped to be immortality or something close, it became obvious the Ixchel and its symbiosis was not so clear cut.

Though the 0.1 percenters may have been blessed others became uncomfortable associating in any way with a mind reader.

Their enhanced abilities led to something resembling apartheid in the workplace; eventually spreading to society as a whole. They met with anything from a cold shoulder to outright hostility wherever they went. Fellow employees complained even going on strike. No-one wanted to work with a man or woman who might listen in on your darkest secrets, the lover you hid from your wife, your worst prejudices, what you really thought of your friends, family and workmates.

So a Trans-mental Department was founded, a place the gifted might work together for the betterment of the I.S.A.

Valorie pushed for its formation and was the natural choice to lead. Employing the most gifted telepaths, the department was now indispensable. She was on Mars to assess the possibility of industrial action by unions.

Workers wanted the same things as usual, more money better conditions, less hours and so on. Valorie was here to weed out the trouble makers, if the Governor could not deal with it she would.

The department employed several of its members on Mars monitoring the situation. All dressed in the same deep red and black uniform, making no attempt to hide themselves. Part of their power was the fact it shot fear into the hearts of normally brave men.

'So where's the Governor?'

'He'll be meeting us in Blue District.'

'Blue District?'

'Tharsis has grown over the years, think of Blue District as a city district.'

The party chatted as they boarded a subway system taking them through the volcano and into Blue District on Syria Planum. Dr Pitt grinned at Faraday for the entire journey, watching him gaze in wonder at all the people on the train. From traders to tourists it was astonishing to think that not so long ago this place was a glorified pre-fab.

After arriving at Blue District the doors opened into a customs area where security checked each person's chip before permitting them to enter.

Approaching a security terminal a young guard viewed Valorie, 'Please look at the wall while I scan your chip.'

Quickly an older member of security moved over, 'She's Transmental.'

'Sorry Ma'am I've never seen a Prophet before,' blurted the young man.

Valorie smiled back 'You can relax, I won't bite.'

The young man looked at Faraday and his guards, 'Are they with you Ma'am?'

'Yes they are.'

Tapping his wrist tablet a barred security gate unlocked, 'Welcome to Syria Planum please enjoy your stay.'

Valorie stepped through followed by Faraday. The old Etonian whispered, 'What did he mean he'd never seen a Prophet before?'

Valorie pointed out an insignia stitched onto the left breast of her jacket. The design was of a human figure holding its arms out, similar to the Cristo Redentor.

'It started as a joke in Geneva however the name stuck.'

Before they might continue Polkovnik Dimitri Kolobklov approached with a man in his 30's.

Faraday and Dimitri greeted each other; Dimitri being the executive officer who brought Ryu to his attention for the original Mars mission. The pair shook hands.

'How have you been Dimitri?'

'Well this assignment has helped me lose weight ... and some of my mind!' replied the man in his 50's.

Faraday laughed.

'How have you been William? Miss Dutta still keeping you on your toes?'

The large Russian bellowed with laughter. Valorie joined in his merriment.

'I didn't come all of this way to gossip,' replied a disappointed Faraday.

'I'm sorry this job can get to you very quickly. I thought it would be a step up from whiling my hours away in Geneva. But if we take hold of it together maybe it won't feel so heavy, what do you say Valorie?'

DR Pitt nodded her head, 'The Trans-mental Department will do our best to prevent stormy seas Dimitri.'

The Russian Colonel quickly turned to his security Chief, 'This is Viktor Orlov he's my head of security. I couldn't run this hell hole without him.'

Viktor saluted Faraday.

'Don't worry about that Mister Orlov,' said Faraday holding his hand out.

Viktor shook his hand, 'It is good to meet you Director Faraday.'

'How has security been on Mars since Doctor Pitt arrived?' asked the old Etonian.

'Much better Director,' at that moment the Security Chief's wrist tablet began to bleep.

Viktor hit his tablet, 'Da?'

A voice with an Asian accent replied, 'Security alert in Green District Mister Orlov.'

The blond haired man let out a puff of wind, 'Did you get them this time?'

'Yes sir, they came to harvest their plants. They're asking for you sir. Grant says if you don't turn up he'll have to shock them.'

Viktor gave Dimitri a coy expression, 'I'm on my way,' then tapped his wrist tablet.

'Green District?' inquired Valorie.

'Someone has been growing lotus in gardens set aside for food crops. It's a minor offence but we can't have citizens planting whatever they want when fresh food is at such a premium.'

Dimitri nodded excusing his head of security.

As Viktor walked off Faraday noted, 'He seems quite dependable.'

'He is,' replied Dimitri, 'put everything onto the grey horse and he'll bear it William.'

The reception area of Blue District was as large as a football field, citizens waited for families whilst others wished friends good voyage. Mars had expanded from just an industrial base to somewhere people spent their holidays touring its great mountain ranges, the first landing sight and contact with the Tlillan.

'I remember when this was little more than a glorified garden shed!' stated Faraday in amazement.

'I must say I'm never bored running this place,' replied Dimitri, 'on that point there is something, more to the point someone, we must speak on.'

'Oh?'

'Oh indeed. He has been in my cells more often than the cleaner.'

'I don't understand.'

'He's one of your men. Every time he's arrested Geneva instructs me to release him the following day. I've requested his transfer more times than I can count.'

The old Etonian fixed a steely gaze on Dimitri, 'Beaumont.'

'That man is intolerable. He creates fights every other night in the Pleasure Dome.'

'Pleasure Dome?'

'Red District,' whispered Valorie.

'Oh God,' groaned Faraday.

'Oh God indeed Viktor had security staff assigned to him, to prevent violent outbreaks. That man assaulted my staff; two of them were in med bay the next day. I tell you I have seen some bar brawls in Moscow but this Beaumont ...'

'I understand Dimitri trust me I understand but Beaumont's skills are required if we're to construct this jump gate to Andromeda on time. When that's done I promise you'll not have to deal with him again.'

'So he just hops in and out of cells for the next 6 months?'

'If we can clear up this sabotage problem you might get rid of that foul man sooner.'

The party reassumed their journey through Blue District.

'We have agents investigating the industrial sabotage problem. They've been scanning workers since the day we arrived,' stated Valorie.

'And?'

'I agree with Viktor this isn't an uprising as some thought.'

'Then what is it?'

'I believe another corporation is sabotaging our current contractors. I think you need to look at who didn't win our contract for the Andromeda jump gate rather than who did.'

The party stepped through some checkpoints and into Yellow District. Security allowed the Governor and his friends through without the usual chip scans.

Yellow Dome was a modest merchant district. A few chain stores from Earth had set up, probably for the prestige more than anything else. Being able to state you had X amount of outlets on Earth paled against a competitor with X amount on Earth and Mars.

Some buildings reached up a few floors coming close to the top of Yellow District's dome which sealed them from the Martian atmosphere.

Faraday looked up at the sun shining through carbon glass, 'It's impossible to understand until you've seen it for yourself.'

'Quite the sight don't you think?' stated Dimitri.

'You know McCann told me it reminded him of mystery, fate and love.'

'You can see Tharsis mountain range from the observation room,' Valorie pointed to a small deck just beneath the dome's apex.

Their group took an elevator to a small room where tourists shuffled taking holographs of themselves with the three extinct volcanoes in the background.

Faraday was struck as to the similarity between these Tharsis volcanoes and the great pyramids on the Giza plateau. Their size and placement was quite a coincidence.

'You're not the first to have thought that,' said Valorie in a cheeky tone.

Faraday gazed out into mystery, fate and love, 'Are you scanning me all the time?'

'No, it's just that some thoughts are difficult to ignore.'

'God help your poor husband!'

'You didn't know?'

Faraday peered at Doctor Pitt, 'Not again?'

'I'm afraid so Will; it's hard to find a good man.'

'Perhaps your psychic abilities will lend a hand next time you make a selection?'

Valorie smiled as she looked out onto Pavonis Mons, 'Now that I have the Ixchel there's no longer any sense of urgency. I'll wait for the next one to come along.'

'Perhaps you could marry Beaumont?' ejaculated Kolobklov.

Valorie glanced at the Governor and raised her perfectly plucked eyebrows.

'Maybe you could adopt him?'

'Only one person can control that man,' said William.

'Then why isn't she here?'

'Ryu is very busy and very married my friend. You'll have to deal with the Frenchman yourself.'

The sun set in the west behind Tharsis mountain range to the delight of tourists snapping holographs.

Dimitri's wrist tablet went off again, 'Da?'

Viktor's voice replied, 'Green District has been dealt with but Beaumont has been arrested again. I have him in Grey District now, would you like to question him?'

Dimitri looked over at his old friend, 'Yes, I'm certain Director Faraday would be interested in observing.'

Dimitri tapped his tablet and smiled, 'Come William I'm sure you'll enjoy reacquainting yourself with an old friend.'

Arriving in Grey Dome Dimitri led his party past security and into an interrogation room. Inside a small grey metal box room Beaumont sat on a chair leaning onto a table constructed of the same metallic substance.

Louis Beaumont groaned, probably from over indulging in a cocktail of alcohol and violence. Viktor had been shouting at Beaumont but the Frenchman replied in an apathetic tone, 'Charge me with something or shut the fuck up you Russian pig.'

Viktor was about to blow up when Dimitri entered, 'Mr. Beaumont … we meet again?'

Louis peered at the table top as he nursed his wounds, 'No need to salute Commissar, just get me a fucking drink before your Cossack gives me a headache.'

'I thought you'd been banned from the Pleasure Dome Mr. Beaumont?'

Louis groaned until a paper cup of water was placed before him. The Frenchman took a sip then threw it across the room, 'I said a drink!'

A furious Faraday stepped into the room, 'BEAUMONT!!!!!'

Louis glanced upwards, 'Shit that drink must have been drugged!'

Faraday pointed the ball of his walking stick at the seated Frenchman, 'How dare you speak to the Governor in such a contemptuous fashion!'

Louis squinted at Faraday, 'This must be one of those crazy nightmares … what do you call it?'

At that moment Valorie entered the room, 'A psychosis?'

'Yes that's it … what the fuck are you doing here?'

'I might ask you the same question Louis.'

'I just wanted a drink!'

'From what I can smell you seemed to have already accomplished that feat.'

'I finished the whisky in my apartment, it would've been fine if this prick,' Louis pointed at Viktor, 'hadn't banned everyone from selling me alcohol!'

'Now why would Viktor do that?'

Louis sneered at the head of security, 'This prick has it in for me,' Louis rose to his feet pointing in Viktor's face, 'Fucking Russians, ask me and I say he's been planting those bombs trying to kill ME!'

As Louis moved towards Viktor two Mars security men grabbed him, thrusting the Frenchman back into his chair. They held him down as Viktor produced a shock stick, a small truncheon which delivered a nasty electrical charge.

'VIKTOR!' shouted Dimitri.

Viktor held the shock stick above Louis' head for a moment. The Security Chief was desperate to teach his nemesis a lesson. The Russian controlled himself retracting the weapon despite a powerful desire to ram it down Louis' throat.

Valorie moved towards Louis motioning the guards away. Viktor's staff released Beaumont and she spoke in a soothing tone, 'Which is it Louis? A psychosis or paranoid delusion? You'd be hard pressed to find someone here that doesn't want to kill you.'

Louis sneered, 'Exactly they victimize me then set bombs …'

The stench of whisky overwhelmed Valorie so much it forced her to turn away when he spoke, 'Enough Louis.'

The Frenchman fell quiet.

'You may not realize it but you are not the center of the universe, not even Mars. These bombings have nothing to do with you, Viktor, Dimitri, William or myself. Do you understand?'

Louis nodded silently.

'If you could relegate your drunken stupors to the privacy of your own apartment everyone would be thankful. And perhaps Viktor might reassign his men from babysitting your drunken brawls to catching the people who are setting these bombs?'

Again Louis nodded.

'Now perhaps you'd like to apologize to Mr. Orlov and Mr. Kolobklov?'

Louis sneered as he stood up, freeing his arms from the security staff, 'They can kiss my sweet ass first!'

Valorie exhaled placing the tips of her fingers upon her forehead, 'Please leave Mister Beaumont.'

The Frenchman exited, the stench of whisky clouding his body and a vile sneer as a mixer.

Viktor watched Louis stagger away, 'I swear that man shall leave Tharsis in a casket!'

'Solve these bombings first ... then he can have a taste of the shock stick,' whispered Dimitri.

Two days later Valorie picked up a thought as she walked through Blue District. Someone was planning on collapsing a dome in White District ... the industrial district.

Unable to locate the origin of the thought she reported it to Viktor. Within hours a device had been discovered and disarmed.

Viktor left the bomb and began monitoring the area, waiting for the perpetrator to return once the apparatus failed to detonate.

Sure enough a man emerged an hour after its timer expired. In moments Viktor and his team swooped in escorting the fellow to Grey Dome; where he now sat in a gun metal cell, previously occupied by a drunken Beaumont.

After more than 24 hours of interrogation the fellow still refused to give up any information. Even his name eluded Viktor's techniques.

Pulling out a shock stick the Russian looked down on his stripped prisoner, hands tied behind his back.

'You will tell me everything you know.'

There was no response from a man in his twenties with short blond hair.

'Until now I have been using approved I.S.A interrogation methods ... but on Mars the I.S.A isn't always here ...' the Russian thrust his shock stick into the fellow's side dispensing a severe belt of electricity.

Two burly Russians looked on as the terrorist screamed in pain collapsing onto the floor. They hauled him and the seat he was tied to back up, thrusting him against the cell wall.

'Vladimir!' shouted the security chief.

In came a man who'd cause a grizzly bear to think twice.

'I want you to take his finger print.'

The prisoner pushed himself against the wall preventing Vladimir from taking his prints.

Vladimir walked over to the fellow, grasped him by the neck and smashed his face on the metal table. The guards untied his arms holding them outstretched on the table.

Vladimir produced a knife placing it above the prisoner's index finger.

'Vladimir will take your finger and process its print. If he finds no match he will return and take another finger ... and another ... and another ... until he has a match ... or you have no fingers remaining,' spoke Viktor in a belligerent tone.

The terrorist replied as Vladimir pushed his face into the table, 'Michael.'

'Yes, Michael what?'

'Michael ...'

Before he could finish the door swung open.

'VIKTOR! WHAT IS THIS?'

Dimitri, Faraday and Valorie stood in the doorway.

Viktor jumped to attention, 'I am interrogating the prisoner he was about to tell me his name, SIR!'

'He was about to tell you what you wanted to hear Mr. Orlov,' stated Valorie.

'In Russia ...'

'This is not Russia Mr. Orlov we have other methods of interrogation; Far more effective than removing digits.'

Viktor nodded towards Vladimir who sheathed his knife and exited the cell.

'I apologize William, I ...'

'Never mind Dimitri no harm done, I only wish it was Beaumont having his tongue cut out!'

The Etonian stepped inside with Dimitri as the guards sat their prisoner back on his seat. Viktor put his shock stick away.

Valorie removed her black leather gloves approaching the prisoner with a soft smile, 'Do you know who I am?'

He refused to answer.

'Never mind you don't need to speak I can hear your thoughts young man.'

The prisoner looked at Faraday and spoke for the first time, 'I have rights! I demand a lawyer!'

'I'm afraid you'll have to wait until one can make the journey from Earth, old boy.'

Valorie placed her hands on his head, 'You've been trained to block mental probes haven't you.'

The prisoner continued to plead with Faraday, 'Get this woman away from me! I refuse to be interrogated by her!'

'I could always bring back that fellow with the knife!'

'Phillip Granger is his name Mr. Orlov,' reported Valorie.

Viktor tapped away on his wrist tablet retrieving the man's details 'Confirmed it says he's a holiday maker from the Scandinavian States.'

Phillip leant back dropping his mind into full concentration. Thinking about a brick wall blocked most deep mental probes. He'd spent a year studying mental discipline in Stockholm before his mission to Mars.

Valorie concentrated on his mindscape going to work on breaking the wall he'd constructed. On discovering a strong emotion she manifested it within his mind.

As Phillip muttered to himself Valorie spoke, 'You had a son didn't you?'

The captive tried to ignore her ploy.

'He died in an accident.'

His muttering became louder.

'I feel the pain you still have … at the funeral … it almost destroyed you didn't it Phillip?'

The man continued muttering an indecipherable mantra.

Valorie whispered a song into his ear, the song they played at his son's funeral. At the same time she manifested the pain and hurt buried inside his psyche for all those years, 'It's alright baby's coming back and I don't really care where he's been.'

The man began to crack as past emotional pain destroyed his mental wall.

'It's alright baby's coming back and I won't turn him around this time.'

The prisoner felt a surge of harrowing memories rip from his past and into the present. Losing control he cracked, collapsing into a pile of blubbering tears on the cell floor.

As he cried Valorie replaced her gloves, 'I have his employer's details. It seems Mister Shinata was not pleased to lose the jump gate contract.'

'Shinata? That bastard! I knew it was him!' growled Faraday shaking his cane.

Valorie smiled, 'Of course you did.'

'Yes well I had my suspicions. He's been pushing for the jump gate ever since the bombings started.'

Valorie peered towards Viktor, 'You can do what you want with him. I'm certain he'll answer any questions you have Mr. Orlov … minus the Russian encouragement!'

'Thank you DR Pitt.'

As the group walked out Dimitri gave his head of security a black look.

The threesome strolled away from Grey District and into Yellow District. Valorie was a little tired and required a coffee.

'Thank you Valorie you've probably saved the entire jump gate project.'

'Then it wouldn't be too much to request an increase in my Department's budget?'

Dimitri raised an eyebrow as Faraday went a funny colour.

'Well I don't know,' stammered the old Etonian.

Valorie sat down at her favorite café, 'William there's no profit in being a penny pincher.'

'I understand. It just gives me a stomach ache whenever expanding budgets are mentioned.'

The three sat down to order drinks.

'Think of the money saved from a collapsed dome. Industry would've been halted for months. The jump gate would've been set back years! When I first requested a Trans-mentalist department you worried over the budget like an old woman. Look at what it's saved you today.'

'You're right. How about setting up a permanent office here on Mars?'

Valorie nodded in approval.

'That's providing it's alright with you Dimitri?'

The large Russian sipped his tea, 'Of course please do.'

Faraday drank tea whilst relaxing into his chair, 'Ahh, this whole thing has been teetering on the abyss. It's a wonder I haven't gone mad or shot myself before now! Or perhaps the world has gone bonkers and I'm the only sane person left?'

Valorie held his hand across the table, 'Don't worry Will … if the world goes into decline I'll always be your danger sign.'

Chapter 23

Arthur made his way through the Teteo's corridors arriving at its Captain's cabin. Without alerting anyone to his presence his eyes reflected the forever sheet of night forcing its door open. Since the Chihuaz Kaeo had not left her cabin. Many worried yet none had the audacity to confront her.

Entranced before a mirror the short Valkyrie fell deep within her own image; as Arthur stepped inside the room its liquid door melted shut.

'If you keep staring at that you'll wear the bloody thing out.'

'What do you want?'

'I came to see how you are.'

'I'm fine, now you can leave.'

'I only just arrived.'

Kaeo moved her gaze from the mirror, 'I'm a monster.'

Arthur observed her terrible disfigurement leaving half her face distorted. A horrific acid burn deformed once perfect features to that of a twisted freak.

Despite her defacement Kaeo did not feel the shock or disgust she'd sensed from others.

'I've seen worse.'

'Well you've seen how I am. Don't forget to close the door behind you.'

'I'm not leaving.'

Kaeo whispered to herself, 'Why me?'

'It will heal in time Sandra said the venom will slowly dilute.'

'No, why am I cursed with you?'

'Cursed with me?'

'I had my own destiny but instead I was burdened. Rather than being free to seize glory I was shackled to mediocrity, teaching a boy to fight like a man.'

'I'll apologise for being a burden on your glittering career after you thank me for saving your skin in the Chihuaz!'

Kaeo pointed at her maimed complexion, 'Thank you? For this?'

The young man replied with a look of confusion.

'I could have died with Kleos, they would have raised monuments in my name instead I am saved by a boy to return a deformed hag!'

'You would have rather died?'

'Yes!'

'I would not have allowed it.'

'You've made me a non-entity.'

'That's not true.'

'But it is … my life is not at risk. With nothing at stake how can I earn glory?'

'Is that all you care for, glory?'

'What else is there?'

Arthur took a deep breath replying in a hushed tone, 'Love.'

Kaeo laughed mockingly, 'Who would love a wretched hag?'

'I love you.'

'Lucky me,' replied Kaeo in a sardonic tone.

'What's the matter? Are you afraid to accept that someone could love you?'

Pointing at her scar she screamed, 'LOOK AT THIS! THEY USED TO FEAR ME, BUT THANKS TO YOU I DON'T EVEN HAVE THAT ANYMORE!'

'Kaeo …'

The short Valkyrie shook her head in despair, as she did Arthur kissed her lips. After a brief kiss she smacked him around the face splitting his lip.

'Before the Chihuaz Matriarchs feared me. Now they fear your retribution I am nothing. I could be a pet, a piece of art work or any inanimate object it matters not the result is the same.'

After hesitating for a few seconds she struck Arthur's face again.

Taking the blow he wiped away blood with a single finger, 'Did that make you feel better?'

'Yes it did actually!'

The scarred Amazon stepped in swinging her knee into his ribcage dropping him to the floor in agony.

'Why don't you defend yourself?'

Arthur didn't reply, only propping himself up to nurse his broken ribs.

The short warrior stormed out of her cabin leaving the young man to make his way to a med bay.

An hour or so later, after receiving medical treatment, Arthur sensed trouble on the Bohr. He disembarked the Teteo via its docking arm and boarded the massive Tlillan station. Rubbing his aching side he strolled its long passage ways eventually reaching an exclusive lounge only Matriarchs of Teteo were permitted to enter. He sensed darkness in the air. Kaeo occupied the lounge and he could not walk by without making certain she was safe.

A tall Valkyrie blocked his path, 'Males may not enter.'

Arthur turned his face to meet her eyes. Once the tall red head recognised who he was she tightened her lips and stepped backwards opening a path. Before proceeding within Cihu appeared from the gloom, despite not being a Matriarch she was permitted to reside within. Her former status and the title of Praetor gave her that privilege. She glared at the young man, 'Make haste!'

Arthur walked through a dim passage into a poorly lit lounge. Inside he picked out Kaeo's silhouette from the gloom. His innate Tlillan vision kicked in focusing all remaining light and illuminating the room as if it were a bright day.

Arthur caught the end of a conversation, from what he understood Kaeo was challenging all comers to a duel. As he entered the short woman drew her sword, 'Who will make the challenge for First of Teteo?'

No-one answered.

Pointing at her burnt profile she shouted, 'I have only one good eye anyone could take me with enough stealth.'

She was correct the damaged eye blurred her vision. Anyone with decent skill in the sword might take advantage by striking her blindside.

Strangely enough none took the challenge yet if someone had and defeated Kaeo she would have risen to First of Teteo but the room remained awkwardly quiet.

As Cihu entered Kaeo pointed in her direction, 'Cihu, do you fear me?'

The tall white haired warrior replied, 'I do.'

'LIAR! You do not fear me.'

'You are my First.'

'I have felt your desire to seize Huey'tlacochcalcatl. If I fall today you may have it.'

Cihu stood in the gloomy room's centre, 'How would I hope to stand against the only Matriarch to be bitten by a Tzitzimeh and survive?'

'Look at me! I'm blind as a Camazotz!'

Cihu peered over her First locking eyes with Arthur.

'Don't look at him look at me,' she continued to point at her face, 'how can you not look at this, does it not disgust you?'

Arthur approached from behind. His hand came out of the gloom to sit on Kaeo's shoulder.

She pushed him away, 'Don't touch me!'

'I'm sorry.'

Kaeo's eyes burnt as bonfires in the night her soul flickering with anger, 'What are you? A poodle? Following me around as a lost animal!'

'I was concerned.'

'Then don't be.'

'What is it you're searching for Kaeo?'

'Someone who isn't afraid of you.'

'They aren't afraid of me.'

Kaeo pointed accusingly at seated Matriarchs, 'They are terrified of you if not I would have been finished long before now!'

'That's just ridiculous.'

The short warrior set her fiery eyes on Cihu, 'Tell him the truth.'

Arthur gave Cihu a puzzled look as he awaited her response.

'Yaaxil speaks the truth.'

Arthur asked Cihu, 'Would you have challenged her if I were not present?'

'I would not.'

'You see?'

'Is that a joke?'

'I was not attempting to be humorous.'

Kaeo brought her blade to bear pressing it against Arthur's neck, 'Perhaps I should kill you?'

Arthur looked down her dark blue blade, 'Then your troubles would be over.'

'Yes, they would.'

'But you wouldn't dishonour yourself by killing a defenceless boy.'

Kaeo threw her sword at Arthur in a fit of anger. The weapon hit him, as he shielded his face, sliding on the floor until it stopped at a pair of boots.

Malikah bent down to retrieve her Marshal's blade. Holding the weapon in two hands she made her way inside.

Glancing at the Matriarchs Xch'uup spoke, 'Leave ... except Kaeo.'

The Tlillan women shuffled out though Arthur remained where he stood.

'That includes you Arthur.'

The young man nodded before following Cihu out of the lounge.

Kaeo looked down at the floor in shame.

'So why am I here Kaeo?'

Stood opposite one another in an empty lounge Malikah returned Kaeo's sabre, 'You seem set on a path of self-destruction.'

'If you fixed my face it might help.'

'I cannot it is your destiny to heal naturally.'

Kaeo snorted in disgust.

'I wanted to ask you something once you'd slithered out from your cabin.'

'What?'

'When you were dying in the Chihuaz you said you saw something.'

'I saw what Arthur was talking to.'

'Describe it.'

'He addressed a woman it was difficult to make out properly but she was a woman ... human.'

'What did they speak of?'

'I don't remember.'

'You must recall something of their conversation?'

Kaeo let out a big huff, 'Something about now being the right time but really that's all and I could be wrong.'

'Do you remember what she looked like?'

'Gold … she was golden her hair and around her eyes. Her eyes were blue but flashed with brilliance.'

'Was she wearing any clothes?'

'Yes, a sort of dress with a golden breast plate over it. She carried a helmet that shone as if it were gold.'

'Could you describe the helmet design?'

'I don't remember … say why don't we just link?'

The two placed their foreheads together and Kaeo's brief memories were transferred.

After taking in Kaeo's experience Malikah opened her eyes and glanced towards the ceiling.

'Well, what do you think?'

'He isn't mad, as to what is going on I have no idea though I intend to find out.'

A few months later the Teteo patrolled the Skin Territory, it took all Arthur's powers of persuasion in convincing Kaeo to enter Kurgudwardum 57. On the boulevard McCann greeted Kaeo, Cihu and Arthur, her scar was quite shocking.

'Pretty gross isn't it?' stated Kaeo in a cold tone.

'I've dated worse,' replied McCann in the hopes it might raise her spirits.

Arthur stepped forward pressing his palms together, 'Namaste Commodore.'

The Englishman smiled, 'So is it Arthurateteo now?'

'Arthur will do,' smiled the young man.

McCann fixed his vision on Cihu and waited. Eventually she pressed her palms together, 'Namaste Censor.'

McCann returned her greeting, 'Namaste Cihuateteo.'

'I am no longer a Matriarch of Teteo, Censor.'

The Commodore peered at Kaeo, 'I'm sure someone will sort that out.'

Ilam and Chan bowed before Kaeo and eventually all proper respect was paid to the correct parties in the proper order.

'What would you like to see first?' inquired Chan.

Kaeo had a very disinterested expression, 'Arthur dragged me here with his constant whining so why don't you ask him?'

There was an awkward moment until McCann spoke, 'I know some people who'd love to meet the mighty Kaeo.'

Thirty seconds after pressing his wrist tablet Hevatsu emerged from the boulevard's bustle. Upon seeing Kaeo she was elated though upon witnessing a walking and talking SI carrying a firearm Cihu was outraged.

'This is heresy!'

'Her name's Hevatsu.'

Cihu was about to continue until Kaeo made a stern gaze with her good eye quietening the former Matriarch.

Hevatsu approached Kaeo, 'Are you Kaeo? From the Chihuaz?'

'I am.'

The former love droid grabbed her hands leading the half Thai across the boulevard, 'I have friends who want to meet you.'

Kaeo allowed the android to guide her into Ninti's bar. Once inside the noise of women shrieking could be heard all along the main boulevard.

The station Marshal questioned Arthur, 'So what's going on?'

'Her injury she feels it has made her vulnerable.'

McCann's eyes shifted between Arthur and Cihu, 'Is she safe?'

'Kaeo believes her position as First of Teteo is in danger but I will not allow it to fall.'

'Why don't you go and join her in Ninti's.'

Arthur made his way across the boulevard.

Cihu looked down at McCann with a condescending Tlillan glare, 'You wish to speak with me Censor?'

'I want to know if Kaeo is in danger.'

'She is not, the Matriarchs fear Arthur.'

'Why?'

'He defeated Mammi in the Chihuaz. They understand he is in love with Kaeo. Arthur would exact a terrible revenge if Kaeo were defeated. It has been witnessed by the Seers.'

Inside Ninti's bar the girls forgot about customers, crowding around Kaeo instead. Arthur watched from a distance, for the first time since the Chihuaz she smiled. All were desperate to touch her, workers and patrons alike. Even Kaeo could not disguise her happiness.

'Do you feel it?' whispered Cihu in Arthur's ear.

'I do,' replied the young man.

'She teeters at the edge of the abyss but you may return her to us.'

'I shall do everything in my power.'

Kaeo peered at Arthur realising she was happy for the first time since the Chihuaz. Quickly readjusting her face she pulled a miserable expression but it was too late, Arthur had witnessed her true state.

'She fears anyone see her true heart,' said Cihu in a hushed tone.

'Why?'

'Kaeo is afraid of opening herself to pain from another as all of us are.'

'I'm not.'

Cihu smiled, 'Because you are in love.'

'And she is not is that what you're saying?'

'She needs love but is too frightened to accept.'

Arthur moved in towards the huddle with Kaeo residing at its centre.

From further out somewhere near the entrance McCann stood with Kurgudwardum 57's Tlillan controllers.

'There that is the paradigm shift Malikah was talking about,' noted McCann.

'Oh? What are you referring to exactly?' inquired Chan.

Ilam replied in a condescending tone, 'Kaeo would have been slain for her mantle. Yet with Cihu and Arthur she is the most powerful Matriarch on Otoch.'

Each worker and customer in the bar, including the owner, had their holograph taken with Kaeo and Arthur. Ninti's bar becoming the most popular nightspot in the Skin Territory.

Later that evening Kaeo took a stroll in Shurruppak's famous botanical gardens. After twenty minutes she stopped by a rock pool. Looking down into the tranquil waters she observed Arthur's reflection. The young man hid high up on an observation walkway.

'You can come down from there.'

Jenkins' son took a slow lift to the ground level and approached Kaeo by the rock pool.

'Why were you following me Arthur? Did you think I wouldn't sense you?'

'I was concerned.'

'My mother died at Bandayuuk, I doubt you are her soul reincarnated!' scoffed his First.

'I apologise, I'll leave ...'

'No, wait here, I have something to ask you.'

'Yes?'

'When I was dying you were in med bay watching me ... weren't you?'

'I was.'

'You spoke with someone else a woman with flashing blue eyes adorned in gold.'

The young man looked down at the floor but before he could reply Kaeo spoke, 'Malikah wishes to know the identity of the woman I saw and touched.'

'I cannot speak on this.'

'Does she pose a threat to me?'

'She would not harm you,' snapped Arthur.

'So she does exist?'

Arthur remained silent staring at the mossy earth.

'Don't worry I won't tell anyone. The Matriarchs already think I've lost my sanity I'm not about to start telling ghost stories.'

'And Malikah?'

'I showed her a little, enough to ascertain your sanity.'

Arthur pressed his palms together, 'Thank you Yaaxil.'

Kaeo raised a smile, 'It's the least I can do.'

'I don't understand.'

'After you saved my life in the Chihuaz.'

Arthur perked up, 'Yes it shouldn't be that long before you are ...'

'No longer a cripple?'

'I was going to say recovered.'

The short Valkyrie smiled, 'I'm sorry for being such a jerk.'

'You're forgiven.'

'Beware of Malikah she seeks the truth and will manipulate any of us to get it,' the short Tlillan sighed, 'but let's not worry about that, tell me where did you learnt to fight?'

'I went to Geneva. Mr McCann brought me to a gym where I picked up some fencing moves.'

'No! The hand to hand!'

'Oh you mean Pankration?'

'Is that what you call it?'

'I learnt it from Mr Clayton and a couple of his friends in Spetsnaz.'

Kaeo smiled at her former student, 'Would you teach me some of those moves?'

'Of course!'

The Valkyrie laughed, 'Calm down Arthur you might regret it later.'

'I don't think so,' replied the young man in a certain tone of voice.

'Malikah saw our destinies intertwine long ago.'

Arthur gave a puzzled look and Kaeo answered him, 'She witnessed my defeat on the floor of the Chihuaz long before it happened,' the short Tlillan folded her arms, 'we were destined to save each other.'

'Save each other?'

'Two people who needed someone to love and someone to love them.'

'Then you?'

The short Tlillan laughed, 'I'm the one who needed someone to love them.'

Arthur clicked onto what Kaeo was saying, 'Ahh and I needed someone to love.'

'Right.'

'Oh well you can't have it all I suppose,' said the young man as he peered into the rock pool.

Kaeo smiled as she grabbed his collar, 'It isn't all bad that kiss you gave me was the best kiss I've ever had in my life.'

The young man grinned as their eyes locked, 'Really?'

'Sure … it was the only kiss I've ever had but still I imagined it to be worse.'

'I suppose that's good.'

She ushered the young man into the forest, 'I tell you what since you're gonna be hanging around me like a puppy dog that's lost its home, you can be my first boyfriend … how does that sound?'

'That sounds good to me!'

Kaeo pointed in his face with her other hand, 'You got lucky with that kiss try it again and I'll take your knee caps out understood?'

'That's fine,' replied a grinning Arthur, 'does that mean I get to call you my girlfriend? Like it's official?'

'This is a plutonic relationship you understand?'

'Sure but do I have to tell everyone else that?'

'Only if they really want to know, you teach me to fight like you did in the Chihuaz and maybe we can have a pizza sometime … you got it?'

'Got it,' replied Arthur with a beaming grin.

'Now tomorrow I want you to teach me that throw you did on the grizzly bear, from the Lassu Territory.'

'Oh you mean the reverse waist lock?'

'Then you rammed him into the floor headfirst.'

'The pile driver.'

'Will you link with me in the gym tomorrow?'

'If you'll let me hold your hand.'

Kaeo held her hand outstretched, 'Go on then.'

Arthur took her hand grasping it softly. The short Tlillan felt bliss welling up inside him such as she had never experienced from another creature, rippling out in all directions and finally splashing into the pool of her soul. Pothos twisted his vine around the pair, tightening until Arthur's yearning did brush against Kaeo's heart. Kaeo observed Arthur's eyes certain they would break into tears. How he held such passion back was a mystery since it filled the Tlillan Marshal. She only watched in wonder whilst his cheeks remained dry.

'I wanted to be an artist you know?' stated Arthur as they walked through a lush forest.

Kaeo scoffed, 'Bah, poets and painters all dreamers.'

'That's easy for you to say your destiny was a path you'd have chosen anyway. Imagine if you dreamt of being a warrior only to be told you had a different destiny. And no matter how hard you struggled you were forced to take another path.'

Arthur halted along a dirt trail. He breathed in moist air of the night forest as several species of insects rubbed legs and wings together in Mother Nature's eternal symphony.

'Do you hear that?'

Kaeo looked around at the trees and shrubs, 'An intruder?'

'The sound of the forest … its breeze rustles the leaves as a conductor directing insects as different sections of an orchestra, listen to them play in sequence.'

Kaeo remained still as she tuned into a subtle ballad of creatures from both galaxies. It was amazing how these insects learned to play their melody sometimes around and sometimes with one another. Never once did sounds clash despite having evolved millions of light years from one another.

'I hear it.'

'How do they know? How do they know their section of the orchestra? Where did they get their copy of the sheet music? How is it they all understand the conductor?'

'They're bugs who cares?'

Arthur raised his face to the branches above.

Kaeo watched as Nyx's veil of darkness descended over his eyes.

The young man raised a free hand into the night air. As he did the insects quietened down no longer playing their natural tune.

For a while the forest was silent then a distant noise of crickets rubbing wings created a deep "dum, dum, dum," sound similar to a violin strum.

Shortly a new section played above them. A creature from another part of the galaxy played a high pitched violin sound over the deep strum.

As the two played alongside each other more entered the symphony. Kaeo could hear Mother Nature's violins beside what must have been a harpsichord.

After a minute the First of Teteo recognised the tune. It was a familiar harmony used in many NET advertising campaigns. She had no idea of who the composer was or when it was created yet it signified a classy and refined product.

As the creatures played in perfect concert her passion increased with the music. Kaeo's soul rose from the deep place it had dwelt since the Chihuaz. The short Valkyrie's eyes fell into Nyx's night as the symphony lifted her spirit aloft. For a few short minutes Mother Nature's orchestra played a violin concerto composed by Vivaldi in F minor ... centuries earlier. Yet it evoked the same feelings today in a different breed as it did then in humans.

As it ended she felt her soul come to rest in a higher place. Nyx retracted her veil and Kaeo turned to Arthur, 'How did you do that?'

'Malikah concerns herself only with what is big. Yet it takes more discipline more will power to control a forest of insects than a star or the crust of a planet. And the result is far more satisfying far more beautiful.'

Kaeo pressed him, 'You still didn't answer me, how did you do that?'

'That is something else Malikah cannot teach you.'

'Will you teach me?'

'If you can learn.'

Kaeo examined the forest around her in wonder, 'I learnt the application of brute force to control large objects ... massive things ... I could even crush a war cruiser. I can control another being force it to do my will. But to control thousands of bugs, that never seemed possible or desirable until now.'

Arthur took a deep breath concerned that he'd already shared too much with Kaeo. Yet she would never betray him, she was the most loyal person he'd known.

'Do you think this is a coincidence?'

'What's a coincidence?'

'That these insects from different star systems in different galaxies when brought together play a symphony?'

'I've never thought about it. I mean they're just bugs aren't they?'

Arthur grinned, 'Are we not little more than tiny insects scurrying around aimlessly when viewed by the Gods?'

The short Tlillan replied in a coy tone, 'If you believe in Gods then yeh, I suppose so.'

'Am I not a God when viewed by a cricket? Does it not look up in wonder at my size and magnificence?'

'So?'

'Andromeda is less than an arm's reach away for the Gods. We are little more than insects to them. They arrange us to play life's symphony to their desire.'

'You mean Xch'uup, right?'

Arthur shook his head, 'There are greater beings than Xch'uup. Gods that even Malikah cannot see. It is akin to looking at all space in one glance, it isn't possible for even the mighty Xch'uup.

Yet there are beings who may do so. Who may arrange the planets and galaxy as they please and we are little more than insects. We see only the leaf or twig we rest on at the moment.'

'That's heresy, you know that?'

'It is the truth. Think of those insects, did they understand what they were doing or why? Do you think they heard Vivaldi as they played their part in the orchestra? Of course not they played for the pleasure of their Gods even though they had no idea.

We are the same. We all sit at our section of the orchestra. We play our instrument without hearing others. From our limited perspective it is not music but a disorganised commotion. Yet the Gods listen with satisfaction delighting in a beautiful symphony of their creation.'

Kaeo folded her arms and gave a look of concern, 'I convinced Malikah you're not nuts don't make me a liar.'

Arthur laughed, 'Malikah, she is as blind as the others. She sees the future and all the possibilities yet she never asks where or why these possibilities exist. Where do the events which don't take place go? Why didn't they occur?

Xch'uup knows there is something but she looks in the wrong place. As an insect she leaps from twig to twig searching out destiny. Counting leaves, logging their place and eventually after many years she has a rough sketch of the branch. Like Columbus discovering the new world and mapping it when in fact Earth is merely a grain of sand in a vast desert.'

'But you can see the whole picture?' replied Kaeo in a sardonic tone.

'No, though slowly I hear other sections of the orchestra. I make out the conductor but for now his gestures and instructions are an enigma. I see pieces of sheet music before me yet the movement eludes me. As for the entire piece I have no idea where it begins or ends however I'm determined to find out.'

'So is Malikah.'

'Malikah has enough trouble waiting for her on Otoch. She will have little time to discover the truth behind destiny in the coming years.'

'Why don't we get out of here before I start talking like a crazy scientist?'

The young man smiled, following Kaeo out of the gardens.

The pair moved onto the main boulevard. Arthur displayed a beaming smile across his face. He was the happiest man alive in the Skin Territory that evening as citizens, merchants and tourists gazed on in wonder at the lucky chap.

From a distance Bazi observed the pair, 'Amar, I believe it is time we return home.'

'We have found the Amelatu?'

'No, but these devils from another galaxy shall do.'

'I understand.'

Bazi flagged down a taxi, a small white vehicle screeched to a halt before them.

'Where you goin' fellas?'

'Docking Arm 12.'

'One guskin mate anywhere for a guskin.'

Amar and Bazi seated themselves on the rear bench.

'Hold on to your jewels gentlemen!' stated the cabby before they rocketed off to their destination at top speed.

Grabbing the chrome bar for dear life Amar and Bazi gritted their teeth as they flew down the boulevard just missing a tree.

'Watch it will you!' screeched Amar.

'Don't you worry; old Faz has never lost a customer yet! Not to a crash anyway!'

'What do you mean?' shouted Bazi.

'No worries mate, it was years ago.'

'What happened?' inquired Amar in an alarmed tone.

'Reactor leak died of Radon poisoning.'

'Radon, is that not an isotope of …'

'Thorium, yeah. Your sitting on the reactor right now, damn thing leaked all over him. He was so crispy his skin turned into crackling!' laughed Faz as he weaved the boulevard.

Amar and Bazi looked down in shock.

'Don't worry lads that thing's as safe as a Telal vagina, safe as a Telal vagina ……'

The End

In memory of Siwaporn Boonprasit

If you wish to contact the Author you may do so via email:
malikachutli@hotmail.co.uk

www.ingramcontent.com/pod-product-compliance
Lightning Source LLC
Chambersburg PA
CBHW071222250626
47163CB00001B/73